STRAIGHT TO THE CHAPEL

BRIDGET L. ROSE

Copyright © 2025 by Bridget L. Rose

First Edition – 2025

No part of this book may be reproduced or transmitted electronically, hard copy, photocopying or recording or any other form without permission from the author, except for brief quotations for book reviews. This is a work of fiction, characters, names, places, and incidents that resemble anything in real life is purely coincidental.

This book is not affiliated with the sport of Formula One. Whilst true aspects of the sport in terms of the format are included in this book, all characters, team performances, as well as the storyline are fictional.

Editing: Bridget L. Rose Books Inc.

Cover Design: Bridget L. Rose Books Inc.

Formatting: Bridget L. Rose Books Inc.

Illustrations 1 & 4: @emilyxvrs

Illustration 2: irdeinfierno

Illustration 3: ask.the.fairies

This book is dedicated to everyone who has been lonely in love their whole life. Your star, the person who finally reciprocates your feelings, will find you, I promise. And when they do, they will burst into your life, steal your heart, and keep it safe forever.

This book is also dedicated to all of the single moms who have ever been made to feel like less of a parent. Don't listen to those people. You are good enough.

Trigger Warnings

This book contains explicit sex scenes, as well as F1 crashes which might be scary for some readers and vulgar language. It contains topics of grief (loss of a sibling and best friend), mental health (talks of her depression that is historic and a scene where he has a childhood trauma response when he fights with his father), and more that may be triggering for some readers. This book also has kink exploration.

Author's note

Hello my dear reader,

As always, I would like to write a little bit about the topics I've explored in this book.

If you've read any of my books before, the topics of grief and mental health won't be a surprise to see for you. However, these are new aspects of mental health that I haven't explored before, and I took them, once again, from my own experience. I don't usually talk about my depression, mostly I talk about my anxiety, but I was diagnosed with mild depression years ago, at the same time I was diagnosed with severe anxiety. I found ways to handle my depression on my own, without a therapist or medication, but I want to clarify that this path, the one I gave Estrella too, is not a universal experience. Nothing I ever write about mental health will be what I consider universal. If you feel seen through her, if you can relate, then that makes me so happy! But I want to make sure that people who perhaps don't suffer from depression do not assume all depression is the same. It isn't. As a matter of fact, I personally had very different experiences with my depression, and I only explore one of them through Estrella. I explore another through my other book that I'm writing right now. All of that is to say, I hope you feel seen, and I hope you will learn more as well if you don't relate. My goal with every book is to spread awareness about important topics, just like James' childhood trauma response you will see in this book, too. That is what happens to me. That is something I struggle with to this day. That childhood trauma, for me personally, is what triggered my anxiety and depression.

I also wrote this book for everyone who ever felt they weren't good enough, especially single parents who were made to feel that way. Through the help of my amazing readers, I was taught about the loneliness, depression, and low self-worth so many single mothers face because of societal stigma. I hope Estrella can show you that you are more than good enough just as you are. That you are doing an amazing job. That you are not alone and so loved.

Thank you for being here. I appreciate you all so much.

All my love,

Bridget

Mis queridos lectores,

Me gustaría platicarles algo.

La diversidad es muy importante para mí en mis libros. He vivido en muchas partes del mundo y tengo el honor de conocer culturas diferentes. De cada país aprendí mucho de su cultura y para mi es muy importante destacar eso en mis libros.

Ese es uno de los motivos que me inspiró a crear el personaje de Estrella.

Cuando era niña tenía un amigo que me enseñó su cultura y encontré una profunda admiración por lo que él me compartía, especialmente por el día de muertos. Me enamoré de las tradiciones y los simbolismos de esa celebración en especial lo que representa la muerte. Ahora que soy mayor, quise hacer honor a esas tradiciones y todas las otras cosas que aprendí sobre México para crear el personaje de Estrella. Mi meta es compartir lo bonito de la cultura y lo que hay en ella como la música que ella escucha, la comida que cocina, las palabras en español que utiliza, y las tradiciones que tiene con su hija Daisy y el resto de su familia. Con la ayuda de muchas personas maravillosas di mi mayor esfuerzo para representar la cultura de Estrella de una manera precisa pero sobre todo con todo el respeto que la cultura merece.

Estoy muy agradecida por todo lo que me han enseñado, especialmente mis lectores beta y el novio de mi hermana. Espero tener la fortuna de seguir aprendiendo mucho más en el futuro respecto a lo que aún no conozco de las costumbres y tradiciones de México, y para mi seria un honor que cuando leas esto sientas cierta conexión y si estás lejos de tu país por algún motivo, puedas sentirte cerca de lo maravillosa que es tu cultura.

-Bridget

Pitstop Series
Team Names

Spark Racing

Playlist

1. Is It Alright? - James Arthur
2. Better Man - 5 Seconds of Summer
3. BESÁNDOTE - Becky G feat. Oscar Ortiz
4. Poco A Poco - Luis Fonsi
5. QUÉDATE BÉBE - Grupo Frontera
6. I Like Me Better - Lauv
7. Dos Oruguitas - Sebastián Yatra
8. BANDIDO - Becky G
9. Maldita Despedida - Reik
10. Mutual - Shawn Mendes
11. That's So True - Gracie Abrams
12. Lonely Heart - 5 Seconds of Summer
13. Hecha Pa´Mi - Grupo Frontera
14. The Alchemy - Taylor Swift
15. Despídase bien - Carin León
16. BESO - ROSALÍA feat. Rauw Alejando
17. TODO - Becky G
18. Recuérdame (Reencuentro) - Luis Ángel Gómez Jaramillo, Rocío Garcel
19. POR EL CONTRARIO - Becky G, Ángela Aguilar, Leonardo Aguilar
20. Ordinary - Alex Warren

And more

You can find the translation pages for all Spanish phrases and words at the back of the book. Happy reading!

Prologue

James

I'VE MADE MANY MISTAKES in my life. Falling in love with my best friend was the biggest. Not only is she now happily married to a man I cannot fucking stand for the life of me, but I'm also a part-time father and full-time Formula One driver. Love isn't in the cards for me. Maybe it never has been and never will be. It feels like I'm slowly getting over my feelings for Val, but I'm also acutely aware that no one will ever *be her*. It doesn't matter how much time passes or how often I tell myself there will be someone else who is even more amazing for me than the woman I've been pining for most of my life.

How pathetic.

I know it is. I don't need to be told I should move on from Valentina. People don't realise how fucking difficult that is when you've spent your whole existence imagining a life with someone. Growing old with the person you've loved more than anything else. My son, Damian, has long taken that spot, but she's still in second place.

Married.

She's married.

And if that isn't like a bullet to the chest, one that peels itself out of me only so I can get shot again every time I think about it, then I don't know what is. As I said, people don't realise what it means to let go of the kind of love I hold for her when I've been carrying it around since I can remember. Watching her get married shattered something inside of me. Hearts can't break, but they can tear, and she tore mine into a million shreds when she whispered "I do" to a man who isn't me.

Again, pathetic, I know.

But it only just happened, too. I'm allowed to wallow in self-pity for a little, right? No one would expect me to simply be happy for her when she was my happy ending for so long. Choices have consequences. I chose not to tell her how I felt. I made that mistake, not Valentina. She isn't the one to blame. She didn't pretend she had feelings for me. She always called me exactly what I am to her. Her best friend. If my head came up with delusions, then that's on me.

Then again, I wish it was her fault so I could be angry with her. So she wouldn't seem so perfect to me, including all of her imperfections.

"Hey," Adrian, my best friend, says as he stands beside me on my veranda. He came over to have dinner with me, but I've been in such a pissy mood, I've hardly spoken. "How are you doing?" he asks, his hand moving to my shoulder and giving it a comforting squeeze. My gaze shifts to the night sky, the light pollution too strong where I live in Monaco for me to see stars.

"I wish I could see the stars shine," I blurt out, and Adrian looks up, too.

"Yeah, so do I," he replies.

Silence fills the space between us until I break it again.

"You've shut yourself off from love before. How did you do it?" I hear myself saying, but it feels like my soul has left my body as I contemplate how the fuck I'm going to keep my chest from aching.

"I didn't have Nevaeh, so there was no reason to open my heart to love like the one you're talking about. Once she stepped into my life, she split me wide open, entangled her soul with mine, and that was it. She is it for me." I nod along to his words, feeling a stinging pain tugging on that fucked up organ in my chest.

"So, you're saying I'm screwed because Val already split me open and now closed me off from everyone else?" I ask, but instead of laughing at how dramatic I'm being, my best friend steps in front of me. He grabs both of my shoulders, his eyes, the same as Val's, staring deeply into mine.

"I'm saying you may love my sister, but she was never meant to be yours. Stop trying to convince yourself she was and open your eyes. There is a whole world out there, a sky full of beautiful stars, even if you can't see them now. Val may have been your first love, but she wasn't your star. You're going to find your own shining bright light, I know you will," Adrian says before letting go of me and pointing at my chest. "Your heart is still in your chest, James, that's why you're hurting right now. If Valentina was meant to be yours, she would have taken it, but she didn't. She left it for someone else to have one day."

"Who?" I ask, tears jumping into my eyes.

"Your happy ending, James."

Chapter 1
Estrella

Three Years Later

"Alright, one more lap, everyone, and then it's time to get off the track," I say and five little thumbs lift into the air, causing a chuckle to leave me.

"Coach, when will it be snack time?" one of my students, Winnie, asks.

"In a moment," I assure her, my eyes focusing on each of my kids to watch them finish their last laps. "Okay, let's go. Helmets off. It's snack time," I call out to my group, and they all park their karts in the designated spots before ripping their helmets off.

Winnie gives me a bright smile before skipping over to her lunch bag. Another instructor, Lori, squeezes my hand as she walks past me, her group now taking over the track.

I sit my kids down at the table and smile as they start eating and sharing stories with one another. They're all about four to six years old, and when they tell each other about things they did this weekend, I can't help but grin.

My group behaves very well most of the time, which is great considering how young they are. The only troublemaker is Damian Landon, a five-year-old with an attitude so big, I have no idea what to do with it most days. He's my student at the racing academy Valentina Romana-Biancheri, current Velocità Rossa Formula One driver, and Leonard Tick, former F1 driver and three-time World Champion, opened a little over three years ago.

I've only been Damian's coach for two weeks, but I had to bite my tongue several times to keep from reprimanding him.

Not only is he the son of famous Hawke Racing F1 driver James Landon, but he's also Valentina and Gabriel's godson. I shouldn't piss off my boss, no matter how much of a brat this little boy is. Then again, if he pulls Daisy's hair one more time, I will put him in a time-out.

I don't give a shit.

"You seem to be doing well here," a familiar woman's voice says, and I turn around to see Valentina approaching, her hand firmly clasped in Gabriel Romana-Biancheri's. The Formula One World Champion gives me a polite smile, but his attention drifts to his wife when she starts talking again. "Are you enjoying it?"

"Yes, thank you so much for the opportunity, Mrs. Romana-Biancheri," I say.

"Mrs. Biancheri will be just fine," Gabriel responds, earning a slap to the arm from his wife.

"Nonsense, call me Val, please," she says, and I can't help but smile when Gabriel lets out an annoyed sigh. "I know you've been trying to get everyone to call me Mrs. Biancheri for years, including all of our friends, but it's not happening," Val adds as they walk away again.

"OWW!" My head whips around in time to see Damian, the little monster, tugging on my daughter's hair again.

"That's enough, Damian! I have asked you nicely to stop pulling Daisy's hair three times already. You're in a time-out after snack time is finished," I say, barely keeping my voice from raising even more.

"That's not fair," the little boy screams at me.

"Do you think it was okay to pull Daisy's hair after I've asked you not to?" I challenge, and his little mouth closes before he breaks into tears.

I can't believe the little monster is crying now because he hurt Daisy, but I let him cry it out until he's calmed down again, pouting at his food.

"Okay, snack time is over. Let's play some games."

Nine of my ten kids are packing away their food while Damian starts throwing around his snack. I let him throw his tantrum until he's exhausted himself. I know he's going to go home to his parents and complain about the mean instructor, but I will be more than happy to address the situation with James Landon when he comes to drop off his son tomorrow morning.

Tomorrow is Friday, and from what Damian told the group yesterday, during non-race weekends, his father takes care of him from Friday through Monday. He also dropped him off at the academy on Friday and Monday morning for the last two weeks.

The fact that I already know so much about this man's life when I haven't even met him is unsettling.

"Mamá, I'm tired," the light of my life says as I wait for the kids in my group to put on their hats and grab their water bottles.

"Only one more hour, Daisy," I say and watch as she wraps her little arms around my leg. For an almost five-year-old, she's pretty tall, but I'm even more so, so her head doesn't quite reach my hip yet.

I notice Damian is still crying, but when my daughter rubs her head where the little monster pulled her hair, I don't feel as bad anymore. He's been pulling hair and pushing the other kids all week. Maybe I'm also a bit more irritated because he's mostly been picking on Daisy, and I will protect my little girl with my life.

I may not have given birth to her, but my sister-in-law trusted me with her daughter three years ago.

My brother, Pedro, passed away when she was pregnant, and Helen died in a hit-and-run a year after giving birth to the sweet angel still hugging my leg. My parents said they would take Daisy, but she was also my kid long before Helen passed away. We lived together after Pedro died, and I raised Daisy as if she were my own from the day she was born.

But I couldn't stay in our old apartment. Not after having lost both of them. It was too difficult, and I had no time to mourn. I had a daughter to raise.

So, I applied for a job in Monaco, packed our bags, and moved from Mexico to this magical country that I've already fallen in love with over the past three years.

Daisy is thriving here. She is learning French in pre-school and speaks it better than I ever will. She also loves racing, just like me. I used to do road racing. My car and I were faster than any other driver on the closed circuits. I was even first place in the National Championship in Mexico, but I left all of it behind to take care of Daisy. And I don't regret any of it.

Training the next generation of racers isn't exactly what I thought I'd be doing so early in my life, but I also never thought I'd have a daughter to take care of at twenty-five, and she's the best part of my existence now.

"One more hour, and then we will go home and stuff our faces with orange slices," I say because those are her favorites.

"Okay, but I don't want to be in a team with Damian anymore. He's mean to me," she says, and I stroke her hair with a small smile.

"Don't worry, *florecita*, he won't pull your hair again."

I will personally call his moms if he does. They're the kindest people I've ever met. I'm sure that when I inform them of Damian's behavior, they will speak to him about it.

"Okay, everyone, let's play a game of football," I call out, causing an eruption of excited laughs and giggles to come from my group.

I love letting them play football, even if they're training to become karting racers. It's great for hand-eye coordination, teaching them teamwork skills, allowing them to socialize, and a million more reasons. My whole lesson plan is built around getting these kids ready to become the best racers this world has ever seen, including Daisy. I'm so proud of her determination at such a young age.

She wants to be a Formula One driver one day, so what better academy for her to attend than the one opened by the first female F1 driver?

Daisy skips over to where Leonora, Leonard and Chiara Tick's daughter, is sitting with another kid.

I watch after her with the biggest smile. This little girl is as incredible as her parents used to be. Nothing can stop her, not even a mean little boy who pulls her hair.

"Damian?" I say as I approach him.

He has stopped crying and is playing with his snack while pouting. I feel bad for snapping at him earlier, so I try a gentler approach.

"I need you to please stop pulling everyone's hair, okay? It's not very nice, buddy," I add, but he gives me an angry look. "You want to play football, don't you?" I ask with a small smile. He's just a kid. He will learn it's not okay to do certain things.

"Yes," he mumbles, his bright blue eyes shifting to the ground.

"Then, please, apologize to Daisy, and you can go ahead and play," I say, so he jumps out of his seat and runs to my daughter, apologizing for pulling her hair.

I smile to myself while splitting my group into two and watching them run onto the grass field to start a game.

It's a hot summer day here in Monaco. Formula One is officially on summer break, so Leonard and Valentina have been at the academy to oversee things almost every day this week. Summer break also means a lot of kids signed up for the training camps. There are eight different groups with twelve different instructors. I haven't gotten to know all of my colleagues yet—I only recently got the job here, before I was at a different academy in France where I had to commute an hour every day—but I've already made a plan to invite Eli to coffee this weekend. They asked me to grab one a few days ago, but Daisy had a doctor's appointment, so I couldn't go.

I have to find a social life for myself. Daisy has friends, and now it's time for me to find some as well.

I shake all of those thoughts before focusing on the football game again.

Everything goes well until the little monster pulls my daughter's hair ten minutes into the game.

Chapter 2
James

For the first time in my life, I'm leading the Formula One World Championship.

I should be happy.

Instead, I've never been angrier at the universe for putting Valentina in second place, mere points behind me. This is her fourth year racing for Velocità Rossa, but this is the first time she's a close competitor for the title. They were struggling with their pace and strategies the year she joined the team, and it's taken them a while to get back to the top.

Adrian is in third while my teammate at Hawke, Cameron Kion, is in fourth. Gabriel is racing for Grenzenlos again this season, but they've been having a hard time keeping up this year. I can't lie. I'm fucking giddy about it. Watching Gabriel, two-time World Champion, struggle in ninth place with a slow as fuck car has the *Schadenfreude* part of me ecstatic. The only problem I see is that my main rival is now the woman I used to be madly in love with, my best friend, and she's a hell of a driver.

She's a better driver than I am.

Pushing all of those thoughts aside, I focus on the road ahead of me. Today is a good day. I have some time off training, and Domi and Nicolette let me have Damian a day earlier than usual.

I can't wait to see my son. He's become the centre of my life. He's the reason I get up in the mornings. He's *everything* to me, and when he tells me he loves me too, I become something else. I become someone who can never be hurt because my kid loves me and that's enough for all the darkness in the world to be replaced by a bright light. I may not be good enough for a lot of people, but I'm more than good enough for him, and that is all that matters.

Yeah, I'm wrapped around that little guy's finger.

He can do no wrong in my book.

I stop my car in front of the large building that's close to the border of France but still part of Monaco. Val and Leonard decided to open their academy here because there is more space for the karting track, football field, and swimming pool they had built into this place. It's a driver academy like no other in every way possible. I'm so proud of them for what they have achieved, I didn't hesitate to invest in their dream when they first told me about their idea. It was a no-brainer. Our sport needed an academy where kids of all backgrounds, ethnicities, genders, and more got a chance.

Racing often favors the privileged, which is why it's so great my best friend and Leonard said "no more."

"Dad!" my son screams as he comes running toward me, his backpack so fucking huge, it flies up and down as he runs.

"Hey, bud," I say and pull him into a tight hug. I missed him so much. I always miss him so much. "How was your day?" I ask as he steps back and smiles like he's never seen anyone as awesome as me.

"My coach yelled at me. Twice," he says, sending a wave of anger through me.

"Why?" I ask softly, even though I feel like yelling at someone.

I feel like yelling at his coach.

"I don't know," he replies and stares at the ground. It doesn't go past me that he's probably lying to me, but no matter what he did, no one yells at my kid.

My eyes shift to my best friend as she waves goodbye to a parent and their kid, looking happier and more at peace with herself than I've ever seen before.

"Val? Can you look after Damian for a few minutes?" I ask as I take my son's hand and walk toward her. My attention briefly shifts to Gabriel, and we give each other strained nods because no matter what he's done for Damian and me in the past, he'll always be the man who took the woman I loved from me.

"Yes, of course," Val replies and squats down to grab my son's face between her hands. He giggles loudly, and my heart warms at the sight, so I force my eyes away again.

I'm on a mission. I will find his coach and tell them never to raise their voice at Damian again unless they want to get fired from the academy. Val would never tolerate her staff screaming at Damian. There is a different way to tell a child not to do something. Raising your voice is the last thing you should do.

I make my way toward the small house outside of the academy. I have no fucking clue who Damian's instructor is, I'm usually too busy being excited to see my son to care about anyone else, but I will figure it out one way or another.

Sweat drips down my back because I came straight from a meeting where I had to wear fancy trousers and a blazer, which is definitely not the right thing to be wearing in Monaco during one of the hottest summer days.

Stepping in front of a group of instructors, my eyes are immediately drawn to a tall woman with wide hips, a smaller waist, and long, toned legs to die for. She has light brown skin and her wavy dark-brown hair is long, but her light-brown eyes have me tethered to her face.

There are tattoos on her arms and legs, spread out and somehow fitting her perfectly. She has heart-shaped lips and a nose that's slightly turned up at the tip. Her cheeks are round as she smiles at someone she's standing with, forcing my attention back to her mouth because I don't think I've ever seen a smile as devastating as hers.

She's beautiful, and when she notices me staring at her, she cocks one perfectly shaped brow.

"Excuse me, which one of you is Damian's instructor?" I ask once I've regained the ability to speak.

It doesn't matter that she's gotten a reaction out of me that no one has since Valentina, that she had my heart skipping a fucking beat. I'm here to get to the bottom of the situation with my son, not to ogle one of Val's employees.

"That would be me," the mystery woman says, and I feel anger coursing through me. Of course it had to be her. It couldn't be anyone else.

Brilliant. Bloody brilliant.

"Might I have a word?" I ask, and she looks down her side at a little girl I only notice now. I bring a smile to my lips for the girl, but she glares at me like I'm the devil.

What the hell?

"*Espérame aquí, florecita*," the gorgeous woman says before letting go of the child's hand and leading me inside the little clubhouse where washrooms and a small kitchen area with a fridge and sink are.

"I don't appreciate you yelling at my son. Do not let it happen again," I snarl because, even if I'm a nice person most of the time, I'm a dragon protecting its egg when it comes to my son's happiness.

"And I don't appreciate you approaching me this way," she replies with a strong Mexican accent, her voice smooth like honey. It's fascinating how I'm getting stuck on these things when I should be focused on telling her off for yelling at my kid.

"If my son comes to me after camp, saying he got yelled at *twice*, you can understand why I'm upset. You don't get to yell at my kid. He's not your son," I say, but she crosses her arms in front of her chest.

"Listen, I'm not here to discipline your son. Raising him to be a decent human is your job. But when I ask him nicely to stop pulling the hair of another child in my group and he continues to do it anyway, I'm going to lose my patience a little. He's disrupting my class and hurting my daughter," she says, and understanding washes through me.

She's protecting her child, I get that. I will speak to Damian about his behaviour as soon as we're in the car, but it doesn't sit right with me that she raised her voice and upset my son. Which is probably where my next words come from.

"I don't give a fuck what he did, you do not yell at my child. It isn't your place." A small smile tugs on the corner of her mouth, pissing me off even more. Why the fuck is she amused? And why the hell does it look so good on her?

"Mr. Landon, how many children training camps have you instructed in your life?" she asks, her arms still crossed in front of her chest, distracting me. I open my mouth to respond, but she beats me to it. "Exactly. None. If you had, you'd know how difficult it is to keep ten kids in line, especially when one of them is a little monster," she says, and I raise both of my brows.

"What did you call him?" I ask, and she grins at me.

"It's something I call all troublemakers in my classes," she explains.

"Not my son. You better correct your teaching methods, or I will speak to your employer about what you've been doing," I warn, and, again, her amusement stays on her face like I told her a funny joke.

She's so infuriating.

"Go ahead and do that, but when nine out of ten parents are happy with my *teaching methods*, and one kid's *parent* is upset because I raised my voice when he misbehaved, I wonder what Mrs. Biancheri will have to say about that," is all she says before leaving me standing there, dumbfounded.

"Hey, I wasn't done speaking to you," I call out as I follow her back outside. She picks up a bag of equipment before carrying it to the small shed beside the clubhouse.

"So? I was finished listening to you. I heard your concerns, and if your son stops pulling hair, then I won't have to raise my voice again," she replies, bending over again to shove the bag inside the cabinet. I do my best not to stare, but I only manage to rip my eyes from her backside several seconds later. "Until then, I'm done dealing with your tantrum. I get paid to be patient with the children when they have one, not you." I almost laugh at that.

Almost.

"You have to be the rudest instructor I've ever met," I blurt out while she straightens out her back.

Her previous amusement leaves her face as she steps toward me. I don't move away as she closes the distance between us until our chests almost touch. Her scent, something floral, bombards my sense of smell until I feel it rush through my bloodstream. She's tall, but I'm even more so, towering over her by at least a head. It doesn't make her cower or back away from this confrontation, though.

"And you have to be the biggest *pendejo* of a parent I've ever met," she replies, and it brings a small smile to my lips. I could get her fired. She knows how close I am to her boss, but she won't tolerate a jerk like me barking commands at her.

"I'll speak to my son, but if I ever hear anything about you yelling at him again, I will—" She cuts me off before I can finish the threat.

"You don't have to repeat yourself for the fifth time. I'd suggest you save your breath to yell at someone else because I won't tolerate it any longer." She juts out her chin, her upper body still almost touching mine. "And don't threaten me again, Mr. Landon. I'll find a different way to handle things from now on. Are you happy with that?" she says and attempts to walk away, but I step in front of her.

"I will be happy when my son gets a new instructor," I say and lean down a little. Our gazes are fixed on each other's, and I try to ignore the way my heartbeat thuds loudly in my ears.

"Then ask for a new one," she replies as she leans even closer and then leaves me standing where I am, trying to catch my bloody breath.

What the hell just happened?

Chapter 3
Estrella

I stare down at the letter Helen's parents sent me, trying my best not to burst into tears.

They're threatening to take Daisy away from me.

Ice runs through my veins at the thought. Helen stated in her will that custody of her daughter would go to me in case anything happened to her. There were no conditions. Daisy is my daughter legally, but now they're saying I'm not fit to be a parent *because I don't have a partner*. I almost laugh at that. They don't think I can handle raising Daisy as a single mom. I've done it for the past three years, and she's been happy, but, all of a sudden, I'm not fit to be a parent?

Tears stream down my cheeks while I fight back a sob. Daisy is sleeping in the room next to the kitchen, where I am sitting at the table. I don't want to wake her. No little girl should have to see her mom crying because her grandparents are threatening to take her away. My hand flies to my mouth so I can muffle my sob. The grief of losing Pedro and my best friend washes over me again until I'm breaking down completely. The fear of losing Daisy now tears apart my heart until it's a pile of shredded pieces inside of my chest.

I promised Helen I'd be the perfect parent for her little girl. She made me swear if anything happened to her before Daisy could understand, that I would let her grow up calling me mamá. So she could have a life filled with more happiness and love than grief.

I love her so much.

Why would they want to take her from me?

Bert and Jennifer have been living their best lives in Florida while mine fell apart into a million pieces. I had to arrange everything for Helen's funeral because they wanted no part of it. I had to fight past my pain because Daisy needed me to be strong. I was the one who fed her at two in the morning. I was the one who changed her diapers and held her until she fell asleep. I was the one who bonded with her while I read her bedtime stories, watched her take her first steps, heard her first words, and so much more.

I'm her mom.

They are nothing to her because they haven't even fucking met her yet.

My sobs slow as anger slowly replaces any other emotion inside of me. There is a phone number at the bottom of the letter, *their number*. I grab my phone and dial. If they think they can take her from me without a fight, they are very wrong. That little girl is my entire world, and I would sooner burn this whole planet to ashes before giving her up.

It's not happening.

Over my dead body.

"Hello?" a woman's voice says into the speaker, and I feel rage settle inside my chest. It fuels me now.

"How dare you threaten to take Daisy from me? How dare you act like you give a damn about *my* daughter now?" I whisper-scream into the phone.

"We've always cared about our granddaughter's well-being, we just didn't have a way to take her from you. Helen's will was undisputable, but we've found a lawyer and judge ready to help based on the premise that you cannot raise her as well as my husband and I can together. One working parent isn't enough to provide a happy life for a child," Jennifer says, and I almost laugh at her because I have never heard anything even remotely as bullshit as the garbage that just came out of her mouth.

Daisy and I have a wonderful life together. She's happy. I'm not missing a partner when it comes to raising her. If I want someone to call mine and fall in love with, it's not because I need them to help me raise my daughter. I'm more than capable of doing a good job on my own. Jennifer won't make me feel like less of a mother, I won't let her.

I *can't*.

"No judge or lawyer would do this if they knew the full story. Daisy and I have a good life together. You can't take that away from her," I say, but then I hear some rustling in the background. A male voice fills the speaker, sending an uneasy feeling through me.

"Listen, Estrella," Bert starts, butchering the pronunciation of my name completely. "You have two options here. Either you find yourself a spouse in the next six months, which you won't, or we will take her from you. Simple as that." Simple as that? Who the fuck could find a spouse in six fucking months?

"Why a spouse? Is a life partner not enough? Because I have a partner," I lie, hoping that they will leave me alone.

"It's not enough. Daisy should have a stable home life," Bert replies, and I let out an unamused laugh.

"You're giving me 'options' knowing full well I can't go through with them," I say, and I can almost see the evil smile working its way onto Bert's disgusting mouth.

"Your choice. As you can see, we only care about our granddaughter's well-being," he says and this time, I laugh out loud.

I wonder if they believe their own lies or if they really expect me to believe them. Either way, I don't give a fuck. I won't do this. They can take me to court if they must, I will—

No.

I'd make Daisy's life miserable. Putting her through all of that would be hell. Custody battles can get ugly and traumatic, and even the thought of making her be in the middle of all of that has bile rising in my throat.

"I will marry a fucking lamp post before I let you take her from me," is all I say before hanging up the phone.

The urge to throw it across the room makes my fingers twitch around the device, but I take a deep breath to slow my racing thoughts. Okay. It'll be fine. I can find a spouse within the next six months. Easy. No problem at all.

I think I'm going to throw up.

There is no way I can convince someone to marry me this quickly. No one would do that, except maybe a really good friend, and I don't have any of those at the moment. A sense of hopelessness fills my chest. Even if I want to spare Daisy the pain of going through the trial Jennifer and Bert are forcing on me, I won't be able to. No one will help me.

Tears shoot back into my eyes, but I blink them away when I see Daisy stepping out of her room, looking all sleepy. It makes my heart break again.

"*No puedo dormir*, Mamá," she says, and I open my arms for her. She steps in front of me, so I pull her onto my left leg. Her head falls against my shoulder as she hugs her plushie close to her chest.

"Do you want me to read you another bedtime story?" I ask, but she shakes her head.

"Tell me one of your racing stories," Daisy replies, and I smile to myself. Telling her about my experiences as an auto racer is one of my favorite things. It adds to her love for the sport.

"Which one do you want to hear?" I say and stand up with her in my arms.

"The one where you won the trophy," she replies and yawns, making me chuckle in response.

I tuck her in again, grinning because she's looking at me with anticipation, as if she hasn't heard the story a million times before.

"So, there I was, at the final race of the season at *Autódromo Hermanos Rodríguez*. My rival was right next to me as we were speeding down *Recta Principal*..." I finish my story even though she falls asleep halfway through my memory.

And as I watch her sleep, I know I'd move all the planets in the solar system to keep my daughter from experiencing any type of pain, especially the one her grandparents are trying to put her through.

STRAIGHT TO THE CHAPEL

I will find a spouse and keep her heart safe.

Chapter 4
James

I don't even know her name. This woman has been stuck in my bloody head for the past twelve hours, and I have no idea what her name is. Damian eventually admitted he had pulled Daisy's hair many times and that his coach had asked him not to do it again. He said he did it because he thinks Daisy is annoying. So, not only am I the biggest wanker for the way I approached his instructor, but I'm also plain stupid for not believing my kid could do something bad.

I'm also desperately trying to ignore the way my body seems to be overheating every time a visual of her slips into my head, all gorgeous legs and amusement on her lips. The way she challenged me and came close enough for me to smell the floral scent coming off her. I've never had this reaction to a person before, not even Val. Then again, I've never been turned on after someone told me to fuck off.

"Daddy, can we watch a movie at the movie place today?" Damian asks when we're walking toward where my best friend is standing with her husband and all the instructors.

"Yeah, bud, we'll go to the movie theatre after I pick you up from camp today," I reply. My son has been picking up my accent whenever he speaks English, but as soon as he switches to French, it's clear as day that he takes after his mothers.

I smile a little at the thought as my eyes fixate on my family.

Adrian and Nevaeh, his wife, are also here today. My male best friend is completely infatuated with her and has been since he first laid eyes on her. She's a very successful sports journalist in the world of Formula One now, and even though it wasn't the sport she saw herself working in, it's the one she fell in love with. Plus, Adrian never has to be apart from her for long.

Looking at them, even Leonard and his wife, Chiara, sends a wave of longing through me. It only intensifies when Leonora hugs her brother, Kieran, and Leonard's gaze softens as he watches his children embrace.

For as long as I can remember, I've been dating casually because my heart belonged to someone else, but I want someone to love. I always have. I want someone who reciprocates my feelings for once. The older I get, the more I realise it might not be in the cards for me, after all. Then I look down at my son and realise I already have one epic love story. I'm pretty lucky.

Not to mention, Marbles and Lollipop keep me very busy when I'm home. They're the two most affectionate, attention-seeking cats in the world, and I love them with my whole heart.

"Hey, bud, remember what we talked about?" I ask as we get closer to my family members and the woman I've been thinking about for half a fucking day. And the most annoying part of it all is the fact that she looks so beautiful, it has my heart racing a little.

Is it anticipation or dread?

I'm not sure.

"Yeah, say sorry to Daisy for pulling her hair," my son replies.

"Yes, bud, please do. It's not a nice thing to do to someone, okay?" Damian nods, guilt written all over his face.

"Okay," he mumbles.

We stop in front of his instructor and her daughter. I place my hands on my son's shoulders and try not to smile at the way her eyes trail over my dress shirt and forearms where I rolled up the sleeves. I have another meeting to attend, so I'm also wearing fancy trousers and styled my blonde hair. She must think I look good because her eyes linger on my body for longer than necessary.

"Mr. Landon, Damian, how can we help you?" she says, faking a smile at me.

"Damian would like to say something to Daisy," I say and pat my son's shoulder to encourage him to speak.

"I'm sorry I pulled your hair, Daisy. I won't do it again." The little girl with bright green eyes, black hair, tanned skin, and a frown on her small face stares at my son.

"*Eres un chico malo,*" Daisy replies, and Damian looks up at me with his blue eyes searching for an answer to his unspoken question. *What did she say?* Since I don't speak Spanish, I look at my son's instructor for a translation, but she merely grins.

"Thank you for your apology, Damian, we appreciate it."

The woman gives my son a sincere smile, and Daisy looks up at her mum. An whole, wordless conversation passes between them within mere seconds. Then, the little girl turns to my son and offers him a wobbly smile.

"Do you want to go play with the ball?" she asks, and my heart warms a little.

"Yeah!" Damian replies.

I give him a kiss on the top of his head.

"Be good," I say, and he flashes me a giant, toothy grin before following Daisy.

"Thank you for speaking to him," the woman in front of me says, her brown eyes full of amusement.

"What's that face for?" I ask because, apparently, I can't stop myself from saying whatever comes to mind.

"You're less of a dick than I thought," she replies, causing the corner of my mouth to curl.

"But still a dick?" I challenge, making her smirk at me. She doesn't respond, merely crosses her arms in front of her chest. "What's your name?" I blurt out because I'm not quite finished speaking to her yet.

"Call me Reya. I don't want you to butcher my full name with that accent of yours," she says, and I let out a surprised laugh.

"You're a handful, aren't you?" I ask, but Reya gives me an unimpressed look.

"Yup," she replies, and I find myself taking a step toward her without meaning to.

"Thank God you're never going to be my handful."

Because I don't think I could handle this woman. She'd put me on my knees and make me beg, and I prefer it the other way around.

"Is there anything else you need from me? Or can I go back to my job, the one you don't think I'm doing properly?" She's still pissed about what I said, and she has every right to be. That doesn't quite stop my next words from slipping past my lips.

"Go for it. I'll keep an eye on you. Make sure you don't yell at my kid again," I reply and tilt my head when irritation replaces any smugness that previously occupied her features.

"I'm flattered. Do all of your son's teachers get such *special* treatment?" she asks, her brown eyes filling with fury.

"Only the beautiful ones who make me want to rip out my hair in frustration." This makes her smile and fuck me, I welcome it back like flowers welcome the sun.

"So you think I'm beautiful *and* I make you want to rip out your hair? Mr. Landon, you sure know how to flirt." There's so much sarcasm in her tone, it's almost like I can reach out and touch it as the words fall from her lips.

"Are you always this... frustrating?"

"Only with men like you." She leaves me standing where I am, my body overheating again because she's just—How can she be so—

I think she might be the reason for my first grey hair to appear.

But I don't stop her. I don't even stare after her because I know I'll look at her arse, and that would make my situation ten times harder. I simply shake my head and turn around to walk away.

Unfortunately, Adrian, Nevaeh, Leonard, Chiara, Val, and Gabriel have clearly all been watching the exchange between Reya and me. They're all smiling too, forcing another blush to my cheeks.

Brilliant.

I take a deep breath and walk toward them. Adrian is the first to speak because of course he is.

"Fucking your son's teacher? How cliché of you. I love it," he says with a big grin while Nevaeh nudges him in the side, rolling her lips to keep from laughing. My best friend merely kisses his wife's temple.

"I am *not* sleeping with her. I don't even know her," I reply, trying not to notice the way Val is attempting to conceal her amusement by turning into Gabriel's chest and hiding her face.

"Hasn't stopped you from fucking people in the past," Adrian replies, and four of them burst into laughter at my expense, everyone except Leonard and Chiara who never smile around me anyway and are too busy keeping an eye on their children where they are playing with Daisy and Damian.

Fucking phenomenal.

Val wipes away her tears of laughter, Gabriel's shoulders shake, Nevaeh walked away to keep me from seeing her amusement, and Adrian looks me dead in the eye. It's like he's challenging me, but we both know he's right. For the past three years, I've shut my emotions off when having sex. It's probably why I've also developed certain kinks, but I'm not going to think about that right now.

"Come on, James, he's just kidding. But if you'd like, I can ask Reya for her number for you," Val chimes in, and I shake my head at all of them.

"I have a meeting to get to, but I will see you all later. Please make sure she keeps my son alive," I add, focusing on Val.

"She's the best coach I've ever met, James. Damian is in good hands." I scrunch my eyebrows together, but I have a feeling she's right. Reya is a great coach and my son was simply being mean to her daughter. Like the parent she is, she was protecting her child, and I can't blame her for that. Hell, I defended my son, too.

The only thing I hold against her are the reactions she's causing inside of me.

Chapter 5
James

Four months later

OVER THE PAST FOUR years in F1, I've become the bad guy of the grid.

The asshole that doesn't leave enough space, drives too aggressively, and doesn't give a single shit about any of the other drivers as long as I win. This image has followed me into this season, but I can't exactly fault them for seeing me this way.

Now that I have a car fast enough to compete for the championship, my full potential has been unleashed. I've always been very consistent, racing more aggressively than others, but now that it's winning me races, I've secured so many haters, I've been booed more often than I can remember.

But it's all I know how to do. It's how my dad taught me to race. And if I didn't, then there were consequences.

When I lost the karting championship after crashing into the wall as a kid to avoid crashing with another child, he didn't speak to me for a week. It's either winning or losing, and losing was never an option for me.

It's the last race of the season. Valentina and I are merely five points apart in the championship. She's leading. I'm starting in first place. Since scoring pole yesterday, I've had hope blooming in my chest. I almost have my first title. If I finish first and Valentina second, I'll win.

But she'd lose. Her first title would be snatched away from her because of... me. The thought makes me shudder.

"Hey. I know what you're thinking, but stop it. You deserve it as much as she does, and you need to focus," my performance coach, Daiyu, says, and I give her several nods, rolling my shoulders to get rid of the tension there. She gives me an encouraging smile, her soft features revealing hints of concern she's trying to hide, too.

"You can admit you don't think we'll win this," I tease, but Daiyu shoots me an angry look, her dark brown eyes showing no signs of amusement. "Valentina is strong, fast, and resilient. More so than I am." It's a fact. I'm not fishing for compliments. It's a genuine concern I have.

"And you're not a quitter. Stop talking like one. I know you're nervous, but this doesn't help," she reminds me, as always being right.

"Yeah, alright. Grab me my gloves, please. I need to get back in the car," I say.

I'm usually the first in the car before the start because it helps settle me. When I'm simply standing next to it, doing nothing, I feel everything tenfold. Sitting in the cockpit silences my thoughts. I've trained to race in Formula One from the age of three. My dad took me karting once, and I never wanted to do anything else after. Every weekend, I asked him to go back to the karting track. Then, as I got older, I watched Leonard Tick win over and over. He inspired me. He's one of the greatest drivers of all time, and I wanted to become exactly like him.

So, I fought. I trained every hour of every day that I wasn't studying. I even graduated a year early because I skipped a grade, but studying more never occurred to me. Racing was all I wanted. Becoming a racecar driver was the only thing I dreamed of being for the rest of my life. There was never anything else.

But I've felt like a failure in this sport for almost a decade. I had achieved nothing more than winning a few races before this season. I haven't gotten a title. I know a big part of that was my team struggling and my years with a low-field team. But Hawke has stepped it up this season. They're finally challenging Velocità Rossa's and Grenzenlos' dominance.

As soon as I'm seated, Daiyu hands me my steering wheel, and I attach it to the front. It locks in place before I get to adjusting my harness belts and the neck strap, ensuring I'm safe. There have been so many advancements in F1 to make it safer for us drivers, the halo one of the biggest. It has saved my life more times than I've been able to keep track of, and I'm so grateful these are priorities for the sport. They still lack in enough other areas.

For example, why is Valentina still the only woman racing?

A year ago, I switched out the members of my team, replaced my male performance coach, race engineer, and strategists with a team of mostly women.

And now look at me.

I'm on the brink of getting my first title.

That isn't a coincidence.

"How are you feeling?" my race engineer, Ximena, asks, and I inhale, taking inventory of all my feelings.

"Like I've been working toward getting this title all season and now everything is on the line," I admit.

What I don't say is that there's a feeling deep inside me, a thought I know will be fact soon, about how this season is going to end.

"Forget all of that. Forget the importance of today. It's just a race, okay? A normal Sunday Grand Prix. No pressure. You've got this, James."

One more deep breath helps me do what she's asking. Push all thoughts aside. Imagine this is a regular race weekend. It might not work for everyone, but Ximena's advice is exactly what I needed to get my head in the game. All I need to do is keep my place. We've got a good strategy. There won't be any rain. Everything will go according to plan. I'll take home the title here in Abu Dhabi for the first time in my career.

The lights illuminating the track look especially bright today as we take our formation lap to warm the tyres and charge our batteries. I'm sweating already, but there is no time to focus on how heavy this heat is weighing on my body. All twenty of us drivers line up at the starting grid again, our engines revving as we get ready for the five lights on top of us to turn on one by one.

I watch them with my heartbeat in my ears.

One, then two, then three. Four. Five.

There's always a moment between when they're all turned on and disappear where I feel the rest of the world falling away completely. I don't worry about my family, my friends, the responsibilities I carry on my shoulders from being a driver, or the risks of this sport.

All I see is the track ahead of me. Hear a clock ticking in my ears. Wait for the lights to disappear.

And then I shoot forward. Once they vanish, I release the clutch and push down on the throttle, pressing the buttons on my steering wheel to shift into gear simultaneously. I have no time to worry about anything else because Valentina has always been the best starter. There's no one as quick as her when it comes to reaction times, and now that she has a car fast enough to keep up, she has no problem following me into the first corner of the track, side by side. I defend and manage to stay in first place, but in the following corner, she's next to me again, fighting me for first place.

There are fifty-eight laps in the Abu Dhabi Grand Prix. Valentina is going to fight me every lap. Every kilometre. She's going to make this the fight of the fucking decade.

"What's the gap between us?" I ask Ximena a lap later. I've got some distance, but not nearly enough.

"The most you had on her was point-five seconds in corner twelve." That's nothing. If she's less than a second behind me when they enable the Drag Reduction System—DRS—then she'll get a speed advantage on me in the designated zones. "Pick up the speed, James."

"Yeah, I'm trying," I grind out, breathing through the strain the G-force has on my body when we move into the first corner for the third time.

"DRS has been enabled," Ximena says a lap later, and I curse when Valentina slips next to me again in the corner. I manage to fight her off, but she's right behind me for the rest of the lap.

This battle could go on for the entirety of the race.

She's told to back off for a little to spare her tyres, but right before we stop for the first time, she picks up the pace again and fights me for first. She overtakes me on the main straight and stays ahead until after the pitstop.

I curse.

"Focus. You have the pace. Go catch her."

Sweat drips down my brow, but I do as Ximena says. Valentina and I both started on medium tyres and are now on hard ones, so we have to be consistent to keep them from degrading and forcing us to stop again. But we both want the win. So, we're giving it our all.

We're two laps from the end. I overtake her in the first corner, but she comes back at me in the next one. I try to cut her off, keep her behind me, but my aggressive defending and racing has gotten me into trouble many times in the past.

Today is no different.

She goes around the outside after the main straight of the last lap, and I go down the inside of the track, my tyres locking up right as I'm about to brake to avoid colliding with her.

"Fuck," I curse when my tyre hits hers. Val slams on her brakes as I keep sliding from the high-speed collision. I spin off the track and straight into the barriers.

"James, are you okay?" my race engineer asks, but the impact has me breathless and incapable of speaking.

My race is over.

The championship title I fought so hard for is... Valentina's.

Lost during the last fucking lap of the race.

Tears shoot into my eyes as I scream, hitting my steering wheel over and over.

Everything I worked for is gone.

All because of *me*.

And the first thing I hear after getting out of my car is the crowd booing for me.

Chapter 6
Estrella

I have two months left.

I've been unsuccessful so far, but six months isn't a lot of time to find someone who'd be willing to marry me. I've been so busy working, focusing on Daisy and her well-being, making Christmas and New Year's as memorable as possible for her, I haven't had time to go out and look for anyone to marry.

On top of that, now that the F1 season is over, I have to see James Landon's stupidly handsome face a lot more, and every interaction we have is a dumpster fire.

"Yell at any more kids?" he asked me yesterday when he picked up his son.

"No, but I've made a bunch of dads cry. Want me to add you to the list?" All he did was smile at me.

Watching him approach today in a green polo, long coat, and black pants that hug his muscular, thick thighs perfectly only makes me angrier. Because why does he have to look so good when he pisses me off so much? It's winter in Monaco. My cheeks shouldn't feel flushed with heat whenever I see him.

I've known this man for a little over four months, and I've fantasized about strangling him more often than that.

"You don't have to greet me every single time you drop Damian off, Mr. Landon," I say right after his son runs past me and straight toward our group. "As a matter of fact, I'd prefer it if you didn't. I don't particularly enjoy looking at your arrogant face." Lies.

"I'm merely making sure my son gets to his class and doesn't walk off without permission. I wouldn't want you to lecture him again." I grind my molars when he gives me a challenging look.

"Actually, your son has been an absolute angel these past four months. You're the one who's been behaving like Satan's spawn. Maybe I should lecture you instead." That damn smirk of his reappears.

"Don't threaten me with a good time, darling."

He walks away without another word, and I roll my eyes before turning to my group of kids and bringing a genuine smile to my face.

"Alright, who's ready to learn something new about racing today?" I ask, earning a round of excited squeals from them.

I don't know when I started bawling my eyes out. It was sometime between watching Daisy leave with Leonard and Chiara Tick and their daughter Leonora for a playdate at their house and putting away my equipment.

As soon as I saw her drive away, something inside of me snapped.

If I don't find someone to marry me, Jennifer and Bert will take her away from me forever. She will drive off, and I won't get to be her mamá anymore.

I sink to my knees and sob into my hands, not giving a damn that I'm right in front of the academy. I can't lose my daughter. I love her so much, more than I will ever love anything or anyone else in this world. If she was taken away from me, I don't think I'd survive it. My heart would shatter, and I'd crumble to dust.

"Reya?"

Valentina Romana's voice fills my ears, but I'm breaking down, and there is no stopping it anymore. Fear has combined with the grief I carry in my heart from losing two of the most important people in my life. It's dragging me underwater until I feel it fill my lungs.

I can't breathe.

"Alright, honey, it's okay. Let's get you off this floor and somewhere more private." I don't want to stand, but she gives me no choice.

This woman is pure muscle, and, apparently, I weigh nothing to her as she heaves me off the ground and helps me walk inside the building. It doesn't matter that I'm almost one-hundred and eighty centimeters and she's much shorter. It doesn't matter that I can't feel my legs. She carries me like none of that is true.

"Sit down," she says, and I do, sinking into the chair in front of what I assume is her desk. "I'll be right back," she calls out before storming out of the room and leaving me to say the same words in my head over and over again.

Please don't take Daisy from me. Please. She's my everything. I can't lose her. I can't.

"Here you go," Valentina says, and I look up to see her holding out a wet washcloth.

"*No siento las manos,*" I say in Spanish without meaning to, but she gives me a comforting smile.

"*¿Puedo?*" she replies in Spanish as well, and it surprises me so much, I just nod my head.

The beautiful woman in front of me drags the towel over my face, wiping away my tears and simultaneously calming me until I find a steady breathing rhythm again. One of her hands is cupping my jaw while the other works on cleaning my face off the pain I couldn't hold back.

My eyes flutter shut at her touch.

"*¿Quieres decirme qué pasa?*" she offers, still speaking in my mother tongue, and I give one slow nod before looking into her green-blue-brown eyes. They're as stunning as the rest of her.

I start from the very beginning, from when I lost my brother and best friend, to me becoming Daisy's mamá and the ridiculous demand Jennifer and Bert presented. Valentina listens closely, her gaze shifting from one of my eyes to the other while her face shows utter disbelief. It must sound as ridiculous as it feels to tell.

After years, now they suddenly give a damn about Daisy, and I cannot understand what the reason could possibly be. Did they realize how horrible they were to their daughter? Did they realize cutting her off because she moved to Mexico to marry my brother was wrong? I have no fucking clue. I wish I did. Maybe I could tell them this isn't the way to ease their guilt. Taking Daisy from me is not going to help anyone.

"What a load of shit," Valentina blurts out, and I laugh in response.

"What the hell am I going to do? I don't know anyone here, let alone someone who would be okay marrying me. Who would want to marry anyone for a reason like this?" And I don't even know how long this marriage has to last. Until I find someone new, fall in love, and then get a divorce to marry the person I actually love? That's fucked up.

But I will do it.

For Daisy, I'd sell my soul to the devil.

"I'm so sorry, Estrella. I can't believe they're making you do this in order to keep *your own daughter*," she says, and I nod along to her words.

"Do you know anyone who'd marry me?" I ask, desperation leaking through in my voice.

"If you'd come a few years earlier, I'm sure my brother would have married you. He didn't believe in the whole concept of marriage," she says and lets out a little laugh. "Well, until his wife came and flipped his whole world upside down. Stubborn ass still hasn't admitted I was right about him finding someone eventually," she adds, and I burst into laughter.

It's clear how close they are by the way her eyes sparkle when she speaks about him. That's the type of pure love I used to share with both Helen and Pedro. The same I share with Daisy. It can't be tainted by anything in the world. It can never be destroyed.

"I would suggest dating apps, but I don't know how safe that would be considering you'd have to disclose that you need to get married within the next two months," Valentina goes on, and I shake my head at her.

"I will figure it out. Somehow," I say and stand up, checking my watch because Eli and I are meant to have coffee today. They must be waiting for me already, and I hate making people wait. I'm always on time, if not a little early.

"I'll try to think of something," Valentina says, but I shake my head.

"There is nothing to do, but I appreciate you taking care of me," I reply, and she gives me a big hug before I can step out of the room.

"We'll figure it out."

Valentina's words linger in my head as I walk outside with my heart heavy in my chest. Eli is standing with sunglasses on their face and a devastating smile on their lips.

I'm supposed to marry someone I love, that's what my mamá and papá wish and hope for me. I'm supposed to tie myself to another person when I'm ready and not a moment before. I'm not supposed to marry a person I haven't even kissed or spent a night with, talking until the sun comes up.

But, here I am, determination in my chest as I step in front of Eli and say, "Can you marry me?"

Chapter 7
James

It's game night at Val and Gabriel's house. Adrian, Nevaeh, Val, Gabriel, and I are all here. I brought Damian to his moms Dominique and Nicolette earlier, and my heavy heart is currently crying in my chest because dropping him off sucks every single time. Apart from me, there is no one who loves Damian more than his moms, but the way I miss him doesn't get easier.

"You want anything to drink?" Val asks, and I look up at her, noticing something's off in the way she looks at me. I've loved this woman too long not to know every one of her tells.

"What's going on? You look upset," I say instead of answering her question.

Studying her face has always been painful in one way or another, but since losing the championship to her, it's become even harder. She used to represent everything I've wanted for my future wrapped into one person I could never have. Now she represents my failures, and the pining pain was much better than this shame deep inside of me.

I hate it.

"Reya told me something sad a few days ago, and I've been trying to figure out a way to help her, but I don't think there is one," she says, immediately piquing my interest.

I might not be that woman's biggest fan, but I don't like the thought of something bad happening to her either.

"Actually, your solution might just be sitting right here," Gabriel chimes in, his accent as thick as it has always been. A small smile tugs on the corner of his mouth when I give him an unimpressed look, but he merely keeps petting their dog, Chase, like the arrogant shit he is. God, I fucking hate him. Not as much as I used to, but enough.

"I don't like the sound of that," I reply. Nevaeh giggles beside me, and I notice her husband's face is nuzzled in her neck. Her cheeks are a bright pink, and there is something about their happiness that makes my chest pull tight until it hurts.

"What's wrong with Reya?" I ask instead of focusing on my feelings.

"Daisy's grandparents are threatening to take her away unless she can find a spouse within the next two months. They said Reya isn't capable of raising her daughter as a single mom," Val explains, and I notice the compassion in her eyes as they fill with tears.

Reya doesn't deserve that. No mother does.

"So, she has to find a spouse within the next two months? Who would ever get married to her in such a short time?" I ask because even imagining it sends a wave of ice down my spine.

What if she marries someone because she's desperate, but that person turns out to be rude? Bad for her? Abusive?

Another wave of shivers run down my spine, forcing the muscles in my back to tense.

"You should do it," Gabriel chimes in, staring me dead in the eye while one of his hands slides onto Val's leg. She wraps her arm around his, watching her husband with wide eyes.

"Why me?" I ask. He's fucking irritating with that half-smirk of amusement on his stupidly handsome face.

"Because I see the way you look at her, and you're not as much of a creep as what she has to resort to otherwise," Gabriel continues, and I let out a breathless laugh.

"Fuck you," I say, but his words are bouncing around in my head.

I would never marry someone I fight with every single time I see them.

Would I?

"Yeah, why don't you offer to marry her? It doesn't have to be forever, and it's not like you believe in marriage anymore," Adrian chimes in, and I flash him an annoyed look. He doesn't notice it. He's too busy staring at the rings on Nevaeh's left hand, the ones he gave her.

All of my friends are married. Adrian, Val, Leonard, even my sister, Mia, got married last year and she always told me she'd never, ever get married.

I don't know what the fuck I'm supposed to do. I have no responsibility toward this woman. We've fought every single time we spoke this far—which has been exactly fifty-two times, but who's counting?—and I don't want to be married to someone I loathe. No matter how I seek her out whenever I can and haven't stopped thinking about her since we met.

I'm definitely not marrying Reya.

I've barely known her for four months.

It's ridiculous to even consider. We might be attracted to each other—at least I hope it's not one-sided—but that isn't enough to marry someone. Even if it doesn't have to be forever... right?

My head is spinning so much, I can't sit still anymore.

"I should get back to Marbles and Lollipop," is all I say before standing up and grabbing my things from the table.

My feet bring me toward the gate area of Val and Gabriel's house until I'm out of sight and can start pacing. No one's forcing me to go through with this. I know that, but I'm still spiraling through every different scenario of what would happen if I told that infuriating woman I'd marry her.

I feel sick.

"James."

Absolutely not. He's the last person I want to speak to at the moment.

"Not in the mood, Biancheri," I reply, digging around in my pocket to get my keys.

"Can you hear me out?" he asks.

"No, thanks."

I check my other pockets, but my keys are in none of them. Gabriel crosses his arms in front of his chest before holding out his left hand, my keys dangling from his index finger. Of fucking course.

I let my head drop and sigh dramatically.

"You're not going to let me leave until you've said your piece, are you?" I ask, and he gives me one of those irritating smirks of his again.

"I think you know the answer to that question, James," he replies, and I snort.

"You want me to marry Reya." I don't know why I say it. He's made it abundantly clear he does. His small nod only irritates me more.

I'm convinced Gabriel was put on this planet to torture me with his presence.

"You're the perfect candidate," he explains and shrugs, his dimples showing as he smiles.

"Okay, either you spit out what you have to say or I will beat the shit out of you to get my keys." And finally fulfil my greatest fantasy.

"Fine, I will stop torturing you and make you see things for what they truly are."

Great. I'm excited.

"You are attracted to Reya, and she's attracted to you, even if you can't stand each other. You don't believe in marriage anymore, as Adrian said, and she needs someone who doesn't give a fuck about it. You're a good guy, and you would never simply watch something like what's happening to Reya unfold. Her daughter's grandparents are threatening to take her away from her mother. I know you won't stand by and let it happen."

My tongue is a brick in my mouth. My vocal cords feel frozen over. No sound leaves me, but I'm also convinced he isn't finished speaking yet. All the reasons he's listed sound noble, but the biggest one for him remains unspoken.

His eyes drop to the ground for a moment.

"Not to mention, you need to finally move on from my wife, and I think Estrella will be good for you. She challenges you, and you need someone who doesn't give you the chance to even look at someone else."

He takes a step toward me, grabs my hand, and slams my keys into my palm. My mind is still stuck on the revelation of Reya's full name when Gabriel keeps talking.

"I think we both know she has the potential to make you feel things you haven't felt since Val. You may not know her well, but the body and heart don't care about how long you've known someone. Your head is responsible for that, and you don't need your head to overthink your feelings in a fake marriage." He stops to grin. "But you may lose your heart somewhere along the way, and isn't that exciting?"

My shoulders sag, but I don't manage to say anything at first.

My body feels too heavy.

"I'll think about it," I say, and Gabriel tilts his head, his green-brown eyes showing sympathy for the first time in a while.

"No, James, you'll do it. If not for Reya or yourself, you'll do it for Daisy, because that little girl has already lost too much. You won't let her lose her mother, too, that's not who you are."

I hate that he's right.

I lay awake in bed for a long time. Marbles is nuzzled against my side and Lollipop is on my chest as I contemplate what I'm going to do about Reya.

Marriage is a big commitment. Legally and emotionally speaking, this is not an easy decision to make, but the image of Reya and Daisy hugging from a few weeks ago keeps replaying in my head. The way that little girl looks at her mother is how Damian looks at me.

And I guess marriage isn't that big of a commitment when you know it won't last forever. When you know you won't fall in love with the person and get your heart broken when they leave. Or choose someone else…

But you may lose your heart somewhere along the way, and isn't that exciting?
Gabriel's words repeat themself over and over in my ears.

"What should I do, Lolli?" I ask when she *meows*, her green eyes studying me.

Marbles and Lollipop are both Norwegian Forest cats, so they have long coats, and I find it soothing to sift my fingers through it. Both of my girls stare up at me with those green eyes of theirs, but that's the only similarity they share. Marbles has a grey and white and black coat while Lollipop has a reddish brown and white one.

Lollipop *meows* again, purring when I scratch her back.

"Does that mean do it?" I ask with a laugh, but because I'm talking to her, she crawls closer to me to rub her head against my chin. "Do you want a temporary mum?" Lolli's head snaps up, her eyes darting to the empty side of my bed.

I guess that means yes.

Oh my God. I don't have to get her a bloody ring though.

Right?

Chapter 8
Estrella

Eli said no to me. The only person I knew here who I would consider a friend told me they couldn't marry me. I can't say I blame them either. What I'm asking... it's too much. No one in their right mind would agree to marry another person they barely know within the next two months so I can keep my daughter. Not to mention, Eli has their own life, where they're in love with their sister's best friend.

My whole face feels numb because I've been crying so much the past few days, I didn't think it was possible to lose ten liters of bodily fluid through crying. Everything feels beyond hopeless. I have enough money to find a good lawyer and try to fight this, but Daisy is still going to have to go through hell because of Jennifer and Bert.

I thought I could avoid all of this.

"Okay, everyone, five minutes left," I call out to my group.

They're all busy playing a game of Capture The Flag. Daisy and Damian have been getting along so well. The little monster hasn't pulled my daughter's hair in four months. It makes me want to thank James, but that's only happening over my dead body.

"Mamá, can Damian and I watch a movie at his house today?" Daisy asks after the second to last child of our group is picked up by their parent. Damian and my daughter have been spending the whole day together, with Leonora too, so I can't believe they want to spend even more time together.

"Sure, if Damian's moms are okay with it," I reply because I already cleaned this morning, went grocery shopping with Daisy last night, and paid the bills during my break today. Everything is taken care of so my daughter can have the Friday afternoon she wants.

Wait.

Friday afternoon.

Oh no.

Oh no, no, no.

"Hey, bud," James' familiar voice fills my ears, and I shudder.

Please, let him be busy.

I have no patience to take my daughter to this man's house today. No matter how good he looks in his dress shirt and jeans, his blonde hair perfectly styled, and a knee-weakening smile plastered on his chiseled face.

"Daddy, can Daisy come over to watch a movie? She's never seen Cars! I have to show her," Damian says, his excitement sending a wave of warmth through me. James' devastating blue eyes meet mine, an unspoken question lingering in them. I fake a small smile and nod.

I'd do anything for my daughter. Always.

"Of course," he tells his son. "We need to speak," James adds while looking at me.

"About what?" I ask because I have no patience for vagueness and innuendos.

"Let's go," is James' only answer.

"No," I say, stopping him before he can leave.

"Are you always this difficult?" he asks through gritted teeth, but I don't falter under his challenging look.

"Only with you." James fights back a smile.

"Well, I won't tell you what we need to discuss out here in the open where anyone could overhear. Either you come with me, or I'll change my mind about the whole thing," he replies, but it's that same vagueness as before that makes me glare at him.

"What whole thing?"

"Come with me and find out." He walks away before I can ask again, and, damn him, my curiosity has me following.

Daisy takes my hand, and I smile when my eyes find her happy grin.

"Are you excited, *florecita*?" I ask, and my daughter gives me several nods.

"*Sí*, Mamá." Tears jump into my eyes at the way she looks at me.

She's the greatest love story I could have ever asked for. I didn't think I'd ever want to become a mother, but now it's a title I hold with pride.

I *am* a mother.

They will not take that away from me.

They will not take *her*.

James and I stand behind his sectional couch for the first ten minutes of the movie, watching our children get along better than ever before. Damian keeps telling Daisy something he finds exciting about the movie, and she keeps watching the talking cars like she's never seen anything better. I can already tell this will be her new obsession.

James' cats are also going to be on her list of new obsessions because she has not stopped petting them once since Damian introduced her to them.

"Come with me, please," James says, but I only offer him a cocked brow in response. "I even said please, Reya," he points out, and I can't help but smile a little at that.

"Yeah, I heard you, and as surprised as I am that that word exists in your vocabulary, I'm still not going anywhere alone with you," I reply, bringing my gaze back to the television.

He takes a step toward me and then another, his hand lifting to brush my hair away from my ear. His fingers tuck the strands behind it before he leans down and his lips almost brush my lobe. Shivers run down my spine, but I don't move.

Why the hell am I not moving?

His voice fills my ear before I can answer that question and everything stops spinning for a moment.

"I will marry you."

Four words.

Fourteen letters.

One promise.

Never in a million years would I have expected him to say this. James Landon offering to marry me is as bizarre as a lion walking on water would be.

"What?" I blurt out, but he merely presses one of his long fingers to his lips to keep me quiet. "Don't *shush* me," I whisper-scream, but he takes my hand to pull me out of the room.

Only once we're alone in his kitchen does he release me.

"Listen, Valentina told me about what's happening to you, and it's unacceptable. I may not like you very much, but I can see how deeply you care for your daughter. You're a good mother, so we're going to make sure no one takes her away from you," he says, crossing his arms in front of his chest and leaning against his stove.

No words leave me. I stare at him because there is so much about what he said that has my head spinning. He doesn't like me, but he wants to marry me so I can keep Daisy. He thinks I'm a good mother. *He thinks I am a good mother to my daughter...*

I start crying without meaning to, sending panic across his previously unimpressed expression.

James takes three strides toward me, raising his hands in an attempt to grab my face and comfort me, but I slap them away before he can touch me. I'm not crying to be comforted. I'm crying because for the last four months, Bert and Jennifer have made me feel like the worst mother in the world. So, hearing James, who doesn't even fucking like me, say I'm a good mother gave me the assurance I didn't think I needed.

"I apologize. I didn't mean to make you cry," James says with that gorgeous English accent of his, and I spin back around to look at him.

"Why would you do this? What do you get out of it?" I ask, my tears finally slowing when I realize I don't want to cry in front of this man.

James gives me a slow, breathtaking smile I have no business admiring.

"Has it occurred to you that I'm simply a decent person?" he replies, and I burst into laughter. It wipes the smile off his face.

"Be serious, James, what do you get out of this?" I ask.

"You want all the facts, darling? Fine," he says, and I choose to ignore the way my heart skips a beat when he calls me "darling" again. "I was in love with my best friend almost my entire life. I've only fucked people for the past few years because dating has become impossible for me. I feel numb inside, and therefore I will be the perfect person for this arrangement. I won't fall in love with you because I'm incapable of doing so, but I'll treat you right. I will be your husband for all intents and purposes, except love. I can't give that to you," he says, but all I manage to do is stare at his mouth as if it would explain the words falling from his lips.

"'All intents and purposes?'" I ask because it's the only thing my brain manages to focus on. His smug smile returns, and I realize what I'm asking him.

"Yes, Reya, we can fuck if you'd like. We're attracted to each other, and if we're going to be married, I don't see why we shouldn't enjoy ourselves," he replies, and I plant my hands on my face, a laugh leaving my lips.

"So, let me get this straight. You want to marry and potentially fuck me because we've been attracted to each other for the last four months, all because you've been in love with someone else your whole life and think you're incapable of falling in love?" I say, and James takes a step toward me. My heart starts thumping against my ribcage, but not in a bad way.

Not in a bad way at all.

"Precisely." I shake my head and lift one of my hands to press against his chest because he's coming so close, the proximity is making my head feel even dizzier.

"There is only one flaw in your plan. You've never resisted falling in love with me. My parents named me Estrella because they thought I was as special as a shooting star," I say to ease the tension, bringing amusement to his gaze.

"Trust me, that isn't something you need to worry about, but I'm glad you're also attracted to me. I mean, I assumed, but it's always nice to know when I pick up on these things correctly," he replies, taking another step toward me. I don't stop him, even though I should.

"I'm not attracted to you, James." I have no idea why the fuck I'm lying.

The Brit brings his face close to mine, his lips barely an inch away. His hot breath on my cheeks sends shivers down my spine, and it takes everything out of me not to close my eyes because he smells so good. I freeze in place when he lifts his fingers to my chin to cup it gently and force my head back. He could kiss me easily like this, but he doesn't. James merely smiles.

"We're going to be married. You will have to stay faithful so Daisy's grandparents know we're serious. Who will take care of your needs if not me?" he challenges.

"I've been taking care of my own needs for years, James. I don't need you," I reply, but it only makes him bring his mouth closer.

"Okay. We'll take sex off the table. We'll just get married, and you and Daisy will move in with me," he says and walks away, leaving me to my spinning head.

"'Just get married.' You make it sound so easy," I blurt out, stepping toward his kitchen island and heaving myself onto the marble counter.

"It is easy, and arse off my counter. Do you know how expensive the marble was?" he asks, and I stare down at the white stone with gray swirls.

"Do you know how expensive my ass is?" I reply, hearing him chuckle.

"Huh. I thought it was natural," he teases, but I merely tilt my head to show him my smug smile.

"It is."

And fuck, it took me years to be this proud of it. I wasn't born with a nice butt. I spent hours in the gym working on it, so when his eyes drop to where my ass is planted on the cool stone and he licks his lips, I grin in response.

"Stop staring at it," I say, and he finally brings his eyes back to my face.

"As you wish, wife," he replies and grabs two glasses from his cupboard.

"I am not your wife. I haven't even said I accept this proposal. Not that it's much of a proposal," I point out and scoff.

"I agree. You haven't even asked me to marry you yet," James says and steps in front of me. "I'm waiting," he says and lifts me off the counter. I let out a surprised laugh.

"You can't be serious," I reply, but he takes a step back and motions for me to go ahead. "Can you marry me?" I mumble, not even looking him in the eye.

"Will you look at me while you ask, darling? At least give me that. People normally get on their knees, you know?" he teases, but I'm done with this whole awful situation now.

I drop onto both of my knees and look up at him before saying, "James Landon, will you please marry me and make me the unhappiest woman?" The gorgeous man in front of me takes a step forward to cup my chin again. I let him do it. I have no idea why I keep letting him, but it would be a lie if I said I didn't enjoy his touch.

"How could I say no when you look so beautiful on your knees?" he asks, his voice low and rough.

My breath has no business hitching. A blush heats my cheeks and cleavage. He runs his thumb over my bottom lip, forcing more shivers to take over my body. I like the power dynamic between us right now. When it comes to sex, I like being submissive.

I like it when my partner takes control, which I tell myself is the reason for my visceral reaction.

"So fucking beautiful, Estrella. Are you sure we have to take sex off the table?" he asks, and I'm so mesmerized by how well he said my name, I forget to keep my walls up for a moment.

"No," I blurt out before regaining my rationality. He drops his thumb from my lip, which also helps me refocus. "Just answer the question, James. Yes or no?" I demand, and he smiles down at me.

"I will marry you, darling, and I will do everything in my power to help you keep Daisy where she rightfully belongs."

And for the first time since all this shit started happening with Daisy's grandparents, I feel hopeful.

Chapter 9
James

"That's the last time I'll get on my knees for you," she says, but desire has infiltrated my mind, and there is no stopping my next words.

"That'd be a shame, Estrella. I very much liked seeing you there," I reply because this woman has affected every cell in my body.

It's only lust, I know it is. I've had sex with quite a few people, and it's always started as this feeling. I don't know Estrella well enough to feel anything else, and after Val and even Annabel, my son's piece of shit mother who abandoned him, there is no room for me to hold any love or trust for a partner. No matter how beautiful they are. No matter the fire inside of them or how much I adore the way Reya challenges me. No matter how keen I suddenly am on the idea of putting a ring on her finger and making her mine. At least for a little while. It won't be forever. I know what I'm getting myself into, and that's bloody appealing.

"James, you should stop touching my hair," the woman in front of me says, and I realise I reached out to play with a strand of her brown hair.

"Sorry," I mumble because the moment has passed. It has to have vanished. I don't know if I could handle it if she kept... drawing me to her.

"We should probably set some ground rules," she starts as I walk over to my coffee machine. Caffeine might not be the right thing to drink right now considering every cell in my body is already vibrating, but I need to busy myself with something so I don't keep staring at her.

"How do you feel about kissing when we're around people to convince them the marriage is real?" I ask even if it's not necessary.

Lots of couples don't kiss in public. Other forms of affection are enough PDA, but I want to kiss her. The part of my brain that's constantly been thinking about her since we met is demanding a taste, and I know I won't be able to fight it off for long if she's my wife.

My wife.

Estrella is going to be my wife.

I shiver all over.

"Sure, but we also have to convince Daisy. I don't want to lie to her, but I think it's better if she doesn't know about this whole charade we're putting on and why. It's too much for a child her age."

"It's too much for a grown person too, Estrella. I'm sorry you're going through this," I say, and she gives me an unimpressed look.

"I don't want your pity, James. Thank you for doing this, but I'm not a damsel in distress that you're saving," she replies, forcing me to drop my head and shake it in disbelief.

"You're not a damsel in my eyes. You're a fighter and a mother who's been put in a horrible position. I can tell you I'm sorry without feeling pity because, trust me, pity is the last thing I feel for you." Admiration, desire, annoyance, and something I don't want to identify, sure, but not pity.

"Will we sleep in the same room?" she asks instead of answering my previous statement.

"We'll be sleeping in our bed, yes, because Daisy would be very confused if she ever walked into our room and we weren't," I reply, sending a wave of heat up my neck. It's logical, but the thought of sleeping next to Estrella every night still has my heart rate spiking.

"You should know, I've never lived with a man before. This will be very new for me, so have patience." I chuckle at that.

"I'm a patient man, Estrella. As long as you don't leave your shit lying around on the floor, I don't care what you do in my house," I say, placing the cup under the stream where the coffee is coming out.

"So, obviously falling in love is on our don'ts list considering you said you can't fall in love and I hope to God you won't be the first person I will ever fall in love with. But I also think that we should put it on our dos list to speak about our feelings. Even if it'll be a fake marriage, I think it's important," she explains, and I nod along to her words.

"Agreed. It'll be easier to tell each other what pisses us off considering we're not planning on keeping each other around," I point out with a small laugh, and she returns it, the sound so smooth in my ears, it makes my heart thump a little harder.

"Fair enough. For the don'ts list, no fucking other people, and no telling our parents that this marriage is fake. Mine would not be able to handle it, and I don't want yours to know how fucked up my life is," she says while I add some cream to my cup of coffee.

Once I'm done, I walk back in front of her—the troublemaker has placed her phenomenal arse back on my marble counter—and force myself to not say anything again.

"Apart from that, I think we should take things as they come. As long as we communicate, it'll be fine," I assure her before raising the cup of coffee to my lips. She snatches it out of my hand and takes a sip before I have the chance to.

"Fine. When do we move in?" she says and takes another sip of my coffee. I grab the cup out of her hand and plant my lips on the same side as hers were a moment before. She watches me like a hawk, her bottom lip slipping between her teeth in response.

"Monday. After, we will get a ring, and in a couple of weeks, we will have the wedding," I say because the sooner we get this over with, the better for Estrella.

"That's so soon," she mumbles, all of her emotions jumping into her eyes.

She doesn't want this. Neither of us truly does, but sometimes in life, we have to do things we never thought were part of our path. I never thought I'd become a dad in my early twenties. I never thought I'd have to watch Val marry someone else. I always thought I'd be a Formula One World Champion by now. Life never runs in a straight stream that follows people's desires. It branches off, curves, and has lots of rocky and shallow areas.

"I know, but we better get married before I change my mind," I tease, but panic crosses her face. I immediately feel guilty.

"You can't back out. I need you to see this through because I can't lose Daisy. So, you will marry me. You already offered, no take-backs," she rants while my eyes scan her face.

"No take-backs, I promise. I will be your husband for as long as you need me to be. You will be my wife."

Wife, wife, wife.

Why does this bloody word keep repeating itself in my head?

"The real reason why we need to get married so soon is because I have to leave for Spain after for pre-season testing," I explain, and her shoulders fall in relief.

"I have never been to a Formula One race," she blurts out, seemingly deep in thought. I smile at her, but her gaze is fixed on my chest.

"I'll take you. As my wife, you'll have to come to at least a few." There is that word again. Wife. I need to keep it out of my mouth.

"Just to be clear, since you like throwing around the wife thing, I will not be your property. I won't belong to you, even if I wear your ring on my finger," she says, and I can't help but smirk at her. Her eyes finally meet mine a second before they roll and she looks away again.

"We'll belong to each other, darling. There is no way around it." There is that possessive side again, too.

Okay, what the hell is going on in my head?

"God, you're insufferable. I can't wait to be stuck with you," she says and pushes off the marble counter.

Estrella is right in front of me then, only about half a head shorter than me. Her long legs are toned and thick with muscle. Her arms are pure muscle too, and her lips are so damn inviting when they're not telling me to fuck off. Who am I kidding? Even then they are. Her brown eyes are something else entirely. So warm and intoxicating and devastating.

Just like the rest of her.

"Mamá?" Daisy says, and I step away without a moment's hesitation.

The little girl says something in Spanish, causing Estrella to cross the kitchen with a grin plastered on her face. She takes her daughter's hand and follows her out of the room.

My future wife only turns her head to mouth the words "I fucking loathe you" at me and then disappears down the hall to the living room.

I think I just made a big mistake.

Chapter 10
James

WINTER BREAK, A TIME between the end of a season and the beginning of another in F1, should be for drivers to relax and rejuvenate so we're ready for the draining season to come. With Estrella and all of my fucking responsibilities to my team, I've had no time to do either of those things.

As much as I love my job and my team, I need one day for myself.

But that isn't possible anymore, not with Daisy and Estrella moving in. Not when I'll have to figure out how to live with a woman who clearly doesn't like me. I don't know what I signed up for when I offered to marry Estrella. Inviting her into my home without an end date. Because there is no end date right now. There is only "convince Daisy's grandparents that our marriage is real so they don't take Estrella's daughter from her." She hasn't even explained why they're doing it—Val told me but made me swear I wouldn't say anything—and I wonder if she'll ever open up about her brother and best friend.

If she'll ever feel comfortable enough around me to share that story.

"You look great, James. Did you finally hire a stylist to help you with your God-awful fashion choices?" Cameron Kion, my teammate at Hawke for the next two seasons and decade-long friend, asks, and I almost snort.

"It's too early in the morning for a verbal sparring, mate. I'm seeing Estrella later, so I'll have to reserve my energy," I say, rubbing a hand down my face. Cameron grins his famous grin at me.

"Four months, and you still haven't figured out how to speak to her without making her angry?" I shoot him a glare so vicious, anyone else would have blushed in embarrassment and left the room. Not Cameron. He finds my reaction amusing.

"She makes me angry. She's infuriating. She insults me one second, then looks at me like she's never seen anyone as attractive as me. It's messing with my head," I say, gesturing a lot more with my hands than is necessary.

"You can be attracted to someone you dislike, James. Doesn't mean they want to marry you. Oh wait—" He cuts off and snickers to himself.

"Ha, ha. Keep practicing. One day, you might just actually make someone laugh."

We glare at each other for a moment before we both burst out laughing. Me at the ridiculous situation I find myself in; Cameron at me.

"Come on. We've got a charity event to attend," he says, breaking the silence once we've both calmed down enough to get a handle on our laughter.

We make our way through the halls of the factory, members of our team running around to get everything in order. From what I've been told, Hawke Racing is hosting a simulated grand prix weekend to raise money for research funds for blindness. Hawke's team principal, Jessica Thorn, let it slip to me that this has Leonard Tick's influence in it, which makes sense considering his mum went blind years ago. He may be retired, but Leonard will never stop trying to change the world. It's why he's always been the man I've looked up to since I was a kid.

"How does this work again?" Cameron asks right as I cover my mouth to let a yawn escape me.

Travelling here this morning at three and having to fly back to Monaco this afternoon to help Estrella pack is going to make today the longest day I've had in a while.

"You've done simulator races before, right?" I ask, and Cameron rolls his eyes at me because we both know the answer to my question. "Well, they've invited a lot of rich people who want to spend money to see us race as well as auction off some old racing suits, helmets, and shoes, I believe." Cameron scrunches his nose up in disgust.

"Shoes? Isn't that disgusting?" he asks with a small laugh. "We sweat a lot in those."

"We? Or *you*?" This time, he does blush.

"Whatever."

We don't speak again. Instead, we walk toward Jessica and her team. Daiyu and Ximena are also here today, and I greet both of them with a hug.

"Nice outfit," Daiyu says with a mischievous grin, and I look down at my dark green dress shirt and black slacks.

"Okay, what's wrong with how I usually dress?" I finally ask.

"Nothing, but it's good to know you can actually dress up," Ximena chimes in, grinning at me. I pull my lips into a thin line, unamused.

"I hate to interrupt, but there are people waiting. Mr. Kion, you will teach Felix how the simulator works, and Mr. Landon, you will teach Evelyn. They are the two fans who have been chosen for today's event," Jessica says as she approaches, handing us team shirts to give to the kids. "You will team up with them. Try to mentor them well. It will impact your team results at the end," our team principal says with a smile before giving us more information about the kids.

Then, she ushers us out of the door and into the big hall where a group of people are already waiting for us. They burst into cheers at the sight of us, standing together as teammates for the first time in our careers. We do our best to smile at all of them before moving over to the kids we're supposed to mentor today.

"Hi, Evelyn," I say to greet the teenager.

"I can't believe this. You're James Landon. You're—" They cut off, covering their mouth with their hands as tears shoot into their eyes.

"It's a pleasure to meet you." I bring a smile to my face. "Are you ready to beat Cameron and Felix in the simulator?" I ask to help them redirect their focus from the overwhelming feelings of meeting me to the excitement of today.

"Ye—Yes. My mom bought me a simulator to practice at home a few months ago, so I have some experience," they say, still looking at me like I'm cooler than I actually am.

I hand Evelyn the shirt Jessica gave us before turning to Cameron and saying, "Evelyn and I are going to wipe the floor with you." He snorts as he guides Felix toward the simulator.

"Can I ask you something?" Evelyn says as I tell them which simulator seat to take.

"Of course. Today you get to ask me all your questions," I assure them, grabbing the headset the Hawke Racing crew arranged for today and placing it on their head.

"How did you feel after losing the title to Valentina last season?"

"Straight for the toughest question, kid," I say with a breathless laugh. "Well, Valentina and I have been best friends since we were kids, so I'm glad that, if I had to lose to anyone, I lost to her. I'd rather be beaten by the first female F1 driver than Adrian Romana," I tease, making Evelyn laugh.

"She's the reason I want to go into racing. Her and Leonard Tick. They're amazing," Evelyn swoons, and I flash them a wholehearted smile.

"Yeah, they are," I reply, adjusting the headset on their head until it's in its proper place. "Now, I need you to focus. Cameron and Felix cannot win after the comment I just made."

"Will try my best," Evelyn assures me. I give them a high five before moving over to my simulator seat, which is right beside the kid's.

All four of us decide on the Hawke Racing Ring circuit because it's long been considered the simplest track on the F1 calendar. While there is no such thing as simple when it comes to Formula One tracks, in my opinion, this one only has ten corners. It'll be the easiest for the kids.

"How are you feeling?" I speak into the microphone of the headset so Evelyn can hear.

"I feel ready to kick their butts." I definitely got the best teammate today.

My eyes drift around the room while we wait for Cameron and Felix to finish selecting their cars and setting up for the race. There are several reporters in here, some from *Spectre Sports* and some from *Griffin Sports*. A lot of the wealthiest people in England are also here, and I do my best to offer a smile to each and every one of the ones staring at me.

"We're ready," Cameron informs us, so we take a few practice laps for Evelyn and Felix before we do a mock Qualifying to determine from which position all of us will start.

I take pole while Cameron takes second, Evelyn third, some non-player-characters positions four through eight, Felix ninth, and then more NPCs fill the rest of the twenty places. I flash my teammate for the day a proud smile, and Evelyn returns it.

Then, we get to racing.

Cameron overtakes me in the first lap, Evelyn following closely behind us. Felix isn't very confident in any of this, but he is laughing like he's having the time of his life.

"Get him, James," Evelyn cheers me on, so I push as much as I can, doing my best to only sightly shove Cameron into the gravel in the second lap of the race.

"Hey!" he complains, but I don't apologize. I keep racing, grinning to myself as he mumbles several things into the microphone of his headset. It's censored because of the kids, but it's still hilarious. "Just you wait until we're fighting each other on the real track," Cameron warns, but I know my teammate. He doesn't drive as aggressively as... well, me. It's not a bad thing, safety first and all that, but he also never takes risks to overtake. He plays it safe, which is why he's never led a championship before. I have. Last season, I was on top, and if it hadn't been for that one mistake, I could have—

Could have, would have, should have. There is no point lingering on the what-ifs and other possible outcomes of things long past.

I don't want to live in the past. I want to move forward.

Especially when I'm leading this race, even if it's only in a simulator.

"Come on, Evelyn. Overtake Cameron," I say, letting out a cheerful sound when they overtake him in the following lap.

"Good job, kid. Now, keep going!"

We fight Cameron until the last lap. Felix has made his way into fourth place, too, and he's laughing at the way Evelyn keeps defending their place from the F1 driver. Right before the finish line, I slow my car, letting my teammate of the day overtake me. I time it well enough to keep Cameron back so Evelyn comes in first, me second, Cameron third, and Felix fourth.

Evelyn's eyes are wide with awe when they realise they won, and I give their shoulder a proud pat before turning to Cameron to see him mouth "you're a softie" to me.

I merely grin.

I'm fucking exhausted by the time I make it to Estrella's flat. Her door is wide open and music is playing so loudly, she doesn't see or hear me until I'm right in front of her. She jumps at the sight of me, placing a hand to her chest as she says several words in Spanish that I'm convinced are curse words.

"For fuck's sake, Landon, don't you knock?" she says and throws one of the pillows she was holding at my stomach. I catch it with a laugh.

"I did, but you were too busy belting out the song to hear me." She throws another pillow, this time at my head. It hits me square in the face because I was too slow. Once it's on the floor, we both stare down at it before slowly dragging our gazes back to each other.

"Huh. I thought F1 drivers were supposed to have great reflexes," she says while I roll up my sleeves, simply nodding along to her words. "What are you doing?" Estrella asks, her brown eyes going wide when I approach her.

"Getting revenge," I point out, but right as I make it to where she's standing, she sprints away with a reluctant laugh escaping her.

"What the fuck?" she blurts out, clearly as surprised by this playful behaviour as I am for being like this.

But we have to bond. I have to find a way to make her feel less anger for me if we're going to survive this marriage, and this is one way to hopefully do so.

Well, unless I fuck it up.

I chase her across her kitchen, wrapping an arm around her middle and pulling her feet off the ground. A squeal escapes her, but she slams a hand onto her mouth to keep any more from leaving her lips, even as I tickle her sides.

"James!" she barks, trying to escape me. "Fine, I'm sorry. I'm sorry, let me go!" she calls out, so I drop her to the floor again, both of us laughing and breathless. She turns around to show me her smile. "Petty fucker, aren't you?" she asks, putting her fists on her hips and placing a glare on her face.

"If I was, Gabriel would have been run over once or thrice by now." That makes her crack a smile again.

"You've got to get over that," she says, leaving me to stand in her kitchen by myself while she goes back to packing.

"So I've been told." I join her in the living room. "Can I help you pack?" I ask, trying to ignore how gorgeous I think she looks in a pair of biker shorts and crop top. She also looks extremely comfortable, and I feel miserable still wearing the same outfit as I did for the event. I didn't have time to change because I rushed to her apartment to make sure if she needed help, I'd be here.

"No. I'm almost finished," she says right as Daisy walks out of what I assume is her room. She speaks to her mum in Spanish before skipping out of the room again, completely disregarding my presence.

"Should we discuss Daisy's routine? So I know what it looks like," I suggest before grabbing one of the blankets Estrella was about to fold. She stares at me for a moment.

Then, she says, "I will be taking care of my daughter, James. Don't worry about her routine." I frown at her instantly.

"We'll be living together. I'll be taking care of both of you. That's just how—" She cuts me off.

"No, you won't. Daisy and I are a unit, and we've been fine on our own for almost five years. We don't need you to pretend to care about us." Estrella walks into the room Daisy disappeared into minutes ago while I let her words bounce around in my head.

They're not my responsibility, but I will do whatever I can to take care of them.

And it won't be because I'm pretending.

It'll be because they deserve it.

Chapter 11
James

SOMETHING'S WRONG. ESTRELLA HAS been silently unpacking several of her boxes for an hour without speaking. To say she's efficient is an understatement. She packed up her whole apartment in a day and hired someone as efficient to bring all of her things to my house so that within two hours, everything was already here. She didn't waste a second carrying it to the designated rooms. I tried to help her, but she told me to watch Daisy, so I've been teaching her a card game.

My eyes betray me because they keep slipping back toward Estrella. The glass doors that lead toward my veranda where Daisy and I are sitting, wrapped in blankets and with the patio heaters on, allow me to watch every single one of her movements.

There's something about her that's been confusing me.

She barely gives me time to think about important things like my job and career, but she's also been giving me less time to think about people I've been trying to forget for years. It's fascinating and makes me want to keep her forever, which is, of course, ridiculous. I merely like that she has the power to take over everything in a way no one, not even Val, has ever managed.

"Do you love my mamá?" Daisy blurts out, and I freeze in place, shifting my eyes back to the little girl who barely looks like her mum.

"Why else would I marry her?" I ask with a smile because it's the only way I don't have to lie to her and am able to keep the truth from Daisy at the same time.

"Do you know my mamá was a racer?" she asks next, and I lower my cards to give her my full attention.

"Really?"

"*Sí*. She raced autos," Daisy explains as she wiggles in her seat, her accent thick as she speaks. "She's a champion back home," the little girl goes on, and I can't help but bring my gaze back to where Estrella is unpacking inside.

She has my full permission to do whatever she wants with the interior. I've never been attached to this house. It's merely a place to live when I'm not racing, but I have a feeling she will turn it into a home before I know what has hit me. Giving up her apartment must not have been easy, so I don't want to limit her by telling her where she can put her things either.

"I think Mamá is really sad. She doesn't want me to know." I don't think Estrella wants anyone to know she's hurting, but it doesn't surprise me that Daisy picked up on it. Children are more intelligent than people give them credit for.

"I'll take care of her, I promise," I assure her before the words even process in my head.

"Because you love her." This child really doesn't hold back, does she?

There is no way in hell I would ever deny it in front of Daisy. I don't want her to think marriage can happen if you're not in love with someone. That's not the way it's supposed to go. I was always meant to place a ring on the finger of the person I love more than anything in the world, not someone I met four months ago and haven't decided if I'll ever like yet.

"Is your mamá why you want to be a racer?" I ask Daisy as she attempts to shuffle the cards for the next round. Her fingers barely manage to hold half of the deck, and I can't help but chuckle at how cute she is.

"Yeah," she says and starts pouting at the cards because they keep slipping.

"Let me help you," I offer, but she frowns at me in response.

"I can do it," she announces, and I grin to myself. Stubborn. Doesn't accept help easily. Strong. Just like her mum.

Marbles jumps onto the table right as Daisy places a card in front of me.

"Come here, sweet girl," I say and lift her onto my lap, petting her head.

"Why did you name your cats 'Marbles' and 'Lollipop'?" Daisy asks once she's done handing out the cards.

"Well, marbles and lollipop are F1 terms," I explain, but the little girl gives me a confused look. "Marbles are the pieces of rubber from the tyres that collect at the sides of the racing line on the track. And lollipops are the signs that tell drivers to stop and go into first gear during a pitstop. They're held by a member of the pit crew." I don't know if my explanations make any sense to her, but she's nodding like she understands every word anyway.

"I like their names," is all she replies before we keep playing, silence filling the space between us.

Eventually, she puts her cards on the table, her eyes suddenly opening and closing more slowly than before. A yawn escapes her, and I check my watch to see it's her bedtime.

"Come on, princess, you need to get some rest," I say and stand up.

My feet bring me to the sliding glass doors that lead into my house, but Daisy takes my hand and waits for me to walk inside first. Estrella halts her movements to watch me and her daughter, hand in hand.

I don't often get to feel like a dad. Five years ago, I wasn't ready to be one, but with Daisy's little hand getting dwarfed by mine, I know being a dad is exactly who I'm meant to be.

I just never knew how badly I wanted to be a full-time dad. It's not until after I tuck Daisy into bed and a pang of longing shoots through my chest that it hits me. I miss Damian. Seeing the little girl fall asleep makes me miss my son even more than I did before. He's happy with his mums, but it doesn't keep me from wishing I could spend more time with him.

It's selfish, I know it is, but feelings are hardly ever born out of rational thought.

Once I'm sure she's sleeping, I place my hand on her head for a moment, thinking about how peaceful she looks compared to the tough expression she usually carries on her face. I can't help but wonder if her mum looks the same, if the weight of the whole world stops resting on her shoulders once she falls asleep.

I guess I will find out tonight.

Fuck, I hadn't even thought about the fact that Estrella and I will be sharing a bed from today on.

"Brilliant," I mumble to myself, running a gentle hand over Daisy's hair before leaving the room we turned into her bedroom. I bought a bed, rug, and some toys, but Estrella unpacked all of Daisy's belongings an hour ago.

I step back into the living room where Estrella is putting a few green throw pillows on my couch. Pain still clings to her features, but she's trying her best to hide it by scowling. I study the way her full lips are pulled downward. This isn't anger. When she gets angry, she smiles, which is as frightening as it is hot. It's as if she knows looking mad isn't even half as terrifying as smiling at the person you're upset with. Scowling means she's trying to hide what I'm certain she thinks is a weakness.

Being sad.

As her future husband, I should walk over to her, take her in my arms, and comfort her. As the irritating man I actually am to her, I stay in place, crossing my arms in front of my chest and watching her. I lean my shoulder against the wall leading into the living room.

The muscles in her arms flex as she picks up a box and places it on the coffee table in front of the couch, and I watch them with fascination and desire spiraling through me in equal measures.

Estrella ignores me for several minutes until she's had enough and drops everything to glare at me.

"Can I help you?" she demands, so I push off the wall and close the distance between us.

"Would you like to tell me why you're upset?" I ask with a small smile I hope comforts her. Or at least makes her open up to me.

"Not particularly," she replies, her brown eyes shifting back to the box she was working on a moment ago. It's a clear indication she's looking for a way to distract herself, but I'm not having it.

"I know this won't be easy, but I keep seeing a million worries cross your face," I explain, taking another step toward her. Her floral scent bombards my sense of smell until it courses through my bloodstream and heats me from the inside.

"Well done, Sherlock, you can tell this situation upsets me," she replies, lashing out at me even though I'm certain I'm not the one she's really mad at.

"Does that mean you're Watson?" I tease, and she cracks a little smile despite herself.

"Don't be a pain," Estrella complains, dropping onto the couch behind her a moment before I'm right in front of her.

"Tell me why you're upset," I reply and sit down beside her.

"Huh, let's see. I gave up an apartment I loved, I have to marry *you*, and I will have to share a bed with you tonight. I'm unpacking and hating every second of it, Daisy is going to see you as another parent and when we get divorced it will hurt her, and, oh yeah, her grandparents informed me an hour ago that they will be attending the wedding."

Her rant comes to an end, leaving me with spiraling thoughts.

Worry spreads through my chest because she's right. Daisy is going to look at me like another parent, and when Estrella and I break up our fake marriage, the little girl isn't going to understand what's happening. Why I won't be there anymore. Then again, if Estrella and I have to be married for years, I doubt I won't become attached to Daisy.

Fuck.

I doubt I won't become attached to Estrella. I may never fall in love with her, but ever since I was little, I've cared deeply about the people around me. Often too much for my own good. Estrella is right. This is going to be more complicated than anything else I've ever gone through… but it'll be worth it when Daisy gets to stay with her mum.

Plus, my heart hasn't properly beaten in years, and it's not about to start because of these two moving in with me.

"I was going to suggest Daisy's grandparents come regardless," I manage to tell Estrella once I find my voice again. "It will solidify our whole pretence. They won't be able to question our marriage if they see me putting a ring on your finger and vice versa," I explain, and her eyes instantly drop to her bare ring finger.

I don't know what comes over me.

My fingers wrap around her strong hand so my thumb can swipe over the skin there. The same, weird possessiveness I've experienced too often around Estrella resurfaces as I think about the piece of jewellery I'll put on her finger soon.

My ring.

She'll be wearing my ring and will be my wife.

Maybe it's because I never thought this would happen for me, maybe it's because there's something about her that has me all over the place.

Either way, the thought of it all makes me feel more at peace than I thought I would.

"We haven't even kissed yet, James. How can we convince a room full of people, including Bert and Jennifer, that we're in love?" she asks, and I peel my eyes off her empty finger to bring them back to her uncertainty-ridden features.

"Is that your way of saying you want me to kiss you?" I ask with a smile, but Estrella rolls those brown eyes at me.

"You really are insufferable. You're about to marry someone you've been fighting with for the last four months, and you don't seem the least bit concerned," she says, snatching her hand out of mine. I wasn't even aware I was still holding it, but now that it's gone, I want to take it back.

"I'm not concerned. We will figure it out as we go. As long as we manage not to strangle each other, everything will be fine."

"Strangling you does sound like a good plan, though." I give her the unimpressed look that statement deserves. "We don't even know each other," she mumbles after a while, dragging her knees against her chest on the couch. It's the first time she appears more fragile than she is.

"Let's see. My full name is James Oliver Landon. My birthday is the fifteenth of January. I have a son I love more than anything, a sister called Mia, and parents who haven't spoken to me since they found out I was going to be a dad. I adore being a Formula One driver. My favourite colour is green. I like most animals and Marvel movies. The biological mother of my child abandoned us when Damian was an infant and left me with trust issues, and, to top it all off, the best friend I was in love with almost my whole life is Valentina. There, those are the most important details you need to know," I rant breathlessly.

I expect Estrella's eyes to go wide, for her to get overwhelmed and run, or anything revealing signs of panic. She does none of those things. Her eyes stay on my face while she rests her chin on her knees.

"That must suck, being in love with someone who doesn't feel the same," she points out, and I let out an unamused laugh. Out of all the things she could have asked me about, I should have known she'd get stuck on that.

"*Well done, Sherlock*," I reply, using her words from before. She smiles at me before standing up and stepping in front of me. Her legs cage in my knees, and I'm so perplexed, I freeze in place. "What are you doing?" My heart is racing.

"May I?" she asks, pointing at my lap. I cock an eyebrow, my body relaxing as I smile at her.

"You want to sit on my lap, darling? Already? I thought it'd take you longer to stop fighting this attraction between us," I reply, a smug smile taking over my face. Estrella glares down at me before bringing a smirk to her face.

"You want me on your lap or not?" she challenges, so I simply bring my hands to her hips and lift her onto my lap.

Her body somehow perfectly fits on top of me, a thought I'm having a difficult time ignoring. Her fingers dig into my shoulders while her parted lips draw my attention to them.

"This would be even better if you'd taken your clothes off first," I blurt out, but she takes my chin between her fingers and cuts off my ability to breathe.

"This whole being in love with your best friend thing isn't going to work for me. This might be a fake marriage, but I can't have you looking at Valentina the way you're supposed to be looking at me. So, from now on, I'm the only woman you get to fantasise about, get to have feelings for, and get to look at longingly. Do you understand?"

Bloody fucking hell.

Her gaze spreads liquid fire through my veins until all the blood rushes south. She must notice because she shifts on top of me ever so slightly, and her eyes fill with lust.

"That's not how it works. You must know that," I reply, fighting her even though right now, I can't even remember why I ever fell for Val.

"I don't care. Make it work," she says and attempts to get off my lap, but I keep my hands on her hips so she stays in place.

"Fine, but let's get one thing straight, darling. The next time you get on my lap, I will be the one giving demands," I say, and she gives me another one of those breathtaking smirks. She leans down until her lips are almost touching mine.

"You like to be in control, don't you?" she challenges, her lips brushing mine briefly with the last word.

Okay, she wants to play? I'll play.

I capture her bottom lip between my teeth and apply the smallest bit of pressure before releasing it again. Her breathing hitches against my skin, sending a bolt of pleasure through me.

I don't think I've ever been this goddamn hard because of a woman on top of me in my whole life.

"I do like to be in control." That makes her smile brightly, so I give her arse a quick, soft slap. "Now, get off my lap. We still have a lot to unpack," I say because if she stays one more moment, I'm going to forget this is all pretend.

I'm going to forget this marriage is a lie.

Most of all, I'm going to forget I don't fall in love anymore.

But when we get back to unpacking, Estrella stills for a moment, her attention shifting back to me.

"My favourite colour is also green," she says with a shy look.

We stare at each other without speaking another word for several long, tense moments before she looks away, back at her box.

I don't manage to take my eyes off her for several more moments, though.

Chapter 12
Estrella

"I WANT THE BIGGEST ring they have," I tell James once we step into the jewelry store. The Brit glares at me with those blue eyes of his, the ones that remind me of a clear blue sky on a hot summer day.

"I want you to have something you can wear without getting stuck on a million things," he replies and walks toward a man standing behind the glass displays.

"How thoughtful," I say, but it sounds as mocking as I intended.

"Come, Estrella, choose something so we can get out of here," James says, only adding to the romance of this whole thing. I squeeze Daisy's hand, and she looks up at me with her eyebrows furrowed.

She doesn't understand anything that's happening. After I told her we'd be moving in with James, she was not happy. She said she likes Damian now, but not enough to live in his house. Only after I explained it's not for forever—and that Damian lives with his moms most of the time—she said she was fine with it.

There was so much attitude in her tone, I couldn't help but smile at my daughter. She's a lot like her dad in that way, and so smart like her mom used to be. She has a part of each of the people I loved most living inside of her, and it's by far one of my favorite things in this world.

"I have to choose a ring," I remind Daisy because I already explained wedding traditions and ceremonies to her. I kept things simple, but it's impossible for her to remember everything, no matter how smart she is.

"Do I get a ring?" she asks in English, and James turns his head to give her a little smile.

"Choose whatever you want, Daisy. I'll buy it for you," he replies, and my daughter lets go of my hand to skip toward the glass displays. She looks at the jewelry with hearts in her eyes, bringing a wave of happiness to my chest.

I love how expressive her face is.

"You don't have to do that," I whisper once I'm close enough so only James can hear me. He bends down a little more to nudge my shoulder with his.

"I want to. You and Daisy are a package deal, and therefore you should both get something," he explains, causing my heart to flutter in my chest. I don't trust this man, but he wasn't lying when he said he was a decent person. He's more than decent.

James is kind.

"Thank you," I mumble, so he nudges me with his shoulder again.

"Let's find a ring worthy of your beauty. Can't have my wife walking around with something simple," he says and walks away to leave me to my spinning head. "Hurry up, Estrella," he adds, and I roll my eyes.

Pendejo.

We look through a hundred different rings, none of them speaking to either of us. They're either too flashy for me, or too simple for James. He wants me to have a ring everyone can see, but it can't be too big either so it doesn't get stuck on things. Considering we haven't found a way to stand each other yet and are just supposed to get married, he seems to care a lot about the little details surrounding it. Earlier, he spent an hour on the phone to get us this great venue for next weekend. *Salle Des Étoiles*, if I'm not mistaken. I don't want to know how much money he's spending on this fake wedding.

"Can I just take this one?" I ask and point at the small princess-cut diamond.

"Absolutely not. It's tiny. How are people supposed to see it?" he asks without looking at me, his gaze fixed on the row of rings in the beige case in front of him.

"Why does it matter?" I challenge while Daisy continues to look at the necklaces she's been eyeing for the past thirty minutes.

"This one," James says and peels one of the rings out of the case.

He takes my hand before I get to look at the piece and slides it down my finger. A perfect fit. I look up at him and hold eye contact until butterflies flap their wings against every organ in my body. The ring is a diamond cut into a star and the rest of it spirals into different lines of smaller diamonds. It looks like a shooting star. A fucking shooting star that he chose because I told him why my parents named me Estrella.

"We'll take this one," James says without even asking me if I like it.

He doesn't have to. I love it, of course I do. This is by far the most beautiful ring anyone could have ever given me, but, for some reason, I can't manage to form the words.

"What do you want, princess?" James asks, looking at my daughter. She points at the necklace with a flower as the charm.

"Can I have this one?" Daisy says, bringing a softness to her tone that normally isn't there. Five years old, and she's already damn great at manipulating men to get her will.

I've never been prouder.

"Sure," James replies before turning to the man helping us and asking for the necklace my daughter wants.

Living in Monaco is expensive. I have the money to afford our life here and buy Daisy anything she could need. Winning races back home earned me enough, but I don't ever spend it on fancy jewelry, especially not here where everything is so pricey. Hearing James spend ten thousand euros on the ring and necklace makes me a little nauseous.

I open my mouth to say something when he stares down at me and grinds out the words, "I don't want to hear it, Estrella."

"Fine, then," I reply, slip off the ring to place it on the counter, and take Daisy's small hand again. "Maybe we should get something to eat so you're not as much of a cranky jerk," I whisper before leaving the shop and waiting outside for him.

Daisy pulls me all the way to the café across from the jewelry store, mumbling something about wanting a croissant. I'm hungry too, so we hurry inside and grab three croissants, which Daisy orders in flawless French.

It's not an eight thousand euro ring, but I feel bad about the way I spoke to James. He's doing all of these wonderful things for me. Not to mention, he had to say goodbye to his son two days earlier than planned because his moms took him on a surprise trip to Paris to see a family friend. I know he didn't have to, he could have told Dominique and Nicolette that it's his weekend, not theirs, but James isn't that type of person. It's something I keep realizing.

It's annoying.

My daughter and I walk back to the jeweler where James is waiting for us, speaking to someone on the phone. Only when I get closer do I realize it's a catering company.

I don't know what the point is of turning it into such a spectacle, but I'm assuming it's to make things seem real. Everything has to be perfect so Bert and Jennifer can't find any holes in the story, or the rest of the world, for that matter. They're not expecting me to go through with a wedding, which might be my only advantage. They will be thrown off-guard, and that gives me enough time to sell my marriage to Formula One driver James fucking Landon.

I don't think I will ever get used to all of this.

My focus is so far on my thoughts, I don't even realize Daisy is poking James' leg to get his attention. As amusing as it is to see him get annoyed, I've taught my daughter how to be patient. I'm about to step in when James hangs up and crouches down to be at eye level with her.

"What's up, princess?" he asks as he digs around in the bag he got from the jewelry store.

"Are you going to be my daddy?" Daisy says, and I stumble two steps backward.

This is exactly what I've been worried about, what I told James would happen. Oh God, I can't breathe.

I try to swallow back my fear so Daisy doesn't see me cry, but when James places the necklace over her head and it falls down her small neck, all of my emotions intensify.

I'm the worst mother in the world. No wonder they want to take her from me. What kind of parent would put their child through more heartbreak when she's already facing a mountain of it once she's old enough to understand her mom and dad passed away when she was still a baby? The kind of parent who'd do anything for their child, but it's not enough in this case, is it?

"I'll be whatever you tell me to be," James replies, and it takes everything out of me not to collapse to the ground and break down completely.

James catches my tormented face. I try to turn away, but his blue eyes hold me in place as a tear drops down and we have a conversation without having to speak.

It'll be okay.

How can you be so sure?

I just am.

You're a pain in my ass.

Tell me something I don't know.

I'm scared.

I don't think he's able to pick up on my last words, but he gives me a compassionate smile as if he did. Daisy puts her hands on James' shoulders to get his attention back on her, and I manage to fight my feelings enough to stop crying.

"Okay! I want you to be a horse and carry me home," Daisy announces, and James doesn't waste a second. He spins around so she can get on his back and then makes some horse noises.

My daughter lets out an excited giggle while James steps in front of me and holds out the bag for me to take.

"Let's go home, Estrella."

Chapter 13
Estrella

It's been almost a week since Daisy and I moved into James' house. My daughter, being the angel she is, has helped me avoid sleeping in a bed with my future husband since the first night. She said she feels strange sleeping here, so I've used it as an excuse to be in her room the whole night. It might make me a coward, but I don't care. I'd rather be a coward than sleep in the same bed as James.

Ever since our moment on the couch, I've been doing my best to stay as far away from him as possible. The way it felt to be on top of him, have him press against me...

I shiver at the memory but push it away when my phone rings.

"*Hola*, Mami," I say as I pick up my mother's phone call. We speak at least once a week, sometimes more if I miss her.

"*Hola, mi amor*," she replies, her voice firm and sure, unlike mine. Ever since I've gotten engaged to James, I've been feeling extremely guilty while speaking to her. I haven't even told her I'm getting married.

"*¿Cómo estás? ¿Y cómo está Papá?*" I ask as I watch James put down Marbles and Lollipop's food bowls. He's still in his pajamas, which consist of nothing but shorts, and I do my best not to stare at his massive thighs or muscular chest.

"We're doing well, Estrella, simply missing you and Daisy. When do you think you'll have a chance to visit us again?" she asks, and I stare down at the ring on my finger, shame filling my chest.

"Probably not for a while, Mami." I fight the urge to burst into tears when she sighs into the phone. It's been two years since I've seen them. I miss my parents more than anything, but for the next little while, I have to focus on what is happening with Daisy.

"Can we come to you instead, sweetheart?" More tears spill into my eyes.

"I don't think right now is a good idea."

Just tell her, Estrella. Lie to her.

"Does this have anything to do with Jennifer and Bert asking us to give them your contact information a few months ago?" She told me that three months ago, but it makes me angry to think about them reaching out to my parents every single time I'm reminded of it.

"There is something I have to tell you," I start, letting out a deep breath. James' attention drifts to where I am on the couch in the living room, so he walks toward me and settles down on the coffee table in front of me. He mouths the words *press mute*, so I say, "Hang on, Mamá," before doing as I'm told. "What?" I ask, a little annoyed he's interrupting my conversation.

James' hands slip onto my thighs and he gives them a comforting squeeze. My stomach takes a tumble in response.

"You love your parents, right?" he asks, and I lower my phone as I focus on his mouth, trying to understand his words.

"More than anything but Daisy," I admit.

"Then tell them. Don't lie to them. It's easy for me to lie to mine because my father hates me and my mother has cut me off, too, but you shouldn't have to. They can handle it, if you give them a chance that is," he says, his eyes dropping to the engagement ring around my finger. Something possessive flits through his eyes, but it disappears right as he removes his hands from my thighs.

"I don't want them to worry," I whisper, but he nudges my chin with his fingers and gives me a little smile.

"The world can be a very lonely place, Estrella. You're lucky to have two parents that love you the way yours do. You don't have to push them away when it's clear as day that it hurts you more than being honest would."

I hate him for saying all the right things right now. I hate him for telling me I'm allowed to still need my parents. I hate him even more for not having been there three years ago when I was falling into darkness and thought I had to go through it all on my own.

"I'll tell them," I say, feeling my heart race with dread.

"Fuck, that just gave me shivers," he replies, and I tilt my head in confusion.

"What did?"

"You doing as I say. I like it. I could get used to it," he says with a playful grin, but I frown at him.

"*Vete al carajo*," I say as he gets up.

"Stop flirting with me, Estrella, and talk to your parents."

I flip him off as he walks away and by the way his shoulders shake, I realize he must know what I'm doing.

Then, I grit my teeth and tell my mother everything. From the letter to James letting Daisy and I move in. It's infinitely easier to rant through the story because of Mamá's silence. My breath keeps running out like I've run a marathon, but really, it's only the emotional toll of the situation weighing heavy on my lungs.

"Oh, Estrella," Mamá says. I can hear in her voice that there are tears streaming down her face. "What a mess," she adds, and I almost laugh.

"I hope I'm doing the right thing," I say, pulling my knees to my chest.

It doesn't go past me that James puts a cup of tea in my hand and distracts Daisy and Damian by taking their hands when they walk out of their rooms and leading them into the kitchen. If he prepares breakfast for them, I'll kick his ass for doing something so sweet and making me like him.

"You're sparing Daisy mountains of fear. No child should have to go through months and months of custody battles."

"So, you think I'm doing the right thing?"

"I think you're doing the right thing for your daughter. But are you doing the right thing for your heart? That depends. Is it safe with James?" she asks. I stand up to walk toward the kitchen and let my eyes drift to where James is standing at the stove with Daisy and Damian sitting at the island. He's smiling at both our kids, looking all chiseled and gorgeous. He catches me staring and winks, sending heat straight into my cheeks.

"Don't worry, Mami. I won't fall in love with him, just like he won't fall in love with me."

James is shirtless in his home gym, which is directly next to the reading room—this man has a fucking reading room with floor-to-ceiling bookshelves covering three of the four walls—where I am. The only wall not covered by a bookshelf is made of glass, so I get to see every single flex of his muscles. The way his light skin shines with sweat. The way his blonde hair clings to his forehead, something that shouldn't be sexy but works on James Landon.

"Do you have to do that now?" I call out, loud enough so he hears me over the music he's listening to through his earphones. James smiles as he takes one of them out of his ear, his muscular chest rising and falling a little faster than usual.

It's awfully distracting.

He steps into the reading room and leans against the door frame, crossing his muscular arms over his chest. His eyes drop to where Marbles and Lollipop are curled up at my feet. They haven't left my side once since I moved in, and I welcome their presence. I grew up with dogs and cats, and I've missed having them around.

"Do you have to read right now? Or did you come in here, see you could ogle me while I work out, and decided to stay?" he asks, his blue eyes sparkling with mischief.

My cheeks heat in embarrassment.

"Well, my daughter is at a sleepover with Leonora, you cleaned every inch of this house this morning, and this is my day off. What else am I supposed to do?" It's a terrible excuse, especially because I came in here to read, but all I've read so far is the title of the book when I pulled it out of the shelf.

"You could have gone anywhere else. You could have even left the house."

He pushes off the wall and takes several strides toward me. My heart stumbles all over itself as he places his hands on each armrest of the chair I'm sitting in, leaning down so we're at eye level. I jut out my chin defiantly, but it only makes him smirk harder.

"So, tell me, wife, why did you really come in here?" His breath coasts my skin, and I'm a little irritated by how fresh he smells after working out for almost an hour.

"I'm not your wife yet," I point out, but he stays quiet, unimpressed with my attempt to avoid his question.

"Tell me," he repeats, but I'm too proud to give him what he wants.

"Over my dead body." James leans away, taking his warmth and intoxicating smell with him.

"That's answer enough for me. Go get dressed, and I'll take you out to lunch before showing you my favorite spot in Monaco," he says and walks away without giving me the chance to respond.

Estrangularé a mi marido.

"Where are you taking me?" I ask, wrapping my coat more firmly around myself.

"Trust me, you'll like this," he says and pulls a spare beanie out of his coat's pocket before placing it on my head. He is gentle about it but doesn't linger. My heart still warms at the way he takes care of me without a second thought, though.

"I don't like you. Why would I like wherever you're taking me?" I reply as I follow him to where he's leading me.

"Stop lying to yourself. You've liked me a little since I bought Daisy her necklace. And taught her how to play cards. And put her to bed. And made food for her yesterday. And—" I cut him off.

"Yes, you have found my one weakness, Mr. Landon. My daughter's happiness. But just because you're nice to her doesn't mean I'm going to start falling all over myself for you," I say, and he stops walking immediately, making me run into his back. "Seriously?"

"Trust me, I'm the last person who'd ever think someone is in love with them," he says, his voice low and full of regret.

Regret to have voiced the words?

Or regret for the life decisions that have brought him to where he is today?

If only we knew each other better so I could ask him.

"James, I—"

"We should get going. We don't want our food to get cold," he says and takes my hand to guide me where he wants to go. His hand is hot in contrast to mine—I've always had cold hands even in hot temperatures—and I hate how much I love the warmth he radiates.

"They're sandwiches. Aren't they meant to stay cool?" I ask, holding up the bag with our food and drinks in it. "And why the fuck am I carrying this bag?"

"Which question do you want me to answer first?" He throws me a mischievous look over his shoulder.

"Fuck you," I mumble, smiling at a person we pass as not to alert them that my future husband is practically dragging me behind him. "I know I'm tall, but even I can't keep up with your long legs." James slows his pace with a chuckle.

"The sandwiches were heated because they have some of the most amazing mozzarella on them I've ever eaten. And you're carrying the bag because you didn't even attempt to pay for them."

"You've gotta be kidding," I say. "You're a millionaire."

"It's about the principle." He throws me a look to show me he's merely teasing, that he doesn't mean it, but I'm glaring at him.

"You're a very frustrating man, James Landon." He cocks his head to the side briefly, then straightens out again.

"Never claimed to be anything else," he mutters before sharply turning right and pulling me with him.

It occurs to me that I could have retracted my hand at the same time he stops walking. My breath catches in my throat at the sight of the most beautiful park I've ever seen. A sign at the entrance reads 'Princess Grace Japanese Garden.'

"Let's eat first and then we can walk through," he says, guiding me to a bench outside of the park before I can study it further.

Silence fills the space between us for several, peaceful moments. I bite into the sandwich, pleasantly surprised at how delicious it is. There are tomatoes, some cold cuts, salad, and, as promised, the most delicious mozzarella I've ever eaten melted inside. I almost let out a moan of pure content, but I manage to hold it back.

My face must tell how much I'm enjoying it because he grins with pride.

"I'd enjoy this sandwich a whole lot more if I didn't have to look at your smug face while eating it," I say, but James is as unaffected by my words as I expected him to be.

"Tell me something about yourself. Something I don't know. Something a husband should." I stop chewing, lowering the sandwich to give him my full attention.

"Why? No one's going to quiz us."

"Perhaps not, but I'd still like to get to know you, if that's alright. I know your favorite color, how you take your coffee, you like reading, and you used to do auto racing. But nothing else about your preferences and hobbies," he says, throwing a piece of bread into his mouth while keeping eye contact with me. I look away to make my cheeks stop heating under his attention.

"Daisy told you I did auto racing?" I ask, not surprised, but a little confused. How much does my daughter share with him while they spend time together?

"Yes, but she didn't tell me why you stopped." I bring my gaze back to his, noting the genuine curiosity in his eyes.

"Daisy needed the one parent she had to prioritize her above all else. I'm not saying she's the reason I stopped racing, that single mothers can't have a career and a child, but I was overwhelmed with the amount of work I had. So, I changed my career. I'm still in racing, but I have more time for my little girl," I explain, staring at the ground because I'm keeping so much from him—Pedro and Helen passing away—and if he sees my eyes, he'll know there is a part of the story I'm not sharing with him.

James has not once asked why Daisy's grandparents are taking her from me. He hasn't asked who her father is. Maybe he assumes I'm her biological mother. Maybe he doesn't. There are so many parts of my life I'm withholding, but I justify it all by telling myself that I don't know this man well. We bicker. We haven't built the kind of friendly relationship that would allow me to open up about the hardest part of my life.

"You're a remarkable, selfless woman, Estrella." His words make me shake my head.

"No. I'm selfish. I took Daisy and escaped to Monaco because I—" *I took her from her home, from the only grandparents that truly love her, because I couldn't bear to look at every little detail that reminded me of the two people I loved most.*

Tears shoot into my eyes, but I swallow hard and blink rapidly to get rid of them.

"Can I ask you how Damian ended up getting adopted by Dominique and Nicolette?" I ask to change the subject, but I almost feel bad when James sucks in a sharp breath that looks as painful as it sounds. "I'm sorry if I overstepped." He shakes his head long before the words have left my mouth.

"It's fine. You're just going to think I'm a massive dickhead after I share my story when yours is so much more admirable," he says, rubbing a hand down the length of his face.

"If it helps, I already think you're a dickhead." James snorts, which only makes me smile.

"It does. Thanks," he says with a chuckle, putting his bread down to give me his full attention, similar to what I did five minutes ago. "When Annabel, his biological mother, left Damian and me, I also thought I'd have to choose between raising him and continuing my career. I wasn't ready to be a father, but Gabriel's aunts... they wanted to be mothers. They were going to have a baby, but they lost it. So, Gabriel came to me and told me what the right choice for everyone was. This way, Damian has two mums with a stable home life, and a father, who loves him more than anything, taking as much time for him as I possibly can. But it was an awfully selfish decision."

Shame fills his gaze, but he never looks away. Never hides.

I admire that.

"You gave that boy the best chance at having a happy, stable life. You have nothing to be ashamed of. Not only does he have three parents who love him more than anything and would burn the world for him, but he also has aunts and uncles that feel the same," I say, remembering how Valentina told me she and Gabriel are Damian's godparents, how Adrian and Nevaeh take Damian on fun adventures when they get a day with him, and how Leonard and Chiara always welcome him to their home when Leonora and him want to have a playdate. "It's just Daisy and me, and sometimes I feel like it's not enough. That she deserves more."

The admission makes my throat feel tight. I've never said it out loud, but I've felt it deep inside for years. The thought of not being enough for her frightens me almost as much as the thought of Bert and Jennifer being right. Because if they are, then I am *not* enough.

I poke at a rock with the toe of my shoe, staring intensely at it when James cups my chin to guide my face back to him. I exhale, a tiny puff of condensation that looks like fog coming from my mouth.

"You are enough. You love Daisy so much, it's the equivalent of twenty relatives loving her." The tears shoot back into my eyes, but they don't fall, not until he repeats, "You are enough."

He wipes each tear away, then goes back to his sandwich. A heavy sigh escapes him before he refocuses on my face.

"It's a bloody shame anyone has ever tried to make you feel otherwise, little star. You don't deserve to waste a second on self-doubt."

"That's high praise coming from someone who hasn't even said he likes me as a person." Another one of those damn chuckles escapes him.

"I don't have to like you to see you for what you truly are." I shouldn't ask. I know I shouldn't. But the words slip free without my permission anyway.

"And what am I?" Those blue eyes meet mine again.

"A shining bright light in a pitch-black galaxy."

Chapter 14
James

After we finish our sandwiches, Estrella and I walk through the park. At first, silence lingers, our previous conversation still hanging between us like a blanket. Every step we take is slow, but I love the way her eyes are full of fascination as she takes in the park. She studies the water as we walk over the bridge, the fish swimming around in it, and the plants surrounding us. It's not as cold as a usual winter day in Monaco, but it's still not exactly pleasant. But the sky is clear and the sun is shining, which always makes me happy.

"So, what's the deal with you and Gabriel? Why do you hate him so much if he helped you in the past?" she asks, realization dawning on her a moment later. "Don't tell me it's because of Val. You realise it's not his fault she chose him, right?" In the past, it would have made my heart stutter to hear these words. Now, I laugh at the way she phrases the question.

"If you were in love with someone and the person they chose was an irritating piece of shit most days, would you like that person?" I ask, making her snort.

"Remember how I said you have to get over your feelings for Val? Well, you have to get over your hatred for Gabriel, too. It's not his fault, and you need to stop pretending it is."

"You don't even know my reasons for why I dislike him," I argue, but it's ridiculous.

Estrella steps in front of me to stop me from walking, her face set in a determined expression.

"Then tell me your reasons. If I think they're not good enough, you have to make an effort to be nicer to him and tolerate him. Deal?" She holds out her hand and I stare at it, still smiling.

"Sure, wife, you have yourself a deal," I say and shake her hand, but she rolls her eyes at the way I address her.

"Still not your wife yet," she reminds me, but I shrug.

"Just trying to get used to the word." It's a big, bold lie that falls from my lips without an ounce of hesitation.

"Alright, give me your first reason," she says as we continue our stroll through the park.

"He told Val I had feelings for her and risked our friendship years ago." This makes her look up at me with surprise.

"Did you tell him you had feelings for her and he betrayed your trust? Or could he see it in the way you looked at her and spoke to her?"

"I don't like this game," I mumble.

"So, the second one. Not a good enough reason, then. If anyone could see it, then it's not a secret." Estrella shakes her head. "Do you have another one, or was that it?"

"Well, you already said him marrying her doesn't count, so I guess I have no reason to hate him as much as I do," I admit with a breathless laugh.

"The question is, Mr. Landon, do you still have feelings for Val now?" she asks, and I open my mouth to respond with the usual lie.

Of course I am over her. She's married. She doesn't love me that way.

It's what I used to tell Adrian, like a robot reciting what they've been told to say. I never meant it, never thought I could.

But as I stare at Estrella and think about the four and a half months of bickering with her, it doesn't feel like that much of a lie anymore.

"I love her now the way I was always supposed to love her. As a best friend. I'm no longer in love with her." A wave of emotion hits me so hard, I almost keel over.

I mean it. I mean every word.

"Good. Then you can let go of your resentment toward Gabriel," she says, placing her hand on my pec and making me realise I stopped walking.

"Why is that so important to you?" I ask, studying her wonderful brown eyes.

"Because he's family, and you can never have too much family." Her attention shifts to my throat, a frown pulling down the corners of her mouth. "I know what it's like to be alone and feel lonely, and I don't wish that on anyone else," she says, her hand dropping from my chest, but I pick it up, rubbing my thumb over her engagement ring and placing it back on my chest.

"I may have been surrounded by the family I found along the way, but the feeling of loneliness is one I'm very familiar with. It's not the same as yours because I did have people, but I've been lonely in love my whole life. My father didn't truly love me, he just loved the potential I had. My mother loved my father more than me. Girlfriends I had in the past didn't love me very much either, not that I can blame them. So, you see, I'm quite familiar with loneliness too."

I shrug when she gives me a sad look.

"Laying awake at night, staring at your ceiling as your hand reaches for the empty side of your bed. Seeing people fall in love and dancing the night away while you stand on your own, watching them find the kind of love you've always dreamt of. Not knowing if you'll ever stop feeling so damn lonely," I add, feeling my chest pull tight from emotion.

"God, we really found each other, didn't we? Two emotionally unavailable people desperate to feel less alone in the world while doing everything we can to protect our hearts," she replies, patting my pec and dropping her hand for the second time. I don't put it back again.

Looking at her right now, with our hearts bared and souls exposed, I find myself leaning toward her instead. Her eyes flutter shut the closer I get, but her phone rings seconds before my lips touch hers. Estrella steps back, pulling it out of her pocket.

"Fuck," she says and holds up her phone to show me Bert and Jennifer are calling. "They do this every month, reminding me how little time I have left," Estrella explains, and I bite my tongue to keep from growling like an animal. I hate them so much already.

"May I?" I ask as I reach for her phone, and she hands it to me with a breathless laugh.

"I don't know what you'll be able to tell them. They know I'm getting married, but they're still calling to remind me."

"They won't again," I assure her before answering the call. "I'll say this once and once only. Stop calling my wife. You have the wedding invitation. We don't want to hear from you until then, understood?" I don't give them a chance to respond. I merely hang up and hand the phone back to Estrella, whose lips have parted in surprise.

"Did you just—"

"Yeah. They better leave you alone now. If not, I'll find a way to send them straight back to where they came from," I say and start walking again.

"And where is that?" I hear the amusement in her voice long before I turn my head to see her grinning.

"Hell."

She bursts into laughter, and I crack a smile, too, loving the way she seems more at ease now than when she first saw the call.

We go back to strolling through the park while she shares a story of her racing career with me. The sound of her voice fills my ears, the excitement in her words beautiful.

I could listen to Estrella talk for days without needing a break.

But, naturally, she's curious about me as well. So, I tell her some stories about myself. Little things since we already spoke about the hardest ones.

It's easy. Despite our rocky start, it's so very easy to talk to her.

And that, more than anything, makes me take her hand again as we keep walking, wanting to be close to her when I know I should keep my distance.

Chapter 15
James

It's book club night.

The club consists of Chiara, Leonard, Val, Gabriel, me, Nevaeh, and a reluctant Adrian, who barely ever reads the book but wants to spend more time with us. We invited Scarlette, Julián, and Cameron to join too when we first started the club a year ago, but none of them are big readers, so they declined politely. However, Scarlette is officially joining for the first time tonight, dragging an uninterested Julián with her. I'm pretty sure the MotoGP racer only tagged along because he hates being away from his wife.

And when he heard everyone was gathering at my house today, Cameron came too, walking in with his book looking brand new and not at all read.

"I read the online summary. That counts," is all he says when I point it out, and I chuckle to myself as I shut my front door again.

Leonora, Kieran, Damian, and Daisy are on the floor in the living room, playing with the Carrera track I bought them yesterday. All four of them love racing, and the way they fight each other so competitively makes me grin.

The next generation of F1 drivers is sitting in my living room, and I get to watch them grow up and one day fight for their spots in the sport we all love.

"James, should we order some food?" Valentina asks as she approaches me, her husband following behind her.

My eyes shift to Estrella, watching her kneel beside Damian and placing her hand on his head to muss his hair. I can't help but smile.

"Sure. Order whatever you'd like." I leave Val and Gabriel standing in my kitchen, walking straight toward my future wife and son.

"To make your car go through the loop successfully, Damian, you have to make it go faster first," she explains to him before asking to have his remote so she can demonstrate.

"Cool," my son says with wide eyes after Estrella managed to make the toy car shoot through the loop on the track. "Can I try again, Reya?" he asks, so she hands him the remote.

Estrella places a kiss on her daughter's head before getting up, but I'm so close to her, she runs right into my chest as she turns to leave them again. My hands find her elbows to stabilise her, at least that's what I tell myself because if I admit I merely want to touch her, have wanted to touch her for the last several months, my broken little heart might just beat a little more evenly than it has in years.

And that thought terrifies me.

"You don't have any sense of personal space, do you?" she asks with an irritated look that she's trying her hardest to conceal. Things have been getting easier between us, but there's still a tension that seeps through in moments like this one. "You can let go now. I'm not going to fall," Estrella reminds me.

"I'm trying," I admit, a pang of longing shooting through my chest.

"Try harder," she replies, stepping away and out of my grasp.

I stare after her as she walks toward Chiara, Scarlette, Nevaeh, Gabriel, and Valentina. A hand claps me on the shoulder a moment before Adrian and Cameron step in front of me. Leonard follows with Julián by his side, but they're both frowning like they're not sure they want to be part of whatever conversation my best friend is planning to have with me.

"So, how's it going with the Mrs.?" Adrian asks, and I roll my eyes at his obnoxious grin.

"How's it going being an idiot?" I counter, but he merely shrugs.

"Still comes as easily as breathing. Now answer my question," he says, earning a small smile from Leonard and a burst of laughter from Cameron. Julián is as unimpressed as always.

"Must I talk about this with an audience?" I ask, but when Cameron looks hurt, I add, "I don't even know how I'm feeling. How am I going to explain it to the four of you?"

"Yeah, guys, give him some space," Adrian says but wraps his arm around my shoulders to lead me away from the rest of them. "In all seriousness, how's it going?" We stop walking so he can grab me by the shoulders and look directly at me. "Are you okay?" I almost laugh.

"Bloody confused is what I am. She tells me she doesn't like me, but we've had a few moments where we... bonded, I think. I don't know. It feels so easy to talk to her, and, fuck, I'm so attracted to her. I've never been this attracted to anyone."

Probably because no one's ever fought with me as much as she has, and no one I've met has been this undeniably beautiful. Plus, she merely accepts things for what they are and... well, tells me how things need to be from now on. Like when she told me I'm not allowed to look at anyone but her anymore.

Best not to think about the fact that I *haven't* looked at anyone but her since we met.

"That's how I felt about Nevaeh. She told me we couldn't be together, but then we grew closer regardless. I was so attracted to her. You even made fun of me for being unable to sleep with anyone else when we weren't even dating."

He chuckles to himself, and I avoid eye contact because besides a brief one-night stand with a man three months ago, one where I couldn't get into the mood and left both of us disappointed, I haven't been interested in fucking anyone.

No one but Estrella.

"What I'm trying to say is, this is a good thing. Let it happen," Adrian adds with a grin, blissfully unaware of my spiraling thoughts.

"I promise not to fight what I'm feeling, even if I have no idea what that is," I say, which seems to make him happy because he gives me a proud grin and a slap on the back.

"Perfect, then we can go discuss this book I definitely read."

"You're full of shit," I reply with a laugh.

"Yeah, well, I probably shouldn't admit that I told Nevaeh to read it to me but ended up with my mouth between her legs every time instead of listening." He leaves me with that visual and sits down next to his wife, kissing her mouth, cheek, and neck.

"Here you go." I almost jump on the spot when Leonard approaches me with a beer, his voice low. "You look like you need it," he points out, and I take it from him with a simple nod.

"Ever had a woman say she hates you but also be attracted to you?" I ask because it's always been easy asking Leonard Tick for advice. He gives me one of his rare smiles.

"That was my relationship with Chiara before we started dating," he replies, taking a sip of his beer. His tattooed bicep flexes with the motion.

"Scar didn't like me at first either. But over time, the feelings between us grew as we became friends. Relationships are never easy, but with the right person, they can be everything," Julián chimes in, nodding at me once before heading toward Estrella and speaking to her in Spanish.

"He's right," Leonard adds, joining his wife on my other couch.

I hate all of them a little bit right now.

"Alright, welcome back, everyone, to our monthly bookclub meeting. This month, we read..."

Valentina's voice fades in my ears as I watch Estrella tug a strand of her long, brown hair behind her ear. She looks at Valentina, listening closely to her words. But I just study her. I study her long hair and light brown skin. The tattoos covering her. Her sharp facial features. Her brown eyes. The way she bites half her bottom lip as she concentrates. How relaxed she looks instead of the tense state she's been in since she moved in.

My heart stutters when she turns her gaze my way, catching me staring at her.

The blush covering my cheeks is out of my control.

"James? Earth to James, are you there?" Adrian says, and I snap back into reality, turning to him.

"What?" I ask.

"Val asked you what your thoughts are on the book two minutes ago." Fuck. I was too busy looking at Estrella to hear anything.

"I thought it was brilliant. Definitely worth the read," I reply, leaning forward in my armchair to place my elbows on my thighs.

"That's all we need to say? There is no quiz on the book? Hell, I could have joined the book club months ago," Cameron says, making my wanker of a best friend burst into laughter.

He doesn't even care when I glare at him.

Then again, I stop caring about his reaction when I notice Estrella grinning at me.

I'm in trouble.

Chapter 16
Estrella

"I don't like the way it flares out at the bottom," Valentina says after I've been stuck in my head for the past few minutes, staring blankly at myself in the mirror.

"Yeah, I don't either. I'm going to try the tighter-fitting one," I announce before turning around to catch Daisy playing with my boss' hair.

"Yes. The one with the low neckline. Try that one," Nevaeh chimes in, and I give her a small smile.

Nevaeh and Valentina insisted on coming dress shopping with me today. They both know this whole wedding thing is fake, but they haven't mentioned it once. Even if it might be the worst thing I could do to my heart, I appreciate them not making me feel as horrible as I should. Plus, it makes it easier for Daisy to be convinced this is real.

Scarlette, Valentina's race engineer, joined us too, and she's been smiling at every single dress I've put on because "they're all just so beautiful." She's a complete ray of sunshine.

Chiara, Leonora's mom, is also here. She doesn't smile much, but a special kind of warmth radiates off her the entire time.

I've been around these four women a lot in the past two weeks, from the book club to the brunch they took me to a few days ago. The friendship they all offer me without a second thought, even during this mess my life has become, makes me deeply emotional.

Chiara has been sharing stories about her art galleries, which I really enjoy. Apparently, she became so successful a few years ago, she opened more locations.

Chiara started in London, but now she has galleries in Monaco, Rome, Amsterdam, and Berlin too. It's why she and Leonard decided to move here two years ago. The Monte-Carlo location is the most profitable one, and the retired F1 driver's academy is here.

Valentina has taken on the role of my maid of honor without me even asking, and it's lifted a lot of weight off my shoulders. She's also entertaining my daughter while I try on dresses so Daisy isn't bored. The more I think about it, the more grateful I become. She's the reason why James offered to do all of this for me, too.

I should invite her over for dinner at my place—

Realization hits me deep in the chest. I don't have a place at the moment. Not one that's mine. How will inviting guests work in James' house? Do I have to ask him for permission? No. No way. I'm not his property. But I'm also not the owner of his house… Fuck, I hate everything about this situation. I hate that I'm being forced to marry someone I don't love, even James who genuinely tries to be helpful. I hate that I'm putting Daisy through so much confusion and potential heartbreak. She's been wearing the necklace James got her since he helped her put it on, and I can see how deeply she already cares for him.

My eyes focus on the skin-tight wedding dress I just slid on, but tears shoot into them at the sight. I'm getting married. To someone who'll never fall in love with me. I take a deep breath to get rid of the tears and to stop myself from spiraling down the same hole for the fifth time today. There is no point. I'll get to know James better. He's already been trying to show me more of himself, and I'll share more, too. We will like each other eventually. It will be fine.

We've already had so many moments when I thought we could even be friends if we kept going down this path.

"Reya? Are you doing okay, honey?" Valentina's familiar voice comes from the other side of the changing room door, and I take another deep breath. "How's the dress?"

The dress isn't too bad. It hugs all of my curves in the right way, and the low neckline makes my big boobs look fantastic. There is nothing special about it, no lace, no frails, nothing. Just like there is nothing special about this wedding.

A sudden wave of panic consumes me because I really don't want to walk down the aisle with Bert and Jennifer watching my every move. My parents won't even be there, which is as much of a blessing as it is a pain. Mamá said she wouldn't be able to lie to Bert and Jennifer if they started asking her questions, so I told her not to come.

I also don't want them to watch me get "married."

"Yeah, this dress won't work either. I'm trying on the other one," I say because I have to get out of this piece of clothing before I become claustrophobic.

"Can I come in?" she says, and I sit on the small stool in the corner of my dressing room.

"Sure," I reply because, at this point, I'd rather not be alone.

Valentina steps into the room with her long, blonde hair falling down her shoulders in cute yet messy curls. Her full lips have a frown lingering on them and her light eyes scan my face with compassion.

I've been pitying myself for long enough, and now Valentina is looking at me like I've just gotten the worst news of my life. Getting married to a millionaire Formula One driver doesn't even come close to qualifying as the worst.

"James is a very good person. He's my best friend in the entire world, and even though he's far from flawless, when he cares about someone, he does so with his whole heart."

She settles on the ground in front of me and pulls her legs to her chest. It's hard for me to believe we're almost the same age but she's already been married for years, is the co-owner of a driver academy, and won her first Formula One World Championship.

"This is not a marriage born out of love, Valentina. I don't expect him to care for me, and he's made it explicitly clear that he *can't*, so his heart is closed off, which is fine because mine belongs to Daisy," I rant without realizing what the fuck I'm saying.

Do I want the possibility of James falling for me? Of course not. We may have gotten along better, but there is still tension, even if that's all sexual. I've fucked people in the past I didn't necessarily like. My brother's best friend is one of them.

After Pedro passed, Simón never reached out to check on me. We had a mutually beneficial sex agreement, but I expected at least a "Hey, I'm here if you need to talk." Instead, I got radio silence.

Pinche idiota.

"Would you like me to speak to him?" Valentina asks, pulling me back to James.

"No. This marriage will be over soon. James and I will figure out the logistics," I assure her and myself in the same breath.

"If you say so. Personally, I think you two could be good for each other."

I frown at her in response, so she lets out a soft laugh.

"We may have been growing closer, but a little over a week of living together doesn't magically fix the negative feelings we were harboring for four months." I don't know who I'm trying to convince, but Valentina seems to believe me as much as I believe myself.

Not at all.

"I saw the way you two looked at each other during our book club meeting. That's not how two people look when they hate one another," she points out, placing a soft smile on her lips.

"Well, we've got a lot of pent-up sexual tension," I joke. I know it's not merely that, not anymore, but lying makes me feel better than admitting so out loud.

"If you say so. Just promise me you won't close yourself off from him. Daisy is the most important person in your life, I know, but you deserve to experience life for yourself, too. I can't imagine how hard being a single mom is, but take a little bit of time and space for things you want, too. Fall in love or have lots of sex, whichever you prefer. As long as you remember you're not just a mom. You're also Estrella Celeste Cortez. Don't forget to live her life, too."

Valentina stands up and places a comforting hand on my shoulder.

She leaves the dressing room while I mull over her words.

For the first time since Helen died, I think about the person I used to be. The fastest racer in auto racing. The champion. The woman who had ambitions she happily left behind to raise her daughter. I don't regret the decisions I've made, but my boss has reminded me of something I forgot long ago.

There is more to me than being a mom to Daisy, and it's time I stop pitying myself for having to go through this wedding. I will take what I want, and, as much as I try to deny it, what I want is to make James Oliver Landon open his heart for me.

Chapter 17
James

"You are a fucking idiot," Adrian says after I've shared what ring I got Estrella, and I roll my eyes when he starts laughing at me. "And in denial. We spoke about your feelings a few days ago and you told me you're confused! How are you confused when your actions speak louder than any words?" I open my mouth to answer, but Adrian isn't finished speaking. "God, what's wrong with you? Please don't tell me it's still because of Val. Or are you using her as an excuse because you're too much of a coward to open yourself up to the possibility of liking Reya?"

I'm about to answer when his laugh cuts me off again.

"Okay, enough. You all convinced me to marry her, and I am, but it's nothing more than that. Now you can shut up and leave me alone," I reply, my eyes catching Gabriel's amused ones as they linger on my face.

This is the last time I tell these dickheads anything. The only reason I started is because I felt bad for how I reacted at the book club meeting when they asked me about how I was feeling.

"Hey, I had nothing to do with this. I wasn't even here," Cameron chimes in, and I bring my attention to the Australian beside me.

"Technically, I also had nothing to do with it," Leonard adds, and I give him a curt nod.

"I had the least to do with it. If my wife wasn't friends with your wives, I wouldn't even be here," Julián says, and Adrian throws him a cocky smirk.

"Please, you love us. It took you a while to get here, but you can't deny it anymore," my best friend says, but Julián merely rolls his eyes.

"So, it's settled," I start to refocus on the topic at hand. "Adrian, you're no longer my best man. Leonard, Julián, or Cameron is, depending on who wants the position," I state, and Cameron sits up quickly, raising his hand in the air.

"Me! I want to do it. I will throw you the best bachelor party in the world," he calls out, and I bring a real smile to my face because Cameron has the kind of personality that brings it out of you. My teammate's smile is as bright as the sun.

"Okay, Cameron is my best man now," I say, pinning my best friend with a glare. That smug jerk flashes me one of his arrogant smiles because we both know, pretend or not, I don't want anyone but him as the best man at my wedding.

"Since when can't you handle the truth, James? I thought I raised you better than that," Adrian says and takes a sip of his water.

"You're barely a year and a half older than me," I point out, but he shrugs as he places his glass down again.

"Maybe, but I've always been more mature than you," he replies, making Gabriel next to him chuckle.

"It seems like you're the one in denial, not me," I tell Adrian, but his attention has already drifted to his phone.

He smiles at his screen, and I realise Nevaeh must have texted him. He plays with his wedding ring as he reads her message before replying to it. I force my gaze away, but, for some reason, it lands on Gabriel's ring next. I've never seen that man without it, not even during a race weekend.

"Did you get a tux yet?" Gabriel asks, and I bring my eyes to his green-brown ones.

"Yeah, yesterday, but Adrian chose it so I might return it and get a better one," I tease, finally getting my best friend's attention again.

"First of all, I dress better than you. Second of all, I chose a fucking Armani suit for you in a sleek black with a green dress shirt that brings out your eyes. I think I know what the hell I'm doing." I cock a surprised brow, but shock soon turns into something oddly similar to amazement when Leonard Tick chuckles at my best friend.

"Touchy subject," he says before standing up and stretching his arms into the air. "Alright, it was a pleasure, lads, but I have to get home. My wife is expecting me in ten minutes, and I don't want to be late." I watch him walk over to Adrian to give his shoulder a squeeze.

"What happens if you're late? She spanks you?" he teases, and Leonard stares down at him with a wicked glint in his eyes.

"I'm only that lucky when I'm on time."

I don't think I've ever seen Adrian's eyes go as wide as they are right now. Leonard walks away, leaving us all with a very interesting visual, but my best friend jumps out of his seat to follow the retired F1 driver. Question after question leaves him as they disappear inside.

Cameron gives my head a little shake before leaving, too, Julián walking out the door with him. Then, it's only Gabriel and me. He's got this knowing smile on his face, and the urge to punch him suddenly intensifies.

"Spit it out," I demand, and he looks away for a brief moment, the tip of his tongue pressing against the inside of his cheek.

"You like Estrella," he says, his gaze skipping back to my face.

"We tolerate each other, nothing more," I reply, but Gabriel's smile only brightens. He seems to find this extremely amusing.

"You don't just tolerate her. I see the way you look at her."

"And how do I look at her?" I challenge, crossing my arms in front of my chest while I wait for a response.

Gabriel stands up at the same moment the front door opens and my future wife and Daisy walk through the door. My eyes fixate on Estrella's beautiful face and they remain there because the happy smile on her lips while she spins Daisy once makes me feel all warm inside.

It's impossible to focus on anything else, even when she catches me staring.

"You look at her like you've been waiting for her your whole life and can't believe she's finally here," Gabriel replies and steps toward the sliding glass doors that lead inside. "You also don't look at Val the way you used to anymore." With that statement, he walks away and leaves me to think about my friends' words.

Am I in denial?

No. I'm not in denial. You can't know whether someone is made for you and you for them after four and a half months of bickering. Can you? How does anyone know anything about love? I fucking hate it.

Either love doesn't reciprocate or it's plain confusing.

"Hey, Daisy and I are going to make dinner. You want to help?" Estrella's familiar voice fills my ears, and I can't help but smile a little.

"Yeah, I'd love to," I reply and follow her inside, trying and failing not to look at her beautiful arse as we step into the kitchen.

"God. If you want to check if it's real, grab a handful, James," she says, obviously feeling my gaze burning her skin.

"Okay," I reply and grab each cheek in one hand, earning a squeal from Estrella. I smile as I let go, and she spins around before bursting into a fit of giggles. The sound almost sends me flying backward.

"I can't believe you just did that," she says, still giggling. I close the distance between us, causing her laughter to die out and her bottom lip to slip between her teeth.

"You offer me a taste, I will take it, darling. I will take anything you give me."

Because I'm a starved man, and Estrella seems to be my salvation.

"We should get started on dinner," Estrella says before moving toward the fridge and grabbing ingredients.

A small hand slips into mine a second later, and I look down to find Daisy smiling up at me. She's been wearing the necklace I got her since the first day, and I wish I knew why it makes me almost as happy as Estrella wearing my ring the whole time.

"Mamá bought a nice dress," Daisy says with excitement lacing her voice. I pick her up and place her on my right hip, doing my best to keep my focus on her and not let it drift to Estrella's tensed-up shoulders.

"Yeah? Will you tell me what it looks like?" I whisper, but Daisy giggles and shakes her head.

"No, that's a secret. You will see it in three days, that's what Mamá said," she informs me while I place her on the marble counter so I can be at eye-level with her.

"Fine, I will wait," I say and let out a dramatic sigh, making Daisy laugh loudly in response.

"You will like it. Mamá looks like a princess," the little girl informs me, and I do my best to hold back my next words, I really do, but they spill out anyway.

"You're the princess, Daisy. Your mamá is the queen."

Daisy and Estrella are dancing around in the kitchen to what she told me is traditional Mexican music. I think it's one way she keeps her daughter connected to her roots, and it's the most beautiful thing I've ever witnessed. Allowing me to stand here and watch them dance around so happily makes me feel like I get to be part of their world, even if only by a little.

I will take whatever I can get.

Once Estrella figured out I'm useless beyond cutting the vegetables and meat when it comes to Mexican cuisine, she shooed me away from the stove. She simply handed me a delicious drink she made called *horchata*, and I've been sipping it while watching her with utter fascination.

Daisy is spinning around to the music while her mum sways her hips from side to side and sings at the top of her lungs. I may not understand a single word, but I love the melody and the way the words sound falling from Estrella's lips.

I force my attention away from her to see Daisy trying to figure out the steps to dance salsa. I push off the counter and join her in the middle of the kitchen.

"Need some help, princess?" I ask, and the little girl looks up at me with her eyes wide.

"You know how to salsa?" she says, making me smile.

"Yeah, I learned it from a friend a long time ago."

In reality, I've been dancing with women in pubs all around the world since I was sixteen, picking up every single type of dance there is. I have a knack for it too, which helps.

"Give me your hands, and I will guide you," I promise, holding out both of my hands for her. She slips her tiny palms against mine, forcing a wave of emotion to spread through my chest.

"*Florecita,*" Estrella starts before finishing the sentence in Spanish and leaving me to wonder what the hell she said.

"What did you tell her?" I ask once they've finished their conversations. My almost-wife smiles at me in response.

"I told her to be careful not to step on your feet since you need them to make your millions." I snort at her words, only making her grin bigger. "Hey, I'm a woman with particular tastes, and I'm starting to like this house. It'd be a shame if you couldn't pay for it anymore," she teases, and I can't help looking around the room.

At the kitchen she has filled with her things. The living room she decorated and made more homey than I ever could. The walls she filled with her memories.

"Hurry, the song is almost over," Daisy complains as she tugs on my shirt.

So bossy.

Just like her mum.

"Okay, Daisy, follow my lead. When I step forward, you step back. When I step back, you step forward. Does that make sense?" I ask, and she gives me an eager nod.

Estrella restarts the song for us, and I lead Daisy through the whole four minutes. She picks up on the steps quickly, and, eventually, we're successfully dancing a simple version of salsa in the middle of my kitchen. I can feel Estrella's eyes on us, but I do my best to focus on Daisy so neither one of us steps on the other's feet.

Once the song is done, Daisy runs off into the living room to watch an episode of her favorite show, leaving her mum and me all alone. Estrella is already looking at me when I bring my gaze to her breathtaking face.

I lift my hand for her as an invitation, bringing a slow smile to my lips.

"Come here," I say and cock my head to the side ever so slightly.

"I already know how to salsa, James," she replies, but I don't lower my hand yet.

"Then come dance with me," I urge, but she turns to the stove to signal she's doing something. "The food can wait a minute, darling. Restart the song and get over here," I say, and she rolls her eyes at me before lowering the temperature on the stove and stepping toward me.

Excitement sends a trail of shivers down my spine when she's right in front of me.

I love to see the bratty glint in her eyes while she does what she's told. I like that she doesn't give me what I want often, but when she does, it's like a shot of adrenaline straight to my heart. I don't know what it is about being in control for me, to have someone do as I want. I know it's normal, I looked into my kinks a while ago, but I have yet to meet a person who won't run when I explain what turns me on.

Pushing all of those thoughts away, especially because she's made it clear she's not interested in having sex with me, I focus on her eyes. My fingers snake around her wrists to drag her against me, and I find the step count in my head before leading her to the music.

Of course, to my irritation, Estrella is a wonderful dancer. She matches all of my steps perfectly until we're moving around the kitchen in the sweetest harmony. My heart is fluttering to the beat because I have never, ever felt this way when dancing with a person.

It feels like I was made for her.

"How did you really learn to dance like this?" she asks, her warm brown eyes meeting mine. There's a vulnerability in her gaze I have a hard time not feeling deep inside my chest.

"I've danced with people from all around the world. They taught me many different types of dances," I admit, shifting my gaze away from her as a bit of shame settles in my chest.

I've been heartbroken my whole life. As a result, I've sought comfort in the arms of any woman—occasionally man—that reciprocated the attraction I felt for them. But it's never been fulfilling. Probably because how is anyone supposed to feel complete when they haven't met their matching piece of the puzzle?

"Can I ask you a personal question?" I place my forehead against hers, closing my eyes.

"We'll be married soon. You should be able to ask your husband anything." That makes her snort, but silence fills the space between us as she leans back to force me to look at her.

"You said people," she points out.

"Yes. I've been with men and women, but I've only started exploring my attraction for men in the last few years," I explain, making her nod.

"So, do you prefer men, women, or is it equal?" A slower song has filled the kitchen, so I drag her against me, wrapping my arms around her.

"I prefer women." Again, she nods. "What about you?"

"I'm pansexual. A person's gender identity doesn't impact how attracted I am to them," she replies. I spin her around once before bringing her back to me. "And I am attracted to you, James, but whenever we're in a room together, I can never figure out if I want to punch you in your smug face or hug you," she says. "We're going to have to work on that."

"Don't tell me. I don't even yell. That's your thing." She nudges me in the side and attempts to walk away, but I chuckle as I grab her wrist and pull her back to me.

"I *raised my voice* at your son, I didn't yell at him. I'm not a person who enjoys screaming," she says, jutting out her chin defiantly.

There's no point arguing with her. In the time I've known her, Estrella has yelled a total of zero times.

"Where did you learn to dance?" I ask after a while of us merely slow dancing in the kitchen while our food simmers on the stove.

"My parents taught me. My father loves to cook, so when I was growing up, he'd ask me to keep him company. He'd tell me stories about his life or turn up the music so we could dance. And when my mother came home from work, she always met us in the kitchen, either telling us about her day or joining our dance party."

There's a heaviness in her voice she's trying her best to hide, but I hear it as clearly as the music playing over the speaker. She's opening up to me again, so I try to ask her about the one thing I know for certain she hasn't shared with me yet.

"Do you have any siblings?" Estrella shuts down on me completely, stepping out of my arms and toward the stove.

"That's enough bonding for one evening, James," she says, turning her back to me and closing herself off completely.

Fuck.

I shouldn't have asked.

Chapter 18
Estrella

It's two days until our wedding, but we're as calm as if we had no worries in the world. We're having dinner like Daisy's grandparents aren't already in Monaco. Like we're not going to have to kiss and act undeniably in love on Sunday. Like everything is the way we've always envisioned it would be.

Lucky for me, James has taken care of everything, and if there are any hiccups, he hasn't told me about them. In a way, being excluded from this has eased things immensely. On the other hand, I'm sad I feel so disconnected from a day that should be happy for all parties involved. But it's for the best this way. The less I know, the better.

"I'm going to put Daisy to bed. Maybe then we can discuss some things about the wedding," James says after my daughter takes his hand and starts pulling him to her room, saying she wants him to read her a story.

There's no need for my heart to stumble at the sight. For my breathing to hitch because she's asked him to put her to bed almost every night this week.

"If we must," I say and clear the table. James gives me a mischievous look before disappearing down the hall.

There goes my hope to know nothing about this wedding. I let out a small groan while I place the dishes into the dishwasher and wait for James to return.

I wonder what he could possibly want to speak about. We're not having bachelor parties. There is no point since this isn't real. We're not tying ourselves together for the rest of our lives, it isn't the purpose of this wedding.

Another groan escapes me because I hate little more than uncertainty about things someone could have told me already.

"What's with all the groaning? Are you in pain?" James asks as he steps into the kitchen. Annoyance grips my very being because of his teasing tone.

"Yes. I'm in mental pain because your throwing out a vague statement about needing to talk makes me nervous. I hate uncertainty," I blurt out. James gives me a comforting look.

"I apologize, darling. It won't happen again. I wanted to talk about the whole kissing and PDA aspect for our wedding," he says, causing my heart rate to skyrocket.

Well, that wasn't what I was expecting.

"Oh," I blurt out while placing the last cup in the dishwasher and turning it on. "What about the kissing aspect?" Heat is pooling low in my stomach, and I do my best not to think about James' mouth on mine.

"I would like to kiss you before we stand in front of everyone we know. Daisy's grandparents need to believe we're a couple, so the kiss shouldn't be messy as if we didn't know each other intimately," James says, and I cross my arms in front of my chest, debating his words.

He's got a point, but kissing him right now sends a wave of nervousness through my chest, one I'm not sure how to handle.

"I know how to kiss, James. We will be fine," I say, but he gives me an unimpressed look.

"Estrella, come here and kiss me," James demands, and I hate that my body melts in response.

"No."

Excitement forces heat through my veins as his eyes darken with a challenge. A smile lingers on his lips, but he remains where he is. Somehow, his gaze on my skin has a tighter hold on me than his hands would. I can't move, can't do anything but try and slow my heart rate.

He shakes his head, allowing me to breathe when his eyes leave my face. His fingers move to his sleeves before he starts to roll them up meticulously, taking his time while I remain in place for some inexplicable reason.

"Make me," I blurt out, forcing him to still for a moment.

"Make you what, darling?" he asks, and I notice he's done fixing his sleeves and is now pulling his dress shirt out of his pants. I love the days he has meetings because he always dresses up.

"Make. Me," I repeat, and another slow smile takes over his face.

"Fine." He nods thoughtfully, thinking carefully about his next words. "If you don't come and kiss me, I'll give you two other options. One, I can put you on this marble counter you love to sit on, spread your legs, and bury my face in your pussy until you can't do anything but moan my name. Two, I can put you on your knees and slide my cock into your mouth until you make me come. Either way, we will be using our mouths," he suggests, making my skin burn.

I wasn't expecting him to be this straightforward with what he wants, but I can't say I dislike it. Part of me is convinced he threw these things out into the open to see if I would run, but I don't want to.

"So, what's it going to be, Estrella? Kiss me or choose between options one and two?" he asks, his feet cemented to the ground, just like mine are.

As much as I'd like to get on my knees for him again, I don't think I'm ready for options one and two. I am, however, ready to know what it's like to have his mouth on mine, to taste him instead of only smelling him like I have since we met.

Will this make an impossibly complicated situation even more so?

Of course it will, but I can't manage to give a shit at this moment.

I've had to be responsible and do everything right for the past five years.

I want to indulge in something wrong for a little.

I take a step toward him and then another until I'm right in front of him. My arms feel as heavy as metal, so I wait for him to make the first move. But he doesn't. His eyes sparkle with lust as they fixate on my lips and then move down my body to my hands.

"Palms against my chest," he instructs, and I finally manage to move them, feeling his hard muscles even through his shirt. His strong fingers wrap around my wrists until he pulls me closer, his mouth hovering over mine. "You smell like spring, darling, and I've been wondering if you taste the same since we met," he whispers into the quiet room, and my eyes flutter shut in response.

"Then what are you waiting for?" I tease, but his mouth crashes onto mine, killing every bit of amusement in my chest and replacing it with pleasure.

Nothing could have prepared me for this.

My taste buds light on fire, and I don't even have words for his flavor. It's simply James. Intoxicating. Like an addictive drug I can't get enough of. I grab his shirt so hard, a gasp escapes him, allowing my tongue to slip into his mouth and explore it at my own, tortuously slow pace.

I don't want to rush this. I want to get lost in his warmth, in the way his hands slide down my back in a lazy caress.

My fingers grip his hair to deepen the kiss. Pleasure consumes my entire being as our tongues tangle and dance in perfect harmony. Fireworks explode in my stomach, leaving a heat that pools between my thighs. James moves his hands to my hips, but I'm not happy with his respectful touches right now.

I need him to *touch* me.

So, I bring my fingers to the sides of his hands and guide them onto my ass. He squeezes it instinctively.

"Estrella," he groans when a little whimper escapes my lips, and I realize how tense he's gotten. His mouth moves onto my neck where he places a trail of gentle kisses. A moan escapes me when his lips find the sensitive spot between my collarbone and neck.

"James," I whimper when he sucks hard on the same spot, sending my mind spiraling.

"We should stop," he says between kisses.

"Probably," I reply at the same moment he picks me up and leads me to the couch.

"Do you want me to stop?" James asks as he sits us down, my clit inevitably rubbing against his hard cock.

"Fuck no," I moan and plant my lips on his again. "Maybe we should put sex back on the table," I hear myself saying, his kiss like a truth serum.

"I never wanted it off the table," he replies, kissing me harder and running his hands through my hair.

"Mamá?"

My heart stops beating at the sound of my daughter's voice. I jump off James in time to see Daisy walk around the corner and into the living room.

"¿Qué pasó, florecita?" I ask, my breathing ragged. My daughter's green eyes are half-closed with sleep as she approaches me.

"I can't sleep," Daisy replies as she hugs my leg for comfort.

"Do you need me to sleep in your bed?" I ask, but she shakes her head. My eyes skip to James, who is sitting casually on the couch with an arm draped across the back of it and a small smile on his face. I glare at him in response.

How can he look so unaffected after we just shared the best kiss of my life?

"Can I sleep in your bed?" she asks, and I beg James with my gaze to answer this for us. We haven't slept together yet. I don't know if he will be comfortable sharing his space with both of us.

But he merely grins at my daughter.

"Of course, princess, anything you need."

I hate him. I hate how wonderfully he treats my daughter. I hate how big his heart is. And, most of all, I hate how he's trying to get me to develop feelings for him when he said he could never have any for me.

Without another word spoken between us, all of us get ready for bed. Daisy and I slide under the covers on one side, but she's right in the middle of us, facing James, by the time he also gets into bed. She's hugging her toy kangaroo to her chest, the one she's had since she was born, while James looks at her with a crease between his brows.

Daisy is quickly fast asleep, so I decide to ask him about it.

"What's with the look?" James' eyes shift to my face, a burning intensity in them.

"I missed my son's first steps, first word, first laugh, first everything. It makes me feel like a fake father. Looking at Daisy, knowing I will be a full-time dad for her even if we're only faking this marriage, makes me... happy. She's a remarkable child raised by a remarkable woman, and even if you don't like me, I don't regret offering to be your husband. You'll like me eventually."

He adds the last sentence with a smile, and I can't help the overwhelming feelings flooding my chest.

"I don't not like you," I whisper, my voice thick with emotion. James smirks at me, the blue of his eyes almost glowing in the darkness.

"We'll manage to be friends." The word sends ice through my veins.

"Friends don't do what we did in the kitchen and were about to do in the living room." James lifts his thumb to my bottom lip, tracing its shape.

"Some friends do, but you're right. We'll never be friends," he says and drops his hand from my face to roll onto his back. He places his arm under his head, looking like some kind of Greek god with his chiseled jawline and muscular build.

"Then what will we be?" I ask because I don't like what he's insinuating.

"Isn't it obvious?" he replies, but I roll my eyes at him.

"Nothing is ever obvious with you, James Landon." I tuck my daughter against my chest for comfort while he tilts his head my way.

"We'll be husband and wife, darling, till death do us part because I'm pretty sure you'll kill me before we get the chance to divorce," he jokes, and I let out a small laugh.

"Why would I kill you? We're getting a prenup."

James rolls onto his stomach to laugh into his pillow while I grin at his backside. Maybe this will work, after all.

Chapter 19
James

"Should we be golfing right now? Don't you have a wedding to prepare for?" Adrian asks when we reach the fifth hole. We started golfing three years ago, and now I truly feel like a rich old man.

"I have everything under control. Well, everything but Estrella's conflicted feelings for me," I say with a small snort, my eyes shifting to my best friend to see his cocked brow and smug smile. "Don't even," I warn, but he merely lifts his hands in mock surrender.

"Jesus. You get so cranky when you're lying to yourself about your own feelings. Why do you do that?" he asks, tilting his head as he waits for an answer.

"Because she's making me want things I can't have," I say as he takes the same position as me. He places his tee a few centimetres from where mine was, and I roll my eyes.

"*Ugh*, stop it already with the 'I can't fall in love' bullshit. Yes, you fucking can. The reason you haven't is because the right person hadn't come into your life yet. I know you pictured your life with Val, but that was a *fantasy*. Estrella is *real*. Do you understand the difference?"

"Don't speak to me like I'm a child, Adrian," I reply, irritation making my tone sharp.

"Then stop acting like one. I also thought I was incapable of falling for someone. Turns out, I was merely incapable of falling for anyone who wasn't Nevaeh. Now, get your head out of your ass. No one's saying you *will* fall in love, but for fuck's sake, you're not incapable of it."

He swings, sending his ball flying at a much better angle than me. His fucking readjusting helped, and I hate him a little for it.

His words, however, send me spiraling. Is the reason why I haven't had feelings for someone else because I have been drilling it into my head that I *can't* love someone else?

Yes.

I've been brainwashing myself for so long, I couldn't even see things straight. Annabel, Emma, and all the other people I dated in the past were with a stubborn man who was trying to convince himself that his heart had long been taken.

But Adrian was right all those years ago.

Valentina didn't take my heart.

No.

I haven't given my heart away yet. It's still there, beating in my chest, and it's more than capable of falling for someone else. The right person. I just don't know if the right person is Estrella or if she will leave me as soon as Daisy's grandparents back off.

A shudder runs down my spine at the thought of never seeing either of them again.

Because the possibility of having a future with Estrella and Daisy makes me feel strangely… content.

I don't want to fight my attraction for Estrella. At the same time, I am scared out of my mind to have feelings for someone who might leave me when this will end.

"God, stop thinking. Steam is coming out of your ears," Adrian says and waves his hands back and forth at my ear.

I slap them away and frown.

"Well, you threw a lot of shit my way. Normal people would expect that the other person needs a second to process the rant," I point out, but my best friend laughs at me in response.

"I've been telling you the same thing for years. Thank God Estrella is making you process what I'm saying. Finally." He adds the last word with a snicker.

"I don't know how Nevaeh stands being in your presence every single day. You're bloody irritating," I blurt out, earning another laugh from him.

"I am irritating and annoying, but *my wife* loves me anyway," he says, obviously using the word to twist the knife because he's happy.

"I'll have a wife tomorrow, too, Adrian. It's not as big of a blow as you think it is," I say with a small smile, but he simply shrugs as we make our way to where our balls have landed.

"Isn't it? I got to worship my wife on our wedding night. You'll probably be worshiping your own hand," he says with a mischievous smirk, and I punch him in the arm. "Hey, ow!"

"You deserved that one," I point out, and he walks toward his ball with a little laugh.

"Yeah, I did."

Estrella is lying on the floor with Daisy, playing a board game.

They're in the middle of my living room, smiling at each other like they don't have a single care in the world. It fascinates me how well Estrella hides what's going on from Daisy. She's so strong, and I'm convinced she still feels weak. Not to mention, she probably blames herself for all of this when she's the last person I'd hold responsible.

How anyone could bring this determined, beautiful, and headstrong woman any pain is beyond me.

For a moment, I simply watch this scene unfold in my living room. Daisy is chewing on her bottom lip as she stares at the board, and Estrella is smiling like

Daisy's a blossoming flower unfolding its petals right in front of her. I'm convinced it's the same way I look at Damian.

A love between parent and child is truly unlike any other.

"*Florecita*!" Estrella calls out before bellowing out a laugh that makes me smile. When she catches me smiling at her, she musters a small one in return. "Would you like to join us?" Estrella asks, but I shake my head at her.

"I have to take a shower," I say and tug at my shirt.

Her eyes drop to my chest, so I stride across the room toward our bedroom, pulling my shirt off my body before I'm out of sight. Knowing her, she was watching me the entire time.

"Do *you* want to join *me*, Estrella?" I call over my shoulder.

"In your dreams, *papi*," she says, and I try not to shiver.

"Trust me, you are a dream," I mumble to myself while stepping into my room and shedding the rest of my clothes.

Chapter 20
Estrella

My wedding might be tomorrow, but I also still have a job at the driver academy. Group lessons stopped a week ago because too many parents were taking their kids on vacation before school restarts, but I still have private lessons.

Like today.

James picked up Damian after his golf session this morning, and he's been watching our kids all day while I went to work.

Another reason why I'm starting to like that frustrating man.

I have three private lessons with kids from my previous groups. Although I'm tired because I haven't slept well in weeks, I manage to plaster a smile on my face for every kid, offering them encouraging words as they sit in the karts.

Seeing their bright smiles, pride on their tiny faces when I tell them they've improved, makes me happy. I don't know if all of them will continue on the racing path for the rest of their lives, but if they do, and I had even the smallest impact on them, then that's enough for me.

It's only after my third private lesson of the day ends and I'm alone, staring at the karts, that I realize how deeply I miss sitting in a racecar. Smelling burning rubber and gasoline. Feeling the power of the machine under my fingertips and feet. There's something heady about racing. And no matter how much I try to convince myself I don't miss it, I do. I miss how free I felt.

Even thinking it makes me feel like a bad mother, and the weight settling on my chest, constricting my breathing, certainly doesn't help.

"Estrella."

His voice is like warm honey spreading through my chest. Smooth and comforting. It's strange how a person you thought you didn't even like could suddenly turn into the only one you want to turn to when your thoughts get heavy.

Not that I would. Sharing how I feel with James may be easier than I'd like to admit, but that doesn't mean I'm suddenly going to lay out all my secrets, leaving me bare and vulnerable.

"Yeah?" I turn around, spotting my daughter and Damian on either side of James. They're both holding his hand, and I do my best to ignore the way my heart flutters at the sight of them.

"Our kids are in the mood to do some karting. Do you feel up for it?" he asks, the three of them stopping right in front of me. Daisy wraps her arms around one of my legs, and I bend down to kiss the top of her head.

"*¿Quieres manejar los karts?*" I ask her in Spanish, and she flashes me a bright smile, the single dimple she has showing with the expression.

"*Sí, por favor,*" she replies in our mother tongue. My eyes shift to where James is watching us with a soft expression lingering on his face.

"Do Valentina and Leonard also have karts for adults?" I ask, which earns me a smile.

"Why do you think they close the academy early on the Friday evenings when we don't have race weekends? We have tournaments," he explains with a chuckle, nodding his head in the direction he wants us to go.

It takes me a moment to swallow down the longing to have what James has every single day. He's had them all for years, and even if they'll involve me in things now, as soon as James and I divorce again, I'll lose it all.

The thought shouldn't sadden me so much. I've become used to being alone. But there's still a sharp pain shooting through my chest that I have a hard time breathing through.

"What's wrong, darling?" James asks, his hand finding the small of my back as we walk by the karting track and to the back where they keep all the helmets and karts for the kids.

"Nothing. Something doesn't always have to be wrong, Mr. I-Fix-Everyone's-Problems-But-My-Own."

I'm lashing out at him, but there is no stopping my words. Sadness and anger and frustration exist in equal measures inside of me, and I don't know how to push past them.

James grabs my arm to keep me from walking.

"Kids, go ahead and choose your helmets and karts. Estrella and I will be right there," James says, and Damian and Daisy sprint toward the karts, racing each other. They've been here often enough to know this place as well as I do.

"What the hell do you want from me?" I snap, ripping my arm out of his grasp.

"Why are you attacking me? What have I done?" I roll my eyes at him, so he takes a step toward me, our chests almost touching. "I thought we were past this, little star," he says, cupping my chin so gently, one might think I'd break any second.

"Past what? Hate to break it to you, but I don't think disliking each other goes away just because we started living together *two weeks ago*." My words are harsh, and I don't mean them, but I'm so scared. I'm so scared of getting hurt. Of losing everything I'm building while we're faking our marriage. Of developing feelings for a man who doesn't want me in the way I need to be wanted. More than physically. I want more. I deserve more.

Pushing him away is my best shot to keep my heart closed off before that happens.

And yet, I don't step away to make him stop touching me. I don't tell him to stop caressing my jaw with his thumb, even when it turns my legs into putty.

"Whatever it is that has you this scared, we can figure it out. But you have to stop attacking me, Estrella. It'll only make you feel guilty afterward." I hate that he's right. The guilt has already started to spread because of what I said to him.

"I hate you so much," I say, my eyes closing right as he tightens his grip on me slightly, just enough to make me feel like he's got me.

Like he won't let me fall.

"We've got to work on that," he replies with a smile. "And you're right. I'd rather focus on helping other people with their problems than deal with my own. I'm only human."

If I kick my fiancé a day before our wedding, will he call it off?
Better not to find out.

"We can fix whatever you're feeling by distracting you. You may not win if we race, but I promise you'll have fun," he says, and a genuine laugh slips past my lips at his arrogance.

"You may be a Formula One driver, but I'm a racer, too. You don't stand a chance against me."

As promised, there are larger karts for adults that James and I pull out of storage. There are even helmets with names on the front, specially designed for the group of friends that are slowly snatching a big piece of my heart. James hands me Scarlette's, saying she'd be the one to least mind anyone taking her stuff. It's a lavender-colored helmet with darker purple stripes running through it. James' helmet is many different shades of green with a hawk painted on it, and I almost smile to myself at the sight of it.

"I'm going to win," Damian announces, grinning at Daisy. She gives him an unimpressed look, one she must have learned from me because it's very similar to how I look at James when he challenges me. Like right now.

"I'm going to destroy you in this," he whispers, making sure neither one of our children hears his bad sportsmanship.

"Give it your best shot, *vice* champion," I reply, and his mouth drops dramatically as he places a hand on his chest. A shocked laugh slips free, but I stand my ground.

"You did not just go there," he says, but I jut out my chin defiantly, something I know he enjoys because it always makes him smile. It also brings our faces closer together, his eyes gluing themselves to my lips.

"Oh, but I did," I reply and step away again.

We all make our way to our karts, James and I helping our kids before we settle down in our own. Excitement bursts through my chest. I fasten the clasp on my helmet before wrapping the seatbelt around myself.

"Five laps?" I ask all three of them, still adjusting in my seat.

"Sure," James replies, both Daisy and Damian nodding eagerly as well. "This is one hell of a way to spend our last night as unmarried people," he adds right as we line up at the start and finish line of the track. No one else is at the academy at this time of day, so we get to enjoy some privacy.

"You mean racing each other?" I ask with a cocked brow, fighting my smile.

"Yeah, each other and our kids," he says with a nod toward where the two of them are bickering about who will win. I grin at them before throwing my soon-to-be husband a challenging smile.

"Catch me if you can," I say and slam on the gas, shooting down the track.

"Mamá!" Daisy calls after me, but I merely let out a cheerful scream before making my way into the first corner.

Almost every kid starts racing in karting. It's where I started too, but over time, as I found a different racing category, I lost touch with how much I love it. Only when I began working at the academy, familiarized myself with it again, did I realize what it meant to me.

What it means to so many kids out there with a dream.

As I race down the track, doing my best to stay ahead of Damian, Daisy, and James—okay, mostly James because I don't really mind if the kids overtake me—I feel the surge of happiness in my chest as clearly as I feel the wind in my face.

Once we move into the second lap, James has overtaken our kids and is chasing me down. I'm laughing and sweating, concentrating enough to keep him behind me but also having a hard time not stopping the kart to fall into a fit of laughter.

I think I forgot how much fun racing truly is until this very second.

And it's all thanks to James Oliver Landon as he chases me around the track.

Chapter 21
James

Estrella beat me, but I've been blaming it on her jump start. In reality, I was too busy staring at her in awe and pure amazement to focus. She just looked so breathtaking and those tattoos of hers make me a very weak man. I haven't gotten the chance to study each and every single one of them intimately, but as soon as she lets me, I will spend hours doing exactly that.

"How did you go so fast?" Damian asks Estrella, poking her leg as we make our way up the steps of the house. "You were faster than Daisy and me."

"Well, I've been racing for more than twenty years," she explains, making my son's eyes go wide. "But I'll teach you, I promise. One day, you'll go even faster than me," she promises, and I feel my heart go all warm and tingly when Damian smiles up at her and takes her hand.

"Okay!" he says, holding onto her.

Daisy grabs my hand, barely walking now that she's tired. I've noticed she gets tired more quickly than Damian. My little guy could be running around the house until midnight if we let him, he has that much energy.

I pick up the little girl and place her on my hip. She wastes no time wrapping her arms around my neck. We went to eat, so both of them are ready to go to bed now.

Estrella unlocks the door with the key I had made for her a week ago, pushing it open a moment later. But something makes her freeze, then push Damian behind her to protect him from whatever is waiting inside.

My heart stops beating, but I can't move past her because I'm holding Daisy. And I can't put Daisy in danger. Fuck.

Luckily, Estrella reacts faster and slams the door shut, turning to me with panic in her eyes.

"Your parents are here," she blurts out, placing both hands on Damian's shoulders.

Never mind my heart stopping. It disintegrates as that information tries to process in my head.

"How do you know what they look like?" I ask because, well, what the fuck?

"I looked through the photo albums you keep in your home library. Is that really important right now?" she whisper-screams at me, and I shake my head.

"No," I reply.

I haven't seen my parents in years. They cut me off when they found out about Annabel being pregnant with Damian, and I didn't dignify them with more than three thoughts. But that also means I completely forgot about them having a key to my house.

I take three strides toward Estrella, handing her Daisy and making sure only she hears me. Daisy looks fast asleep on her arm, but I want to protect Damian from my parents. Especially my father. Even before he left, he wasn't a good parent. He's always expected too much of me, unreachable things a child should never have to feel shame for not being able to accomplish.

"We're going to go inside, and I need you to put Daisy and Damian to bed, please. I don't want them to get in the middle of the crossfire," I say, placing a hand on her cheek. It's only as I reach for her that I notice my hand is shaking.

"Of course. I'll take care of him," Estrella assures me.

"Thank you."

With a deep breath, I push the door back open, stepping inside my house to find my parents sitting in the living room. Estrella takes Damian's hand and leads him to his room while I make my way toward the mother who gave birth to me and the father who traumatised me more often than not.

"What are you doing in my house? I don't remember giving you permission to ever enter again," I say, crossing my arms in front of my chest as I stand in front of them.

My father looks angry as he gets up and walks toward me. I brace myself for whatever he has planned to do when my mum's hand wraps around his wrist to stop him.

"Why is it that we have to find out you're getting married from a friend of ours you invited to your fucking wedding?" he asks, his English accent stronger than mine.

"Last I checked, you cut *me* out of *your* lives, not the other way around. I have no responsibility toward you," I remind him, even if it breaks my heart to see Mum flinch.

My father's glare is pure evil.

"Do you know how deeply you've upset your mother? What you've done is inexcusable!"

Says the man who once left me at a fucking supermarket car park when I didn't win a karting race. The man who punched one of my former mechanics in the face for "sabotaging" my race, even though he had nothing to do with the pit crew not properly attaching my tyre. The man who made me feel small every single day of my life.

"You cannot simply get married without telling your parents. How dare you?" my father, an older version of me when it comes to appearances, asks, and I almost laugh aloud.

"How dare you show up here on one of the rare nights I have my son? How dare you threaten my little girl's mental well-being? How dare you scare my wife?" I ask, the words rolling off my tongue a little too easily. But I have to sell the story. I have to convince them this is real.

For no other reason do I say these words.

"Little girl? Wife? Do you hear yourself? You're not even married yet. That child of hers is not yours," my father says, attempting to step toward me again, but Mum holds him back. Her green eyes are trained on me, regret and remorse clear as day in them.

"Yes, I hear myself, Father. But what I'd rather hear is what the hell you're doing here." I cross my arms, trying to stand my ground.

Childhood trauma is an interesting thing. I've had an easy enough time ignoring it when the physical reminder, my father, wasn't in my life anymore. But now that he's standing here, confronting me, my hands have started to shake. My heart is racing. I can't breathe properly.

I've been around people who have anxiety and panic attacks. They live with those mental illnesses on a daily basis. Some days are better, others are worse. For me? My bad days only happen when I have to speak to my father.

"We came here to discuss your disgusting behaviour," he says.

"And what you did was breaking and entering. If Mum wasn't here, I'd have called the police."

It's a lie. I don't think I could ever call the police on my parents, no matter how fucked up all of this is. From the day I was born, I was trained and told to love them. Every child is. But what they don't tell you is that once you love a parent, unloving them is nearly impossible. Even when they don't deserve your love.

"You've always been a spoiled, little boy, but now you're a twenty-eight-year-old man, James. It's getting pathetic."

"Alright. Thank you for your compliments, as always. Now, get out of my house before you scare my family," I say and point toward the door. My parents make no attempt to move toward it.

"James, I—"

My father cuts my mother off before she can finish her sentence, which only makes me angrier. Mum has always been a gentle soul. She never yelled at me, Dad did enough of that for the both of them, and was always kind to everyone we met.

My father is the bully.

"You've embarrassed us in front of our friends, James. You have to apologise," he says, and this time, I do laugh out loud.

"Are you having a laugh?" I ask, but my father twists out of Mum's grip to grab me by the collar.

"Appearances are everything. Take responsibility, and it'll restore our good name among our friends. Can you do that or is that too much to ask of you, you little shit?" he says, tightening his hold on me.

"I'm going to give you five seconds to take your hands off my husband. If you're still touching him by the time I reach one, I'll remove them for you, okay?" Estrella asks, and I turn my head just enough to see her standing in the area between the living room and kitchen.

"Who do you think you—" She cuts him off.

"Five." The word comes out low and threatening, in a voice I've never heard her use.

"Now, hold on, you—"

"Four." I could push my father away, but I kind of want to see what she'll do if he decides not to let go.

"What are you going to do? Push me?" Dad asks, but Estrella merely shrugs.

"You'll find out in three seconds."

"Let go of our son," Mum says, but he doesn't listen to her either.

"Two," Estrella chimes in.

I don't know if it's her confidence or the danger she radiates, but Dad releases me and takes a step back.

"Good. That wasn't so hard, was it?" she asks, faking a smile. "Now, how about you give your wife the chance to speak to her son while I escort you out of our home? Or would you rather I release this recording of you almost strangling your son so all of your rich, little friends can see who you truly are?" Estrella asks, pointing at the phone she propped against the vase on the shelf beside her.

It must have perfectly recorded the whole confrontation.

"No wonder my son hasn't introduced you to us. You're—"

"Finish that sentence, Dad. See what happens." It's my turn to threaten him.

He can insult me as much as he wants. But one bad word about Estrella, and I'll forget he's my father. No amount of shaking hands and childhood trauma can prevent me from unleashing my anger then.

"We'll leave," Mum says, my heart sinking at the defeat in her voice. "I'm sorry we came here. I only wanted to congratulate you. I hope the two of you have a very happy life together." My throat constricts as a wave of emotions floods my chest.

"Mum..." I trail off, not knowing what to say. Not that it matters. She hands me the key I gave them before pushing Dad toward the door.

Estrella watches them closely, her body only relaxing once the door is shut again. I don't mean to sink into a squat, but the moment has overwhelmed every fibre of my being and there is no stopping the bodily reaction.

"What do you need?" Estrella asks, kneeling down in front of me and placing her hands on my knees.

"You heard it all?" I ask, and she gives me a careful nod. "Then you know there is nothing anyone can do to give me what I need. Because what I need, deep down, is memories with my father that aren't tainted with his anger."

Estrella studies me for a long moment, compassion stitching itself into every centimetre of her face. I look to the left of her to keep from seeing it.

"Perhaps, but that isn't something I can give you. So, let me rephrase." She tilts her head to the side to make me look at her again. "What do you need that I can give you?" she asks, and, for the first time in my life, I feel so safe speaking about what it is I truly need from someone.

"Feel like watching a movie?" Estrella flashes me a wonderful smile in response.

"Absolutely."

It takes everything out of me not to pull her against me when we settle down on my... our bed. From tomorrow on, everything I have will be ours for the foreseeable future. But I don't even mind the thought anymore.

I'm even looking forward to it.

Except—

"Isn't it bad luck for us to spend the night before our wedding together?" I find myself asking. She turns her head my way, an amused expression on her features.

"Bad luck for our fake marriage?" she asks, but I merely shrug. "I wouldn't have pegged you for a superstitious person."

"I'm usually not," I admit. Estrella pats my arm a few times before leaning back on her side of the bed again.

"It's not meant to last, James, so I wouldn't worry about it." She's right.

And still...

"I'm going to go check on Damian," I say, completely disregarding that we haven't even started the movie.

"Will you be back?" Estrella asks, giving me a confused look.

"I don't know. He might need me."

I don't go back to our room. I stay in my son's, sharing his tiny bed with him for no particular reason.

None at all.

Chapter 22
Estrella

It's my wedding day.

Woohoo.

I slept about three hours last night because Daisy woke me in the middle of the night, telling me she had a nightmare and couldn't sleep.

Valentina is currently frowning at my under-eye bags with a concealer in her right hand. Even when she's about to scold me for not sleeping before such an emotionally, physically, and mentally draining day, she's devastatingly beautiful. Her curly, dirty blonde hair is in an updo with sunflowers stuck into the braided sections. Her trained and curvy body is hidden beneath a silky, long, red dress she chose as my maid of honor. I let her pick whatever she liked because I wanted her to be comfortable. And she looks breathtaking. She painted her eyelids in a combination of yellow and brown tones and added half a dozen sunflowers on the crease.

"Who did your makeup?" I ask before she can complain about my eye bags. A slow smile spreads across her face and replaces the frown that previously occupied her nude-painted lips.

"Gabriel drew the sunflowers, I did the rest," she says.

"It's lovely," I say, looking up when she points a finger at the ceiling. Valentina dabs a makeup sponge under my left eye, and Nevaeh tugs on a strand of my hair as she twists it into place. "Ouch," I complain, immediately causing her to hover over me so I can see her apologetic expression. It's even cuter because it's upside down.

"Sorry, sweetie," she says and massages my scalp where she pulled the strand of my hair. "Your hair is so thick. I'm jealous," Nevaeh adds, bringing a grin to my face.

"I love my hair. It's the only thing I got from my mother." The reminder of her not being here wipes the smile right off my face, and Val gives me a comforting smile.

"Have you seen Daisy's grandparents?" Chiara asks, stepping in front of me in a sleek black suit with nothing underneath her blazer. Everything is hugging her body in the right places, and while it looks like it fits snugly, the curvy, short woman with bright green eyes moves around with more grace than me in sweatpants. Leonard bought it for her, and I have to hand it to him, he has impeccable taste. Chiara looks sexy, dangerous, and stunning all at the same time.

"No, not yet. I've been avoiding everyone. I haven't even looked at the venue or what James has done with it," I admit, and the Italian woman gives me a small nod.

"It's beautiful. He's had stars put everywhere, dahlias, green and white place settings, and other floral decorations. It's nicer than my wedding," Valentina says with a soft laugh before adding, "Don't tell Gabriel I said that. He spent weeks preparing the perfect wedding for us." She hands me a glass of water and tells me to take a sip before she gets started on my lips.

"It's not your fault your wedding was a mess, no offense," Nevaeh chimes in

"None taken. It's not every day that your mother, who abandoned you as a child, tries to kill your future sister-in-law by burning down the house where you were staying," she says, and I wish I hadn't taken a big gulp of water.

It takes several moments of Scarlette slapping my back and me coughing to get the water into the right pipe.

"I should have warned you a little," Valentina says with a small chuckle once I'm able to breathe properly again.

"Yeah, I agree." My words come out a bit hoarse.

"So, you see, marrying a gorgeous, English, millionaire Formula One driver isn't as bad," Scarlette replies from where she's steaming my dress now, and I snort in response.

"Definitely not."

Everything quiets as Nevaeh and Valentina get back to work on my hair and face. Scarlette is removing the wrinkles from my dress and Chiara helps her. I'm about to tell them all to stop making such a fuss because this wedding is only pretend, but my mouth clamps shut before any words leave me.

It feels nice to be pampered. I can't remember the last time I had anyone take care of me like this. For the longest time, I didn't mind either, but there is no way I could tell any of them to stop when hardly anything has made me feel this at peace in a long time.

A harsh knock on the door pulls me out of my trance.

"Estrella Celeste Cortez, open this door before I bust it down," a familiar voice calls out in Spanish from the other side of the closed door. All of my senses heighten as panic floods my chest.

Oh my God.

What the hell is he doing here?

"Reya, who is that?" Valentina asks, and I realize she understood his aggressive demand because she speaks Spanish, too.

"Do you need us to send whoever that is away?" Scarlette asks, her Spanish also flawless. From what I've gathered, she learned it from her husband.

"No. It's someone from my old life," I reply and stand up, admiring my hair and my subtle makeup before striding toward the door.

Out of all the things to happen today, I didn't think his showing up would be something I had to deal with.

Another aggressive knock sends me forward faster than before.

"Estrella!" he barks, and I let out a low sigh.

"*¡Ya voy,* Simón*! Cállate la boca, idiota,*" I call as I fumble with the door knob.

My shaking hands won't allow me to open the door for my ex-friend-with-benefits. I take a deep breath to get some control back, opening it only slowly.

"*¿Qué quieres?*" I demand in Spanish, but he pushes past me, frustration seeping into the room. All four women go on high alert, and Chiara steps in front of Nevaeh, Scarlette, and Valentina. She's a trained fighter, and, right now, she looks about ready to rip Simón's head off if he makes one wrong move.

"Not another step," Chiara warns in Italian, but it's close enough to Spanish for me to understand her.

Which means Simón also understood.

"Back off, lady, this doesn't concern yo—"

He shouldn't have raised his hand to point at her because now he's pressed face-first to the wooden floor, one of his arms wrapped across his back. Simón wasn't even able to finish his sentence before Chiara had him pinned to the ground. I do my best not to burst into laughter.

"Get off me!" Simón calls out, his voice filled with discomfort.

"Chiara, it's okay. He's not a threat," I assure her, but her green eyes show suspicion.

"He was yelling and storming in here like a threat," she replies, and I cover my mouth to keep from laughing.

"*No te atrevas a reír,*" Simón says.

"Sweetheart." Leonard's voice fills my small dressing room, catching his wife's attention.

"Be right with you, *amore*. Just have to make sure this guy doesn't hurt my friends," she says, and my chest warms a little at the protectiveness coming from her.

"Okay, but make it quick, Starling. I found that place we were looking for," he says and leaves the room like this is the most normal thing in the world for him to witness.

"Place?" Scarlette asks, and Chiara gives her a little smirk.

"Don't worry about it."

Only the most innocent-minded people would fail to pick up on what they meant based on the Italian woman's facial expression.

"Now, let's try this again, little boy. What the fuck do you want and why the hell are you storming in here like you're going to war?" Chiara asks Simón, and I finally manage to unfreeze my legs and get them to push me forward.

"Chiara, it's okay. This is Simón. He was my brother's best friend," I explain, and she finally lets go of him only to push herself upright by pressing his face into the ground again.

"Jesus, woman. I don't know whether to be scared of you or turned on," Simón says as he stands up and massages his shoulder.

"I'm married and not even a little flattered," Chiara replies as she looks him up and down with distaste on her face. He merely gives her one of his panty-dropping smiles that I've taken too literally in the past.

Simón is gorgeous. He has brown eyes, light brown skin, and short hair with wavy curls. His muscular and tall frame has made my mouth water in the past, but all I feel for him at the moment is anger. He disappeared when I needed someone the most.

"Could we have the room for a minute? Please?" I say to the four women I'm becoming immensely fond of. They all give me an unsure look before glaring at Simón and then doing as I asked. Chiara is the last to step out of the room, but she stops in the doorframe and turns slowly to look at Simón again.

"Touch her without her consent, and I'll cut something off. You don't need your dick or balls, right?" she threatens, and I cover my mouth once again.

Simón gives her another smile, not in the least bit threatened even though she had him pinned to the floor like he was a little doll.

"I do need 'em, *guapa*, sorry," he says to Chiara, and I let out a small snort.

"*¿Para qué? Son igual de inútiles que una bolsa de arena en el desierto,*" I say in Spanish, causing Valentina and Scarlette to burst into laughter since they're clearly not out of hearing range yet.

Simón shoots a glare in their direction before focusing all of its rage on me.

"Let's stop playing games, shall we, *planetita*?" Simón says, using the nickname I hate more than anything.

He's been calling me little planet for years because he thinks it's funny since my name means star. It's as hilarious now as it has always been. Not at all.

"I'm not playing any games, *sapito*," I reply, causing him to frown.

I've been calling him little toad because when we were kids, he used to chase them around. I kicked him in the shin more than a few times for it.

"What are you doing here, Simón?" I say when I realize he didn't answer my question.

His eyes focus on me as he says, "I'm here to stop you from making the biggest mistake of your life. Marrying a man you met only months ago? What the hell are you doing? Marriage is sacred, *mi amor*," he says, his anger subsiding a little. His eyebrows pull together in worry.

"Don't '*mi amor*' me, and don't come in here after you disappeared years ago while I was hurting and needed you by my side."

Okay, maybe I don't hate Simón as much as I always try to convince myself. Maybe I cared for him, and saying I hate him is easier. I liked the way he made me feel, the way he worshipped my body, and let me take out my frustration with him. We worked, even if it was in a fucked up way. We made sense, even when we weren't supposed to. But I don't think I'll ever be able to forgive him for what he did. I was heartbroken, and he left me when I needed him.

There is no returning from that.

"I'm so sorry. I truly am. I know you were grieving so much more than me, but when my best friend died, something in me snapped. It was like losing my other half, and I didn't know how to cope. Then, Helen passed away so soon after, and I fell into my darkness. Daisy and you didn't deserve someone like me to hold you back. I knew disappearing would be better for you," he explains, and I suck in a sharp breath as I shake my head.

There is no point arguing with him over what he did or how he handled everything years ago. I have more important things on my plate.

"I know what it feels to fall into depression, Simón. I get it. It's horrible. It's something I don't wish on anyone, but we could have talked to each other. I went to therapy, and you could have gone with me, if that would have helped. There were so many options, but you chose to run. It broke the trust between us and there is nothing you can do or say to bring it back."

It feels so good to finally get all of that off my chest, to tell him what I've been wanting to say for years. But that doesn't change what's happening and what I'm going to be late for.

"Now, I have a wedding to attend, if you don't mind," I say and attempt to move past him to get my veil, but he grabs me by the elbow and brings me against his chest.

My body instantly melts into the contact. His scent, something rugged and strong I've always adored, fills my nose until he's intoxicated me. That's always been the problem with Simón. He's got a strange effect on my senses and my head. He draws me in until I don't know how to untangle myself from him.

"Actually, I do mind," he says and cups my face with his hands. "Estrella, what's going on? Why are you marrying a stranger?" I cross my arms in front of my chest to put a buffer between us, but when his piercing eyes meet mine, there is no fighting against my emotions anymore. "Hmm? Tell me, *mi amor*. Tell me what's wrong, and I'll fix it," he promises.

I tell him about Bert and Jennifer, about their threat to take Daisy from me, and James' offer to marry me so I don't lose her. Every little detail flows from my lips, bringing more and more rage to his features. His grip on my neck remains steady the whole time, but I can tell this is by far the worst scenario he envisioned for why I'm marrying James.

The comfort of him being here, a small trinket from my past even if it's a complicated one, is strong enough to make my heart beat a little steadier.

"So, you see, I have no choice. It's either this, or I'll lose Daisy. Marrying James is the only way," I explain, still fighting the tears so as to not ruin my makeup.

Valentina would strangle me if I did.

"You're not marrying him. If you're going to marry anyone, it'll be me," Simón announces before briefly pressing his lips to mine and then storming past me.

A bit dizzy from what the fuck he said and the kiss, I barely manage to hold him back.

"Absolutely not. I don't care if you apologized, Simón. You're too late. How do you think it'd look to Bert and Jennifer if I married someone else now?" He opens his mouth to reply, but I beat him to it. "Not good, Simón, not good at all."

"I don't give a fuck. We'll get a lawyer. Everything will be fine. No one will take Daisy from you," he says, grabbing my arms again.

"No. I'm not putting Daisy through any of that." He lets out a small growl and then throws his hands into the air out of frustration.

Under different circumstances, I'd enjoy being able to speak so much Spanish again, but this conversation is anything but enjoyable.

"For the love of God, Estrella, please don't do this. Please. I know I fucked up. I know I shouldn't have left. I'm sorry. Just, please, don't marry another man, especially not one you don't know. Baby, please. We can figure it out together."

His lips crash onto mine again, and I don't step away. I should. I know I fucking should. I'm wearing another man's ring, I'm about to marry him.

Letting Simón kiss me is a new level of wrong.

James and I aren't actually dating, but we did talk about being exclusive, and I can't do this to him. I can't melt into the kiss, not with so much on the line.

The worst part is, the door flies open, and James walks into the room before I manage to step away.

Chapter 23
James

"What's going on?" I ask Val as I approach Estrella's dressing room.

"Someone from Estrella's past showed up. I'm pretty sure they're fighting," she explains, her arms wrapping around her front in a hug.

A few years ago, I wouldn't have hesitated to hug her and find a way to wipe the concern off her face. Today, I'm barely even registering the fact that she might need me and solely focusing on Estrella being in any kind of danger.

"I'll check on her," I say, the protective part of me going into full-activation mode.

"Wait, I hear them talking," Val interrupts, placing her hand on my chest before I can step past her. "He's begging her not to get married to you. Says he'll marry her instead," my best friend explains, and, suddenly, I'm angry.

Whoever this wanker is will not be marrying Estrella.

I'm marrying her. End of discussion.

"That's good, right? You don't have to marry her if he will," Val says, interrupting my thoughts.

I don't reply. My hand grabs hold of the door knob before turning it to open the door and finding my fiancée with another man's mouth on hers. The jealousy coursing through me invades every part of my bloodstream. It's uncalled for since we aren't an actual couple under any circumstances, but, as much as I tried not to, I've started to like this beautifully stubborn woman. I like the way she looks at me, the way she demands my attention without accepting only half of it. I like how she turned my whole life upside down.

"If I were you, I'd get your hands off my wife before I remove them," I warn the short man with dark, wavy brown hair. He's quite a bit more muscular than me, but I'm much taller. And probably angrier.

"Or what? Is rich, pretty boy going to hurt me if I don't?" he challenges.

"Would you like to find out?" I'm not a violent person, I never have been. Right now, though, I'd very much like to beat his face in.

"Listen, asshole, Estrella isn't marrying you. You're no one to her, and I'd rather die than see her pretend to be in love with you in front of all of these people."

Half a smile touches my lips.

"That's not your decision to make, is it?" I reply, bringing my gaze to Estrella, who's been watching our exchange with shame written all over her face. It bugs me that her lipstick is a little smudged. *I* want to smudge it. I want to be responsible, and knowing I wasn't has me more frustrated than I have a right to be. "Up to you, darling. Say the word, and I'll call it off."

No, I won't. She'll choose me. I know she will. I've seen the way she looks at me, felt what I do to her. And for once, I want someone to want me as much as I want them, and I want to marry Estrella. I want to help her keep Daisy and get to know her better at the same time.

"Simón, can you give us a minute?" Estrella says and pushes *Simón* toward the door. His eyes shift from me to her.

"You have five minutes before I'm throwing you over my shoulder and carrying you out of this fucking room," he warns and storms past me.

Estrella steps in front of me immediately after the door closes.

"I'm so sorry. I'm so fucking sorry, James. Simón is someone I thought I'd never see again. He abandoned Daisy and me during the worst time of our lives, and I thought that would be it. Then, he showed up here, acting like a knight in shining armor even though I don't need saving. And I have you. But he didn't listen and then he kissed me, twice, and the second time I don't know what happened. I didn't step back, but I don't want to kiss him. I'd much rather kiss you, and—"

I cut her off by smashing my lips to hers.

For a split second, she tenses, but then her hands lift into my hair and she melts against my chest. I'm reeling from the thought of smearing her lipstick. Plus, I'm a little pissed and want to make sure the only taste in her mouth is me.

Her lips part, and I lick across her bottom one before pushing my tongue inside her mouth to taste her. Estrella's scent is enough to weaken my knees, but her taste has a different hold on me. It demands I remain upright and get more, as much as I can. Let it light my taste buds on fire. It makes me want to lick every single centimetre of her body, to memorise her because I've never felt this drawn to another person.

Ever.

The stars in the universe may be too far away to have a gravitational pull on me, but the one standing right in front of me is close enough to have plenty.

Once she's out of breath and reaching for the waistband of my expensive suit, I pull back and cup her face to tilt her head back. Her brown eyes are fixated on mine as the dominant part inside of me grabs hold.

"James," she whimpers as I trace her jaw with my thumbs, pressing down firmly. She needs more, I can feel her lust in my bones, but there is a more urgent matter at hand.

Clarifying what the fuck I want.

"I don't like that he kissed you, little star. But if you want to marry him instead of me, tell me now because once we say those vows, we will be married for however long it takes. You will be mine, and I will be yours. No other person touches you, let alone kisses you. I'm not a man who is capable of sharing the person he takes into his bed for good, Estrella. I don't want us to play games, unless they involve sex," I rant, my fingers still caressing the soft skin on her chin.

Her breathing hitches when I take a step closer, bringing my chest flush against hers.

"We may not know each other for as long as you've known him, but I will *never* leave when you need me most. I've got you and Daisy."

I'm making a hell of a promise, but I mean it. I mean every word.

"I don't know how you're going to top those vows," she whispers, and I give her a small smirk.

"Why don't you let me worry about that?" I suggest, bringing a shy smile to her lips.

I love it when the woman who is all fire and flames turns into a shy person. It's like I have some sort of superpower when it comes to her.

"Why do you keep taking care of things? Of me?" Estrella asks, her fingers snaking around my wrists where they are resting on her face.

"Because I have a feeling no one's taken care of you in a long time."

Because despite my best efforts, I care about you.

"Sounds like you do care. I thought you were incapable," she says, her eyes fluttering shut when I lean down to brush my lips against the corner of her mouth.

"It's all pretend."

Why the fuck did I say that?

Why am I still lying to her?

She's going to knee me in the balls because I'm the biggest fucking dickhead on the planet. Instead, her hands drop to my thighs as her nails dig into my thin trousers. My cock jumps to attention, growing painfully hard behind my slacks.

"Maybe, but you can't pretend your dick's not throbbing for me right now."

Fuck. I don't have to tell her she's right. The evidence is right between us, and her gaze drops to it before she licks her lips.

"I really hope you're as fun as you look," she says to my groin before looking up at me with mischief in her eyes. "I was never going to choose Simón, James. He's my past, and while you're not my future, I'd much rather pretend with you than live in constant fear that he'd leave again," Estrella explains, her fingernails slowly tracing upward.

I'm fucking furious. Part of me wants to strangle Simón for what he did to Estrella and another part is getting lost in her touch. In the electricity she's shooting through my whole body. In the pain of my aching cock as it pushes harder and harder against the barrier of my trousers. I want to slide them down, let him jump free, and bury myself so fucking deep inside of her, Simón will be a distant memory.

When she grazes my cock, all rational thought leaves my mind. It's consumed by the desire to tattoo myself onto her skin so she never forgets how good I make her feel.

"*Planetita*, we're leaving," Simón says as he storms back inside the room, preventing me from putting my mouth back where it belongs.

On Estrella's.

"I'm sorry, Simón, but I told you I'm not going anywhere with you," she says, and those words send a wave of possessiveness through me.

She's choosing *me*.

"Please, Estrella. Let's go," Simón begs, and I can see it right then and there.

He cares for her, maybe even loves her, but he fucked up. He let her go when she needed him most, and if I learned anything from leaving Val when things got tough, it's that you stay. No matter what.

"She said no, Simón. Don't make me get Chiara," I warn because she once beat up the man that vandalised her art gallery years ago. He was in the hospital for a week.

"Don't do this, baby. We can figure it out. You and me. Like it was supposed to be. I love you. I love you so much, Estrella, please, don't marry him," he says, sending my heart into a frenzy because she fucking hesitates.

Tears fill her eyes as she looks at him, and I realise how stupid I am. I may have told her I can't fall in love, but she didn't warn me she can't either because she's already in love.

With another man.

"I have to get dressed, Simón. James and I are getting married, and I need you to leave before you ruin everything. I will not lose Daisy."

As happy as I should be with her words, she's only saying them to keep up appearances in front of Jennifer and Bert. Maybe I'm not the one pretending, but she is. It's all an act.

"Excuse me," I say and leave the room without another word.

My chest is burning, so I take a deep breath to push past the unnerving sensation. There is pressure behind my eyes, but not from unshed tears.

It's the start of a bad headache from being one dumb man.

No one chooses me because they want me. They choose me when I'm a means to an end. Annabel chose me because she wanted to have Damian and then leave him with me. Emma, my ex-girlfriend from many years ago, chose me because she liked the way I fucked, but she didn't want me for more either. Estrella chose me not because she wants all of me, including my baggage.

I'm simply a solution to all of her problems.

"Daddy!"

My heart swells in my chest at the sound of my son's voice. I see him and Daisy sprinting down the hallway toward me. Damian's arms fling around my neck after I squat down to greet him. It feels like I haven't seen him in weeks, even though I dropped him off at his mums' place only hours ago.

"Hey, bud," I say, and then Daisy's arms are around my neck, too, and both kids are hugging me like I'm the best thing in the world.

And, right now, it's all I need to distract me from feeling as unwanted as I always have.

Chapter 24
James

I'VE INVITED A LOT of people to witness our wedding ceremony today. Some of my parents' friends, people from my F1 team, a few trusted reporters, and friends of friends. Bert and Jennifer are sitting near the front of the altar, looking around suspiciously. My eyes almost roll because of how ridiculous they look.

And no matter how fake this ceremony is, I'm nervous. Palms sweating, breathing uneven kind of nervous.

"You look as scared shitless as I felt before my wedding," Adrian says as he approaches.

I have yet to make my way down the aisle, to stand in front of everyone who thinks this is real and the people who know it's not. I can't breathe properly. Marriage doesn't mean what it used to for me, but the infuriating woman still getting ready is dangerous for my heart. I can't let her in.

"At least your marriage was real. You were allowed to be nervous. I shouldn't be," I reply and straighten out my jacket. I may have made fun of Adrian's fashion choices, but he chose a nice tux for me. All sleek and black and cut to highlight my trained form, especially my thighs.

My best man steps in front of me, compassion in his eyes.

"You *are* allowed to be nervous. You're allowed to feel anything you want to feel. This may not be a real marriage, it may end in a year or two, but you're still tying yourself to another person. May it be purely on paper, or something more—" He cuts off to shoot me a challenging look. "—it doesn't matter. It's still a bond." He fixes my tie with care, then steps back again. "And if all fails, just fake your death and block her number before disappearing." I do my best not to crack a smile at his awful joke.

"You're terrible. Have you ever done that to someone?" I ask because as ridiculous as he is, I welcome the distraction.

"No. I was always very clear about what I was looking for. But you're getting married to someone you don't love, so it's a bit of a messier situation," he replies, and I shake my head.

"Thanks for the reminder," I grumble.

"Welcome. I'm always here for brutal reality checks and unhelpful advice."

He's so full of shit. Adrian has always had this way of being exactly the kind of person anyone needs. If I need a friend, he will be my friend. If I need a shoulder to lean on, he'll give me both of his. If I need a brother, he will prove to me that blood doesn't make you siblings.

Adrian is full of himself beyond measure, but he's also the kindest soul in the world.

"What have I missed?" Cameron asks as he approaches too, making Adrian crack a smile.

"Nothing much. James getting cold feet, having an existential crisis. The usual," Adrian replies, and I smack his arm with a frown.

"I was not—" Cameron cuts me off, only addressing Adrian.

"Is there any chance you want to switch seats? I'll go to Velocità Rossa, and you can have my seat at Hawke," he says, both of them pretending like I'm not standing next to them.

"I can't believe anyone would put you two together. You have nothing in common. How will you work as a team?" the Monegasque tells the Australian while I furrow my brows.

"Yeah, I don't get it either. We're complete opposites. I'm good-looking, a natural talent in other sports, spend my time doing important things, and James, well he..." Cameron trails off, but he doesn't have to finish the sentence for Adrian and me to understand him.

"Ha, ha. You are so funny. Maybe when you lose the championship to me this season, stand-up comedy can be your alternative career path," I suggest, making his blue eyes narrow. He glares at me before we both start laughing, Adrian watching us with a quirk of his lips.

"Ready to get married?" Gabriel asks as he approaches.

Nervously and still with sweaty palms, I run a hand down the front of my tux.

"Stop that. You're going to crinkle the fabric," Cameron reminds me, but if I don't give myself anything to do, I might start sweating in more places than my palms.

"I might have a panic attack," I warn, my heart racing. Adrian's back stiffens as he looks at something behind me.

"You might want to wait until after you've spoken to your mom," he says, grabbing Cameron's elbow to guide him away and toward the altar. Gabriel offers me a compassionate smile before disappearing, too. Leaving Mum and me by ourselves.

"Hi, Mum."

She steps toward me, her grey-brown hair flowing with every step she takes. She's much shorter than I am, so when she stops in front of me, I have to tilt my head down to meet her green eyes' intense gaze.

"I'm sorry for showing up unannounced. Estrella invited me," she explains, making my breathing hitch as my heart stumbles all over itself.

"She did?"

"Yes. She said she noticed how much this distance between us hurts me, that it wasn't my decision," Mum says, her eyes filling with tears. "Your father is a hard man, James, and stubborn, too. He's been so angry about you having a child so young, when you had your whole career ahead of you. Every time I tried to go to you, he'd scream at me. I had no idea how to keep my relationship with you when he—" She cuts off and sucks in a sharp breath. "The why doesn't matter. What matters is how sorry I am. And when Estrella called me, I knew your father's anger wasn't enough to keep me from coming to your wedding."

Mum takes a step toward me and places her hands on my arms. Tears fall down her cheeks, sending a sharp pain through my chest.

"I want to be a part of your life again. I want to get to know Damian, Daisy, and Estrella. I want to do better than I have before," she says, and I swallow down the tears shooting into my eyes. "Do you think you can forgive me?"

It's an easy question. And I have an equally easy answer. Because the little boy in me is broken, and having Mum back in my life could heal the parts of me she broke by vanishing.

"Of course, Mum." I wrap my arms around her and hug her to my chest.

I lived with my father for eighteen years of my life before I moved out. He never physically abused me, but the emotional and mental abuse left scars deep inside of me. And yet, I still loved him. I still wanted to make him proud. I still thought his approval was the most important thing I could ever have.

My mother is married to him. Despite everything, she loves him, and I know how difficult that is.

"Thank you for coming," I add after stepping back.

"If it wasn't for your wife, I wouldn't have," she admits, and the reminder of what Estrella did for *me* sends a wave of emotion through me that I don't know how to deal with. I'm still so frustrated with her, but I like her a little bit more at the same time.

It's fucking with my head.

"Yeah, she's something else," I reply with a smile, my mother nudging my chin with the back of her fingers.

"She's remarkable. I may not know her well, but I do like her quite a bit already," Mum admits with a shy grin that makes her pale cheeks blush. All I manage is a smile because, well, so do I. "Do you think it's okay if I walk you to the front?" she asks, so I step to the side and offer her my arm.

"I think that would be lovely. Thank you, Mum." My words make more tears jump into her eyes, but she blinks them away as she takes my offered arm and follows me down the aisle.

Eyes attach on us instantly, and it's only when I notice Bert and Jennifer raising their brows in surprise that I realise why Estrella did this. It wasn't so I could have my mother here, which isn't an entirely good thing either considering we're lying to her. It's so this marriage looks more believable in their eyes.

No, it's not.

The voice in my head saying those words sounds as frustrated as the voice that keeps reminding me this is fake.

"What did Estrella say that made you want to come today?" I ask, needing to hear her tell me this was selfish. That Estrella only asked her to be here for her own agenda.

What she says is so much worse.

"She said that, as a mother, she'd never want to miss her daughter's wedding. She said she'd give anything to be at Daisy's, so she'd never keep me from yours. That I'm more than welcome, if I wanted to come."

No pressure. Estrella put no pressure on Mum to be here today. She merely connected with her on a maternal level. This wasn't for selfish reasons. This was for me. And it was also for the woman who gave me life.

Fuck.

It doesn't matter. I'm still upset with her. Even if it's not nearly as much as before. God, I'm getting whiplash from my conflicting feelings.

Once we reach the altar, we shift until we face each other. Mum fixes the boutonnière where it sits above the left side of my chest, a hint of pride on her face as she looks up at me.

"I'm so glad you found the one person you want to spend the rest of your life with, James. I know you've been looking for them for a very long time, and I'm glad you found them in a wonderful person. Well, two people, I should say," she adds, turning her head in time for us to watch Daisy with her little flower basket, throwing the petals on the ground to mark the way for Estrella.

"I love you," is all I say because guilt has my heart in a deathly grip.

"I love you, too. From here, across the galaxy, and back, my beautiful boy." I press a kiss to Mum's cheek, watching her for a moment as she finds her seat at the front.

Damian is now following behind Daisy, also distributing flower petals. He told me a few days ago he wanted "to be a flower girl too," and I told him there's nothing I'd love more. Watching them both make their way to me makes me emotional all over again. I give Daisy a hug when she comes running toward me in her green dress. Damian is wearing a little tux, and I can't help but smile from ear to ear at how seriously he's taking his job. Once he has no more petals left, I press a kiss to the top of his head and watch him run to his mums.

Daisy looks at me, uncertainty in her blue eyes. She doesn't know where she should go.

Valentina, Nevaeh, Scarlette, and Chiara have yet to walk down the aisle, and they'll all be standing on Estrella's side. Cameron, Adrian, Leonard, and Julián are all already standing on my side. And she doesn't know her grandparents.

"You can stand with me Daisy," I offer, but Cameron lets out a huff.

"Daisy, don't you want to stand with your cool uncle Cameron instead?" The little girl's eyes shine a little more brightly at his words. She looks up at me as if asking for permission, so I give her a nod. She's gone and in Cameron's arms seconds later.

Then, the bridesmaids make their way down the aisle.

The first one to walk down is Valentina. She has a bright smile on her lips, her red dress swaying with every step she takes.

Chiara is next in her perfectly tailored suit with nothing underneath her blazer. She's frowning, as always, but she winks at Leonard when she catches his gaze.

Scarlette follows after, a long lavender-coloured dress with frails from her waist down hugging her body. She has pieces of lavender stuck in her hair, too, the scar running down her lips an accessory in itself that somehow makes her look even prettier.

Nevaeh walks toward us next, her velvet, orange dress perfectly cut for her curvy body to show it off. I hear Adrian sniffle beside me right as she smiles comfortingly at her husband, so I turn to see my best friend fighting back his tears.

"It's not even your wedding. Why the hell are you crying?" I ask, but he doesn't look away from Nevaeh as he replies.

"I'm reliving the memory of our own wedding in my head, dipshit. Leave me alone." I almost burst into laughter at that.

But every piece of amusement disappears as Estrella steps toward the aisle.

My heart palpitates so strongly, it knocks the breath out of my chest.

She looks devastating. Her dress isn't white. It's sage green, and it fits her body and skin tone perfectly. The chest part is a corset, but the bottom half of it flows around her long, trained legs. There are flowers woven into the lace covering the lower half of the dress, and I almost take a seat when I see the slit on the left side, exposing part of her tattooed leg. There are straps hanging on her shoulders, but the corset is pushing up her breasts wonderfully. And fuck me, the rest of her gorgeous tattoos are on display.

This dress and this woman were created to bring a man like me to their fucking knees.

Her brown hair is in a complicated updo, and her makeup is light, subtle colours that match her dress. Estrella's eyes are full of the same kind of nervosity I feel deep inside my chest, but I give her a reassuring smile, telling her we've got this. Together.

This wedding couldn't look any more real than it does. The venue, the bridesmaids and groomsmen, the fucking priest. This is as real as it gets. So I don't have to take the extra step and pull her to me, kissing her lips when she's close enough, but I want to sell it as best as I can.

Not because Estrella looks more breathtaking than anyone has a right to. Not because I'm so mad at her, but I also can't deny that she chose me. Not because I actually like her.

"James," she whispers as I pull back again, my cheeks heating when I realise what I did.

"Just selling it," I whisper back, winking at her.

God, I'm lying through my teeth.

Chapter 25
Estrella

STANDING IN FRONT OF James at the altar while we said our fake vows to be very real married was worse than I thought it would be. He smiled to sell our story, but there was a coldness to his gaze, one I knew I was responsible for.

When Simón told me he loved me, I hesitated.

It threw me so off-center for a moment, I could do nothing more than stare at him in disbelief. I was shocked to what lengths he'd go to convince me not to marry James. He didn't love me. As soon as he'd said it, I knew it was a lie to manipulate me, but I was too surprised to point it out, and, to be fair, I didn't feel like arguing with him anymore.

I chose James. I don't want to be in a fake marriage with anyone but him.

James probably doesn't see it that way. All he saw was me hesitating, and I hate that I'm the reason for the hurt look in his eyes now. Even when he kissed me in front of everyone before and after we vowed to love each other until death do us part, it felt different. It felt like he was closing himself off, and I have no idea how to make him understand Simón and I are nothing.

James wanted to take care of me. For the first time since we agreed to this whole thing, it sounded like he might care for me, but all our progress has been thrown out the window. It doesn't matter how often he kisses my temple or lips to convince people we're in love, I know he's unhappy with me.

I'll have to figure out a way to make it up to him later. It's supposed to be our wedding night, after all, and I'm still a bit worked up from his kiss earlier.

For now, I have to keep focusing on avoiding Bert and Jennifer by talking to the guest James invited.

He did an outstanding job with the decorations. Valentina wasn't kidding. There are stars hanging from the ceiling in the reception room and the table settings are classy, white, and green all around.

James invited people from his Formula One Team—pit crew members, marketing people, reporters, and even the team principal of Hawke, Jessica Thorn, and Mia. She and her husband have been speaking to *my husband*—fuck, I'll need to get used to that—since we finished our slow dance where James pressed his cheek against my temple and sang along to the music.

I refuse to let what happened with Simón come in between what James and I could have. He's my husband now, and we'll have to figure out how to work through our problems. I may have demanded we take sex off the table at the very beginning, but we both realized it's bullshit ever since we kissed for the first time. I even knew it when I knelt to propose.

It felt too right, and now I finally know how to prove to him I want him.

"Mamá, can Leonora, Kieran, Damian, and I go play?" my daughter asks, tugging on my hand.

I've been keeping her glued to my side for the past hour, unwilling to allow Bert and Jennifer a moment alone with her. They haven't introduced themselves to her, but it's mostly because I asked my new friends to keep my daughter as far away from those people as possible.

"Of course, *florecita*. Go play and have fun," I encourage her, leaning down to press a kiss to the crown of her head.

I should have known the second she's no longer by my side, her grandparents would appear in front of me, ready to slice my head off with their threat to take my daughter from me.

My smile crumbles to dust as I see Bert's wrinkled face, silver hair, and bright-white-teethed smile. Jennifer's face grabs my attention next. She's a beautiful woman. Her natural features are highlighted by the slightest amount of makeup, and I hate that she has the same blue eyes Helen had, that Daisy has.

"Estrella," Bert says, butchering the pronunciation of my name. In Spanish, the double l is pronounced like a y, not two ls. This conversation hasn't even started, and I've already had enough.

Running away becomes a very appealing option, but I have to stand my ground. They can't sense any weakness from me or they will eat me alive.

"You know how to pronounce her name, Mr. Johnson. I suggest you say it properly," James says before appearing behind me, one of his hands sliding onto my right hip.

Two reactions take place in my body. One, comfort seeps into my soul because I don't have to deal with the people who are threatening to take my life from me by myself. Two, electricity shoots through my veins until my blood catches fire.

"However, if you're too stupid to say it, then call her Mrs. Landon." A tingle trails down my spine, and I find myself leaning into James' hard chest.

I also really like that his name is mine now, even if it won't be for the rest of my life like other people intend for it to be. Estrella Celeste Cortez-Landon is a mouthful anyway.

"Watch yourself, young man," Bert warns, but I feel James' chuckle vibrate through me.

"You're at *my* wedding, harassing *my* wife. You don't get to tell me how to speak to you, not after everything you've put Estrella and Daisy through. We weren't planning on getting married until next year, but now you've forced us to throw our life plans on their head and do things at your speed. Wrong fucking move, in my opinion." God, I love it when he's like this. Firm, unforgiving, and angry with the people who hurt me.

"In all fairness, son, the existence of your relationship was unknown to us until we received the wedding news from Estrella's parents."

Again, Bert mispronounces my name on purpose. James practically growls, but I place the back of my hand on his chest to stop him from ripping Bert's head off. I notice Jennifer growing uncomfortable next to her husband. I furrow my brows for a split second before refocusing. She's, surprisingly enough, not my biggest problem at the moment.

"Listen, Bernt," I start, and he squints his eyes at me for using a wrong name. "I am married. Daisy has a stable home life with two parents who love her very much. James has the income of a millionaire, and I make a great salary, too. No judge in the world would take Daisy away from me, not even one you've bribed. You have no case against me."

I think it's ridiculous they had one before either. Being a working, single mom doesn't make you any less of a qualified parent, but these people and their old mindsets don't seem to have gotten that memo.

A groan almost slips past my lips, but I swallow it as soon as it tries to escape.

"Maybe, but I'm going to prove this marriage is fake. No one's ever heard of you in the Formula One world, Estrella. That seems suspicious for a girlfriend of last season's vice champion. No rumors, no tabloids saw you together, nothing. You orchestrated this whole thing to get rid of us, but guess what? We're not going anywhere. We will take Daisy from you. You have my word," Bert snarls before grabbing his wife's hand and pulling her out of the room.

Tears shoot into my eyes, but I do my best to swallow them.

I got married to James. They're supposed to leave us alone. I did what they wanted, but I should have known better. This isn't about wanting what's best for Daisy. It's about taking her away from me, and I wish I'd know why now, all of a sudden, it's so important to them to raise her.

"Speak to me, little star. What's going on in your head?" James asks as he steps in front of me, all gorgeous and serious.

He looks pissed, but not at me. Not anymore. He's angry because he saw to what lengths these people are willing to go, and neither one of us knows how to get rid of them.

"I'm so scared," I whisper, fighting to keep from crying. "I can't lose my daughter, James. She's all I got." My voice trembles as the words drop from my mouth in fear. James cups my face, his light blue eyes on mine.

"No one's going to take her from us. We're a unit, and I promise you, the only way Bert and Jennifer will take Daisy is over my dead body," he assures me before letting me wrap my arms around his waist to seek comfort.

He might still be upset with me deep down, but James is not the kind of person to let someone who's hurting stand alone. He's the type of person to fling their arms around you and hold you close until you know you're safe.

Because he will keep Daisy and me safe.

I have no doubt about it.

Chapter 26
Estrella

AFTER OUR HUG, JAMES kept his distance from me as much as he could. We played the happy couple better than I thought we would, but I know he's still upset with me, and I can't stand it any longer.

Daisy is having a sleepover at Leonora's, which means James and I are all alone. The lingerie I bought for tonight is already under my dress—the second one because my wedding dress was too heavy after a while. Although I did like the way he was looking at me when I was in my main dress, like I was a shining bright star illuminating his world.

At least until he remembered the moment in my dressing room and the expression vanished.

"James," I start while he's taking off his cufflinks and placing them neatly back inside his drawer.

"Yes, darling?" His voice is a few degrees colder than usual, and I hate it.

"I don't like that you're upset with me," I blurt out, and his shoulders tense for a moment, his jaw ticking with something I can only identify as frustration.

"And I don't like being a second choice," he explains, understanding washing over me.

Valentina didn't choose him.

Annabel didn't choose him.

His parents didn't choose to stick around when they found out he would be a father.

All his life, people have not been choosing him, and he thinks I made a choice between him and Simón where James was the second choice. He wasn't. Simón wasn't even a choice I was considering. I didn't want him.

I wanted someone else.

I *want* someone else, and there is little I won't do to prove him wrong.

"Let me prove to you that you were *not* a second choice," I offer.

"How?" he asks, still not looking at me.

Without hesitation, I walk into the middle of his—our?—bedroom. I slip the straps off my shoulders, letting my dress pool at my feet. I kick it to the side before sinking to my knees behind James, giving myself to him in the only way I think will make him understand I want him.

Not Simón.

Not anyone else.

Just him.

My lingerie, a sage green set made up of lace that barely covers my nipples and pussy, digs into my skin. I become acutely aware of how naked I suddenly am, my ass covered by nothing because I'm wearing a thong.

My garter presses into my thigh while I wait for my husband to turn around and see me on my knees for him. Anticipation creeps up my spine. I've always loved this. Submitting. Letting someone take control.

It doesn't feel degrading, which I know many people assume it would.

For me, it feels liberating, empowering. I get off on submitting, and I know James gets off on dominating.

He is still facing his dresser, but I see his knuckles turning white as he grabs the wood. He knows what I'm doing, and he's trying to practice self-control because he's still upset.

That won't do. That won't do at all.

"Like this. If you'd like to as well," I say, and his back tenses.

"Of course I'd like to, Estrella. There's nothing I'd like more right now," he replies, turning around to see me on my knees.

Fire licks up my spine as an unbearable pressure builds in my clit from the way his gaze caresses my skin. He takes a few moments, taking me in while casually leaning against his dresser with his arms crossed in front of his chest. His strong forearms, coiled with muscles, catch my attention for several moments too long.

"I'm sorry about what happened," I start, swallowing hard as I go on. "I married you. I'm *your* wife. I'd like you to fuck me until I feel that way, too," I say, bringing my hand to the waistband of my panties to play with the fabric. His eyes drop low, watching my every move.

"What a filthy mouth you have, little star. Makes me want to fuck it," he says so casually, my heart flutters in response. I'm so turned on, I'm shaking.

"Then do it."

Use me, fuck me, anything. I've been so turned on because of this man since we met, I'm convinced a little brush will be enough to make me come.

"What do you want? Sex for a night?" he asks, and I swallow hard.

I can't admit I want more.

I can't be more vulnerable with him without getting any vulnerability in return.

So, I say, "For now, yes." He nods several times. "Touch me," I beg.

James shakes his head, his chiseled face pulling into an easy smile as he tilts his head. His blue eyes are burning into mine, causing my breathing to hitch.

"No, not yet. Before I touch you, we need to establish our ground rules," he says, and I lick my lips when he slowly rolls up his sleeves one at a time.

"Can you touch me while we make the rules?"

I'm begging, I know I am, but my body hurts from how much I want his hands on me. James pushes off the dresser and takes a step toward me, sending my heart into a frenzy.

"Are you aching, darling? Does your pussy need me?" he asks, and I nod in response.

One of his hands moves to the crown of my head where he gives my hair one quick stroke before bringing his fingers to my jaw and holding tight. He tilts my head upward until I'm looking at his face again.

"Lucky for you, I get off on making women come. Not so lucky for you, I'll do it until you can't take any more and beg me to stop. So, we need a safe word. Choose something you won't forget under any circumstances," he demands. "We can use red, yellow, and green if that's easiest," James adds, making me swallow hard.

"Red flag. I want red flag as my safe word." An easy term for racers. It means immediate stop, and I like that it's just ours. "Red flag, yellow flag, green flag."

"That's good," he praises, caressing my jaw until my eyelids flutter shut.

I roll my hips forward, searching for any sort of friction, which he notices instantly. A little smirk tugs on the right corner of his full lips. It's annoying how beautiful he is.

"You hold all the power, okay? If you don't want to do something, we won't. Is there something you know you don't want to do? Pain? Position? A certain kink you don't enjoy? One you do enjoy and want us to do?" he asks, his expression careful.

"I don't have a lot of experience with kink. I know I like to submit, but I've never had a partner to try out certain… fantasies with," I admit, my whole body shaking.

"Okay, we will go slow," he promises me. "Are you comfortable with me taking full control? What I say goes, but only in our bedroom, I promise," he says, adding the last part even though I know he'd never expect obedience outside of sex.

"Yes." His eyes grow a little dark at that.

"Okay. I want you to call me 'sir.' Are you comfortable with that, too?"

"Yes, sir," I reply without hesitation. I'm shaking all over.

"I don't like inflicting pain with paddles or whips, it's not one of my kinks, but I enjoy spanking. And, right now, I would love to spank your phenomenal arse for kissing another man before our wedding. Is that too much for you?" His thumb trails over my bottom lip as he waits for my response.

"No, sir, it's not too much."

No one has ever spanked me before, but I can't say I haven't been intrigued by the idea. Simón liked being rough in bed, so I've gotten to experience combining pain with pleasure.

I like it.

"I didn't like seeing his mouth on you, Estrella. I don't want anyone else to kiss you, not while we're married," he says.

"Yes, sir," I reply with his thumb still on my lip.

"Good girl."

I didn't even have to tell this man that I like being praised. He just knew.

I whimper when he squats down to be at eye-level with me and grazes his other hand over my pussy.

"What's this?" he asks, brushing over my clit. I swallow hard as he pinches it.

"Clit piercing," I manage to croak out.

"To increase pleasure?" he asks, his mouth moving closer to mine.

"Yes, sir."

He lets out a slight hum before standing up again and breaking skin contact. He runs one of his hands down the length of his face as a breathless laugh skips past his lips.

"You're driving me absolutely wild, Estrella. I need you to pull your panties to the side. Let me see," he instructs, and I don't waste a single second.

My fingers pinch the fabric and drag it to the side, exposing my needy clit.

"Fuck, you're such a good girl for me, Estrella. It almost makes me consider not spanking you," he says, his eyes focused on my pussy. Half his bottom lip slips between his teeth as he drags his gaze back to mine. "Play with yourself for me, little star. Let me watch you," he says, and I bring my fingers to my clit to rub it.

Pleasure seeps into my veins, especially when I see his hard cock pressing against the front of his slacks.

"That looks painful. Are you sure you don't want me to take care of that for you?" I ask, still rubbing my clit because he hasn't told me to stop.

"Remember how I said I get off by making you come?" I nod, earning a smile from him. "Then let's get you off my uncomfortable floor and onto my lap," he says, holding out his hand for me. I slip mine into his and let him pull me up against his chest.

"James," I whimper when he presses his thigh between my legs, allowing my clit to rub against him. It's even better because instead of my fingers, it's his very muscular and hard leg.

"I could make you come like this, couldn't I?" he asks, and I moan when he grabs my hips to roll them against his thigh.

"Yes."

He stops his movements, grabbing my chin again. I almost whine in complaint because the pleasure was building, bringing me embarrassingly close to my orgasm already.

"Yes, sir," I correct when he gives me a challenging look.

"Better," he praises, giving me a slow kiss.

His tongue plays with mine while I grind against his leg to get myself off. When he realizes, he digs his fingers into my sides to stop me.

"Naughty girl. I didn't allow you to come yet, did I?" I shake my head, but a mischievous smile dances onto my lips.

"Can I please come, sir?" I ask, but I know he won't let me.

"On my lap first, darling." I follow him to the edge of the bed before dragging myself across his lap. "Can you handle ten, or should we start with five?"

Feeling confident, I blurt out, "Ten."

Maybe part of me thinks I deserve a little punishment for kissing Simón back. Maybe part of me wants to be sure he won't be mad at me on any level afterward.

"Red flag, Estrella. Repeat it back to me."

"Red flag."

"Good. Ready?"

"Yes, sir," I reply, feeling his hands on my ass a second later. I expect him to spank me right away, but instead, he trails a finger over the tattoo that runs down my spine and groans. "What?" I ask, turning my head enough to see him staring at the tattoo.

"I don't think I'm ever going to last while fucking you from behind. Shit, Estrella," he mumbles, tracing the line of flowers running from the top of my spine all the way down. I shiver visibly in his arms. "I won't last. Not with this tattoo and arse that looks even more perfect bare," he mumbles to himself before his palm connects with my butt, sending a hot pain through me. "Count out loud for me, little star."

"One," I say, sucking in a breath while I try to decide if that was painful or only took me by surprise.

His palm connects with my ass a second later, forcing a moan from my lips.

Fuck, that feels... good.

Chapter 27
James

"Count, darling," I remind Estrella as she bucks her hips against me, looking for a place to rub her clit against.

"Two," she breathes out, and I reward her by placing a kiss to the slope of her back where she's bent over my lap.

"Give me a flag," I demand, and she lets out a breathy laugh.

"Couldn't be greener."

I slap her arse again, hearing her moan and watching her grab the sheets in response.

"Three," she cries out, bucking her hips forward again. "James, I need—" She cuts off when I spank her again.

"What do you need, darling? Tell me," I demand, my cock so fucking hard right now, I have to be careful not to let her graze me. Coming in my pants because of how turned on I am is not how I want to spend the night with this amazing woman.

"I need to come. Please," she begs, and she sounds so fucking sexy, I give in.

My hand trails between her legs and pushes her panties to the side, finding her soaking wet for me. My cock stirs in my pants, demanding I slide myself into the paradise my finger is slipping into right now.

Her walls clench around me as I stroke her G-spot, feeling her quiver on top of me. Never having felt anything like it, I barely hold myself back from thrusting against her to get some friction myself. The blood is pulsing in my cock as I slip another finger inside her and she clenches again.

I almost lose it.

My fingers glide over her clit where I rub tight, fast circles around that dangerously delicious piercing, making her scream on top of me.

"Flag?" I demand, and she starts shaking, getting closer to her orgasm.

That won't do, not yet. As much as I like to make the women I'm with come, we're not finished with her "punishment" yet. Not that I think it's much of a punishment considering the way she moans.

"GREEN!" I remove my hand before she can come, her trembling slowing as Estrella lets out a complaining grunt. She cocks her head my way and opens her lips to complain, but I spank her for the fifth time, a little harder than before, causing her to grab the sheets again. "I hate you," she mumbles, grinding herself against my thigh.

"Count, Estrella," I say while she tilts her head to the side to lay it on the mattress.

"Five," she mumbles, her plump bottom lip slipping between her teeth.

I notice the skin on her arse is now a bright red, but hearing her moan with every single slap encourages me to keep going.

"Fuck, oh God, eight," she says moments later as I lean down to nibble on the skin above the curve of her perfect arse.

"Two more and then I'm fucking your beautiful pussy so hard you'll feel me with every step you take tomorrow," I say, biting her arse a little.

"Please," she begs, and I spank her again and then once more, getting impatient and so fucking hard, I can't wait any longer. I need to sink into that wet heaven between her legs, and I need it right now.

"On your back, little star. Spread your legs wide for me and play with your pussy, but don't come. If you come, you don't get my cock tonight, okay?" I ask, and Estrella tilts her head to show me she's nodding. "Say it," I demand gently.

This woman smiles at me.

"Yes, sir."

She slips off my lap to get into position, wasting no time letting her thighs fall to open herself up for me. Her long fingers slip over her sweet pussy, which is already wet with arousal. A sigh of relief leaves her the second her middle and ring fingers stroke her clit.

"Use your left hand," I command, and she raises her head just enough to cock a brow.

"Why?" she asks, clearly confused because she's right-handed.

"Because I like the way my rings look on your hand, and I want to watch you fuck yourself with your ring finger," I explain because there is no use hiding that information.

"Yes, husband," she says before going back to fingering her pussy with her left hand. My cock jumps at the sight and at the way she addressed me, so I start undressing.

My fingers undo the buttons of my dress shirt while my eyes stay on the way Estrella is caressing her sensitive, pierced clit and drives her fingers inside her wetness. I fight back the urge to groan at the sight because I've never seen anything so fucking beautiful than her acting out my wishes while wearing my ring and smiling like she's never been happier.

It takes every ounce of my self-control to keep undressing and not touch her again.

A moment later, her movements slow, telling me she was close but stopped herself before she came.

I love that Estrella enjoys being submissive in the bedroom. We're equals inside and out, but this side of me, where I need to be in control, doesn't surpass sexual situations. I like being dominant because I know this is a power exchange. Estrella is willingly giving me control, but she's the one holding it all. What she wants goes. As long as she enjoys me being in control, I will be. If she decides she wants things to be different, they will be. So, even though she's submitting to me, we're equals on every level, and the power lies with her.

At least that's how it works for me.

"Good girl," I praise her, and she flashes me another one of those smiles that takes my breath away.

"Thank you, sir."

My mouth waters at the sight of her pussy swollen with need, and I move before I'm finished undressing. I hook my arms under her thighs and drag her to the edge of the bed, making her squeal.

"Flag?" I ask, taking a deep breath.

Fuck. She smells like heaven. I press my nose to the inside of her thigh before tracing small kisses along the length and toward her needy pussy.

"Stop asking me. I have a safe word, don't I?" She's right, but I also like reassurance. I need it. I want her to feel as comfortable as possible so that by the end, she has no regrets.

"Tell me what to do again, and I will put you back over my knee, Estrella," I warn, and she smirks down at me, already thrusting her hips forward to get my mouth closer.

"I'm sorry, sir," she replies, but I know full well she isn't the least bit sorry. She merely wants to come, and she wants me to use my mouth to do it.

"This is how it's going to go. I will fuck you with my tongue for as long as I want, making you come as often as I can. Only when I've had enough will I stop and fuck you with my cock. Or, of course, if you use your safe word. Okay?" She gives me an eager nod, and I shake my head with a grin as I lower my mouth to her demanding clit.

Estrella has no idea what she signed up for.

The first lick is like a lightning bolt shooting through my entire body, electrifying my cells and veins. A moan escapes me because, fucking hell, she tastes incredible, and when she writhes against me in pleasure, I only get more turned on. Hearing a woman moan, watching her come apart, is a pleasure like no other for me. There is nothing better, but I do like the occasional overstimulation, and right now, that's what I want to do. I want to see how much pleasure I can bring her before she can't take more. I want her crying out for me, begging for me. I want her to know she's mine without a sliver of a doubt. Because while we're equals in every way, she belongs with me for as long as this fake fucking marriage lasts.

I take my time, leisurely licking along the length of her pussy but completely ignoring her clit at first. She's trembling and writhing against me, and her complaining grunts when I lick anywhere but where she needs me most make me smile. Her fingers slide into my hair and she tugs and tugs, but I don't budge. Estrella tastes addictingly good, and I will take my time exploring her until I've had my fill.

Which may be never.

"James, please," she begs, and my lips move to the soft skin on the inside of her left thigh.

"Don't rush me, little star," I warn, my voice low and rough. She lifts her head enough to stare at me between her legs, causing a moan to leave her.

Estrella likes the sight probably as much as I love being here.

"Please, make me come. Then I won't ask you to rush anymore. I promise," Estrella says while I nibble at the skin on her thigh. I debate giving in for a moment, but part of me likes edging her a little, too. It'll make her come much harder, ensuring she'll never forget me. Ever.

I use the tip of my tongue to flick over her swollen clit, playing with her piercing and watching her back arch off the bed in response. Her nails dig into my hair. She starts trembling, but I grab her hips and hold her down so my tongue can fuck her right through her orgasm.

Estrella's entire body shakes with pleasure, but I don't stop. I keep licking and pulling her clit into my mouth until she's sobbing out a "please." I ease off for a minute, giving her a little bit of time while I swipe my tongue along the length of her pussy, tasting her orgasm.

A groan leaves me before I can stop myself, and I find myself reaching for my cock to give it a hard stroke.

"Fuck," I moan against her thigh, feeling pleasure coil through me. I thrust into my hand with every lick, seeking a release to the pressure in my cock and balls.

Estrella cries out for the second and third time within mere minutes of each other, sweat collecting on her forehead. I kiss her thigh for a bit before diving back in, with my fingers this time, and making her come for the fourth time. For some reason,

I'm already very in-tune with her body, and everything I do to her seems to push her right over the edge.

The thought of the reason for that being her attraction for me almost makes me come in my hand, so I stop my thrusts.

"How long has it been since someone made you come?" I ask, waiting for her to come down from her high. "Tell me, little star. Is that why you're so eager to come again and again, or is it because I'm touching you?" I ask as I wrap my arms around where her legs have been resting on my shoulders. I press a light kiss to her swollen clit, and she hums in response.

"It's you," she whispers, causing the last of my restraint to snap.

I kiss my way up her body, and she takes my mouth as eagerly as I expected her to. My arms barely hold me upright when she moans at the taste of herself on my lips. Her legs wrap around my hips, bringing the head of my cock right to her entrance.

"Let me get a condom," I tell her between kisses, but she merely keeps kissing me as she nods eagerly. I let out a small chuckle as I press half a dozen more kisses to the lips I want to lose myself in and then lean over her to reach my drawer.

After retrieving a condom—we both showed our negative test results to each other before signing the prenup and Estrella told me she's on birth control, but we both don't want to take any risks at the moment—my fingers make quick work of the foil and slip it down my aching cock.

"James?" Her soft voice hits my ear like the sweetest song.

"Yes, darling?" I stare down into the brown eyes I know I'll inevitably become attached to if I'm not careful.

"Thank you for marrying me," she adds, letting her vulnerability come to the surface. I don't know what to say or do. The tips of my fingers find the top of her left hand before I lift it to my mouth and press a kiss to her ring finger.

"Anytime, Mrs. Landon," I reply with a small smirk, but she pulls my mouth back down to hers to extinguish my amusement.

I lower myself more until I find her entrance again, letting my cock slowly sink inside, inch by inch. She's so ready for me, I slip in almost easily, but once I'm sheathed to the hilt and we both moan happily, she tightens her walls around me. Little explosions of color go off behind my eyelids, and I suck in a sharp breath to keep from coming.

"Oh God, you feel so good, James," she says as her nails dig into my arse cheeks. "More, please, more," she begs, grinding her hips to get me to move. I pin them to bed, my hands bracketing each side, before I slowly slide out of her until I'm barely inside.

"You're such a good girl, begging nicely," I say and slam into her so hard, she arches her back off the bed.

"Holy fuck," Estrella breathes out, and I smile to myself.

My thrusts only get harder and deeper. Estrella clings to me like I'm her lifeline while our bodies find a rhythm so perfect, it has me questioning everything.

It's never felt this... all-consuming before.

I like making people come, but making Estrella come? The thought alone threatens to push me over the edge. I fuck her even harder, until she cries out my name so loudly, I'm convinced all of Monaco can hear her.

She falls apart a second later, her walls clenching around me as she trembles through her orgasm. Estrella tugs me right over the edge with her, and I come so fucking hard, I see stars for a moment. Her name leaves my lips as my cock pulses and fills the condom with my cum.

The waves of pleasure don't stop for a long time, but, eventually, I pull out and fall onto the bed next to her. She rolls onto her stomach and half onto me, resting her chin on her hands on my chest. An easy, satisfied smile is on her lips, and I can't help but caress them with my thumb.

"We should shower, Estrella," I say when a strange sort of panic fills my chest.

She's going to make me fall for her, I already know it. Estrella won't give me a choice. And then she'll leave. Once Jennifer and Bert get off her back and Daisy is not going to get taken away with a million percent certainty, they will leave me.

Fuck.

If there is a way to distance myself, I have to do it.

But not tonight. Not after we had the best sex I've ever had. Not after I was rough with her. Aftercare is by far one of my favorite parts of having sex, and I'm going to take care of her.

Tomorrow, I can continue panicking.

"How was this for you? Too much?" I ask because communication is important after sex.

"It was amazing," she replies, clinging to me a little harder. Panic floods me again.

"Come on," I say and hold out my hand after slipping out of bed. Estrella watches me with those big, brown eyes of hers.

"I can't feel my legs," she says with a little laugh. A smile threatens to break out across my face as I close the distance between us and scoop her up in my arms. She lets out another laugh. "You don't have to take care of me," she says, placing her hand on my cheek to cup it.

I tense before I can stop myself, but if she notices, she doesn't point it out.

"I know, but I would very much like to," I say, and she settles in my arms.

I take my time washing her in the shower, placing a cream on the sore skin on her butt after. Estrella watches me closely but doesn't say a single thing. Making sure she's okay is my highest priority. Her happy smile has my fingers shaking the entire time because, goddamn it, I like her so much.

It should make me happy.

Instead, I've never been so terrified in my entire life. Even as we lie in bed together, Estrella safely tucked against my side, I'm barely able to keep from shaking.

She'll leave me.

I'll care for her, and she'll choose someone else eventually.

I have to protect myself, no matter the cost.

Chapter 28
Estrella

"Mamá!" Daisy screams as she runs from Chiara's side and right into my arms. I hug my daughter to my chest. I know we were only apart for a day, but any duration of time makes me miss her so much.

"Thank you for bringing her home," I tell Chiara, and she flashes me... well, not quite a smile, but as close as it gets for her.

"Of course. Daisy is a darling, she's always welcome at our house. Leonora and Kieran love her," she replies, and I grin up at her.

"Mamma, can we play with the Carrera track?" Leonora asks, pointing at the one James bought Damian and Daisy. Chiara gives me a questioning look, so I smile reassuringly.

"Sure, but only for an hour, then we have to meet Daddy at home to get ready for our trip to Spain," Chiara tells her daughter, and I nod along to her words, realizing that this weekend is a pre-season testing weekend. James and I haven't discussed it yet, but I also haven't seen him today.

He's definitely avoiding me.

Who else leaves the morning after their wedding night without speaking to their spouse?

Then again, this isn't a real marriage. Just because we had sex doesn't mean we're going to act like husband and wife. Neither of us agreed to do so in private. Yesterday was amazing. Best sex of my entire life, but it was just sex.

Expecting more from James isn't fair, not when I don't even know what the hell I want. I want him, yes, but what the fuck does that entail?

"So, how are you feeling?" Chiara asks after we've sat down on the couch. Our kids are playing with the track, so my attention is on them even while I reply to my friend's question.

"Fine, thank you," I say, catching the way she studies me with amusement sparkling in her eyes. "What?" I ask, and Chiara takes a sip of her water.

"You look more than fine. You look like you had a bunch of orgasms and a good breakfast," she says so dryly, I can't do anything but stare at her with my mouth agape.

"Why would you think that?"

"I see it in the way you keep smiling when you're not paying attention to controlling your facial features. It's quite amusing," Chiara explains, smiling faintly.

"Goddamn James Landon," I mumble, the grin fighting its way onto my face.

"Where is he?" She looks around as if she could spot him wandering about the house.

"He left before I woke up." The words feel sour on my tongue. "But it's okay. We're not really married, so I'm surprised we even had a real wedding night," I blurt out with a nervous laugh, which dies the second I see Chiara's irritated expression.

"He wasn't there when you woke up?" she asks, her usual scowl in place. I shake my head. "And you haven't seen him since?" Again, I shake my head. "He's avoiding you."

God, she doesn't bullshit. I love it as much as I hate it.

"But why? We had great sex. He came so hard, it took him several minutes to come back to reality." What is this woman? Some kind of truth serum inflicting person?

"Then he's not avoiding you, he's avoiding his feelings. Ugh, men," she says and rolls her eyes. "I love my husband, but when he first had feelings for me, he ran the other way. Then again, maybe so did I. Feelings are a shitshow waiting to happen, after all," she adds, talking more to herself than me, I think.

The sound of the front door shutting drags my attention from Chiara. James strolls into the living room with his golf bag slung across his shoulder, not the one with the clubs but the one where his water, towel, and change of clothing hide.

Our eyes meet for a split second before he tears his away and rushes into the bedroom.

"I think you should speak to him. Marriage 101, always talk through what's bothering you because if it piles up, it blows out of proportion," Chiara says, causing my eyes to shift to Daisy instantly. "Don't worry, I'll take them for ice cream so you can have the house to yourself. We'll be back in an hour." Chiara is on her feet and over to the girls before I can protest.

She's right. Whatever is bothering James, we need to discuss it. I thought we had a great night yesterday, but if he didn't feel the same, I have to know.

Chiara, Leonora, and Daisy are out of the house minutes later. I don't waste a second before tiptoeing into the bedroom. James is sitting on the bed, working on undoing his shoelaces. He doesn't lift his head to look at me, his expression cold and unfeeling.

"I don't understand what happened. We were fine last night. I thought we made up," I say, crossing my arms in front of my chest.

"I'm not sure I know what you mean. You wanted one night of sex, and that's what we had. Have I not done as you wanted?" God, I hate this version of him.

"Was my pussy so good it scared you shitless?" I ask, catching him by surprise. He finally looks at me, a bit of warmth replacing the ice-cold intensity of his gaze.

"Has anyone ever told you how dangerous you are, little star?" he asks, shaking his head in disbelief.

"Is that why you disappeared this morning? Because I'm dangerous to your heart?" I ask before I can stop myself. His head drops again, and he sucks in a sharp breath.

"The way you make me feel scares me," he admits, his voice strained as he stands up to put his shoes neatly into his closet.

"You can't hide from me for the entire duration of our marriage, James. You're my husband. You will have to play the part when we're not alone," I remind him, following him.

"I know," is his only response before he rips his shirt over his head and places it in the hamper. "I'm sorry," James says as he appears in front of me again. "I shouldn't have left this morning, but I can't do this whole feelings thing, darling. I did it before, and my heart can't take it again," he says, and since I appreciate his honesty, I bring my hands to his face to cup his cheeks.

"I'm not her, James," I reply, and he smiles.

"Trust me, I know. Doesn't change how scared I am though," he admits, stepping back. "I would say give me a little time, but we both know this marriage won't last longer than it has to."

His willingness to be vulnerable with me has my heart swelling with emotion.

"James—" I start, but uncertainty fills me, cutting me off.

What the hell am I going to say?

"It's okay, I understand." He lets out a breathless laugh. "I need to be the one to take sex off the table again. Being with you that way on top of everything else, it's... it's too much. I can't do it." He removes his pants, and I wish I could form words.

It's too much for me, too, but I don't want to stop. I want to explore us.

"We don't have to have sex. Not all relationships require it. We can still... see where this could go in other ways." He studies me, then shakes his head.

"No, darling, I need distance. That's what I'm trying to say. We will play the part, but I can't... I can't do this."

The heart I haven't given him starts aching as if he'd punched it in the face, making something horrible set in.

My defense mechanism.

"You know what, James? Fine. We will build a fucking pillow wall in our bed and stop talking unless we're in public. It's better this way anyway." Tears jump into my eyes, but he's got his back to me. It gives me time to blink them away so when he's facing me again, I've gained control of my feelings.

Rejection always hurts, even if it's from your fake husband.

"Okay," is all he says, his emotions locked down completely.

I know this wouldn't be a conventional relationship, but there's an end date already. How bad could it be to feed into whatever it is that's already between us?

"I think it'd be best if you and Daisy join me for pre-season testing in Spain. So we can finally be seen together in public," he says, cold and distant again.

"Sounds great. I'll pack our bags," I reply, attempting to storm out of the room when his fingers snake around my wrist to stop me. "What?" I snarl, irritated with him.

"This is for the best, little star. For both of our sakes." I let out an unamused laugh.

"Run and hide, James. This isn't a cat-and-mouse game. I won't chase you. I appreciate you marrying me, and if an image is all you want us to be, fine. But don't pretend this is a decision we've made together. You're the coward, not me."

There is nothing left to say, and I don't want to hear his excuses, so I rip free of his grip and leave the room we're going to have to share until we've dealt with Bert and Jennifer.

Chapter 29
James

WE'VE BEEN IN SPAIN for the past three days, and Estrella and I have barely spoken four words to each other. She's been busy showing Daisy around Barcelona, and I've been working non-stop. By the time both of us are usually back at the hotel, she's already asleep, and I'm left watching her like a fucking creep because I soak up every moment I get to look at her face.

Pre-season testing is a nice distraction.

Cameron and I are running around tirelessly with our teams, trying to work out all the kinks to make our cars go faster than anybody else's on the grid. We've set record times so far, but my engineers keep telling me they have to make more adjustments.

The season will start soon, and I'm excited to get back to racing. While I'll be away from Damian more than I am right now, it'll also give me some space from Estrella.

"Is the honeymoon phase over already?" Cameron asks, a bright smile covering his face.

My eyes wander to where I was hoping Daisy and Estrella would be, but they haven't been here for any of the testing sessions. I'll have to speak to my wife about that. We have an image to uphold, and she can't pick and choose which part of this fake marriage she wants to be real. Having the paper isn't enough. Not even having the wedding seems to have been enough.

"I never got to go on a honeymoon. Maybe that would have helped my odds of making my wife want more than one night with me," I say, but the lie tastes bitter on my tongue.

Estrella said I'm the one running, and she's right. She may have only asked for a night with me, but the next day, she was fighting my decision to push her away to protect myself. But there is no way I can tell Cameron I want to date my fake wife without an end date.

"Do you know what's cute? The little crinkle that appears on your nose when you lie," my teammate replies, pointing at my nose. His smile stays in place, even as I swat his hand away.

"You're unbearable," I mumble as Daiyu approaches me to urge me back into the car.

"You still love me, mate. I make you laugh harder than everyone else," he reminds me, and I hate him a little for making me smile despite myself.

"One season as your teammate might actually be the death of me," I say as I walk away, but he bursts into laughter, which makes me chuckle, too.

"Yeah, either it'll be me, or that goddess-looking wife of yours."

Touché.

The car feels fantastic today. My team made some adjustments yesterday that have me flying over the track. And the sound this car makes... it makes me shiver.

It sounds like a bloody rocket ship.

My body vibrates with adrenaline, with the thrill of speeding down the track at three hundred and something kilometres per hour. Ever since I started racing, my heart has adapted to the up and down of the sport. It drops when I approach corners at high speed. It stops entirely when I need to concentrate. It races when I'm proud of a lap I've set or before the start of a race.

I know it beats the same way most of the time, doesn't physically drop or beat out of my chest, but it feels that way and it's not unpleasant. I like the way I love this sport like nothing else. It's a unique kind of love reserved for the one thing I've always wanted to do. Even when it breaks my heart, when I make mistakes that cost me the title I've worked so hard for.

It's not always a good thing, not something I'm proud of, but racing feels like a fundamental part of who I am.

How is a person meant to willingly give this up?

"How does it feel?" Ximena asks right as I finish setting the fastest lap time ever set at the Circuit de Barcelona-Catalunya.

"It feels like a dream," I admit, my breathing wonderfully uneven.

"It looks great on our end, too. Bring the car back to the pits," she replies.

Following my race engineer's instructions, I drive the car back, throwing Cameron a quick, little salute when I see his car halfway out of his garage. He lifts his fingers to make a heart with them, nodding his head my way as if to say it's for me.

I shake my head as I laugh.

"Take a quick breather. Then, we're going to go back out there with a different setup and run as many laps as we can, okay?" Ximena asks, and I nod several times, making my way out of the car.

A shooting pain goes through my left knee as I jump out of the car, making it buckle. Daiyu catches me before my arse hits the ground, and I curse in my helmet because what the fuck just happened?

"Daiyu, my knee is—" I cut off when I attempt to put weight on it, which sends another wave of pain through me.

"Okay, come with me. I'll take a look at it," she says as we make our way to my private room.

She helps me onto the table where I get massaged, then helps me take off my racing suit. I groan through another wave of pain as we slide it down my legs.

"Sorry," my performance coach says. She takes off my shoes and then lifts the fireproofs I wear underneath the suit. Daiyu frowns at my knee instantly, her brown eyes lifting to my face to reveal the concern in them. "It's swelling already. I think you have to go to the hospital," she says and applies the slightest amount of pressure that makes me grit my teeth, grinding my molars together.

"Daiyu, I don't have time to be injured. The season is starting in four weeks," I remind her, but she gives me the unimpressed look that statement deserves.

"What you have time for and what is happening are two different things. We're going to the hospital, and you're going to listen to everything the doctor and I say. Do you understand me?" she asks, panic filling my chest.

"What if something's really wrong?" I say, fighting through another wave of panic.

"We will only know once they've done an X-ray." She steps back and starts gathering our stuff. "You should call your wife. Let her know where you're going," she reminds me, and the thought of having an angry Estrella by my side, who has every right to be upset with me, is making me as nauseous as it is helping me breathe.

I don't have to be alone.

If she decides to come, that is.

Fuck, what if she doesn't?

My trembling fingers find my phone, dialing her number. I take several deep breaths because I feel stupid for overreacting when I don't even know what's wrong yet.

My wife picks up the phone after several rings, her voice as distant as it has been for almost a week now.

"Yeah?"

"Daiyu is taking me to the hospital. I hurt my knee getting out of my car, and we're going to have it looked at. I thought you should know in case I'll be back late," I say, trying not to put pressure on her to come to the hospital.

But this woman always finds a way to surprise me.

"Send me the address of the hospital. Daisy and I are coming." She hangs up without giving me a chance to respond, which is just as well. I'm having a hard time breathing past the swelling in my chest and knee.

Both extremely painful in their own ways.

"Daiyu, I think I'm going to need some help walking," I say because standing up, even though I put most of my weight on my other leg, still hurts like several thousands of needles are pricking me.

"I'll call the paramedics," she says when she reappears in my room.

The panic in my chest returns tenfold.

Whatever is wrong with me needs to be fixed in the next four weeks. It's bad enough I probably won't be able to test the car anymore. Our reserve driver, Mai Bui, is probably going to step in for me until I'm back, but I need to get better as soon as possible.

I've already lost one championship.

I can't lose another, not when we've got the fastest car on track right now.

Not when we're going to dominate this season.

Not when I've got something to prove to myself and everyone who called me worthless when I lost last year.

Chapter 30
Estrella

Worry has wrapped its hand around my throat, squeezing with every step Daisy and I take. Rationally, I know James is going to be fine. He said he hurt his knee, not his neck or any vital organs. Plus, I'm still mad at him. He's been pushing me away and avoiding me for a week, ever since the morning after our wedding night. But rational thinking rarely applies to complicated feelings, which is exactly what I have for my fake husband.

I find his performance coach, Daiyu, a trained woman with long, black hair and deep brown eyes, sitting in the waiting room, talking to someone on the phone in Cantonese. Daisy looks up at me when I squeeze her hand, and I flash her a reassuring smile. I don't want her to worry. I shouldn't even worry.

James will be fine.

"Hello, Daiyu," I say as I approach her, and she hangs up immediately, holding out her hand to shake mine.

"It's nice to see you again, Estrella." We met briefly at my wedding, but we didn't have time to talk because Cameron started dancing in the middle of the dance floor and dragged James onto it too. It was too adorable not to watch.

"How is he doing? He sounded freaked out over the phone," I say softly, only loud enough for her to hear. Daisy isn't paying attention to our conversation, she's studying all the different people running from one place to another around us, but better to be safe than sorry.

"He was definitely panicking. If it's worse than a sprain, I don't think it'll heal in time for the start of the season."

Fuck, that's not good. He'll be devastated if he begins the season on the sidelines.

A nurse walks out of the room closest to us, their eyes finding mine and then Daiyu.

"I'm looking for a Mrs. Landon," they say and then look around the room. I step up to them, forcing a smile.

"Yes, that's me." Daisy's hand is still in mine, but when the nurse tells me to follow them, Daiyu places a gentle hand on my arm.

"Leave her with me. I'll take care of her," she says, and I realize she's saying it so Daisy doesn't have to sit in the doctor's office.

"Thank you," I tell Daiyu before squatting down to grab my daughter's face. "*Ahorita vuelvo. ¿Está bien? Quédate con Daiyu,*" I say in Spanish, kissing the top of her head.

I may not know Daiyu well, but James and her are as close as a performance coach and driver can be. He trusts her, so I do too.

My husband is sitting in a chair on the opposite side of the one the doctor will occupy, one of his legs bouncing up and down from nerves. So, his left knee must be the hurt one.

Without thinking, I place a hand on his shoulder and squeeze it as I settle down in the seat next to his. He doesn't even jump at my presence, but his shoulders fall and his leg stops bouncing as soon as he feels my touch. His head drops, so I rub his neck, trying to comfort him more. We may not be on speaking terms at the moment, nothing more said between us than what is necessary, but I don't want him to go through this without having me by his side.

"I'm spiraling," he admits, his eyes pressed shut and his breathing shallow.

"Okay, then get out of your head. Stop thinking about the what-ifs and focus on what's real," I say, cupping his chin the way he does with me and tilting his head my way. "I'm real, and I'm right here," I add. His blue eyes open to study my face.

"Are you real? Because I can touch you, try to convince myself that you're really here, but I don't understand why you would be. I don't deserve it," he replies, leaning away to break skin contact.

STRAIGHT TO THE CHAPEL

I poke my own cheek as he watches, then my sternum, stomach, and legs.

"I feel pretty real to me," I say, trying to distract him. "And I'm here because I'm your wife. Real marriage or not, that means something."

His gaze softens, and he lifts his hand to my face. Right as he's about to touch me, the doctor walks in, so my husband drops it again, the panic visibly rushing back into his body.

"Well, good news, Mr. Landon. It's only a mild sprain. Bad news, you'll have to take things slow for the next three to four weeks and wear a knee brace," the doctor says, and I appreciate that she doesn't beat around the bush. "Try to stay off the leg as much as you can. Since you have a performance coach, I encourage her to make a plan to help you recover. I'll forward her the diagnosis."

James lets out a breath of relief, his hand grabbing mine almost out of reflex.

"Thank you, doctor," he says, squeezing my fingers. I look down, hating the way electricity keeps shooting through my veins long after he's stopped touching me.

Stupid James Landon with his stupid intoxicating touch.

After we're done with the doctor, James and I get up to walk out of the room, but he's limping. He tries to hide it, and I roll my eyes at the stubborn man and grab his arm to place it around my shoulders.

"What are you doing?" he asks, putting all his weight on his good leg to lean away from me.

"Helping you, asshole. Now lean on me," I reply, placing his arm more firmly around me.

Daisy takes his hand as soon as she sees him, and we say goodbye to Daiyu before making our way to the rental car James got me, my husband having received crutches to make it easier to walk.

I help him inside, then place my daughter in her car seat. She's so sleepy from our day of sightseeing, her eyes close as soon as she's in the backseat. I smooth a hand down her hair before fastening her seatbelt and making my way to the driver's side.

As soon as I get in and turn the car on, James turns his head to look at me.

"Thank you for everything," he says, his expression sincere.

"Don't thank me yet. I still have to pick up the painkillers the doctor prescribed and get your knee brace. We also need to do something about your smell." I navigate out of the hospital parking lot and drive toward the closest pharmacy where his prescription can be picked up.

"What's wrong with my smell?" he asks and sniffs his shirt.

"You reek of rubber and sweat. You were in the car all day, James, what do you expect? To smell of roses and rainbows?" He snorts and shakes his head, leaning it against the headrest.

It's only when we're all back at the hotel, Daisy dragging her feet because she's so tired that I realize how exhausted I am, too. James is walking beside me on his crutches as I push past the feeling because he must be even more so. And in pain. And uncomfortable because he's still sweaty from earlier.

So, my top priority is taking care of him so he can rest.

I put Daisy down for a nap, finding James where I left him in the big bedroom of the hotel suite, holding himself up with the help of the chair that stands in front of the desk they put in here, his crutches against the wall now. His eyes track my movements as I walk across the room, grabbing a fresh pair of his underwear, a shirt, and some sweatpants.

"You don't have to take care of me. I can wash myself," he says, but there is no anger in his words. Nothing but what he said to me earlier. That he doesn't think he deserves this kind of treatment from me.

"You can also shut the hell up and let me help you. Which is it going to be?" I ask, placing my fists on my hips because I'm so sick and tired of this man and his foul attempts to keep me at arm's length.

His eyes sparkle with amusement as he considers me.

He doesn't say a word, which is all the answer I need.

"Perfect. Let's get you cleaned up. And stop with that bullshit word 'deserve.' You deserve kindness, no matter how we feel about each other. Why is that so difficult for you to understand?" I ask, and he looks me dead in the eye as he says some of the worst words I've ever heard anyone speak.

"Because as a child, when I fucked up or got hurt, my father only kicked me when I was down. He never took care of me. This injury? He would have punished me for it. Would have called me every bad name for being so weak." My heart aches at the thought of a little James being treated so horribly by his father.

"Your dad is a piece of shit that should be very careful the next time I see him." This makes him smile.

"Yeah," is all he says at first, but then he adds, "You know, as a kid, when you don't know anything else, you just take the hits. You think that's love. My father didn't physically harm me, so no one said anything. The only bruises I carried were the ones on my heart because I still loved him so much, you know? I wanted to make him proud more than anyone else, but it broke me. Not that I ever told anyone."

He shakes his head, and I find myself taking a step toward him without thinking.

"So, you see, little star, when it comes to getting injured, I know nothing else but my father's way," he says and swallows hard, avoiding eye contact with me. I don't stop walking until I'm right in front of him, taking his hand in mine.

"Then let me show you another way," I say and help him to the bathroom where I lower him onto the rim of the bathtub. "May I remove your clothes?" I ask, trying to ignore the way my heart stumbles at my words.

"Yes. Thank you."

He keeps his mouth shut the entire time, and I do my best to keep my eyes off him as much as I can because James Oliver Landon is a masterpiece. Every inch of him. And the sight of his—

Nope, I'm not looking at it. I refuse to be reminded of our wedding night. Because every time I remember it, I also remember the morning after, and he's in a vulnerable position right now. I don't want to get angry with him again.

I fill the tub with some lukewarm water before helping him inside. He groans in complaint, his knee not cooperating.

"This is going to frustrate me for the next three to four weeks," he mumbles, straightening out his leg as much as he can in the bathtub.

"You have to take it easy, James, so you can start the season with every other driver. Okay? You can't be your usually stubborn self and ignore your body's limits." I run some soap down his muscular chest and over his shoulders, doing my best not to notice how much my touch is affecting him.

Even with the evidence right in my line of sight.

"I'll do my best," he mumbles as he settles against me where I'm kneeling at the end of the bathtub. "Thank you for taking care of me, wife."

"It's nothing to thank me for. You will pay me hourly." He bursts into laughter.

"Of course I will. What's your rate?" James asks, his eyes closed as I massage shampoo into his hair.

"One thousand dollars an hour." He smiles from ear to ear, looking like he doesn't have a care in the world. I hate myself for how much I enjoy putting that expression on his handsome face.

"Send me the bill, Estrella."

I wash the shampoo out of his hair and get the soap off his body, but even once I tell him I'm done, he makes no attempt to stand. He merely keeps his head resting on my shoulder and his eyes tracing the lines of tattoos on my arm.

"Will you tell me about your tattoos? What they mean?" I stare down at the snake where it wraps around my forearm, the same one my brother had.

"No, I don't think I will. That information is reserved for people who don't push me away," I reply. He tilts his head to look at me, regret covering his features.

"I'm sorry."

"Saying sorry won't fix shit, James, not when you keep doing it."

Chapter 31
James

Estrella has been taking care of me for the past three weeks. Without a single complaint, which she'd more than deserve to voice. I'm a difficult patient. I can't sit still. I always do too much without asking for her help. I'm stubborn. But my wife has been so patient. If she finds me in the kitchen trying to make a coffee, she merely stares me down until I go back to bed.

She stopped helping me shower a few days ago, and as much as I tell myself I don't miss it, I do. Spending time with her even when we hardly speak is addictive. The more I get, the more I want. Maybe that's why every morning, when I roll over to look for her on the other side of the bed, disappointment washes through me to see her gone. But what is always there, what irritates me more than words can describe, is her wedding ring resting on her bedside table.

Every morning.

And every morning, I pick it up, carry it to whichever room Estrella sits in, grab her hand, and slide it back into its proper place. She glares at me every time but never says anything. I don't say anything either. I'm satisfied with the fact that she keeps wearing her engagement ring, and if I have to bring her the wedding band each morning, then so be it.

While I'm never alone because Marbles and Lollipop always stay with me, Daisy has made it her mission to be glued to my side for weeks, too. She keeps trying to entertain me so I don't get bored sitting around. She brings me books whenever she notices I've finished one. Estrella must be the one handing them to her because she always either brings me the ones with spines that are in perfect condition—unread books—or with spines that look like they've been through hell and back—my most read books.

Daiyu made a plan to help me recover, so we've been doing lots of exercises for my knee for the past three weeks, making sure my body doesn't get too stiff from sitting around so much. Lucky for me, I sprained my left knee, so I've been working in the simulator too, using only my right leg. Normally, I race with both feet. It's easier and allows for better control, but I'd rather adapt for now than not train at all.

The season begins in a week. I have no time to sit around without training.

"How are you this good while injured? It makes no sense," Adrian says over the headset I have resting on my head. SIM racing has become very popular among quite a few of us drivers. We stream it online for the fans as we race each other.

Today is one of those days. Our stream is live, and Adrian, who is the best out of all of us when it comes to these things, is racing against me, as well as a few other friends and racers from F2, F3, and F4.

"Jealousy isn't a good look, Adrian," I tease, and he bursts into laughter.

"Well, you'd know," he replies, making me roll my eyes at him, even though he can't see me and I can't see him.

Cocky dickhead.

"Which track are we choosing now?" I ask all of the drivers.

Three different voices fill my ears at the same time, and I almost smile at the chaos that ensues. I stay silent, waiting for them to make up their minds and grinning at the camera, at my fans. I'm petting Marbles' head, too, and she purrs happily. She loves sitting on my lap while I'm doing SIM racing, but I can only have her there in between the races. Like right now.

"James?" Daisy says, and I watch her walk toward me with the kangaroo plushie she needs to sleep hugged to her side, rubbing one of her eyes.

"What's wrong, princess?" I ask and turn my body to face her as best as I can.

"Where's Mamá?" she replies, still rubbing her eye.

"She went to work. She will be back soon, I promise," I assure her, and the next thing I know, her little arms wrap around my neck as she hugs me for the whole world to see.

I hug her back, smiling at this little thing. Because it is meant to be a little thing. A child hugging their parent. Except I'm not her dad. Not really. And she's not my daughter. No matter how much it's starting to feel that way.

It feels the way it does when Damian hugs me.

And that thought frightens me above all else at the moment.

It's probably just because I miss him. Whenever he starts school again, I only get to see him from Friday evening to Sunday noon.

"Can I sit with you?" Daisy asks as she pokes the side of my glasses, her blue eyes wide open and her bottom lip pushed forward in a little pout.

She knows I can't deny her a single thing when she gives me that look, so I pick her up and place her on my right leg before saying, "Sorry, everyone, I'm out of the next race. My little girl and I will just watch," into the headset microphone.

"Boo, you're no fun," Adrian replies, and I almost snort.

I won't comment on the fact that he and Nevaeh have decided to try having a biological kid. It's not my place to announce it to the world, but I send him my witty comeback via message. The sound of his laughter fills my headset moments later.

After turning off everything except the screen so Daisy and I can watch the race, I gently place Marbles on the floor and wrap my arms around the little girl. I just watch her with utter fascination. The way she points at the screen with her eyes wide open in amazement. The way she hugs her kangaroo to her chest as she tells me how cool this is.

"Why does it do that?" Daisy asks as we watch the flap for the DRS open on the rear wing of the F1 car.

"It makes the car go faster," I reply before going into a bit more detail for her.

"*Es algo bueno,*" she says once I'm done explaining, but I don't understand Spanish, so I have no idea what she said. I doubt she even realises she switched to her mother tongue.

"*Sí, florecita, es algo bueno.*"

I hate the way my heart thumps in excitement every time I hear Estrella's smooth voice. The way it beats so wonderfully uneven at the sight of her leaning against the door frame of my simulator room, watching her daughter and me bond over racing. All long legs, warm brown skin, tattoos, and sports clothing that hug her wide hips and slimmer waist perfectly.

I meant what I said to her. She doesn't feel real to me sometimes.

Hell, most times.

But I'm so fucking glad she is.

Even when she's not talking to me. Even when we still won't work. Even when I'm not even entirely sure she doesn't hate me.

"Can you teach me Spanish?" I ask when Daisy and I are standing in front of my wife.

"No," is all she replies, taking her daughter's hand and leading her toward the kitchen.

"Why not?" I ask, following them with my knee still bothering me. It isn't exactly painful anymore, but it's not pleasant either.

"*¿Por qué? Porque eres un hombre muy difícil y no quiero pelear.*" Daisy giggles, which only makes me more confused.

"Estrella—" I start but she cuts me off.

"Daisy, please go play with your toys. James and I need to have a conversation."

As soon as her daughter is gone, she turns to me and grabs me by the front of my shirt.

"What is your goal, James? Huh? Why are you spending so much time with Daisy, bonding with her over books and racing? Why do you want to learn Spanish?" she asks, gripping my shirt so hard, I stumble forward a little. My knee cries in complaint, but I don't say a single thing.

My racing heart is all I can focus on.

"What is so bad about me wanting to be closer to both of you? You and I are married. Daisy is your daughter, which means, right now, she's—" She pulls on my shirt again, bringing our faces so close together, her heavy breaths coast my lips despite our height difference.

"Don't finish that sentence. I will break your nose," she warns, her chest rising and falling so quickly, I realise she's as scared as I am.

Of these unspoken feelings between us.

Estrella releases me, stepping away and taking her enchanting scent with her.

"Bert and Jennifer have been radio silent since the wedding. I don't think we have to go through with this for much longer," she says, and my heart drops into my stomach. The thought is like an electroshock travelling through my whole body.

I open my mouth to respond when the doorbell rings, dragging my attention away from Estrella. My heart drops from my stomach to my feet when I open the door to reveal Daisy's grandparents.

Speak of the fucking devil.

"What the bloody hell do you want? You're not welcome on our property," I say, attempting to shut the door again when Bert places his foot in my door to stop me.

"Let's have a conversation, James. I promise you'll want to hear what I have to say."

He bulldozes into my house, dragging his wife with him. She throws me an apologetic look that surprises me so much, I take a step to the side. It's the same look my mother gives people when my father is a pretentious prick.

"Sit down, son. This is mostly a conversation for you," Bert says, and I raise both brows at the back of his head.

"Oh. No," I reply, laughing a little. "Here is what we're not going to do, Bernard. We're not going to bark orders in someone else's house, okay? Can you understand that with that walnut-sized brain of yours?" He spins around, anger on his features. I spoke to him like he is a child, but he's going to prove me wrong by throwing a big boy tantrum.

"You think just because you're a rich asshole who gets overpaid for driving fast cars that you're better than me?" he asks, getting closer until he's in my face. I stare down at him with an unimpressed expression.

"No, I think I'm better than you because I don't try to break up families. But the millions, good looks, and fame certainly don't hurt." I smirk at him, which only infuriates him more.

Estrella appears next to me, and I realise she must have put Daisy in her room to keep her from hearing this conversation. Something her grandparents keep forgetting is that their granddaughter has not met them. They are strangers storming into her home, and that's terrifying. It's why Estrella keeps doing her best to hide her daughter from them.

"You have such a smart mouth, but I wonder what you'll have to say when I take Daisy away from both of you. Because the lawyer I hired advised me to get a private investigator and look into your past," Bert says and points at my chest.

"So? I have nothing to hide." I cross my arms and watch him with distaste.

"Oh no? What about giving your son up for adoption?" My arms drop down my sides as anger replaces any other feeling inside me.

"He has nothing to do with this. James still has shared custody," my wife chimes in.

Estrella takes my hand when I ball mine into a fist. It's the only thing keeping me from picking up Bert by the collar and dragging him out of my house.

"Our lawyer thinks otherwise. He said we have a good case, one we can win to get custody of Daisy," Bert says.

I wonder if the PI that he hired to look into me—to find public information and waste his money—has connections to a contract killer. It's a drastic and illegal move, yes, but this man is seriously starting to piss me off.

"How much money will I need to pay you so you go away? Hundred thousand dollars? Two hundred?" Estrella squeezes my hand and looks up at me like I've lost my mind.

"How about ten million? Then, we'll leave you alone for good."

So, this is about money. Money I have, but there is no way I will pay this man ten million dollars. I'd rather spend every cent I have on lawyers.

"What the fuck is wrong with you?" Estrella asks, shaking her head in disbelief at the man threatening to take her daughter away. "You're doing this *for* money?"

"Money does beat getting back at your family for taking our daughter away," he says and Estrella takes a step back as if he slapped her across the face.

"This is what this is all about? You're blaming my family for Helen falling in love with my brother? Because you cut her off as soon as she moved to Mexico? That wasn't our fault. It was your doing, you racist, disgusting, piece of shit." I wrap my arms around her middle to keep her from lunging at Bert. Holding her back is the only thing holding *me* back.

"Ten million. Or we'll spend the foreseeable future in court."

They storm out of the house moments later, Jennifer throwing another apologetic look at us over her shoulder. I have no time to linger on it because Estrella sinks to the ground, bursting into sobs and tears. With my knee screeching in complaint, I sink down beside her to wrap my arms around her and hold her, tears jumping into my eyes at her pain.

"I can't do it anymore, James. I did what they asked. I married you. I moved in with you. I've given Daisy as much of a stable life as I could. It's not enough. It'll never be enough for them. Not until they get their revenge." Her entire body shakes with a sob.

"We will figure it out, I promise." I smooth her hair back, but Estrella lets out a dry laugh.

"Yeah? How the fuck will we do that? We can't even figure out how to be in a room together," she replies and moves out of my embrace to look at me.

"We will do better," I promise.

"Stop making promises we can't keep, James. You're still scared of feelings, and I'm still unwilling to wait around for a person who can't even commit to the *idea* of liking anyone other than the girl he was in love with most of his life."

She gets up and walks away before I can apologise to her again, which is just as well. Estrella is probably as tired of hearing it as I am of having to say it because of my stubbornness.

I have to do better.

By Estrella and Daisy.

A little by myself, too, because I can no longer be stuck.

This year, I'm getting my first title.

And allowing myself to fall for my wife.

Chapter 32
Estrella

IT'S THE FIRST RACE of the season, and Daisy and I decided to join James in Australia. It made him so happy, which I tell myself is because we could bring Marbles and Lollipop with us.

Plus, Daisy missing a few days of pre-school isn't that big of a deal to me.

James and I have found a good lawyer to deal with the paperwork Bert and Jennifer have already sent over. I tried to understand what it said, but I'm pretty sure most of it was bullshit. From James' groans and mumbled curses as he read the papers, I'm convinced that even for someone who understood the more technical terms, it was a case pulled out of someone's ass.

Something I've realized since we got married is that James is incredibly smart. And if that wasn't sexy enough, he wears these glasses while reading that make me want to do sinful things to him.

"Are you okay? You've been zoning out for a few minutes," James says, nudging my shoulder with his.

There is a smug smile on his face, which is the only reason I don't remind him of how he said that he'd "take care of my needs" but I've never been hornier than I am right now. I hate him a little for it, especially because after the night we had, I haven't been able to satisfy myself as thoroughly as he fucked me.

"I hate you," is all that comes out of my mouth as I glare at him. A surprised laugh escapes him at my words.

"So you've said, darling. Any particular reason for why you hate me right now?" he asks, lightly brushing the back of his fingers along my arm. Shivers run down my spine immediately.

I lean toward him and he meets me halfway, intrigue in his eyes.

"Yes, but I'm not telling the person who's responsible for my current frustration," I reply and lean away again, but he reaches out to cup my chin, holding me in place.

"Sexual frustration?" His gaze turns several shades warmer as he looks at my lips then back up to my face. A lump forms in my throat as desire travels through my body.

"Well, what do you think? It's been over a month. On top of that, you look delicious in that racing suit, which only bothers me more," I say and shove away from him, grateful for the distraction of Daisy walking inside the garage with Nevaeh.

She offered to take my daughter to one of the stands to get a shirt, and I couldn't say no after Daisy said "please" and gave me her puppy dog eyes. She's perfected them over the years to make sure she gets everything she asks for.

"Thank you for letting me take her. We had so much fun," Nevaeh says and kisses me on each cheek as well as hugging James. She leans down to hug Daisy, her eyes filling with tears.

I'm about to ask what's wrong when she blinks them away and straightens out her back.

"Thank you for taking her," I reply as she walks away.

She winks again, then makes her way back to the Velocità Rossa garage where she's working with the team. And her husband.

"*Florecita*, you look so cute," I say as I take in the Hawke Racing shirt she's wearing. James' number, nineteen, is written on the left chest area as well as in a big font on the back. The blue, red, and white of the team make up the shirt, and I smile at the proud look on Daisy's face.

"I'm wearing James' shirt. It's good luck," she says, catching my fake husband's attention. He squats down beside her and grins approvingly.

"I'm going to win today because you're wearing it, princess," he says, poking her stomach to make her giggle. He stands up and steps in front of me, smirking at me until I'm fighting to keep the heat from entering my cheeks under his attention. "Do I get a good luck kiss, wife?" I narrow my eyes at him, not sure what game he's playing.

"How about no kiss and I resist the urge to kick you in the balls?" He snorts.

"Ever the romantic," he replies, throwing Daisy one more smile before heading off to start the pre-race process. I don't mean to watch his tight ass as he walks away, but the racing suit he's wearing just hugs it *so right*.

"*¿Mamá, puedes repetir los nombres de todos los equipos?*" my daughter asks, so I squat down next to her and wrap my arm around her middle.

"*En Fórmula Uno hay* Velocità Rossa, Hawke Racing, Grenzenlos, Spark Racing, Alfa Adrenalina, Klein Racing, Aerodinámica, Tempête Racing, Zeitgeist Racing, *y* Carousel Racing." She nods along to my listing of the F1 teams.

"*¿Y el* Qualifying? *Cómo funciona?*" she asks, so I explain it to her as well.

I tell her James qualified first yesterday, snatching the first pole of the season. I explain that in Qualifying, the rest of the nineteen drivers also set lap times that got them places nineteen through second in tiers Q1, Q2, and Q3. Five drivers got knocked out in each tier, so the ten drivers that entered Q3 fought for the top ten places. This isn't the first time I've explained this to her, but she's still having trouble remembering it all, which is normal. The technical side of Formula One can get very difficult.

"Okay," Daisy replies, nodding a few times as her eyes drift around the room, taking in all of her surroundings.

"*Tomen, estos son para ustedes,*" Ximena, James' race engineer, says in Spanish as she hands us some headphones.

I place my daughter's on her head. They're a little big, but they will protect her from the loud noises in the garage. Daisy bounces on her feet in excitement, giggling when I put on my headphones too and make a funny face at her.

"What are they doing now?" Daisy asks a few minutes later, poking my leg.

"They're preparing to listen to the Australian anthem. It's normal before every race."

My daughter is so smart, but I don't know if all of this makes sense to her. Especially because she asks me why some of the drivers still warm up while standing next to their cars. I tell her that some of them are practicing their reaction times—like the French driver racing for Tempête Racing is doing with his performance coach dropping tennis balls—and others are trying to get everything in order—like Gabriel fixing his racing suit or Valentina fixing her balaclava and helmet.

Watching them settle back down in their cars takes me back to when I used to race in mine. When I was fighting for the win, the title, the honor. I was so good at it, I had sponsors on top of sponsors. I loved auto racing with my whole heart. And there is a pang of longing in my chest as I watch all of these passionate racers get ready to fight for the win.

Instead of lingering on it, I take my daughter's hand and smile at the excitement covering her whole face. If I was still racing, I'd have missed so many things. I've missed enough moments with her already trying to be everything for her and forgetting to live in the moment. Being a single mother means you're constantly doing your best to be two parents at once, trying to give your child everything they could possibly need. I've missed out on the small moments.

It's something I've only noticed now, since James has given me the time and space to spend more time with my daughter without having to worry about things like groceries, cleaning the house, or laundry.

I hate him a little more right now for making me smile while thinking about him.

"*¿Qué están haciendo ahora?*" Daisy asks as the drivers leave the starting grid on the track.

"They're taking their formation lap. It helps them warm up their tires so they stay better on the track. It also charges their batteries and helps the drivers see the track conditions," I reply, but this time I'm sure she didn't understand me well because those were big terms.

"The tires get better grip?" I stare down at my child with my mouth agape.

"Yes. How do you know that word?" She gives me a proud smile.

"James taught me." My heart warms in an instant.

"He did?" She gives me one big nod then turns her head back toward the screens.

A combination of frustration and adoration travels through me until my head spins. Because, on one hand, I think it's so sweet he's teaching her more things about the sport she loves more than anything else. On the other, he's making this so much worse. Daisy will get even more attached and when we end this fake marriage, it'll break her heart to never see him again.

"Mamá. Mamá, *mira*," Daisy says and pulls on my shirt to make me focus on the moment. I look at the screen where she's pointing, my eyes catching the first light as it turns on above the drivers.

I hold my breath until all five lights are on, hold it until they vanish again and...

The first race of the season begins.

Chapter 33
James

My car shoots forward as quickly as I want it to, my reaction time the best out of everyone else's at the front of the grid. Val, who qualified second, is on my arse, almost ramming into the back of me in the first corner. She doesn't. She never does. I think in the years she's been racing in Formula One, she may have been the cause of three collisions. She's an aggressive racer, but she follows the rules and respects the rest of the drivers to the best of her abilities.

It's fucking impressive, in my opinion.

But Gabriel is a fantastic racer, too, and unlike last season, his Grenzenlos matches his driving skills. He's already fighting his wife for second place, which is convenient for me. I use that opportunity to create a gap big enough to get her out of DRS range.

Checking my mirror, I see Adrian's Velocità Rossa fighting to overtake his brother-in-law. Cameron should be right behind them, but I can't see him and I have no time to look for him when another corner approaches. I downshift and hit the brakes with my left foot, ignoring the slight pulling I still feel in my knee.

It's been doing much better, but I'm pushing it by racing today. My doctor told me he thought it was best if I waited until the second grand prix. Like the irresponsible adult I can be when it comes to healing injuries, I ignored my doctor. I have no time to still be injured.

I rested. I recovered. Now, I'm going to win this race.

I'm going to get my first title by the end of the season.

I've got a wife and daughter to make proud now as well as a son, even if my two girls don't want me forever.

Even if my wife looks at me with so much contempt, I shiver every time.

"You've already got two seconds on Valentina. Keep pushing, James. You're setting good lap times," Ximena says, encouraging me to continue doing exactly what I have been so far.

Laps later, I'm five seconds ahead.

A few more laps pass, and I'm almost ten seconds ahead.

"What's happening? Why are they so far behind?" I ask because, even though we've been setting fast lap times in practice and Qualifying, ten seconds in less than twenty laps is something that hasn't happened in Formula One in decades. The top three teams have all been very close together for a while now.

This? This is new territory.

"They're setting lap times slower than yours. Val lost almost a whole second to you in the previous lap." *A whole second?*

"Remind me to send our engineers and mechanics some gifts for making this beauty," I reply, letting my car fly down the track and through every corner.

We started racing on medium tyres, but I've been managing them so well that we only do our first pitstop on lap twenty-three. All the other drivers have already pitted, but their attempt at an undercut—pitting earlier than me to set faster lap times and close the time gap—didn't work either. I'm five seconds ahead when I rejoin the race.

"We're still going with strategy A, Ximena?" I ask, laps passing by without a single threat from any of the other nineteen drivers.

"Yes," she replies, her voice firm and even.

"This car is just lovely," I say to Ximena after I've regained my ten-second lead.

It's ridiculous to have such a lead, no one to fight, at this stage in the race. I'm not complaining, but I'm so surprised, I can't stop letting out shocked laughs when Ximena tells me my lead is increasing. I make sure my radio is off before I let them burst free.

"Where's Cameron?" I ask, trying to find something else to focus on.

"He's working his way up to second place. He's already in fourth," she replies, and I'd nod if I didn't have to fight the G-force as it hits my body in the seventh corner.

The Australian Grand Prix is fifty-eight laps long. We get all the way to lap fifty, long after my second pitstop, when Ximena speaks in full sentences to me again. There aren't any track limit warnings before that, nothing except the occasional update on how big the gap between me and the rest of the grid is.

"Cameron is now in second place. He's setting better lap times than the others, so the gap is closing. You can push more, worry less about the tyres. They're looking great on our end."

"On it."

I push the car as much as I can without being foolish. There's no need to take corners riskier than before. No need to subject the car to any time on the gravel. No need to lose seconds to carelessness. I've been reckless before and it cost me the title. I'm not about to repeat the same mistake, even if this is just the first race of the season.

"Three laps. Lap times are looking great. Keep going." I almost welcome Ximena's voice. Silence while I'm focused on fighting off my competition is best, but with a twenty-one second-lead on my teammate, the silence is almost painful. Well, as much silence as I get with the dulled sounds of my car's engine as I race down the track.

"One lap. You're now twenty-two seconds ahead," Ximena says, and I let out a deep breath as I try to go for the fastest lap of the race to earn an extra point.

Every corner, every straight, feels like the beginning of something I could only dream of. A dream I've been harbouring since I was a child. A dream I fuelled by adding gasoline to the fire last season, but it burned out before it could fully form. Even letting myself hope this season will be different might be naive, but as I cross the finish line, snatching the first win of the year, I let hope infiltrate my system.

"Fuck yeah! Come on!" I scream inside my helmet, making sure to hit my radio button so Ximena can hear me celebrating.

"Well done, James. That was a flawless drive," she says, and I can't help the way proud tears fill my eyes.

"Well done to you and the team, too. This car, Ximena, it's a rocket ship." I thought the same during testing, before my injury, but I was proven right today.

"Don't celebrate it too early. We still have nineteen races left," she says, but I hear the smile in her voice, the same as the one currently making my face hurt from the amount of facial muscles it uses. "Cameron came second," she adds, only increasing my joy.

This is my teammate's home race. I know he was hoping for a win, but even working his way up to second after starting fifth behind the top three racers of last season is brilliant. And a one-two finish for Hawke is always an accomplishment to be proud of.

Slowing down during my cool-down lap allows me to wave at every single one of my fans currently screaming for this victory. It also lets Cameron catch up to me so we drive side by side, celebrating together.

But, of course, the wanker lifts his pinky at me, an inside joke between Adrian and me that our whole family knows now. When I was a kid, Adrian broke my pinky while we were karting—he says it was my fault, I blame him, so the truth is probably somewhere in the middle—and I had to wear a cast that prevented me from putting the finger down for weeks. So, instead of using our middle fingers, we used our pinkies to tell each other "fuck you." It prevented us from getting into trouble since no one knew except Val.

"Don't go into the pits. They've placed the signs on the track at the start line. The interviews will be conducted there, then you'll go to the cool-down room after," Ximena informs me, and I do as I'm told, grinning the whole time.

When my car is parked at the first place sign, I take a second to slow my uneven, excited breathing. But it's useless when I see Estrella with Daisy sitting on her hip and her arms wrapped around her mum's neck waiting along with the rest of my team at the sidelines.

They're waiting for... *me*.

I get out of my car, stepping on the nose of it to raise both hands in the air before forming them into fists. My team screams for me, but I rip my helmet off and run straight for Daisy and Estrella.

In my excitement, I barely hold myself back from coming at them full speed. I stop in front of them, my heart racing in hopes they will be happy for me. Estrella might be angry, but I know this stubborn woman. She has a passion for racing and so does Daisy. So, they both start grinning when I stop in front of them, and the sight has tears filling my eyes.

I barely blink them away when Daisy reaches for me, wanting a hug.

"James, James! You won!" she cheers as I take her in my arms and lift her over the barrier separating my team and me, hugging her firmly.

My eyes lock with Estrella's brown ones, the pride in them a validation.

"Do I get a kiss now, wife?" I whisper, making her roll her eyes.

"Of course, husband," she says with a fake smile, but as soon as I cup her cheek to lean down and kiss her, she mouths the words, "I hate you."

I kiss her anyway, tasting the lie on my tongue. She may not like me very much at the moment, but she doesn't hate me anymore. We've been through too much for her to still harbour those strong negative feelings.

Her mouth tastes like things I've never let myself feel before, and it takes all of my remaining strength to step away. I enjoy the way her eyes remain closed for two seconds longer than mine, the way she sways on her feet a little.

"Thank you for celebrating with me, princess," I tell Daisy when I lift her over the barrier and toward Estrella again. She's still wearing the headphones I told my team to give her, but she seems to understand me well enough.

"You raced good," she says, patting my shoulder like a grown-up.

"Thanks," I reply, kissing the side of her head before finally moving on to the rest of my team, who've been patiently waiting for me.

STRAIGHT TO THE CHAPEL

I've never prioritised anyone over my team. Not my parents when they came to races. Not my sister. Not even Val before she was racing. The thought hits me hard when I see Daiyu and Ximena smirking at me, but I ignore their smug looks as I make my way through every team member, either hugging or high-fiving them.

I'm a married man. In order to keep up the fake image, I have to show that I prioritise my family.

It's all for show.

At least to the outside.

My heart and soul have a hard time remembering that.

Cameron approaches me as soon as he's done celebrating with his team, and we exchange a few congratulatory words before I spot Valentina jumping out of her car. She doesn't go to her team. Instead, she steps toward my car and inspects it like it'll tell her how the fuck I gained twenty-two seconds on the rest of the grid. I shake my head at her, but all of my attention drifts back to Estrella who's bouncing Daisy up and down on her hip in happiness. Continuing the celebration even though I'm not standing with them anymore. They're both still smiling and it warms my heart to see my two girls, who've gone through so much, look so happy.

"Earth to James? Hello?" A hand appears in my line of vision, and I tilt my head down to see Valentina in front of me.

"Sorry. I was…" Well, I was staring at my fake wife and her daughter, wondering how I can convince them to join me at every race so that when I win, they celebrate with me.

"Yes, staring at Estrella, but I need you to tell me something," my best friend says, crossing her arms in front of her chest.

"Tell you what?"

"Tell me what the fuck just happened!" She points at my car and laughs. "What the hell is that? That can't be a Formula One car." I burst into laughter and, though she smiles at me, I can tell she wants an answer.

"FIA checked it. It passed all the regulation tests," I assure her, leaving her standing where she is when I'm being waved over to get weighed and prepare for the post-race interview.

My smile only brightens when I see Leonard holding a microphone, which means he'll be the one conducting the interview. This is the first time he's back in the F1 world in any way since he left, but I have a feeling it won't be the last time.

Last year, he let it slip that Robert Fuchs, Nevaeh's dad and current Grenzenlos team principal, mentioned retiring soon and that he asked Leonard if he was interested in the position. While I don't know if Leonard wants to be a team principal right now, I saw the glimmer of excitement in his eyes as he spoke about it.

Maybe one day.

After getting weighed, I take several sips of my water, Cameron winking at me as he wipes his sweat with the towels they give us. He's got his famous sunshine smile plastered on his face, and I shake my head as I put my team's hat on, making my way toward the person holding a microphone for me. I take it from them with a smile, then step in front of Leonard, a massive camera pointing at me to broadcast this interview to the world.

"Congratulations on your win, James. It's well deserved. You were consistent the whole race. Your team's strategy and pitstops were brilliant, too. How do you feel about it?" he asks, and I bring a smile to my face, wiping my sweat with the sleeve of my racing suit.

Many people cheer for me. Others boo. I'm so used to it at this point, I let the negativity roll off me. They're going to hate me even more if I keep outperforming everyone else.

"The car felt great. My team and I were very happy with the performance during the free practices and Qualifying already, but the pace we had throughout the race was more than we were expecting," I reply, my cheeks hurting from how much I'm smiling.

"Twenty-two seconds is a big gap, bigger than any gap we've had between cars in F1 in decades. How was it leading the race that way?" Leonard asks next, and I let out a deep breath.

"Honestly, I'd rather lead twenty-two seconds than battle for it every step of the way, but I think most drivers would feel this way." A nervous laugh escapes me, but I'm not quite sure how else to speak about what happened here today. This is as much of a new territory for me as it is for everyone else. But I know a lot of people won't be happy with me because of today.

After wrapping up my interview, Cameron is up next and then Val. Once we're all done, we go to the cool-down room where we're allowed to take a minute to breathe and collect ourselves before the podium celebrations.

"Velocità Rossa needs to fix the issues we're having so we can catch up with you," Val says once she joins Cameron and me in the room. "And what happened to you? Why didn't you go catch him? Don't you have the same car?" She's teasing Cameron, and he lets out a loud laugh before suddenly cutting off to throw her a playful frown.

"You get your broken humour from your brother, Val," he says, so she sinks into the chair beside his and lightly punches his arm.

"Cheer up. At least you came second in your home race."

"Says the woman who has won her home race how many times?" he asks.

"Me? Only every year since I started racing." She chuckles to herself, sitting up a bit straighter with pride. I envy those wins. I haven't won in Silverstone yet.

Maybe this year I will.

Maybe I'll fail again.

My eyes shift to the big screen in the room, watching the replays of the race. A lot of drama unfolded in the midfield, but I love watching Cameron fight his way into second place, going up against three of the best drivers in Formula One history.

"I know. I'm fucking awesome," he says, getting up to stretch. "Now, let's go. I've got a trophy to be handed and champagne to spray."

Chapter 34
Estrella

WATCHING JAMES GET HANDED the first-place trophy is one thing. Seeing him wink at Daisy and me from the podium with that proud smile on his face is another. But what shouldn't be real is the way my lips still tingle long after he stopped kissing me.

As soon as the trophies have been handed out, the champagne gets sprayed, concluding the celebrations on the podium. Daisy and I make our way back inside the garage, but we're soon ushered out of the motorhome so James' crew can start their post-race procedures and pack up as well. Those things take a while and I bet none of them want to stay later than is necessary.

So, Daisy and I decide to stroll around to look at the stands again. There are so many with merchandise, artwork, and more, and she said something about wanting a keychain in the shape of a Formula One car with the Australian track attached to it as well.

But I should have known better.

James kissed me for everyone to see. He held Daisy. He made our relationship very public since we married, sharing pictures of us on social media, too. People know who we are now, and as soon as we approach the first stand, a wave of fans comes up to us, crowding us. My heart drops, the fear of something happening to Daisy taking over my whole body.

I lean down and pick her up while fans scream at me.

"Can we have a photograph?"

"Aren't you James Landon's wife?"

"Can we get a picture with you?"

The questions are simple enough, not even rude in any way, but the people huddled around us have Daisy crying in my arms in fear. She gets easily overwhelmed in crowds, and no matter how many times I ask the people to give us some space, they don't listen.

"My daughter is crying. Please, move back," I announce as more people shove papers and pens my way. Panic seeps in as Daisy cries harder, but I can't see an exit. There are people all around us in a circle, still saying things I can't hear.

Fuck, this is my fault.

I didn't think.

I should have known.

I—

"Hey! Back the fuck away from her. Can't you see you're scaring her daughter?" A somewhat familiar voice booms out before a very angry Julián "Storm" Alvarez pushes through the crowd of people to get to Daisy and me.

Two security people follow him, guiding the people away from us.

"*¿Estás bien?*" he asks as soon as he's in front of me, but I shake my head as tears fill my eyes. One of his hands slips onto my shoulder and he gives it a gentle squeeze, his permanent frown more of a vicious scowl right now. "*¿Te lastimaron?*" he goes on in our mother tongue, but all I manage to do is shake my head again. "*Está bien. Vamos. Las llevaremos de vuelta a su hotel.*"

It's a good thing he's speaking Spanish with me because I don't think my panicked brain could understand my second language at this moment.

"But Daisy wanted a keychain with an F1 car and the track. I couldn't get it for her." My voice is as shaky as the rest of my body.

"Next time. For now, I want to make sure Daisy and you get to the hotel safely," he says.

My tears finally fall as he leads me away and back toward the VIP area. Julián doesn't notice, and I hope Daisy doesn't either. She's still clinging to me, making more guilt shoot through my chest.

This was my fault. I made her cry because I didn't think. She was in danger because I hadn't considered the consequences of kissing James for everyone to see, of making our fake relationship so public.

As much as I try not to let self-loathing consume me, it's hard not to feel like the worst mother in the world when my daughter hasn't even found a way to stop crying.

I *am* the worst mother.

After I bathe Daisy and put her to bed, I take my time showering, too. More tears fall until I feel numb inside. My system is on autopilot as I dry off and slip into a set of pajamas. As I make myself tea to calm my nerves, maybe even help stop my hands from shaking. As I settle down on the sofa in the massive hotel room with my knees pulled to my chest.

Every doubt I've ever felt about what kind of a parent I am creeps in, making me cry all over again. Bert and Jennifer may have wanted to take Daisy as a means of revenge, but maybe they're right about me not being a good mother. I thought I was. I thought I could be everything for Daisy, but I'm simply not enough.

A sob bursts out of me at the thought, so I cling to my legs and rock back and forth on the sofa. Loneliness slithers back into my chest. This feeling, this looming darkness and sense of hopelessness, it's all I felt when I first became Daisy's legal guardian. After I lost Pedro and Helen. It was this depression inside of me that tore me down day after day. It was the reason I went to therapy.

Nothing calms me now, just like nothing ever calmed me the nights I was in this same position on my couch, sobbing and crying until numbness kicked in and left me staring blankly at the wall. I sit in misery, wondering how I'm ever going to fix what happened today. Daisy was already afraid of crowds. She'll be traumatized now.

And it's all my fault.

All my doing.

"Estrella?" My eyes shoot open at his panicked voice. "Daisy?" he says next, even more panic seeping into his tone. "Come on, where are my girls?" James mumbles those words, but I hear them as clearly as the shattered pieces of my heart trying to put themselves back together. "There you are, thank God," he says when he finds me on the couch, and I look up at him to see the worry on his handsome face. "Where's Daisy? Is she okay?"

No words leave me. I haven't spoken much since it happened, except the few words to Julián earlier. I simply nod, so he gives my hair a gentle stroke before rushing toward Daisy's room, probably to make sure for himself that she's okay.

A few moments pass before he walks back toward where I am. I take in his disheveled appearance, his blonde hair all over the place and his team shirt thrown on haphazardly. He kneels in front of me, one of his big hands slipping onto my thigh.

"Darling, speak to me, please." I simply sit there as more tears fall, not saying a word. "Julián called me to tell me what happened. It wasn't your fault. None of us knew it would—"

"No! You don't get to make me feel better." Anger replaces the shock I felt, making me stand up to get away from him. "This was my fault. I didn't *think*. I put my daughter in danger. This is my fault, and I don't deserve to feel anything but the guilt inside me." I'm whisper-screaming at him, trying not to wake Daisy.

"This was not your fault," he says softly, stepping toward me and reaching out to take my shaking hands when he notices how badly they're trembling.

"Yes, it was. This was my fault, and my daughter deserves better than a mother, who—who—" I cut off to sob. I cover my mouth, but my anger is soon misdirected toward the one person trying to make me feel better.

"Estrella, this shouldn't have happened. I should have arranged for security. The fact that I didn't makes this my fault," he says, but all I can do is laugh. He takes another step, attempting to take my elbows and pull me to him, but I wrestle out of his gentle touch.

"Don't comfort me. I don't deserve it. I'm the worst mother. I've been doing all I could to give Daisy the best life, but it's never been enough. Nothing I've done has ever been enough. I failed my little girl. I thought I could do right by her, be all she needed, but I keep making mistakes," I rant, my anger returning tenfold when he tilts his head and gives me another soft look. "And you! You just had to make everything so much more difficult."

I shove at his chest.

"I thought this would be a simple fake marriage, but nothing is simple about us. We're a dumpster fire. We're messy and we can't even be in a room alone together anymore."

I shove his chest again, but he lets me. He doesn't budge, which only frustrates me more.

"It's my fault. I agreed to marry you. It's on me. Daisy loves you already, and breaking her heart will be my fault. No decision I make is the right one. None. And I'm so tired of it all. I'm so tired of the way we avoid each other. The way you take care of Daisy when it's not your responsibility. The way you look at me even when you push me away."

One more shove, and I'm finally angry enough to do it so hard, he takes a step back.

"Most of all, I'm tired of the way you kiss me like you want to keep me forever when we both know this is only temporary," I say and attempt to shove him again, but he grabs my wrists this time, stopping me.

He uses his hold on me to drag me against his chest. One of his hands slips onto my throat, but he doesn't press down. It's as much of a gentle touch as every other one he's given me tonight. It's merely to make me look into his eyes, but his gaze is too intense. I feel the tears return, so I close mine.

"Look at me," he demands, and, damn him, but I love this side of him. The firm, I'm-taking-what-I-want-and-what-I-want-is-you side. "You *are* good enough," he says, and the tears drop. "Say it, little star. Say it for me."

"I can't," I blurt out, crying even harder.

"Yes, you can, darling. Tell me you're good enough. Tell me you're the best mother that little girl could have ever asked for. Tell me you're worthy of all the good things this world has. Then, I'll let you go."

"But I don't want you to let me go." The words are out of my mouth before I have a chance to hold them back. "For tonight. Don't let me go for tonight." He presses his forehead to mine and nods.

"I won't. I promise. But I still need you to say all of those things out loud. Please," he says, so much vulnerability and desperation in that single word, I obey without overthinking it.

"I'm good enough. I'm the best mother Daisy could have ever asked for. I'm worthy of all the good things this world has." He nods in approval.

"There's my girl." I melt into him at his words and the way he presses a soft kiss to my forehead. "Today was not your fault. I'll make sure this never happens again. I'll have security with you every race weekend you attend." He kisses my forehead again, then wraps his arms around me, his scent filling my nose until I melt against him.

"Okay," I reply against his shoulder, the word muffled.

"I was so worried about you two. I'd have come sooner if my press officer let me go, but they're a stickler for the rules, so I couldn't convince them to ditch the interviews." I chuckle, making James join me.

"I'm sorry I shoved you," I say, but I can feel him shaking his head.

"Don't be. I love the fire inside you, Estrella. When I came in and didn't see it, I was even more worried." I hug him harder, and he does the same.

"Thank you for helping me get it back." His cheek presses against my temple as he runs a hand up and down my spine. "Should we talk about that kiss today?" I ask, trying to think about anything other than how guilty I still feel. Less so after speaking to James, but still guilty.

"Sure. Anything you want me to take care of because of it?" he asks, smug as always.

"I hate you," is all I mumble in response. He steps out of the hug to cup my cheeks in his hands, and I hate my eyes for fluttering shut.

"You keep saying that, wife, but I have a feeling you like me a whole lot more than you want to admit." His blue eyes are scanning my face when I open mine again. "Or is that just wishful thinking on my part?"

"Wishful thinking," I reply, and he grins even more brightly at me.

"Are you sure?" He holds up a keychain with a Formula One car and the Australian track dangling from it.

"How did you know?" I take it from James, trying to ignore how right it feels when his hands move to my hips to guide me against his chest.

"Julián told me. I went to get it as soon as I was done." I hold it up between us, meeting his gaze. "You can tell her you got it for her. We don't want to give her more reason to like me," he says with a sad laugh as he steps away from me.

My mouth opens, but no sound comes out, and he doesn't force me to speak either. He merely gives me one more kiss on the cheek before taking my hand and leading me toward our hotel room. We may have not built a pillow wall between us, but it's almost like there was an invisible one there for the past two months.

Not tonight.

Tonight, I let him help me strip out of my clothes until I'm in nothing but my panties. He does the same, until his glorious body is in front of me only covered in a pair of dark green boxers.

His eyes trail down my body in the same way mine scan his, studying every ridge, vein, freckle, and birthmark.

James is painfully beautiful when he's wearing clothes. He's downright devastating when he's not wearing any.

"Our relationship may be messy, but I need you to know I will never regret offering to marry you. I never have, not from the moment I said the words." James reaches out to trail a hand down the tattoo on the left side of my body; a tree that sprawls out on my ribcage and back. "It was supposed to be fake, but, fuck, Estrella, my feelings for you are the realest thing I've ever experienced." My heart stumbles all over the place at his admission.

"How do you know it's not a result of the faking? How do you know they won't leave as soon as we get divorced?" I ask because this is ridiculous. He's been pushing me away this whole time.

"Because even the thought of never seeing you again, never seeing Daisy again, has me sick to my stomach, and that means something," he replies, his eyes glued to the tattoo on my collarbone.

On the words "*Nada Es Más Importante Que La Familia*" written across it.

"Do you think we could… I want to explore that. I want to explore these feelings and stop running from them. My friends have told me to allow myself to feel everything I want for you, and I lied to them and said I would. But I haven't. I'm so scared of you not falling with me, I never allowed myself to jump off the side of the cliff."

Never mind a stumbling heart. Mine has stopped beating entirely.

"What would that even look like? Do you want us to go on a date? Do you want to simply start fucking again? What is it that you want?" I ask, shaking my head in disbelief.

"I want to make it up to you. Then, yes, I want to take you on a date. Several, actually. If sex is something you want us to keep exploring after these dates, then I also want that. If you want to tell me I've lost the plot and never speak of this again, I'll understand. But, please, don't ask me to stop fighting for this when I have a feeling it could be the best thing to have ever happened to me."

Standing here, naked except for my panties, I should feel like the more vulnerable one. But he's giving me all the power, he always is, and I know deep inside of me that I feel the same as him. The thought of never seeing him again makes me just as sick.

"Daisy comes first. No matter what. She's the most important person in my life, and her happiness comes before all else, which means it'll come before whatever relationship we have." He smiles at me.

"I fully agree." I fight back my own smile.

"I expect some groveling for these past two months. For how cold you were after we had sex." Without a second of hesitation, my dominant man drops to his fucking knees.

"You'll get as many apologies as you'd like, darling. As many as it takes. From now on, I'm going to do right by you. And by Daisy," he says, his hands snaking onto my thighs as he looks up at me.

"Please, you spoil my daughter. You have nothing to make up for there, so you can use all of that energy on me," I say, crossing my arms. He's still grinning, the ass.

"You got it, little star." He leans forward to kiss the top of my thigh. "I'm sorry," he whispers, then kisses it again. Shivers run down my spine in an instant.

"That's a good start," I croak out, hating my traitorous body for wanting to give in to him so easily. "We should go to sleep," I add, whispering now, too, because any strength I had left leaves right after he stands up and runs his hands over my ass. It's a light touch, nothing more than a brush really, but there's something about James' hands on my body that does things to me. I feel them in the deepest parts of me.

"Whatever you want, wife."

"Sleep, husband. I want some sleep."

Like the respectful man he is, he doesn't argue. He merely takes my left hand in his and kisses the rings, the ones he got me, and then picks me up and places me on the bed. He slips in behind me, and I expect him to move against me immediately, but he doesn't.

"This fucking spine tattoo, Estrella," he mumbles, so I smile to myself. He traces it, even places a kiss on it, but when I shiver, he leans away again. "Sleep, right.

Okay, let's sleep," he reminds himself, pulling me toward him so my back touches his chest.

He very noticeably keeps his groin away from me, but I don't comment on it. I can't muster the words when he places one of his arms under my head and drapes the other over my stomach, his hand sprawled across my ribcage close to my breast.

"James?" I ask after a moment of silence.

"Yes, darling?"

"Congratulations on winning the race. Your first of many victories this season, I'm sure." He nuzzles his face into the crook of my neck, and I can almost feel him smile against my skin.

"The most important one will be getting rid of Bert and Jennifer, but we will win that, too, I promise. No matter what it takes."

His determination is the only thing keeping me from falling apart. It has been since he first told me we're a unit and I didn't have to fight them alone.

"Thank you," is the last thing I say before sleep finally consumes me.

Chapter 35
James

My fist connects with the front door of Dominique and Nicolette's home, excitement making my heart vibrate. It's been almost three weeks since I got to take my son home for a weekend. We spent some time together after the Australian GP because I had a week off, but the Bahrain and Saudi Arabian Grands Prix were stacked, so I haven't had a chance to spend time with him since.

The first three races of the season have gone smoothly. While the rest of the grid hasn't managed to catch up to Hawke, Cameron has been consistently second. Last race, we were barely three seconds apart, which was a major improvement from the gap in the first race. I still won them all, but I'm sensing I'm about to get a whole lot of competition from my teammate.

Dominique, a curvy, tall woman with beautiful curly hair, dark skin, and brown eyes, opens the door for me. A serious expression lingers on her lips, and my heart immediately stops its excited, uneven rhythm.

"What's wrong?" I ask, reaching out to place a comforting hand on her shoulder.

"Come on in. There is something we should discuss." I follow her without hesitating.

Nicolette, Damian's other mum, approaches me and gives me a hug, something she's done since they adopted Damian. She has long red hair, light skin, and light brown eyes that are filled with just as much concern as her wife's.

"Okay, you're both scaring me. What happened? Where's Damian?" I ask, more fear settling in my chest.

"He's fine. He's sleeping. Come, sit. There is something we want to ask you," Nicolette says, taking my hand and leading me to the kitchen table.

"You're not going to ask me to give up my visitation privileges, are you?" Tears fill my eyes before I can stop them. Nicolette's eyes widen, and Dominique shakes her head.

"Goodness, no, James. We would never do that. Damian loves you just as much as he loves us. You're a very good father." It gets infinitely more difficult to swallow back my tears.

"Then what's wrong?"

"Well, nothing is wrong. At least, we don't think there's anything wrong with him. We went to the doctor, and Damian was diagnosed with ADHD," Dominique says. I sink back in the chair and let out the breath I've been holding.

"Okay. I think I'm going to need a bit more information," I say.

"We've been noticing for a while now that he has trouble sitting still and focusing. He's also shown some impulsive behaviours, fidgeting when he sits, and so on. We went to two doctors in the last three weeks, and they both agreed that Damian has ADHD."

I think about Nicolette's words. I think about Damian pulling Daisy's hair. I think about his hyperactivity. He *can't* sit still. They're right.

Feeling like a bad father is a daily occurrence for me, but I've never felt worse than I do right now. I noticed, but I didn't really notice, not in the way they did. Worst of all, I'm so familiar with this neurodivergence and if I'd spent more time with him, I'd have seen it, too.

"Yeah, my sister has ADHD, so I know how this works. He's going to go on medication?" Dominique and Nicolette both nod at the same time. "And what about therapy?" I ask next. "Behaviour therapy helped my sister," I add, and the two women give each other a quick look before turning back to me.

"Yes. We wanted to discuss that with you. We think it's the best route for him to take. He's been very upset recently, so we think it's definitely best if he starts as soon as possible. Especially with pre-school. Damian hasn't been able to sit still and complete a task his teacher has given him since the year started."

The urge to run to my son and hug him as tightly as possible makes my chest constrict. I can't imagine how frustrated he must feel. How scared. This is all so new to him, and I wasn't even fucking there to help him.

"Since the year started? It's almost over now. Why did you not tell me about this sooner?" A sense of betrayal fills my chest. We're meant to be co-parents. I'm meant to be able to rely on them to tell me what his teachers say.

"You were fighting for the title and then preparing for the next season. There isn't really a good time to tell you these things," Nicolette says, and I feel like a bad father all over again.

"I don't care if my head is hanging on by a thread. I don't care if the world hangs in the balance. My son comes first, and I need you to tell me these things as soon as you have even an inclination of what could be happening. ADHD is hereditary. My sister has it. I could have helped. I could have been there," I say, my chest constricting all over again, this time for a different reason.

"We're sorry. We spoke a lot about that since we found out, and you're right. We should have told you. It's inexcusable that we didn't." Nicolette nods at her wife's words, and both of them reach out to wrap their hands around mine.

"Parents are encouraged to go to parent coaching to learn the best ways to respond to his ADHD behaviours. We would very much like it if you came with us. We will make it work with your travel schedule. You'll just have to take some time a week for the eight to twelve weeks of the program. Is that going to work?" Nicolette asks, and I stand up to straighten out my back.

"Yes. I'll make it work." Even if I have to move heaven and Earth.

"Thank you." Both of them smile before Nicolette gets up and moves in front of me. She grabs my arms and squeezes once, her brown eyes full of the kind of comfort I need at the moment. It has words tumbling from my lips that I never wanted to admit to them.

"I should have seen it, too."

She hugs me the second I'm done speaking. I hug her back, needing comfort. Dominique and Nicolette have been family for years, and sometimes, you just need a firm hug from people you let into your heart.

"Let's find a way for you to spend more time with him. I think that would make both of you a lot happier," she says, and Dominique gets up to hug me, too.

"Can I take him to a race or two this season? Estrella and I've discussed it already, and she said she'd be happy to have both kids while I'm racing," I say when we stop hugging.

"Of course. She's your wife now, after all," Dominique replies, and Nicolette shakes my shoulder as realization dawns on her.

"I forgot you got married. Well, fake married," Nicolette corrects. "How's that going?"

"We've had a bit of a rocky start, but I'm taking her on a date today." Both women grin.

"Not so fake anymore, is it?" Dominique asks, wiggling her brows at me.

"I haven't faked a single feeling for that woman since we met. This marriage might have been born out of convenience, but it doesn't force me to feel the way I do, which is as frightening as it is exhilarating," I admit, letting out another nervous laugh.

"Well, good for you. You deserve someone who looks at you the way she does. Plus, the sparks that flew between you at the wedding almost made my dress catch fire," Nicolette adds.

"Are you sure you don't want to pick up Damian tomorrow so you can have date night without the kids around?" Dominique asks, but I shake my head.

"No, no, the date I have planned includes the kids. Daisy and I've been planning it for two weeks, and we're going to surprise her mamá today. I want Damian there, too," I explain, watching both of them give me the kind of look only a happy mother can muster.

"Well, then. Let's talk about Damian's medication. I'll need to tell you the dose and when to give it. As a matter of fact, let me write it down for you so it's easier to keep track," Nicolette says as she steps toward the kitchen island where a pen and paper rest.

Damian walks out of his room a moment later, his hair all over the place. His face lights up at the sight of me, and I kneel down so he can fling his arms around my neck.

"Hey, little warrior," I say, my old nickname for him slipping out.

"Daddy, I have to show you the toy Mama and Maman bought me," he says, Nicolette calling something after him in French as he runs back into his room. Dominique follows after him, and I look at Nicolette.

"If you really want to impress Estrella on your date, choose something to bring her that you want to give her on every single date. Start a tradition right then and there. I did that with Domi, and to this day, I bring her something related to doves for every date." She cocks a challenging brow at me, and I smile.

"That's why you call her 'colombe,'" I point out, making her nod.

"Have any idea what you could bring Estrella?" is all she replies, and it's my turn to nod.

"Something befitting her name."

Chapter 36
James

"Tell me where we're going," Estrella says as I fasten the seatbelt of Daisy's car seat. Damian is already in his, kicking his legs as he waits for me to hurry up.

"No," I reply once Daisy is buckled in. She pokes my cheek, and I twist my head to playfully bite her finger, making her burst into giggles.

Estrella turns her head to look at her daughter and me right as I close the door, and I wink at her. She tries to fight her smile, but it's useless. It covers her whole face and softens her eyes until she momentarily forgets she wants information from me.

Marbles and Lollipop have decided to each occupy one of the kids' laps, and Damian and Daisy are holding onto my girls as they talk about something that happened at preschool.

"How long is the drive?" Estrella asks as soon as I'm in the driver's seat, wrapping my own seatbelt across my chest.

"About two hours," I reply, turning on the car without glancing her way again. I can see the way she glares at me in frustration out of the corner of my eye, though.

"Can you survive two hours with me constantly asking where we're going and two children in the back?" she challenges right as we make it onto the road leading to France.

"You won't have two hours to ask me because there is something important we need to discuss." My tone must give away that this conversation is nothing to be joked about, so Estrella turns my way, offering me her attention. One look in the rearview mirror tells me Damian is busy talking to Daisy about the new toy he got and won't be paying attention to our conversation.

"Damian was diagnosed with ADHD. He's on new medication that may have some mild side effects, but they should go away within a few weeks, according to the doctor. He will also start behaviour therapy, and Nicolette and Dominique have asked me to go to parent coaching once a week for eight to twelve weeks, so we can learn the best approaches to responding to his ADHD." My voice is low and my words come out fast to ensure only my wife hears them.

For a long moment, she stays silent, her brown eyes scanning my face as she processes what I've just told her. She opens her mouth several times to say something but seems to think better of it and closes it again.

"Tell me what's on your mind, little star. Since when don't you?" I ask with a smile, making her frown.

"I'd like to go to parent coaching with you, if that's okay. I'd like to learn as well. We're still dealing with Bert and Jennifer, and if we have to stay married for another year or longer, I will be around Damian a lot, too," she says, reaching out to place her hand on where mine rests on my gear stick. Again, she thinks better of it and retracts her hand, but I place mine on her thigh and give it a gentle squeeze, briefly eyeing the rings wrapped around her finger.

Mine.

"I'd love that, darling." For more reasons than I'll ever admit.

"Okay, cool," she says as she looks away from me and out of the windshield. Half a smile curls the corner of my mouth.

"Cool," I repeat with a small chuckle.

Estrella shakes her head, her brown hair moving with the action. I squeeze her exposed thigh again, loving the way goosebumps appear on her skin.

"My brother had ADHD."

For months, she has locked that information away from me. To this day, she hasn't opened up to me about her brother, hasn't told me she adopted Daisy after he and her best friend passed away. She hadn't even told me she wasn't an only child. And why would she? We've only just begun to truly let each other in, and I haven't pried once about why Daisy's grandparents are trying to take her away from Estrella.

I've only ever received that information from Valentina and then Bert when he couldn't keep his big, disgusting mouth shut. He made Estrella open up about her past, and as much as she's tried to avoid speaking about it, she knows that I know the story. I didn't ask her about it. I didn't question it once, and my wife is smart enough to have figured out that my lack of surprise at Daisy not being her biological child means I knew.

It's an unspoken fact that has lingered between us since Bert and Jennifer left our house.

"He was also on medication, which helped him a lot. I hope it'll do the same for Damian," she adds, and I turn my head to see she's still staring at the road ahead, her whole body tense from this conversation.

"Was he a racer, too?" This makes her snort.

"No, my brother failed his driver's license test three times. He hated driving and he wasn't very good at it, either," she says, smiling to herself. "Helen, his wife and my best friend, was, though. She raced motorcycles, but just for fun. She stopped when she had Daisy and was planning on starting back up again once our little girl got older, but..." Estrella trails off, sucking in a subtle, sharp breath. "Well, she passed away before she had a chance," she says, turning her head away to stare out of her window instead.

"Thank you for telling me about them. I can't imagine how difficult that is," I reply, lacing my fingers through hers.

"It's even more difficult because you're such a pain in my ass most days," she teases, and I chuckle as I tickle her side, making her giggle and shift in her seat.

Silence replaces our words, but Estrella holds onto my hand with both of hers, and I take that sign of affection as encouragement to keep this conversation going. Because I want as many pieces of her life—past, present, and future—she'll give me.

"Will you share more stories about them?" I ask, my voice still quiet to make sure our kids focus only on whatever they're talking about in the back. I also have the radio on— Grupo Frontera playing because they're one of Daisy's and Estrella's favourite artists.

I've made a list of all the artists I hear them playing.

In number one, we have Grupo Frontera. They play them the most.

In two, Becky G, but mostly her new music.

In three, Carin León.

Estrella finally looks at me again.

"Only if you tell me where we're going," she challenges, and I shake my head with a grin.

"We're going to France," I say right as we pass the sign that tells us the same thing.

"That's not fair." I squeeze her hand as I tilt my head her way.

"Deal's a deal," I remind her, and she smiles despite herself.

"Fine, but I hope you're ready for some heartbreak. Because I have lots of it," she says, holding onto me as she tries to make her words sound more lighthearted than she feels.

"Give me everything, Estrella," I say and hand her the earrings in the shape of stars that I bought after Nicolette's advice this morning. "I want it all."

We arrive at *Circuit Paul Ricard* two hours later. Estrella's eyes are wide as she wiggles in her seat in excitement.

"Tell me I'll be the one racing this time," she says, covering her mouth a second later.

Estrella and Daisy have only come to a single race this season, but I saw the way my wife stared at the cars and race track like there was not much she wanted more than to be the one driving. With no one racing against her today, it's much safer. I know she's worried about something happening to her because she's all Daisy has.

Well, at least she used to be.

I think Estrella has yet to see that she and Daisy are not alone anymore. They have me. They have Valentina, Gabriel, Nevaeh, Adrian, Leonard, Chiara, Cameron, Scarlette, and Julián. They have a family in Monaco now, and it's the kind of family that would cross every line to protect them.

I would cross every line for them.

"Yes, you will be the one racing around the track, and I will be watching the kiddos," I say as we get out of the car, and she runs over to my side to wrap her arms around me. When she leans away again, I notice the tears in her eyes. "Best date ever?" I ask with a little grin, and she closes the distance between us to plant her lips on mine.

My knees nearly buckle at the taste of her. She tastes floral and like something solely Estrella, an explosion of stars. My arms wrap around her middle on instinct, and hers fling around my neck, but she steps back long before either of us is satisfied.

"The kids," she whispers, her eyes still closed as she lingers in my arms for a moment longer.

"The kids," I repeat, nodding a few times to get rid of the desire to kiss her again. Kiss her to make up for the months I didn't. For bickering with her instead of asking her out the first day she told me I'm a "*pendejo*."

Estrella is still grinning when she undoes Daisy's seatbelt and lifts her out of the car. She directs it my way right as I help Damian undo his.

"Do Daisy and I get to race, too?" he asks as soon as he's out of the car, and I ruffle his hair once with a smile.

"Not today. Today is about Estrella getting to race again, okay, bud?" Being the good kid he is, he merely nods and takes my hand, not arguing once. "I love you," I add, kissing the top of his head.

"Love you, too," he says, but he's pulling me toward Daisy and Estrella.

I have a feeling he adores those two as much as I do.

Chapter 37
Estrella

I'm trying my hardest to stay calm, but I'm shaking because of how excited I am. Pulling up the racing suit James arranged for me, I let a wave of nostalgia settle deep inside of me. I think of the days I used to do this for a living. When the crowds in my home country would cheer my name.

I was the first woman to race for any team. But I wasn't the last, and the thought of more women making it into such a male-dominated field has me smiling for a different reason.

Once I'm dressed and ready, I rejoin James where he's standing with our kids.

My husband catches all of my attention. He looks gorgeous in his black sweater and dark blue jeans. His sleeves are rolled up to expose his trained forearms, making my mouth water a little. James only becomes more attractive when he picks up my daughter and places her on his hip while talking to Damian about something.

He keeps exploiting my one weakness: my daughter.

And it's not even on purpose. James seems to truly care about her happiness and well-being, which makes my heavy heart beat a little more evenly every single time they interact.

Yesterday, Daisy and James spent the whole evening playing games so I could have "some alone time." As a single mother, "me time" was really "me and Daisy time" most days. Since marrying James, he's done his best to give me one day a week to do self-care.

When Daisy is at preschool, I'm usually too busy getting everything in order to take time for myself, so he does this instead.

"Are you ready, darling?" he asks once I'm close enough, and I give him an eager nod.

"I'm so ready," I reply, approaching them in my racing suit.

"Mamá, you look so pretty," Daisy says when I'm in front of them, and I place one hand on Damian's head and the other on my daughter's cheek.

"Thank you, *florecita*."

I kiss her cheek, then flash James a smile before he gestures toward the crew of people standing beside a Hawke Racing sports car. It's white, blue, and red, like the team's colors, and my heart skips a beat at the sight of it.

"Is this a new model? I didn't know Hawke made these kinds of cars." From what I know, Hawke Racing doesn't make cars outside of Formula One.

"They're trying out something new," James replies. "They've seen how successful Spark Racing, Velocità Rossa, and the others are, so they're dipping their toe in the water with this model. You're one of the first people to try it out," he explains, and I almost sprint toward the car to inspect every inch of it.

It's stunning. The spoiler, the suspension, the carbon diffuser, and the body itself are sleek and unique. It's designed with smooth edges, and I think I fall in love with a car for the first time in years because fuck, this is a nice model.

I can't wait to see how fast it goes.

We're in the garage designated to Hawke Racing at *Circuit Paul Ricard*, and the crew that James hired for today is helping me get everything ready. They check the car, then give me a helmet to put on and some gloves. They usher me into the car moments later, and before I know it, I'm driving it out of the garage and onto the track.

As soon as I'm racing down the track, the familiar sense of weightlessness the adrenaline rush causes fills me from top to bottom. I'm strapped in as tightly as possible, but I might as well not have anything tying me to the car considering how free I feel right now.

A scream rips out of me as I drift into the first corner. Driving at high speeds down a track, braking hard as I move into corners, drifting, all of it has my heart racing.

It's always felt like I was made for this. Like there was nothing in the world comparable to the feeling of being in control of such a dangerous machine. I know the risks of racing. I've always known them. They were part of the reason I gave it up when I became Daisy's guardian.

Being her mom is the greatest thing in the world.

Racing is a close second for me.

For so long, I've seen myself solely as a mom. It's hard not to when it takes up so much of my life. It's the reason I was alone for the first four years I had Daisy. I had no friends, my parents had their own grief to deal with, and I was dealing with depression while trying to keep everything together for my little girl. I was a mess. I functioned just enough to support us and raise Daisy, keeping the darkest parts away from her.

One of the hardest parts of being a single mom?

You have no time for yourself, but even if you do, finding people who want to be around you is beyond difficult.

It's only after James introduced me to his wonderful family—the one he chose, not his parents—that I realized there is a different way. That there are people who care. People who don't mind the baggage because being there for you is more important than anything else. They don't think of it as me pulling them down with the weight of it. They simply help me carry it all.

"How does it feel?" James asks me through the earpiece I was told to put on earlier.

"Like a dream. I think Hawke Racing is onto something with this model," I reply.

It does feel like a dream. It drives like it was made for me, which is ridiculous considering this isn't even a finished model, simply a prototype of a sports model Hawke *might* bring out. It's incredible. It's faster than any of the cars I've raced in the past, and, even though I'm probably going to be fucking sore tomorrow from the G-force, I could race for hours in this.

It's everything. And I like James Oliver Landon a little bit more with every lap.

"Do you think Hawke Racing is looking for test drivers? I'd take that job in a heartbeat for these cars," I say with a smile.

"There's no harm in asking."

He was right.

Best date ever.

After I had to get out of the car, James took the kids and me to dinner. I couldn't stop talking about how incredible it felt to be behind the wheel again, and he listened to all of my rants with a smile on his face and a proud glimmer in his eyes.

I liked him even more in that moment.

James booked a hotel near the track, and we came back here twenty minutes ago to a happy Marbles and Lollipop rushing to the front door to greet us. He bathed Damian and put him to sleep, and I took my time doing the same with Daisy. Like me, she couldn't stop talking about how exciting today was. How much she loved watching me race.

I kiss her forehead once I've tucked the blanket under her chin, her tired eyes fluttering shut before I've even turned off the light. Damian is already fast asleep, so I tiptoe out of their room, walking toward James' and mine.

We've slept in the same bed for weeks now, but he's always kept his distance because he wants to do this the right way.

Taking me on our first date today was his first step, at least from what he told me.

But he promised me that if sex was something I wanted to keep exploring *after* the dates, then we could. That he'd want that, too.

So, I make my way toward the bathroom where I hear the shower running. The door is slightly ajar, so I carefully knock. I hear a grunt and step inside, thinking it's his grumpy way of telling me to come in.

It wasn't.

It was a sound of pleasure while he stroked his cock in the shower. The glass doors hide nothing, giving me a clear view of his muscular arm flexing in synchronization with his pumps.

My mouth waters at the sight of his thick length so hard and on display for me that I don't even realize James is looking at me while fucking his hand.

"Estrella," he says, his voice low and almost warning.

"I'm sorry, I didn't know you were—" I cut off, finding myself moving without meaning to. Trying to get closer to him.

"What are you doing, darling?" he asks, still stroking himself.

My body catches fire, arousal licking up my spine. The longer I watch him fuck his hand, the more I wish I could replace it with my mouth.

"I'm not sure, but I'd very much like to join you in the shower," I blurt out, and he stops briefly, an internal battle happening inside him and reflecting in his eyes.

"I want to take this slow, Estrella, do it right. One date isn't taking it slow," he says, his hand dropping from where it was wrapped around his cock.

"I don't care," I reply, swallowing hard. My eyes keep drifting from his face, down his muscular chest, all the way to his massive length. "Please, sir," I beg, his eyebrows pulling together as the battle intensifies.

Then, his expression gets that dominant edge I love.

"Undress, darling. Come in here and take what you need," he says, and I almost sigh at the familiarity of this. I've missed it.

My dress falls to the ground, and I slip off my panties, stepping toward the shower a moment later. He opens the door for me and holds out his hand. Anticipation almost makes my toes curl. James pulls me inside and against his chest, his mouth capturing mine.

A moan leaves my lips at the taste of him on my tongue. I know it's hardly been five hours, but I've missed his mouth on mine. I wrap my arms around his neck and step on my tiptoes to deepen the kiss. He tastes so good, I have a hard time peeling myself off him, so I don't try. Our naked bodies, now slippery wet, slide against each other while his tongue explores me. My right hand slips down his body, over the hard ridges of his abs, and toward his hard cock.

"May I?" I ask before touching him.

"Unless I tell you 'red flag,' you can touch me as much as you want." With a smile, I grab it, giving it a sloppy stroke that makes him take both of my wrists in one of his hands to pin them over my head and against the glass shower wall. "But if you're going to touch me, do it properly, little star," he instructs against my lips, and I smile in return.

"Yes, sir," I reply in a low tone. "You have to release my hands so I can do so, *papi*."

He kisses me, ignoring my comment. His hard cock presses against my stomach as he explores my mouth, then uses his to trail kisses down my neck. James sucks my left nipple into his mouth, tugging so hard on it that my knees buckle and a low cry escapes me.

"Fuck, James," I curse as he cups my other tit. "Please, I want to make you feel good. Let me," I beg, and he finally releases my wrists.

I don't waste a second before sinking to my knees in front of him. The hot spray of the water hits my back in a steady motion, calming my racing heart.

"I would like to suck your cock. May I?" I ask, looking up at him while my hands rest on his thick thighs.

He places a hand on my cheek, causing my eyes to flutter shut as he trails his thumb along my jaw. His touch is soft and gentle, and I forget about the rest of the world.

"You're such a good girl, asking politely, but I prefer to give you head," he says, his eyes only half-open now that I'm stroking his cock again.

"But I'd still very much like to," I reply and rub the head of his cock with my thumb. His grip on my jaw tightens in response.

"Okay, but I'm not finishing in your mouth. I want to finish inside of you, darling," he says, using his index finger and thumb to pull my chin down and part my lips. He nudges his cock into my mouth, and I almost let out a happy sigh. "You're on birth control, little star." I nod eagerly while sucking him down even though it wasn't a question. My clit throbs with need. "How would you feel about not using a condom so I can fill you up?" He slides out enough to give me a chance to answer.

We both got tested before we got married, just in case, and we were both negative. We didn't want to risk it before, but I have an IUD, which is one of the safest birth controls there is.

Plus, I want to be with this man more than I've ever wanted to be with anyone.

"Very good," I admit, smiling to myself as he pushes his cock back into my mouth.

I know he likes to be in control, so I don't try to take over and simply let him fuck my mouth.

"You're so beautiful, Estrella," he whispers while I relax my jaw even more to take him as deep as possible. He groans as I swivel my tongue around his head and then suck hard. "Fucking hell," he moans, finally letting me take control as his hand falls from my face.

I keep going, keep switching between licking, sucking, and stroking him. James is putty in my hands, and I love the fact that a man who is so set on being in control is letting loose with me.

It's fucking intoxicating.

"Keep going, darling, you're doing so well," he praises, forcing a moan out of me. "Fuuuck!" He places his hand on each side of him in the shower and groans my name. "Wait."

The command comes a minute later, and I obey instantly, stopping my movements and watching him slip his cock out of my mouth. James leans down to capture my lips in an aggressive kiss and lift me at the same time. My legs are wobbly with desire, and the flames lighting me on fire, inside and out, don't get extinguished by the water in the shower.

If anything, the opposite happens.

"Let me see you play with yourself while I slip inside you. Use your left hand," he says as he picks up my left leg and pushes me against the glass wall. The cool material makes me squeal ever so slightly, bringing a satisfied smirk to James' lips.

"Has anyone ever told you how sexy you are when you're dominant?"

His blonde hair is wet, but the curls are somehow perfectly in place anyway. The light blue eyes he keeps studying me with are full of lust, turning them a much darker shade. His lips, so full and plump, show hints of satisfaction I can't get enough of.

"No. Not many people appreciate the fact that I get off on being in control," he admits, gently caressing my left breast. He nudges the head of his cock into me, and I gasp at the thick feel of him. "It's why I want you to know, I'll always give you a safe space to explore your kinks. You tell me what you want, and I'll give it to you." James slides an inch inside of me, and my lips part as I moan. "All your fantasies, Estrella, I want them all. I'll make them all come true," he says, sinking even deeper inside of me.

"James, fuck, oh God," I blurt out, pleasure clouding my mind.

"Can you take more, darling? I'm not halfway inside yet," he says, and I stare down between us in shock.

"You're not?" I'm breathless. I've had him inside of me before, but he feels so much bigger today for some reason.

"Not yet," he replies with a strained smile. I meet his gaze a second before one of his hands cups my breasts again so he can squeeze my nipple. His other one lifts my leg higher, spreading me wider for him.

"Give me all of it," I say right as he sinks all the way inside of me, kissing me to swallow the scream of pleasure ripping out of me. Having him inside of me without a barrier has me quivering in his arms. I've never been with a man without a condom, but fuck, it feels good.

"Keep rubbing your clit, Estrella. Let me feel you come around my cock," he says, but my head merely falls against the shower wall while I keep trembling.

It's been almost two months since we fucked, and my body is so charged from what we've done so far, I feel my orgasm building merely from feeling his cock inside of me. He slides out a little, rubbing the head of his cock against my G-spot, and I slam a hand over my mouth as an orgasm blindsides me. I shake through it, James holding onto me as I feel the waves of pleasure shooting through me.

"Fuck, Estrella, I don't think I'll ever get enough of making you come."

He cups my chin to make me look at him. I obey without him having to say anything. His eyes are filled with the kind of possessiveness he always looks at me with when he slides his ring onto my finger.

"I've never fucked anyone without a condom, but I fear once I see myself drip out of you, it's all I'll ever want to do," he admits, kissing me again as he pulls out just to drive into me again.

My knees buckle fully this time. James holds me up as I moan into his mouth once more.

"Your fucking body, Estrella. It will be the death of me," he says, fucking into me so hard, I see stars. "You will be the death of me," he mumbles, my nails digging into his back as he continues his hard thrusts.

"You already said that months ago," I tease breathlessly, pleasure seeping into every inch of my body.

"And I was right. I won't survive you. Not with my heart intact." I'm about to reply when he picks up his pace, groaning from pleasure.

All words leave me as another orgasm builds. His fingers dig into my ass and mine dig into his back. It only makes him go harder and faster. Apparently, I'm not the only one who enjoys a little pain with pleasure.

"Right there. Yes, right there," I chant, clinging to him and enjoying the way his skin feels pressed against mine while we're grinding against each other. So desperate for our releases, even if I already had one of the most intense orgasms of my life.

He rubs my clit, playing with my piercing, and I orgasm immediately.

"That's my girl. Squeeze my cock," he encourages, and I do as I'm told, squeezing my walls around him.

One last hard thrust has him spilling inside me, his body shaking in perfect synchronization with mine.

His forehead drops against mine as we both come down from our highs. He stays inside of me for a little while longer, rocking back and forth to make me quiver even more.

"Too much?" he asks, his touch gentle as he caresses my ass, then my breasts, and lastly my cheeks.

"No. It was perfect." He kisses me the second the words have left my mouth. "So perfect, I want to do it again," I admit, and he drops his nose to my neck, inhaling deeply. "I want more."

"You deserve more. You deserve everything you want for being such a good girl, Estrella," he replies before picking me up, turning off the shower, and carrying me to our bed.

Chapter 38
James

EVERY PIECE OF ME aches in the best way possible. Estrella's naked body is pressed to mine, our skin slick with sweat. We've been fucking for hours, neither one of us getting enough of the other. Well, Estrella mostly. I feel like an old man, hardly keeping up with her stamina. But I fucked her so well, she's finally sleeping after her—sixth?—orgasm. My cock feels as spent as the rest of my body, but I haven't been this content in a long time.

She's like pure adrenaline, and I can't get enough of her.

Then, right as I want to take some time studying every single tattoo on her body, my phone rings with a new message. I want to ignore it, and usually, I would, but I've been expecting to hear back from the lawyer all day.

My heart stops as I read the contract Bert and Jennifer's lawyer sent mine. Words like "Child Neglect" and "Abusive Behavior" catch my attention, and I sit up in bed as I read the whole rubbish legal document. They're accusing Estrella of neglecting and abusing Daisy. This is the case they're making, and their evidence is Estrella being a single mother with a full-time job. There is no evidence for the abusive behaviour part because of course there isn't. Estrella doesn't abuse Daisy. She doesn't fucking neglect her either, but these people don't care about that.

"James, what's wrong?" Estrella asks, one of her hands slipping onto my back. She sits up and looks over my shoulder, so I hand her my phone to read the document. "They're taking me to court. In America. Unless, of course, I pay them the ten million dollars Bert demanded." Estrella's voice is strangely monotone, as if she feels nothing at all about the words she just read.

"Yes. Unless we find a way to get rid of them for good."

I watch Estrella as she slips out of bed, nodding several times as she grabs my shirt and slips it over her head. There is no time to admire how wonderful the sight of her in my clothes is because she gently places my phone on my bed before sinking to the ground. She doesn't cry, doesn't scream, doesn't do anything but sit there, staring at her hands.

"They're going to make me stand in court while they accuse me of neglecting my daughter and abusing her. They're going to pull evidence out of their asses and take her away from me." She lets out a small laugh I know she doesn't mean. "They're going to rip me to pieces and make Daisy sit through it all," she adds and bursts into laughter. "All because they cut off their daughter for falling in love with my brother." She breaks down into more laughter.

I watch her for a moment, waiting for the inevitable tears. Because that's what usually follows after a fit of laughter to cover up pain. At least that's how it works for me. It's what happened the day Annabel abandoned Damian. Once I was alone and trying to process it all, I started laughing and laughing until I was bawling my eyes out.

But Estrella doesn't cry. No. Rage consumes her instead.

"I'm going to kill him. I'll get Chiara to help me. She seems like the kind of woman who knows how to make it a slow and painful death," she says, glaring at a spot on the ground as she seems to really consider this option.

"Get Valentina to help you, too. She's got enough hatred for the male population for what they've put her through while chasing her dream to last a century," I reply, snapping Estrella out of her angry trance and making her blink at me.

"What the hell am I going to do, James? This is what I was trying to avoid by marrying you. Isn't it enough revenge to have made me get married and throw my life on its head? Why are they still doing this?" she asks, the pure defeat in her tone and face enough to make me slip out of bed and onto the ground with her.

"Because Bert is an evil man," I reply, not throwing Jennifer's name in there because I have a feeling she's only doing this for her husband. Which is fucked up, too, of course, but it reminds me a lot of the situation Mum is in. Always sticking by a horrible man because she's not ready to realise the man she fell in love with has turned into a completely different person.

"I'll pay him the ten million." The words are out of my mouth before I can stop them.

Initially, I didn't want to pay him. I didn't want him to get a cent. But I'd rather pay him all of my money than see Estrella get insulted and her character ripped apart to find any fault in her that they can exploit. She doesn't deserve that. She deserves peace of mind.

"No. I can't ask you to do that," she says, shaking her head.

"You're not asking, Estrella."

"Yeah, I would be. Plus, what if he decides that isn't enough? What if he wants more later? It isn't a viable solution," she replies, but she lets me take her hands and pull her to me.

"Let me make it one. I'm privileged enough to keep making a lot of money. So, let me use what I have to make sure that little girl stays at home, where she belongs with us," I say, watching her eyes soften. She takes my face in her hands, kisses me once, and then leans away.

"Ten million dollars is not something you simply give away, *bebé*," she replies, wrapping her arms around my neck and holding me tightly. "We tried to avoid this, but it's happening anyway." Estrella leans back, her deep brown eyes on me. "I'm sorry, but you'll have to stay married to me until this is all done with," she says as if that's our biggest problem.

We could lose Daisy to Bert and Jennifer if they manage to convince everyone that Estrella is a neglecting, abusive mother. We could lose the life we're so cautiously trying to build. But there is no use fighting her on this when I know it isn't my place to force her to let me pay or take an approach she doesn't agree with.

I may be dominant during sex, but that's only then. Ignoring Estrella's wishes and doing what I want to do is not how I want this relationship to work. There is a decision we will both be happy with, and even if there isn't, at the end of it all, this is Estrella's decision.

I only get whatever she's willing to give me.

"Don't apologise. We'll stay married," is all I manage to say because I'm fighting back irrational words that have no business being voiced.

"What does your lawyer think we should do?"

"Well, he wants us to fight instead of settling because he'll get more money," I explain, making her nod several times. "What do you want to do? Fight this out in court or find a different way to settle it that doesn't include him getting ten million dollars from us?"

Us? Me. Estrella doesn't have that kind of money, so I'd be the one paying. And I certainly didn't mean us as in what is mine is ours. We signed a prenup making sure what's mine stays mine, and the other way around. I can't forget that. This is a *fake* marriage.

"There is no way to settle it outside of court that doesn't include money, is there? I mean, what can we show about Bert and Jennifer that would prove *they* are the unfit guardians?" she asks, but her eyes widen in realization a moment later.

"What is it?" She kisses me and smiles against my mouth.

"I have an idea, but I'll need you to trust me and do exactly as I tell you to," she says and stands up, holding out her hand for me.

"Usually, I prefer it the other way around, but sure," I tease, and the hope blooming inside her has her giggling. "Anything you need from me, wife, I'll give you. I promise."

Chapter 39
James

Daisy and Estrella are finally back to attending a race, and I have been smiling all weekend because of it.

Today is media day and the track walk.

It's hot here in Baku, but I'm enjoying the humid air. Well, so far. I haven't been in the car yet. That part of the weekend is starting tomorrow during the free practices.

Cameron's and my team have given us a couple of bicycles and told us to stay together while we do our track walk. There are cameras attached to the handlebar, which means this is all for content to be put on the social media platforms. Knowing that this is for entertainment, I leave the old man—yes, I know he's only a few years older than me—behind and ride ahead.

He calls out something like, "James and I were told to stay together, but, apparently, he forgot his manners at home and is ignoring those instructions," and I burst into laughter while making noises like an F1 car as I pick up speed.

"Catch me if you can, Cameron," I call over my shoulder. I notice him picking up his speed as well until we're racing, both of us bursting into laughter at our immaturity.

Well, sometimes, especially when it feels like the world rests on your shoulders, you need to act a bit immaturely to cheer yourself up. If racing your teammate down the track while making social media content is the worst I do, I'll take it.

I need a lot of cheering up at the moment.

Estrella and I have been plotting for weeks. Bert and Jennifer live in Miami, so we're still figuring out a way to execute her plan and get rid of them once and for all. This year, Miami is a few weeks after the summer break, so we've still got a bit of time to figure out the logistics. Until then, there is nothing Bert and Jennifer can do so quickly. A custody battle takes time, especially if you're forcing people to make their way to another continent to fight it out.

Two more races have passed since our first date. Cameron won one of them while I came in second, and I came in first in the other one, Valentina in second. I'm leading the championship by a lot, by far more than any F1 driver in the past decade even achieved against their rival.

It's still such a heady feeling to win races on top of races, with strategies that work, starts that secure my first place for the rest of the race, and a reliable car. But the other teams, Velocità Rossa and Grenzenlos, have caught up to Hawke. There are no more races I finish with a twenty-second lead.

We're closer together again, and I have to fight for every win.

Half an hour later, I'm sitting on the sofa they provide in the room where the press conference is being held. Reporters filter in as well as the rest of the drivers. Cameron and I were the first ones there, but Adrian and Valentina follow soon after. They're bickering about something, and Val rolls her eyes at her brother before waving him away. He merely chuckles at the back of her head.

"How's married life?" Adrian asks as he drops down beside me, and I pat his thigh once.

"Good," is my only reply because we're in front of a lot of reporters.

Plus, I've already told him that Estrella and I have been growing closer this past month. Granted, we don't get to spend a lot of time together because of our busy schedules, but whenever we are together, it's good.

It's better than good.

It's Earth-shatteringly amazing.

Estrella is remarkable in a way I've grown to adore more than most things. She's kind, resilient, tough, courageous, a wonderful mother, a devastatingly beautiful person inside and out, and so smart. She makes me laugh so much, and whenever she's in front of me, I can't look away. I can never look away from my wife.

Especially as she falls apart on my tongue. My fingers. My cock. Or on the toys we've been trying out.

"Hey, need a pillow or something?" Adrian says, waving his hand in front of my face to get me to snap out of my thoughts. I lean back and cross my legs to hide what he meant.

"Need a punch in your smug face?" I reply, smiling threateningly at him.

"We're both married, James. Quit flirting with me. You missed your chance," he says, and I burst into heartfelt laughter.

"You couldn't handle me, Adrian."

"Not since you put on all of those muscles. Your thighs alone would crush me," he says with a nod toward where I crossed my legs, my ankle resting on my knee.

I've never been in better shape in my life, and even though every gram matters in F1, putting on muscle has personally helped me with enduring the G-force and my stamina.

"Drivers, are you ready?" I turn to look at the person who just spoke, then glance at Adrian, Cameron, Val, and one of the Zeitgeist drivers, Javier Morales.

He's a rookie who started racing only this year, but the twenty-two-year-old Mexican has shown a lot of potential already. My teammate also looks at Javier, but his eyes linger on the rookie's lips. Javier catches the look, smiling at Cameron in a way that makes me grin to myself.

Cameron and Elijah, his boyfriend of about five years, split a year ago, right after my teammate found out he was cheating on him. He's been weary of entering a relationship since, because of his newly acquired trust issues and also the heartbreak, but the rookie caught his attention from the first race. He introduced himself to us, his hand lingering in Cameron's for several seconds longer than he shook my hand.

He seemed as affected by my teammate as Cameron was by him.

"We're ready," Valentina answers for all of us, and I smile at the first reporter to take a microphone and stand up to speak to us.

"First question is for the current championship leader, James Landon," the reporter says, and I hold onto the microphone I was given a little tighter. "Since you've gained a significant amount of points already, especially more than any of the other drivers, you've started receiving more negative comments. How do you deal with that?"

The question catches me a little off guard. For a while, the fans' treatment of me has been something that was just accepted. No one has bothered to ask me about it, and my team advised me to never talk about this unless I was asked, to avoid more negativity. Until today.

"Honestly? I've made my peace with the fact that there always has to be a bad guy in Formula One. It keeps it more interesting for the fans, I think, and I'm happy to keep being that person for them if it makes them enjoy it more. I know who I am as a person, so the negativity doesn't get to me as much. I don't really care. Maybe I'm misunderstood, maybe they truly do believe I'm the same person off track as I am on the track."

The reporter cocks their head in surprise.

"As long as no one comes for the people I love. They can attack me all they want, but if someone harasses my wife and daughter again, I promise you, I'll actually turn into the bad guy."

Three heads turn my way, shock on every single one of their faces. Adrian's eyes are wide. Valentina's mouth is agape. Cameron's eyebrows have risen all the way up to his hairline.

"Thank you," is the only response I get from the person who asked the question, and the room stays silent for a long moment as everyone tries to catch their jaws off the floor.

I've been waiting for a chance to poach this subject since I heard about what happened to Daisy and Estrella. Maybe this will finally get everyone to leave them alone, both online and when seeing them in person. It's one thing to have a few fans ask nicely for a picture. It's another entirely to make my girls feel unsafe by crowding them in and screaming at them. And that will never happen again. I've sworn to protect them with everything I've got.

Even after she breaks my heart and takes it with her.

For some inexplicable reason, Gabriel is waiting outside of the press conference room, leaning against the wall with a sketchbook and pencil in his hand. Assuming he's waiting for Val, I simply walk past him, but the wanker starts talking to me as soon as he spots me.

I get what Valentina sees in him. He's a handsome fucker. He's that rugged kind of attractive that I used to be—I don't see anyone but Estrella anymore—attracted to. Those dimples of his only add to his looks, just like his curly hair and self-assured smile.

"Hey, James," he says, smirking at me. *Dammit.*

"You heard everything I said in there, didn't you?" He closes the sketchbook and pushes off the wall to approach me. He grins to himself.

"Have you lost your heart yet, James? Or is it all still for show?"

"You're unnecessarily interested in my life," I say, avoiding his question.

"And you're deflecting. Answer my question. Was I right?" I try to be angry or irritated, but I'm neither. Not anymore.

How could I be?

I'm dating my fake wife, who seems perfect for me in every way possible. It feels like everything has started making sense since Estrella and Daisy came into my life.

"We're not going to become best friends just because I'm grateful to you for making me do this," I say, and he practically bounces on his feet in joy.

"Aha! I knew it. I fucking knew it. Mate, you are so welcome." He clasps my shoulder and keeps grinning like he's won the lottery.

"I'm not thanking you," I say, but he shrugs as he drops his hand.

"You don't have to. I'm glad I could shove you in the right direction. All I've ever wanted is for you to be happy, James."

I open my mouth to argue, but there's no point, is there? When I was at my most hopeless, at my lowest, it was Gabriel who showed up at my door. He told me his aunts wanted to have a child and that they would love to take Damian. It was Gabriel who helped me reconnect with Val after I left, despite hating me and wanting me as far away as possible. It wasn't to make himself happy. It was to make *her* happy, and I would be lying if I said it didn't bring me peace, too.

"But it certainly doesn't hurt that I look at no one but Estrella now, does it?" I ask, making him chuckle.

"No, it doesn't. It also doesn't hurt that you don't look at me like you want to run me over with your car anymore." This makes both of us burst into laughter, and I find myself genuinely enjoying a conversation with Gabriel Matteo Biancheri.

Chapter 40
Estrella

Today is Qualifying, and I'm sweating because of how nervous I am for James. His lap times during yesterday's practices weren't ideal, and even if he improved in the session this morning, I don't know if it'll be enough to get him pole. Cameron, on the other hand, has been fast during all of the practices. He's been catching up in the championship standings, too.

Daisy and I watch James get ready to get into his car, talking to various members of his team. He's been extra focused this weekend, never smiling or getting distracted.

Well, he gets distracted a little bit every time he looks at me, but after a heated moment of him staring at my lips, then eyes, he goes back to work.

No one's ever cared for me the way James does. Chaotically, overwhelmingly, and undeniably with his whole heart. It's the same way he cares for Damian, Daisy, Val, Adrian, and the rest of his family.

I wonder if he sees us like that. Like part of his family.

Legally, we are, but I just wonder if he feels the same in his heart. It certainly feels that way when he doesn't hesitate to spend any cent, second, and piece of energy he has to help me figure out a way to get rid of Bert and Jennifer for good.

"Mamá?" Daisy asks, poking my cheek to get my attention. James arranged for a table and some chairs for us this race weekend so Daisy didn't have to be on her feet the whole time.

"Yes, *florecita*?" I reply, bringing my attention to her blue eyes.

"James looks angry today. Can I draw him something to cheer him up?" she asks, and I feel my heart tumble all over itself at her question.

"Of course. I have to go find someone who has some paper and pens. Can you wait here with Daiyu?" I say, running a hand over the crown of her head. She nods several times, so I get up and walk toward James' performance coach. She's standing off to the side now that James is talking to someone else. "Can you keep an eye on Daisy for a couple of minutes? I have to go find some pens and paper," I explain, and her smile is answer enough.

"Yes, sure. I love hanging out with Daisy," she replies, walking toward my daughter.

Daisy lights up at the sight of Daiyu, which is all the reassurance I need before walking out of James' garage. I don't even know where to start looking or who to ask, but as soon as I'm out of the motorhome to look somewhere else, I spot Valentina running around. When her eyes catch me, probably noticing how lost I am, she sprints my way.

"I have two minutes, unless you need more time to talk about whatever has you frowning," she says, and my chest warms at the comforting smile she offers me.

"Daisy asked to draw James something, but I don't know who to ask for supplies," I admit, letting out a nervous laugh.

"Oh, come with me. Gabriel is an artist, but my husband has become horrible at remembering to bring paper and pencils with him in case inspiration strikes, so I carry spare."

She takes my hand and leads me toward her garage. Isabella, Val's performance coach, gives us a confused look, but my friend is pulling us all the way to her private room. I don't have any time to argue when she walks straight toward her bag, taking out a sketchbook and some colored pencils as well as a bunch of regular pencils.

"How's this?" she asks, and I grin at her.

"Perfect. You're the best, thank you," I reply, and she returns my happy expression.

"Glad I could help. If you need anything else, don't hesitate to ask." Val gives my shoulder a gentle squeeze.

"You've done more than enough already. I hope it didn't inconvenience you," I say, suddenly feeling shy and a bit breathless from the heavy weight resting on my chest. Val's smile fades as she processes my words.

"You are family, Estrella. You are never an inconvenience." I almost snort out of reflex.

"It's not a real marriage, Valentina, remember?" The woman in front of me, the Formula One World Champion badass, gives me a frown that somehow makes her even more beautiful.

"The marriage might not be real, Estrella, but the friendship we've been building over the past year, since you started working for me, is. The way my whole family has started to care for you is," she says, then pauses to take a step toward me and grasp my hand in hers. "The way James looks at you is. This marriage may have started out of convenience, but I doubt James' feelings for you are anything but convenient for him at this point." Val chuckles, but my heart is racing so fast, I don't manage to return the sound. "But they're good for him. *You* are good for him. Fake or not, my best friend has never been good at hiding his heart. He wears it on his sleeve, or, when he looks at you, in his eyes."

She kisses my cheek before leaving me to my own spiraling thoughts. He told me he feels something for me, but if Valentina sees it, if she can confidently say all these things to me, then it feels all the more real to me.

"I'm so fucked," I mumble to myself.

Daisy is drawing with the headphones on her head, not caring about anything that's happening because she's so focused on what she's doing, but I can't tear my eyes off the screens.

We're in Q2. Five drivers have already been eliminated from Qualifying in Q1. Val and Adrian's Velocità Rossas have been struggling all weekend, and their lack of pace is reflected in them currently occupying places thirteen and fifteen. If they don't set a faster lap time and make it into the top ten, they won't make it into Q3, which means they won't be able to fight for pole.

"Mamá, the table is shaking," Daisy says, catching my attention. I stare at it to see that my bouncing leg has made the table tremble.

"*Lo siento, bebé,*" I say with a little laugh before doing my best to keep my nerves from making my leg bounce again. "Come on, Romanas," I mutter under my breath at the same time Gabriel sets a lap time fast enough to snatch third place for himself.

Cameron and James are first and second, which is the only thing settling me at least somewhat. That is until Q3 arrives, and James and Cameron start battling for P1. Adrian and Val have made it into the next session of Qualifying too, along with Gabriel; Javier Morales and his teammate at Zeitgeist Racing; Gabriel's teammate, Jack Malec; both of the Spark drivers; and one of the Tempête drivers.

There are ten minutes left, and I resist the urge to start biting my nails. It's a bad habit I had as a kid, one that earned me a vicious glare from my father every time he caught me. He never yelled at me. Neither did my mother. But he communicated his displeasure about certain actions with a very specific look.

I smile at the reminder, then frown when I think about how much I miss my parents.

The Mexican Grand Prix is in a few months, so Daisy and I could see them. Maybe James will even want to join us...

Cameron takes provisional pole a couple minutes later, and I cover my mouth as I push my chair away from the table so I can bounce my legs without interrupting Daisy's drawing.

The seconds tick by as I grow more and more restless. James is in second place. They only have time for one more fast lap before the end of Qualifying. I watch as James drives back into the pits, his crew dragging his car into his garage.

They work on it for several long moments before he heads out of the pits again, on his way to set his final lap time. I stand up when my nerves get the best of me. The headphones I'm wearing allow me to hear everything between James and his team, but he's been uncharacteristically quiet this Qualifying session.

"He seems distracted," Daiyu says, and I almost jump at the sound of her voice. My eyes shift to where she's standing next to me, worry creasing the area between her brows.

"Today?" I ask, but she shakes her head.

"No, he's been distracted for weeks now. I don't know if leading the championship is so overwhelming, he can't quite manage to concentrate on the individual races, or if it's something else altogether," Daiyu explains, silencing me. No words escape as my shoulders sink in defeat.

He's *been* distracted.

Daisy and I are distracting him.

This damn custody battle Bert and Jennifer want to drag us into is distracting him.

We're the problem.

No.

I'm the problem.

Tears shoot into my eyes right as James crosses the finish line for the last time, his lap not fast enough to take pole. Cameron takes pole instead.

I manage to fight the tears as James pulls his car into the pitlane and climbs out of it. I watch my fake husband pull off his helmet and balaclava as he stands close to his team, an expression of defeat on his handsome face. When he catches Daisy and me walking outside to stand with his team, a smile replaces his frown, and he stalks over to us with determination.

"Thank you for being here," he says and kisses the top of Daisy's head before bending down to brush his lips over mine.

"I'm sorry you didn't get pole," I say, but he merely shrugs as he grins at both of us.

"Doesn't matter. Tomorrow is another day, and as long as you two are here, I've already won, haven't I?" The tears come back, but he kisses me before he notices them. My eyes stay closed long after his mouth leaves mine, making sure he doesn't see how badly I'm overthinking.

Even when that's all I can do.

"James, I drew this for you," Daisy says, holding up the drawing she made him. James takes it from her, tears filling his eyes as a bright smile covers his face.

"Is that supposed to be me?" he asks, biting down on his bottom lip, probably to keep from laughing. Daisy didn't draw stick figures. She drew him as something akin to a broccoli person, and if I wasn't so lost in my head, I'd laugh at him trying not to laugh. Then again, he looks so emotional, I don't feel amused in the least. James has told me he doesn't often get to feel like a father, and Daisy has just done something very childlike for him.

"Yeah, you tomorrow," she says and points at the first-place podium she drew that is really a cookie with the number one at the front of it.

"Thank you, princess. I'm going to frame this and hang it on a wall at home," he says, kissing her temple before handing me the drawing, kissing my lips, and leaving to do his post-Qualifying procedures.

Guilt is still a living and breathing thing, clawing at my chest and ripping me apart thought by thought. Second by second.

I'm going to have to tell my husband to focus on the rest of the season and stop helping me win this battle against Bert and Jennifer.

If I don't and he loses the championship because of *me*, I'll never forgive myself.

Chapter 41
James

Estrella and I sit in complete silence as we attempt this new date idea she had. We each have a canvas on a little easel stand and every few minutes, her timer goes off, telling us to switch. I'm not exactly an artist, but, of course, Estrella is wonderful at it.

I have yet to find something this woman doesn't excel at.

The new pair of earrings I bought her—shaped like daisies—decorate her ears, making me smile. For every date, I have bought her a pair of earrings. I always try my best to make it something related to her. Stars, daisies, green diamonds, something racing-related, and more.

Daisy is already fast asleep while we paint, so I don't have to bite back my curse words when I get frustrated at what I'm creating.

I started my canvas off by drawing a simple blue base, and when she gave it back to me, she had drawn a perfectly depicted plane. She started her canvas with a field of grass and a clear blue sky, and when I gave it back to her, it had two trees on either side that looked like I went for an abstract style of art instead of a realistic one. She didn't comment, didn't smile, nothing.

My wife and I have been married long enough for me to know something's bothering her.

Fake wife.

Fake wife, but, perhaps, real girlfriend. We have been dating, after all. We said we'd give it a chance, and that's exactly what we've been doing. We've gone on dates.

We've explored each other's bodies and found little ways to drive the other wild with need and desire.

But things are never that easy, are they?

"We need to talk," she finally says, and my heart retreats into the deepest depths of my body, hiding in fear of the hurt she might inflict any moment now.

"No, thank you," I reply, and she looks up from her canvas, furrowing her brows at me.

"What do you mean 'no, thank you,' James?" she asks, stopping her painting.

"If this is about us, we're not talking. Unless it's to discuss how good we are together. Even when we were hardly speaking, when you were taking care of me while I was injured, we were good for each other." She gives me an unimpressed look, as if to call me out on my lie. "Fine, I'll speak for myself," I say and stand up, ignoring the alarm going off on her phone.

She turns it off a second before I squat beside her, my heart moving all the way into my throat to keep me from speaking. It's warning me, telling me to keep the next words to myself, but I've already married her. What more can I do to tether myself to this woman that I haven't already done? I laid myself bare. I gave her all my secrets, guilt, and shame.

"*You* have been good for *me*. More than good. You've been the answer to all of my questions. The answer to why I couldn't move on from feelings I was harbouring for years. I couldn't move on because I needed you to burst into my life and *demand* I move on. I needed you to show me feelings can be reciprocated," I explain, hating the way tears fill her eyes.

I don't want to make her cry.

My hands cup her face, and she closes her eyes as soon as I make contact with her cheeks, tracing the apples of them.

"Haven't I been good for you, my beautiful little star?" The question is filled with so much vulnerability, I can practically hear my heart shrieking in fear.

"You have been, James. You've been everything. Even when you were running from me, from us, you've always done everything in your power to take care of us. But that's the problem," she says and stands up to put distance between us.

"Darling, I'll need a bit more explanation to understand why you're so upset. You know Daisy and you mean a lot to me."

It's more than just them meaning a lot. It's been almost a year since I've met both of them. I've lived with them for about five months. We've been married for a little less than that. I've grown attached to them in a way I tried so hard to prevent. I thought I could protect myself from developing deeper feelings for Estrella, but it's as useless as using an umbrella made out of paper while walking in the rain.

This woman in front of me, the one person I don't think I could have ever protected myself from, certainly didn't give me a chance. She shoved her way into my heart, and so did her daughter. It's hard to run away when you're stuck in quicksand. Only the quicksand is the feelings I've avoided like a bad case of the flu for most of my adult life.

Estrella throws her hands in the air and shakes her head repeatedly, as if that would help the words come out of her mouth.

"You're distracted," she says, exhaling deeply as more frustration becomes visible on her entire body. "Daisy and I are a distraction, and if you lose the title because of us, because of this fucking custody battle Bert and Jennifer are dragging us into, I'll blame myself forever. And you'll blame me, too. Why wouldn't you? It'd be my fault," she rants, placing her hands on her legs as she bends over and shakes her head again.

"Estrella, look at me," I say, but she doesn't. So, I step toward her, bend down until my shoulder can touch her lower abdomen, and throw her over it.

"JAMES!" she says, but I'm already walking toward our room in the suite. "Put me down," she says, and I obey, dropping her on the bed. She looks up at me with pure shock. "What the hell are you doing?" she asks as I take off my glasses and then my shirt.

"Arms up, darling," I command, and she hesitantly follows instructions. I slide my shirt over her head, then settle down on the bed next to her, pulling her onto my body.

"I'm very confused," she whispers but nuzzles her face into the crook of my neck. "Damn you and your scent for having this effect on me." She inhales deeply while I slide my hand into her hair and massage her head.

"You are not responsible for anything that happens on the track. I have trained my whole life to separate my work from my life at home. You are not the reason I'm distracted. While you and Daisy are my priority, every F1 driver is able to shut that part off. We run on adrenaline and our heightened emotions in the car. I promise you, if I seem distracted, it has nothing to do with you, Daisy, or the custody case, okay?"

My words make her sink even more into the embrace, her breathing evening out with every second we cuddle on the bed.

"I hate you," she mumbles after a moment of silence, surprising a laugh out of me.

"I know," I reply, kissing the top of her head. "What for this time?" I ask, running a hand down her arm and admiring the snake tattoo that wraps around her forearm. My gaze trails upward until I reach the racecar tattooed on the inside of the same arm.

"For finding the right words. For reassuring me. For being you. I just hate you. I don't need a specific reason," she teases, and I burst into laughter.

"Have I earned the right to hear about your tattoos yet, darling?" I ask once I've stopped laughing and silence filled the room for several comfortable moments.

"Why do you want to know so desperately?" she asks, but her question is followed by her leaning back to show me her soft smile.

"Because they're a part of you, and I'd very much like to know each and every one of them." She sits up in the bed, her brown eyes filled with something I can't quite identify.

Fear? Adoration? Love? Regret? Hesitancy? Maybe it's all of it. Maybe it's none of it. Maybe it's wishful thinking on my part when I see love in her eyes.

We're not there. She's not there. I'm not... fuck, I don't know where I am.

"Most of these tattoos are exact replicas of my brother's," she says and removes my shirt and her tank top at the same time, leaving her chest completely bare. Then, she slips her shorts down her body, panties now the only thing covering her. I swallow hard, my hand reaching out to touch the tattoo painted across her ribcage.

"That one was his tattoo for Helen," she explains, her hand covering my fingers where they run over the fine lines of the tattoo. It's several daisies stacked together in an intricate design with leaves and single petals falling down her body.

"When they first started dating, she used to wear these daisy earrings with a matching necklace. From that day forward, my brother called her his daisy. His *florecita*."

Realization dawns on me, but Estrella keeps talking before any words leave me.

"My brother was an engineer, so he was used to being around dangerous equipment. He designed, built, and tested most of his projects, and one day, one of the tools he was using—" She cuts off, more tears filling her eyes. My thumb stays on the tattoo as I wrap my other finger around her and squeeze gently to tell her I'm here. I'm not going anywhere. "Helen was pregnant at the time it happened, and when she gave birth to Daisy, she knew right away what she wanted to call her. She wanted something to remind her of Pedro," she goes on, and I hold my breath as a wave of grief that isn't even mine hits me in the chest.

"That's why you call her *florecita*," I say, probably butchering the word, but Estrella gives me a thoughtful smile.

"It felt right, you know? This way, my little girl will always have something from both of her parents," she says, grabbing my hand again and guiding it to the next tattoo.

I watch her, completely mesmerised by how strong she is. She's lost so much, had to be so strong throughout the whole process for her daughter, and she never even says anything about that. That's just the way things were, and she never looked back.

My little star lives with one of the hardest things a person ever has to experience, grief, and she does it all while raising a child. A child she never planned on adopting, but one that has become the centre of her world.

"This one was Pedro's tattoo for our parents," she says next, stopping my hand right over the tree that's painted across her other ribcage. "His had their names on it. Like a family tree, but I haven't finished mine yet." She doesn't linger there. Estrella moves my hand up her body to the words sprawled across her collarbone.

Nada Es Más Importante Que La Familia.

"Nothing is more important than family," I translate, looking up at her.

"Yes."

She doesn't ask me how I know that, and I'm glad she doesn't. I've asked Val to teach me Spanish, and between her and Julián, who's also helping me learn, I've picked the language up a little, but not even close to well enough to impress Estrella yet.

"This one is an *alebrije*," Estrella continues, bringing my attention to an animal that looks like a combination of a panther and bird. It also has antlers, and the intricate design of the tattoo is drawn on her upper left thigh. "Pedro's favourite day of the year was *Día de los Muertos*. He was a very spiritual person, and he said it would always make him feel very connected to the family members we've lost. He told me that once, when he walked by the cemetery on the second of November, he heard the voices of the souls of the people who passed away," she goes on, tears forming in her eyes. "I haven't been able to go back to Mexico when we celebrate this day since he died."

My hand reaches out, and she leans into my touch as soon as I make contact.

"Daisy and I always have our *ofrenda*, but I haven't been able to go back and visit their graves. I don't think I'll ever be strong enough to stay composed for Daisy, for my parents."

There is not a second of hesitation that passes before I say, "I can come with you and give you as much strength as you need. I can take Daisy and give you the space to grieve. I'll do whatever you need, *be* whatever you need, little star."

She says nothing, but she flings her arms around me and holds me close until she stops shaking. Even then, I hold onto her for a little longer, just to make sure she's okay.

We spend the next twenty minutes talking about the rest of her tattoos. The snake on her arm was her brother's tattoo as well, and he got it because he was fascinated by them. The shooting star on her left wrist was his tattoo for her. The tattoo running down her spine was something for herself, not a tattoo for her brother. But the rest of the tattoos are all for him. The roses running from the middle of her thigh all the way up to the side of her butt. The bird flying out of the opened cage on her other thigh. The head of a stag with more flowers surrounding it.

There are so many more, small ones that I give as much attention to as the big ones, and I could spend another hour or ten listening to Estrella talk about them all.

It doesn't go past me that the longer I touch her, the more I run my fingers over her naked skin, the more goosebumps appear. But it's only when she stops talking, no more designs to explain, that I look up at her. Her breathing hitches as I bring my hand back to her ribcage.

"Thank you for sharing this part with me," I say, still looking at her. Estrella bites her bottom lip to hide a smile.

"Thank you for giving me a safe space to do so," she says, running her fingers through my hair and making my eyes flutter shut. "You should sleep. You have a long day tomorrow."

Estrella's breathing hitches all over again as I trail open-mouthed kisses all the way from her breasts to her neck, jaw, cheek, and then hover my lips over hers.

"What are you doing to me, little star? With every word you utter, you pull me in deeper. With every kiss, I feel more tethered to you," I say, kissing the corner of her mouth, not quite giving either of us a proper taste. Estrella shivers.

"Then tether yourself to me," she says and grabs my face, tilting it to press her mouth perfectly against mine.

I lose myself in that kiss. I taste her, nip at her bottom lip, and chuckle when she giggles happily against my mouth. She helps me out of my shorts, too, until we're almost naked and wrapped up in each other again. Half of her body is draped over mine while I fight the urge to drag all of her onto me. I want her as close as possible, and while I'm already grateful we're skin-to-skin, I crave more. I'll always crave more of her.

"Good night, *bebé*," Estrella says, resting her head on my shoulder.

"Good night, little star." Her nails run up and down my chest before she rests her palm flat against my neck.

If I die right now, with Estrella in my arms, I'd die the happiest man on the planet.

Chapter 42
James

It's race day here in Baku. Cameron is starting from first, but I'm in second and ready to fight him for the win. Val qualified third, Adrian is in fourth, and Gabriel is in fifth. Grenzenlos has been struggling a lot, even if they were dominating again the season after Adrian won his second championship with Velocità Rossa.

"James, we're gonna keep an eye on the overheating issue we had all weekend, but it should be fixed after the team's adjustments. I'll let you know in case of anything, but I'm going to need you to be even smarter today, okay?" Ximena says, the subtext clear.

Don't fight Cameron unnecessarily. We're one team, and we win and lose together as one, too. However, this is still a fight for the championship. So, I am going to fight for the win.

I'll be a lion hunting down its prey in my Hawke.

"Got it," I reply, releasing the radio button as I take a deep breath, then let it back out.

The formation lap is minutes of heart-racing, shallow-breathing misery. I don't know why I'm so nervous. It feels like if I mess up the start, beating my teammate will become even harder, especially because I won't be the one who deserves the win more.

While I've gained some fans since my first race of this season—some people really like seeing me win—I want to deserve my win.

For my team. For my fans. For Estrella and Daisy.

I weave from side to side to get more heat into my tyres during the formation lap, charging my battery at the same time. The track conditions are exactly what we were expecting, no surprises there, and I take one more deep breath before we line back up on the grid. Cameron's car is facing mine ever so slightly, so I position mine facing his in the same way. It's nothing more than a simple tilting of the wheels in the other driver's direction, but it's an aggressive move. It's meant to cut off the driver that has a slower start, to overtake them.

Ballsy move on Cameron's part.

Makes me like him even more.

But then the rest of the world vanishes as the lights above me turn on one by one. I wait until all five appear, wait even longer for them to disappear, before releasing the clutch, hitting the throttle, and shifting into gear. My start is better than Cameron's, but I have no time to feel surprise at his slow reaction time as we head into the first corner.

Because he's fighting me, trying to get back his first place.

The G-force hits me hard as we keep racing, just like it always does, but it feels worse when I'm racing against someone else. Sweat drips down the side of my forehead within a lap.

Cameron is still on my rear, but DRS hasn't been enabled yet, so he doesn't get the speed advantage he's looking for by staying within a second behind me. By the time the second lap comes around, I've managed to gain a second on him. That's important. If he can't overtake me more easily with DRS, then our team is going to tell *him* to back off to spare his tyres.

But there is no driving away. No twenty-second lead like I had during the first race.

I barely have two seconds on him when he gets called in for his first pitstop.

"Ximena, they're trying to undercut," I say, waiting several moments for her response.

"Box, box on this lap, James." My tyres haven't given up on me yet, they'd still have a few laps in them, but we can't risk it. If Cameron makes up those two seconds before I pit, then I will come out behind him.

My heart is racing as I enter the pits, praying that everything will go smoothly enough so I reenter the track still in first place. I hold my breath as I stop, praying to whoever will listen that my pitstop goes well and I come out in first place.

My crew works quickly and moves out of the way about two seconds after I've stopped, the green light for me to leave appearing a moment later. I dart away from my team and drive toward the pitlane exit, talking to Ximena.

"That seemed fast. Tell me I'll come out ahead," I say, practically beg, but my voice is firm enough to hide the weakness I'm feeling deep inside.

The weakness of my fear. Of feeling like I'll never be good enough. Never amount to all the things my father wanted me to achieve.

I drive back onto the track, barely shooting in front of Cameron as he makes his way toward me. Sucking in a sharp breath, I hold it as we move into the corner, our tyres almost touching as he tries to overtake me. But he has warmed-up tyres. Which means he has more grip and ultimately more speed. I'll have to defend like never before to keep him behind me and simultaneously get some heat into my tyres.

Cameron backs off before we run into each other, realizing I was further ahead when we went into the corner, but there is no time to let out a sigh of relief. He's still in DRS range, and with that extra speed advantage in the designated zones, I'm fucked.

My teammate could and might overtake me.

"Downshift later in the corners. Use the momentum on your exit," Ximena says, and every muscle in my body screams at the G-force as we keep racing.

I'm not new to hard racing, which is exactly what Cameron is doing when he dive-bombs me in the next corner. I barely manage to avoid him and stay ahead, but it's a close thing.

Way too fucking close for my peace of mind.

We race down the main straight again during our second lap of battle, Cameron attempting to use his DRS advantage to overtake me again. He attempts to go down the inside, so I move in front of him before we take the corner to cut him off, and—

He runs right into the back of my car.

The impact hits me everywhere, knocking the air out of my chest. There is nothing I can do but give myself over to what's happening until we move into the run-off area and his car moves away from mine. I spin in circles before finally hitting the barrier, my hands releasing the steering wheel to keep them from getting hurt.

It's only once I've stopped moving and can take several breaths to ease the shock and fear rolling through my system that I manage to hear Ximena speaking to me.

"James, are you okay?" She sounds like she's asked that question several times already.

"Yeah," is the only thing I manage to respond.

Then, anger sets in and adrenaline returns tenfold to my body. I catch sight of Cameron getting out of his car and make my way out of mine to approach him.

"Have you lost your bloody mind, Cameron? What the hell was that?" I scream at him as I approach him. He lifts his visor to reveal he looks as angry as I feel.

"You fucking swerved!"

"No, I didn't. I was in my racing line the whole time," I reply, both of us throwing our hands around and yelling at each other because our emotions are running high.

"Bullshit, James. This was your fault," he says, getting right up in my face. I'm not a violent man. I never have been.

Have I imagined running Gabriel over with my car more than a dozen times? Sure.

Have I actually done it? No.

Because I don't like harming anyone.

But Cameron is pushing my character at the moment.

"Step away from me. You've done enough. You've ruined both our races. Let's not ruin our reputations, okay?" They already see me as the bad guy. I don't need to give them more reason to paint me as the villain.

"Fuck you," he says and shoves past me, his shoulder hitting mine with so much force, I grit my teeth and groan quietly in my helmet.

I watch him shoot me a dirty look after we've made our way off the track because he took his helmet off, but I just shake my head in response.

We both need to cool off and talk about it after if we want to save the friendship we've been building for years, the one that's grown even more since we've become teammates.

But neither one of us is in the right headspace to talk without our feelings getting in the way right now.

Chapter 43
James

My wife is so cute when she's scowling at me. I can't help but grin at her, committing the image of her—her fists on her hips, tattoos on full display in her sweet, green summer dress, curves I want to dig my hands into, and beautiful features downturned into an upset expression—into my memories forever.

"You're not fine," she says, so I reach out to touch her, but she steps out of the way before I get the chance to make contact.

"But I am," I assure her, ignoring the way my body aches all over.

I already got checked and cleared, but Estrella is giving me the type of look that says she doesn't care if the doctor said I'm fine, if *I* assure her that I am. She's worried about me, which only makes my feelings for her run even deeper.

"No, you're not," she insists.

"If I admit my whole body hurts, will you kiss me?" I ask, and, finally, the smallest of smiles slips onto her face.

"Yes. I love hearing I was right," she replies.

"You were right. I'm not fine. But it's nothing my wife can't make better by putting her mouth on me," I say, and she doesn't miss the double meaning of my statement. No, she places her hands on my face and trails them down agonizingly slowly.

Estrella brushes her fingers, especially the ones with her rings on it, over my left nipple which is still covered by my fireproofs.

"Here?" she asks, her mouth moving toward mine as she speaks.

"No." I smirk, my body almost shuddering when she continues trailing down her hand.

"Here?" She stops at my abs. I shake my head.

"Try again, little star. Find the right spot," I instruct, my body suddenly full of energy.

Her hand drops to my groin, but she does nothing more than rest it there.

"Here?" Her lips brush against mine as she says the word, but I shake my head again.

"No, darling," I say and raise my hand to her lips, tracing her bottom one with my thumb. "Here," I add right before I kiss her fully, deeply, letting her taste consume me. Her tongue slips into my mouth to explore me, and I return her kiss just as eagerly. I could kiss this woman a million times and still wonder if I'll ever get enough of her.

"James, it's time for the team meeting," Daiyu says as she knocks on the door of my private room.

"I'm coming," I reply, keeping my lips off Estrella long enough to say those two words.

"Then stay and let me pull up my dress and climb on your lap," my wife says once we manage to separate our mouths, and I squeeze her butt. Considering how worked up I am from her teasing touch and soft lips, it wouldn't take very long.

I stand up to tower over her, and she bites her lips at the hungry expression on my face.

"We'll have to wait until we get to our room. Then, you can make me feel better about my horrible race finish, if you'd like," I say, my words making her breathing hitch.

"I don't know if I can wait that long. I have a very attractive fake husband," she replies, but I frown because I hate that she still thinks there is anything even remotely fake about us.

Maybe I'm naive for thinking this could be a real marriage after not even half a year of it being "fake," but we work. Daisy, Estrella, Damian, and I are a family whenever we're together, and that feeling has become so addictive that I find myself craving it every chance I get.

Cameron and I sit across from each other at the table in the conference room our team arranged so we could discuss what happened. I'm glaring at him and he's glaring right back at me. After the race ended, I went to look at the footage with my team. I still don't see what I did wrong. I didn't *weave*, if I had, the FIA would have given me a penalty. It's against the rules because it's dangerous. Cameron ran into the back of my car because his left tyre locked up.

That's a fact.

He braked too late.

That's another fact.

Our teams are waiting for us to speak to each other, and they know it's best not to pressure us into breaking the silence before we're ready. Unlucky for Cameron, I've been ready to confront him since I watched the replay.

"I don't know why you're so upset with me. You saw the footage," I say, but he merely shakes his head and looks at his performance coach, Parker, like they can keep him from taking the blame. "Cameron, do we have to watch it together? I will if it allows you to see what I saw. You locked up. You didn't move to overtake me because of it and hit me."

"You've always been a hard racer, James. You push and push and push, never getting blamed or even a penalty. It's not bloody fair, and you know it," he says, and I realize what this is all about. This is built-up tension finally releasing.

"I'm sorry." The words catch him completely off-guard.

"What?" he asks, still not sure if he heard me correctly.

"I'm sorry it feels that way, that *I* made you feel that way. It wasn't my intention. I'll do better," I promise, but Cameron merely leans back, dumbfounded.

"Just like that?" he asks, and I shrug.

"I don't want to fuck up this friendship and work relationship. You mean a lot to me, so yeah. Just like that," I say and cross my arms over my chest.

"But it was my fault," he mumbles, and I nod.

"This time, yes, it was. But it was racing. I think we can all agree it'll never happen again." I give him a look that speaks louder than any words, and he looks away ashamed. "We'll do better. Okay?" I'm still pissed, but there is no point in prolonging a fight with someone I love.

"Nah, it can't be this easy, mate. I've been acting like a defensive prick."

Both of our teams exchange glances, not sure what to make of this situation. Honestly, I don't either. All I know is that I want to go back to the hotel where Estrella and Daisy are waiting for me to have dinner. I want to cuddle up with my wife and daughter while we watch a movie.

Daughter?

Fuck.

An alarm goes off in my head because I can't look at Daisy that way. I can't even look at Estrella as my wife, but I use the excuse of the paper tying us together as a good enough reason to keep calling her that. To see her as such. But Daisy? I cannot start looking at her as my daughter. My child. Someone that takes priority above all else. I can't look at Daisy that way, especially not without asking Estrella for permission. She didn't sign up for us to become a family. She told me she was scared of Daisy looking at me like a parent because of how much it'll hurt if or when this ends.

If? When?

Never have I hated the English language more than when it reminds me that this ending is a very real possibility.

"James?" Cameron asks, and I realise my chest has pulled tight with fear.

"Yeah, I'm with you. Are we good? I need to get back to the hotel."

"We're good, mate. Thank you."

Cameron stands up and extends his hand for me to shake, but I walk around the table and pull him into a hug instead. I need the comfort to help ease the panic whirling around in my body. From my chest, down to my stomach, all the way into the tips of my fingers before moving to my throat to constrict my breathing. It's everywhere.

"To an incident-free remainder of the season," I say, and Cameron pats my back.

"Well, if you can keep the back of your car out of the nose of mine," he jokes, but I step back to give him an unimpressed look. He blushes and lets out a laugh. "Too early?"

"Yup," I reply, shaking my head.

"I'll try again tomorrow."

Despite myself, I burst into laughter until we're both consumed by it, Cameron bending at the waist. After the horrible day we've had, our emotions are all over the place, and we need this.

I'm still leading the championship. He's still second. Val is a close third with Adrian in fourth and Gabriel in fifth.

But we have a buffer.

It's between Cameron and me.

And as much as I want to save this friendship, I'm scared it'll break as soon as the championship is finally decided.

Chapter 44
James

THIS YEAR, SILVERSTONE IS directly after Baku. I don't know why the F1 calendar has been thrown around this way, but I'm excited for my home race. It's the last race before summer break, and I'm ready to spend every moment Estrella isn't working with her and our children.

But for today, I have to focus on the race.

I only qualified fifth because Javier Morales crashed right during my final fast lap in Q3. I'm nervous, but having Daisy and Estrella here for the second race in a row helps settle me.

"I love the Drivers' Parade," Adrian says, pulling me out of my thoughts.

"Yeah, because people are practically chanting your name," I reply right as I attempt to walk toward the old-timer Spark Racing sports car—since Spark is a British team, they sponsored these cars for the parade—but his words stop me.

"They chant your name now, too, James. Haven't you been listening?" my best friend asks with a soft smile, and I swallow back a wave of emotion hitting me directly in the chest. I place my sunglasses on my eyes and fumble with my team shirt.

As I sit, I think about the people cheering my name. They've always outweighed the haters, but I've been so programmed into believing I'm the worst, it's hard to remember that. My dad made me feel this way my whole life. It's all I know. No. It was all I *knew*.

So, I close my eyes and let the screaming fans boost my confidence as they call out my name. I open my eyes to wave at them and see the posters they've made for me.

Each of them is a work of art in its own way, and if I could take a picture of all of them, I might just never forget how much people love me again.

Once we're back at the starting line, all of us drivers get out of the cars and walk toward our garages to get ready for the race. I still have to get changed and warm up with Daiyu, who's already waiting for me with all of my things.

I catch sight of Estrella and Daisy talking to my team principal. My wife is laughing, the look of joy so beautiful, I actually stop dead in my tracks to take it in for a moment. It's rare that Estrella looks this carefree. She doesn't have a lot of reason to feel this way with Bert and Jennifer still a looming threat over our heads.

"Come on, James, we don't have time for you to get lost in Estrella's eyes," Daiyu says, interrupting me before I can spiral down into my dark thoughts.

"Coming," I mumble, forcefully dragging my eyes off my girls to follow her.

There will be enough time to hold them and assure myself everything will be fine. For now, I need to get ready to win my home race. And I have a feeling it will be anything but easy.

It's raining. I hate racing in the rain. Unlike Mr. I'm-Perfect-At-Everything, I am not good at racing when it's pouring. I'm not bad, but not being good is horrible enough in F1, especially when I'm supposed to chase down said perfect racer. But Adrian isn't my only threat. Ms. I'm-The-Best-Racer-The-World-Has-Ever-Seen is also ahead of me.

And so are Gabriel and my biggest rival and teammate, so, truly, I'm fucked.

"Alright, James, I'm going to need you to take a deep breath," Ximena says, her words flowing from the earpiece straight into my head.

"Why?" I ask, a bit perplexed by her words.

"Because I can see how tense your shoulders are from here, which is saying a lot," she says as if it's the most obvious thing in the world.

"I'm soaking wet, uncomfortable, and terrified. Pardon me for having tense bloody shoulders." It's not raining hard. If it was, then we wouldn't be racing right now. It would be postponed, but, unfortunately, that isn't the case today. It's raining just enough to soak every part of me but not for water to accumulate into puddles on the track.

"Take a deep breath, *estúpido*. Don't make me go out there and force you," she says, and I can't help it. I chuckle.

"Nice pep talk, Ximena." This makes her snort.

"I'm not here to give you a pep talk. That's your wife's job," she says.

"Well, then put her on," I reply, still smiling because this conversation is helping me calm my nerves. Any mention of Estrella is enough to settle the deepest turmoil inside of me, even if it's only for a little.

"No can do. That's against the rules, but I can tell her you said hi and that you miss her."

I don't tell her not to, nor do I speak again. All of my attention drifts to the lights illuminating simultaneously where they hang over the start line of the grid. My heart stumbles a little, even though it's just the signal for us to take the formation lap.

"It feels like I pissed myself," I tell Ximena halfway through the lap.

"It's barely drizzling. Stop being a whiny baby," she replies, but I hear her snicker before she releases her radio button.

"You want to come sit in this fucking car?"

"Watch your language, James. You don't want a punishment from the FIA for cursing, do you?" I roll my eyes at her question.

"They wouldn't start punishing us for that, would they?"

"You never know." I clamp my mouth shut to keep from laughing at the absurdity.

STRAIGHT TO THE CHAPEL

Rain continues to hit my visor, but the track isn't that bad. Ximena is probably right. I'm just being whiny, but who would ever enjoy being in full racing gear and being wet?

Answer: no one.

Well, maybe Adrian. I wouldn't put it past him.

"Okay, we're on wets, but the rain seems to be clearing up on the monitor, so I'm assuming we'll be switching to intermediates very soon. Maybe even medium or hard tires," Ximena says right as the grid lines back up on our designated spots.

"Understood," I say, trying to wipe a bit of the rain from my visor.

The sound of roaring engines fills my ears as all twenty cars wait for all five lights to appear and then disappear again. My heart finds a perfectly uneven rhythm for several moments, so I take three deep breaths.

One to settle my uneven heartbeats. One for courage. One to go into tunnel vision.

The start is important. I need to overtake at least one of the drivers ahead of me. Otherwise, I'll spend the next fifty-two laps fighting my way from fifth to first *and* trying to stay there. Ahead of the best drivers in the sport.

Fuck me.

The lights on top of us are all on right as I take another breath for concentration. I hold it, my fingers itching to shift into gear and my foot twitching to slam on the gas. But we wait.

And then.

The lights disappear.

I've always been a better starter than Adrian. It's one of his weak points, so we race down the straight and into Abbey side by side. Valentina disappears ahead of us, and if I had the mindset to curse, I would, especially because the way the rain distorts my vision through the visor is making me want to bash my head against a wall.

God, I'm starting to sound as dramatic as Adrian.

The immediate strain the G-force takes on my body doesn't help my irritation when my best friend shoots ahead of me in the next corner. It's only when we reach National Pits Straight that I move beside him again. He fights me off, but I slip beside him in Maggots again, stay there all the way as we go straight into Chapel before finally overtaking him.

He may be a skilled driver, but so am I.

And my car is bloody fast.

Once I'm finally ahead of Adrian, I chase down Val.

It's a brutal battle. Her Velocità Rossa is slower than my Hawke, just like Adrian's, but she is a strong defender, if not *the* strongest I've ever raced against. The rain keeps pouring down, too, so we're all going slower than we would if it wasn't. It becomes less about who has the fastest car and more about who can drive the best on the slippery track.

We arrive at lap twenty when I finally manage to go down the inside at Chapel. This must be my lucky corner today because I move ahead of her and manage to make it stick. We go wheel to wheel, and I do my best to stay on my racing line, but it's so fucking wet in this corner, I end up forcing Val to go wide.

"Fuck," I curse, checking my mirrors to see her re-enter the track behind me.

I can't take a breath of relief yet because I still have to hunt down Gabriel and Cameron, but it feels like a huge accomplishment to have finally made it into the podium places.

"Okay, James, that move on Valentina is under investigation. You might get a penalty for causing a collision," Ximena informs me, and I grind my molars together.

"Understood."

"Rain is supposed to stop in three laps. Push your tires. I want to go with plan A," Ximena says right as I notice Gabriel making his first pitstop.

"Are you certain that's the right move? It's raining," I say, holding my breath.

If the track is dry, one-stop strategies are called for in Silverstone. If it's wet, you do two. That's the rule.

"Trust me on this," is her only reply.

Lucky for both of us, I do trust her.

I just hope her hunch doesn't end up fucking us over.

Now that Gabriel has pitted, I'm in second, and Cameron is ahead of me by two-point-eight seconds. Apparently, his strategy mirrors mine.

I'm racing down the track for the twenty-third lap when the rain finally stops. That's when a sigh of relief escapes me. But it doesn't last very long.

Another two laps pass when I hear my race engineer's voice again.

"James, you've got a five-second penalty," Ximena says right as I fight my way into DRS range.

"What?" I ask, but she doesn't answer me. So, I just say, "Yeah, alright. Send them my bloody thanks and let me get back to work."

Shit, fuck, shit.

How the fuck am I going to overtake Cameron and create a five-second gap between us?

"How are the track conditions?" Ximena asks next, and I barely bite my tongue to keep from shouting at her for interrupting me while I'm getting my speed advantage to fight Cameron.

"Getting too dry for these wets," I reply, pressing my DRS button as we shoot down the main straight.

"Okay, then box, box on the next lap," she says, making my heart stop.

"What? No! I need to overtake him," I reply, groaning as we move through the next corner because my body, even though it's running on adrenaline, is so fucking tired.

"James, think," Ximena says, and I let her words sink in, truly sink in.

If I pit now, I'll have better tyres. I'll get to set faster lap times. I'll undercut him. He will come out behind me, but Gabriel will be ahead of me again.

"We'll serve it during the pitstop, right?"

"No, they want to put it onto your time at the end." *Fuck.* The fucking people in charge and their desire to do whatever they please.

"Understood. Tell me, what tires did they put on Gabriel?" I ask, making my way through the straights and corners.

"Intermediate." I hear the fucking smirk in her voice. I don't know what Grenzenlos was thinking, putting him on intermediates, but it plays in our favor.

It's all I need to know before making my way into the pits. My pit crew seems to be lightning fast as they change my tyres. From wets to hards. These will hopefully get me to the end of the race. If I manage them well.

As predicted, I come out behind Gabriel.

Also as predicted, he has to stop a lap later again because he's too slow on his intermediates. The racing line is dry enough now. Intermediates won't help.

I race down the track, taking chunks out of the gap between Cameron and me. Because the gap is closing quickly, he's called into the pits sooner than I think he'd want.

Cameron comes out behind me.

"What's the gap?" I ask Ximena.

"One-point-nine seconds," she replies.

Which means I have work to do.

There are twenty-two laps left. I need to gain another four seconds on Cameron to keep my first place. Unfortunately, my teammate is fast. The most time I get per lap for the next five laps is point-one second.

"Gap?"

"Two-point-seven, James," she replies.

I have fifteen laps left.

"Is he catching me?"

"No. Focus. Set your lap times, but I need you to be careful in corner twelve. You've just received a warning for track limits."

We don't speak for a while after that. The only communication I have with my race engineer is her giving me updates on the time gap between Cameron and myself.

Ten laps later, I have four seconds on him.

My tyres are starting to give up on me.

"How are Cameron's tyres looking?" I ask, breathless and sweaty. My suit is still wet from the rain.

"Degrading. Yours are older, but they look better. You're doing a good job, you tyre whisperer. You can push a little more," she says, so I do.

For the last five laps, I give it everything I've got without exceeding track limits again. I push so hard, it almost feels like I'll pass out as soon as I leave the car.

And when I cross the finish line for the last time, my country explodes into celebrations.

But I can't celebrate.

Not yet.

"Ximena, talk to me. What was the gap?" I ask her, fear in my chest.

"Five-point-one, James, you had more than five."

I start crying. I don't mean to, but I've never, ever won my home Grand Prix before. People are screaming my name. Without meaning to, I think about how proud my father would be right now, but I shove that thought aside to focus on everyone else that will be proud of me.

Damian will be ecstatic.

Adrian and Val will cheer for me.

My girls will be overcome with joy, so I focus on getting to them.

Tears are still falling down my cheeks when I park my car in front of the first place sign in the pits. I take a moment to sit and collect myself, but it's useless when my eyes find Estrella and Daisy, my wife crying at this victory, too.

Jumping out of my car, I don't even bother taking my helmet off. I simply run to them. My team is screaming, and I hug them all, but first I hug my girls. Since I can't hear them well with my earpieces in, I move on to hug the rest of my team first. Only once they all patted my back and hugged me do I take my helmet off and move back toward Estrella and Daisy.

Cupping her cheeks in the way I always do, I kiss my wife on her lips without hesitation. I don't know if I taste her tears or my own, but it doesn't matter. Nothing matters but the way she kisses me back.

"I'm so proud of you," she whispers right as I nuzzle my face in her neck. My other arm lifts to hug Daisy, too.

I almost say it. I almost tell her how I feel, say those three little words because of how high my emotions are running, but this is neither the time nor the place. So, I simply lean back, kiss Estrella's lips one more time, and then place a kiss on Daisy's temple.

"Good job, Daddy!" she exclaims, and my knees buckle immediately. It's only because I reach for the barrier separating us that I don't sink to the ground.

"Thank you, princess," I reply and hug her again.

She called me "Daddy."

She thinks of me as her father.

I never thought I could have two major victories in one day.

Estrella squeezes my arm, and I look at her to see she's also still crying.

This was supposed to be fake. This was never meant to last. This was a relationship born out of convenience, not love. But it was love that I got in return. And I'm not letting them go. Not unless they truly don't want me, and I hope that's not the case.

But then, how could I think anything else?

I'm the man whose feelings have never been reciprocated.

"James!" I turn around, watching an angry Valentina storm my way. She slams her gloves on the ground before ripping her helmet off. Once she's right in front of me, she lifts her index finger to point threateningly at me.

"Val—" I start, but she cuts me off before I can apologise.

"No, don't 'Val' me. Estrella, cover Daisy's ears," she says, and my wife doesn't hesitate to do so. Then, my best friend keeps yelling at me without really raising her voice at all. It's terrifying. "You push me off the fucking track one more time, and

I will take you out when we're not in our cars. I don't give a flying fuck how long we've been friends, I will teach you to fear dive-bombing me. Got it?"

Yeah, I messed up. There is no denying it. She didn't have to threaten me.

"I'm sorry," I say, but she shakes her head.

"That means shit to me right now. You fucked with my race, and all you got is a five-second penalty. That's bullshit, and you know it." She walks away right as I open my mouth to respond again.

"Uh oh, James is in troubleeee," Estrella says to Daisy, and I can't help but crack a smile at the way the little girl giggles.

Nothing in the world seems to matter when I take in Estrella's smile, too.

Chapter 45
Estrella

"We only get one shot at this," I say, looking each of the four women sitting at the table at James' house in the eye. "If they suspect what we're doing, it'll never work," I add, my hands shaking a little. Marbles purrs in my lap, rubbing her head against my arm to get me to keep petting her. I stroke her fur, letting the way she's become so attached to me comfort me.

I came up with this plan to get rid of Bert and Jennifer, to stop this custody battle from ever fully forming so we don't have to go to court, but I'll need their help. I can't do this without these four powerful women.

"Just get me in a room alone with them, Estrella. I'll take care of this for you," Chiara says, and the serious expression on her face makes me let out a nervous laugh.

"We're not killing Daisy's grandparents," Scarlette says and pokes her friend in the arm.

"Who said anything about killing? There is always the *seriously injure* option." That makes me chuckle.

"Violence is not an option," Nevaeh says. "It'll just get traced back to us."

"They wouldn't be able to trace it back to us. Have any of you heard from Leonard's old teammate Jonathan?" Chiara asks next, and I furrow my brows at her question.

"No?" Valentina says, looking as confused as I feel.

"Exactly," Chiara replies, crossing her arms as she leans back in her chair and gives each of us a look that says "see, my way works." Three out of five jaws drop at the table, but Scarlette rolls her eyes at the woman beside her.

"Okay, relax, Jonathan is alive. He was looking into joining NASCAR a few weeks ago."

Scar shoots Chiara a warning glance, but there's a hint of amusement on her face that I've never seen before. Scarlette is as bright and colorful as a rainbow, and Chiara is a slightly violent, grumpy thunderstorm.

"For now," Chiara whispers, and I almost fall out of my chair laughing.

I adore them all so much.

It's frightening because I'm so scared that as soon as James and I end our fake marriage, they'll all choose him. I mean, they've known him longer than they've known me. They love him more, but I'm not ready to lose everything I've built during this fake marriage.

"Estrella, honey, do you want to share what is going on in your head?" Valentina asks, reaching across the table to wrap her fingers around my balled-up fist.

"We will make your plan work," Nevaeh chimes in, giving me a comforting smile.

"It's not that. It's just—" I cut off to suck in a sharp breath, letting it out with a laugh. "You've all become important to me, and I'm scared I'll lose you when James and I end," I admit, my legs bouncing up and down from nerves. Marbles jumps off my lap because of the movement, and I feel even worse.

I have never shared my feelings like this. They all seem so fearless and strong, and I feel the opposite of that. My heart is hurting, and the family I've found here that has been a huge comfort to me is not even mine. It's James'.

At least that's what it feels like before Valentina opens her mouth.

"We are not going anywhere. Our friendship and love is not conditioned on whether you stay married to James. It is conditioned on whether you want us around, and as long as you do, we will be here. I told you this only recently, Estrella. You and Daisy are family. That will never change," she says, making a lump form in my throat that I have a hard time swallowing past.

"Yeah, you're stuck with us, sweetie. I know you didn't have a lot of people before this marriage, but no matter what, you have all of us now. You don't have to be scared. We promise we won't leave you behind. If we go anywhere, we're dragging you and Daisy with us," Nevaeh chimes in, and Scarlette gives an approving nod.

"*Estamos contigo, corazón, en las buenas y en las malas. Siempre nos tendrás a tu lado, siempre,*" Scar adds in Spanish. Chiara leans forward, propping her elbows on the table as she looks directly into my eyes.

"No man can come between us, especially not James. And I swear to God, if he ever hurts you, I'll—" Scar slaps a hand over Chiara's mouth and laughs.

"Sometimes, it's better to leave things to the imagination," she says, and I start laughing all over again.

"All I'm saying is, you have nothing to worry about, *bella*."

I drop my face into my hands to hide from their gazes and swallow back the overwhelming emotions pooling in my eyes. A hand appears on my upper arm, and I split my fingers just enough to see Nevaeh leaning forward and offering me comfort.

"You are not losing anyone else, Estrella. You've lost enough," she says, and I cover my eyes again because, this time, there is no holding back the tears.

Four sets of arms make their way around me, hugging me as I sob into my hands.

I'm not alone anymore.

I'm not alone anymore.

I'm not alone anymore.

Maybe if I chant it often enough in my head the information will eventually settle deep inside of me. But it's still so unbelievable. I don't know how to get used to having a group of people catch me when I fall.

"You're all to blame for these tears, by the way," I say once they step out of the hug, and Neveah wipes one away with a soft laugh escaping her lips.

"Don't worry, when Valentina, Scar, and Chiara took me in, I was also overwhelmed by the amount of love they threw my way. Unconditional and nonjudgmental. You'll get used to it," she assures me, but Chiara lets out a snort.

"I did judge you for your taste in art. You liked Colin Arden," she says and shudders.

"You only say that because he opened two of his art galleries right beside two of yours," Scar says, which makes Chiara shoot her a glare.

"Yeah, that *figlio di puttana* was trying to steal my business."

"Which is why I don't like his art anymore," Nevaeh assures her with a grin.

"Speaking of rivals," Valentina chimes in, trying to redirect the conversation. "I have been informed that you were asking about becoming a test driver for Hawke's new sports cars." A smile creeps onto my face at the memory of racing down the track in that beautiful Hawke.

"I said that more as a joke. What does that have to do with rivals, though?" I ask, a little curious to hear what else she's thinking.

"Well, what if it doesn't have to be a joke? Velocità Rossa is looking for test drivers for their sports cars. They haven't found anyone they want to permanently fill that position."

"Are you serious?"

"Yes. If you want, I can see if they're interested in interviewing you, maybe even letting you 'test' test drive," she says with a smile that makes even more hope bloom in my chest.

"But what about my job at the academy?" It's summer break, so we have a lot of business.

"It's safe, no matter what. I just thought that maybe you missed racing, so I wanted to offer," Valentina explains, and I let out a deep breath.

Test driving would be much less dangerous than racing against other drivers, but it would still allow me to be in the car. When I asked James if Hawke was looking for test drivers, I didn't think anything would come of it, but I should have known that if I asked Valentina, she would move heaven and Earth to find a way to help. To get another woman back into racing.

"Are you trying to steal my wife from my team?" James asks, catching me off-guard. My head whips his way in time to see Daisy running toward me.

"Mamá, Daddy bought me a huge kangaroo," she says, and I look past her to see my fake husband holding a kangaroo-shaped plushie that's almost the size of him in one hand and another giraffe-shaped one in his other. That one must be Damian's because the little guy keeps looking at it with excitement sparkling in his eyes.

I am also going to go ahead and keep ignoring the way Daisy calls James "Daddy" because if I let that truly process, I'll break down. This is what I was worried would happen, so I'll just blame it on Daisy being around Damian so much. Damian calls James "Daddy," so it makes sense Daisy sees him that way, too.

My logic is as flawed as my argument that this marriage is still fake.

"Are you eavesdropping?" Val asks, raising both her brows as if to tell him she's got him there. Which she does. The tension between them since last race's incident doesn't go past me, or anyone at the table for that matter, but I know James will find a way to make it up to Val.

"Perhaps, but only because you're trying to poach Estrella." I snort at that.

"Why? Hawke Racing has not hired me," I remind him as I hold onto Daisy's hand.

"Not yet," James replies with a wink. "Come on, Daisy, let's get ready for bed. Your mamá will tuck you in after," he adds, and my little girl runs straight toward him.

Whenever I have girls' night, I insist on being the one to tuck Daisy in because I always feel so horrible for choosing to spend my free time with anyone but her. It's gotten easier because everyone in my life has been telling me to take some time for myself, including my mother, but I think deep down, I'll always feel a twinge of guilt regardless.

"Reya," someone says, and I look down to see Damian approaching me with his stuffed toy dragging on the floor.

"Yes, sweetie?" I ask as he drops his head against me.

"Can you tuck me in, too? Dad doesn't do it as nice as you," he explains, which has my heart beating unevenly for several moments.

"Excuse me, ladies. I'll be back in a little," I say as I stand up.

Damian takes my hand, waiting for me to lead him to the bathroom where James is supervising Daisy as she brushes her teeth. If no one makes sure she actually does it, she will brush them for ten seconds and that's it. Damian is the same, so James hands his son his toothbrush with a firm look that says more than any words could.

Once they're both in their pajamas and ready for bed, James kisses the top of my head and lets me know he needs a shower.

"Who wants to be tucked in first?" I ask, and Daisy and Damian simultaneously scream, "ME!"

I end up tucking Daisy in first because Damian assures me he can wait. My daughter is fast asleep long before I even bring the blanket up to her chin, and I grin at the smile she wears on her face even in her sleep.

She must have had a great time with James and Damian at the carnival at the border between France and Monaco. I wanted to go, too, but I needed to speak to Chiara, Nevaeh, Scarlette, and Valentina, and it's difficult to find a day they're all in Monaco. They're too busy kicking ass and taking over the world.

"Reya?" Damian asks again right as I bring the blanket to his chin like I did with Daisy. "You're really cool," he says.

"You know what? So are you. I think you're the coolest little man I've ever met," I reply, tickling his sides until he giggles.

"What about my dad? Am I more cool than him?"

"Oh, absolutely." He gives me a toothy grin.

"I'm hurt," James whispers into the room, grabbing Damian's and my attention. He's standing in the door, leaning against the frame in nothing but some lounge pants and dripping wet hair.

"Then stop eavesdropping," I whisper back, making him chuckle.

"To be fair, Daisy told me you often share your racing stories with her before she falls asleep, so I was hoping to overhear you share one with Damian." I shake my head at him, disbelief and amusement battling to take over my features.

"Oh yeah, I wanna hear," Damian chimes in. I let out a sigh and pat the other side of Damian's bed, waiting for James to make his way there before I start talking.

"Six years ago, I was head-to-head with my rival in the championship standings. It was the last race of the season, and I was peeing my pants because of how nervous

I was," I say, making Damian giggle. James watches me with fascination. "We switched places for most of the race. I was first, then he was first. It was exhausting. I never sweat as much as I did that day. When a race is mentally and physically draining, it's hard enough to push past the exhaustion. Add the emotional side to it, wanting to win, and it becomes ten times harder to stay focused." I pause, watching James nod along to my words.

"I know exactly what that feels like," he admits, shame filling his eyes.

"I almost lost that day. I had lost the championship every year before that, whether it was by a lot or a little, it didn't matter. I lost. But that day, everything felt right. I knew the title was supposed to be mine. There was no doubt. It was only about how I would get there." James is hanging onto my every word.

"And how did you?" I notice Damian is fast asleep, but I have to answer James' question.

This isn't only my memory anymore.

This is about his future.

"I fought harder than I ever had before. I fought for myself. And I fought for the people I love. Their strength gave me what I needed." I cup his jaw, and he immediately leans into my touch. "It showed me I deserved that win, and no one was going to take it from me."

Chapter 46
Estrella

James has taken Damian, Daisy, and me on a family vacation.

Is it the best thing we can do a mere week before we're supposed to show up to court where a judge Bert and Jennifer probably bribed will decide we're not fit to raise Daisy?

Maybe not. But our plan is already in motion and all we need is to attend the dinner those evil people agreed to have with James and me.

Plus, Damian and Daisy are in preschool for another year since they both turn six after the school year starts. James and I agreed as long as they're not in elementary school, missing a couple of weeks to enjoy time with their family is fine.

Valentina gave me time off to go on a vacation with my family. On top of that, Dominique and Nicolette encouraged James to spend two weeks with Damian—a week of exploring Disney World here in Florida and a race week—so he didn't feel so disconnected from his son anymore. We've been going to parent coaching with Damian's moms too, and they always invite us to dinner afterward, so James has gotten to see his son more frequently already.

I've never seen my husband so happy since we met, with all of us around. It's almost like he can't quite believe we're real, but he's not trying to escape the fantasy. If anything, he seems to fall deeper with every moment we spend together. Or maybe I'm the one who keeps falling deeper, especially as I watch James walk ahead with Damian on his shoulders and Daisy's hand clasped in his. I take out my phone and snap a picture.

"God, they're so cute," Nevaeh says as she appears next to me, holding one of those massive churros they sell here.

"I know. I can't stand it," I reply, smiling despite my words.

"Tell your face that," Chiara replies, holding Leonora's hand. I notice Leonard walking a step behind her with Kieran. He looks a lot like his mother, but his eyes and hair are all Leonard.

"You know, considering you crashed my family vacation, you should be on your best behavior," I tell Chiara, but she cocks a brow and directs her scowl my way.

"We didn't crash your vacation. We simply told our kids about you going to Disney World, and they insisted on us joining," Leonard replies, and I almost burst into laughter when Kieran shoots him a devious look. "And I don't just mean Leonora and Kieran," he adds, nodding toward someone walking behind us.

"Oh my God, this place is amazing!" Adrian announces, his voice full of joy. I turn around to see him wearing Mickey Mouse ears and carrying a dozen plushies and souvenirs. "Why have we never come here before?" he asks Nevaeh, who gives her husband a soft look.

"Probably because I was afraid you might want to buy the place, and our bank account cannot support that," she replies, but she's grinning and grabbing his face to kiss him as soon as he stops in front of her. He kisses her back as fiercely.

"*Te ves feliz*," I say in Spanish once Julián walks toward us.

He's frowning, but he looks absolutely adorable wearing the same ears Adrian is. He's holding Scarlette's hand, but his sunshine wife is smiling so brightly, it blinds me for a moment.

"*Odio estas pinches cosas de turistas*," Julián replies, so Scarlette gives him a light nudge in the side. He simply snakes his arm around her and kisses the top of her head.

"He's always like this. If it were up to him, all we'd do is go on bike rides," she explains, which finally brings a small smirk to his face, an expression I've never seen on him before.

"*Bueno, no es lo único que haríamos,*" he adds, making a viscous blush take over Scarlette's face. Luckily, the only person who can understand us is Valentina, and she's too busy looking at Gabriel like a sunflower looks at the sun to listen.

"You're unbelievable," Scar murmurs, shaking her head.

Julián shrugs, then goes back to strolling around with his wife tucked against his side. I stare after them for a moment, a sense of longing hitting my chest when I realize they never have to wonder when their marriage will end. They went into it wanting it to last forever, no end date in mind.

A bond never to be broken.

Mine was only ever meant to be broken.

And it's something I have to keep reminding myself of because when James slips his hand from my waist to my stomach and pushes until my back is flush against his chest, I forget everything else. Then, his lips move to my cheek, trailing kisses toward my mouth and simultaneously tilting my head so he can claim my lips.

"I was waiting for you to follow us, but you never came," he says between kisses, making me smile against his mouth.

"I'm sorry, *bebé*. We have a lot of friends, and they distracted me," I reply, and it's that "we" that almost makes me shudder. It sounds like we're an actual married couple. And we aren't a "we," we're barely anything at all.

"I'll send them all away if it means I'll get one hundred percent of your attention," he replies, and I smile all over again.

"There is no need. I'm all yours now, *papi*," I say, and he steps back, his hand reaching out to cup my jaw in the way he always cups it. His thumb on one of my cheeks and the rest of his fingers on the other.

"Are you?" His eyes, blue as the sky currently is, are serious and full of something I'm not sure how to decipher.

I open my mouth to respond when Damian appears between us.

"Daddy, Daisy and I want to go on the carousel, but Uncle Adrian said we can only go if you also get on it," he says, putting his small hand on James' stomach. It takes the F1 driver a moment to manage to look away from me, but then he gives his son his full attention.

"Did he now? Well, good thing is, bud, I'm your dad. So, I get to make the rules. And I say you can go if you convince Uncle Adrian to get on the carousel with you," he replies, and I burst into laughter when Damian runs back to the Monegasque, tugging on his shirt.

Adrian listens closely to Damian before looking up and shooting James a dirty look. His best friend merely smiles back at him. Then, he turns to me and takes my hand, the intensity of his gaze enough to knock the air from my chest.

"James—" I start but cut off because I'm not certain what to say.

"You look absolutely devastating today, did you know that?" he asks, making my tensed-up shoulders fall as they relax.

"Thank you," I reply, feeling heat rush into my cheeks. "You look very handsome, too."

He does look very handsome. He's wearing something simple, shorts and a plain shirt, yet he looks as breathtaking as always. Maybe it's because his face is so chiseled, his lips are so full, his eyes are so bright, and his blonde hair is always perfectly styled. Maybe it's simply because of my feelings for him.

Maybe it's both.

"Come on. As funny as it will be to watch Adrian join Daisy and Damian on the carousel, they need to be supervised. I trust Adrian with them as far as I can throw him," he says, and I chuckle as I follow him toward where Nevaeh and Adrian have taken our kids. Daisy is holding onto Nevaeh and Damian is holding Adrian's hand, making my chest tighten all over again.

I don't think I'll ever get tired of the way this group of people have taken my daughter and me in, after we've been alone for so long. After I fell into a depression because of how lonely I was without any friends or family. It was a decision I made, but I couldn't breathe back home. I couldn't look anywhere without seeing Pedro and Helen. I felt them everywhere, as if they were watching me. It was an overwhelming grief I couldn't handle, and I didn't want to raise my daughter in that environment. This way, she's away from all of that pain.

She can be free.

And that's all I've ever wanted for Daisy.

We go on almost every ride. We spend hours at the park, and by the time nighttime comes around, Daisy and Damian are practically asleep. I'm carrying my daughter and James is carrying his son all the way back to our suite. We place them in the twin beds in their room, lingering for a moment as we watch them, passed out and with smiles on their faces from how happy they've been the whole day. Marbles and Lollipop stroll into the room, jumping on their beds and curling up at their feet. It's a ritual they do every time the kids share a room. Almost like they're protecting them.

"Why are they so cute?" I whisper to James, and he takes my hand in his, still watching his son.

"I don't know, but I love them so much." My back goes stiff at his words, and I feel him tense too when his fingers wrap even more tightly around mine. He's never said that before. I know he loves his son, but hearing he loves Daisy?

My knees almost buckle.

"James, you can't say that," I remind him, but he guides me out of the room because this is not a conversation we should have where Daisy could overhear us if she wakes.

We've done a good job keeping her in the dark about all of it. She doesn't know her grandparents are trying to take her away. She doesn't know James and I are fake married. She doesn't know anything that could either scare her or break her heart, and I want to keep it that way. At least until she's older.

James closes the door to our room and finally responds to my statement.

"Why can't I say that? It's true," he says.

My heart is hammering in my chest. I step toward him until our chests brush. His is falling and rising so quickly, I realize he's nervous. Only after taking a deep breath for courage does he speak again.

"Just like it's true that I've fallen in love with y—" I slap a hand over his mouth, stopping him from finishing the sentence.

"Don't," I whisper. "Don't say that. This isn't real. This will end after the dinner, if our plan goes well. We will get a divorce and this will end," I remind him, looking up at him and doing my best to swallow back the tears.

"Is that what you want?" he says against my hand, or at least I think it's what he says.

"I know we've been dating to see if this works, but it's one thing to go on dates when you can decide to go your separate ways if it doesn't work, and it's another entirely when you're forced, *through a marriage certificate*, to stay together. Maybe we're simply caught up in the moment and as soon as we get a choice, we'll never want to see each other again," I say, fearing the possibility of my words. James' fingers snake around my wrist, lifting my hand.

"How can you look at me and say that, Estrella? Haven't you felt what I've felt for the past seven, no, twelve months?" Of course I have. I have felt *everything* with him, but it doesn't change the facts.

"We made a deal. Marriage and exclusivity. You're *forced* to feel this way for me. I didn't allow you to look at anyone else. When that ends, when that isn't true anymore, how can you know for certain you'll still feel the same?"

I know I will. I know James is the person I could see myself growing old with, if only we gave ourselves the chance to fall in love without any responsibilities we've made to one another.

Who am I kidding?

I've been falling in love with this man since he told me he'd marry me.

I've been falling in love with him for so long, I didn't even realize when it became a fact instead of a possibility.

I love James Oliver Landon.

I love him like the stars love lighting up the sky alongside the moon.

I love him so much, I'm scared he won't love me as soon as he's a free man again.

I can't lose anyone else, but forcing him to stay in this marriage once we pull off our plan is cruel.

"There is no changing your mind tonight, is there, my little star?" he asks, and I shake my head.

"There is no changing my mind because there is no way you could ease my worries. Because *you don't know*." He gives me a thoughtful look, tracing my features with his gaze.

"Then we will wait to decide anything until after we're rid of Bert and Jennifer. Once we have a choice, you'll see I will choose you. I'll choose you time and time again, darling, because you're the person I've been looking for my whole life." He takes another step toward me, but my heart hurts so much, I can barely stand it. "You're my little star."

"Please stop," I beg, and he nods several times.

"Tell me what you need from me, Estrella." He cups my chin again, making my eyes flutter shut.

"Make me forget. For tonight, please make me forget about all of it." James rubs his thumb along my bottom lip, kisses me briefly, and then pulls back again.

"Get on your knees, wife. Let me take your mind off it," he says, his voice low and firm.

Excitement runs down my spine as I sink to my knees without hesitation. It's a relief to be allowed to let go. To release the tight hold I have on control.

"Yes, sir," I reply as I lower myself.

James gives my hair a soft stroke as he towers over me.

"Good girl."

Chapter 47
James

I thought I knew what it felt like to be in love. I was so convinced it was what I felt for Valentina my whole life.

I was so fucking wrong.

This all-consuming, ever-evolving, and agonizingly beautiful feeling I have whenever I'm with Estrella or even think about her…that's what being in love feels like. Like a reprieve, a place your heart finds its home in. She didn't even tell me if she reciprocates my feelings. Maybe Estrella will be another person who doesn't feel the same for me as I do for them but, fuck, now I know what it truly feels like.

It feels like salvation.

And having Estrella on her knees, her palms on her thighs and her eyes trained on the floor like the perfect little submissive when we both know as soon as we step out of the bedroom, she's the one in charge has me questioning things I never thought I would. Like how the fuck I'm going to drop to my knees, beg, and fight for this woman to keep me in her life.

"Look at me, darling," I say softly, and she doesn't waste a second, lifting her head so her eyes meet mine. She's so beautiful. Those eyes of hers… I think I could stare into them forever.

"You look so handsome," she says, but she doesn't reach out to touch me. She merely waits. "I love it when you get like this. You're a dom, but you're a soft dom. Always taking care of me and my pleasure. Always praising me."

My knees turn to putty.

Humiliating a submissive isn't what gets me off. I like the power play, but I love the praise more. The partners I've had in the past have never seen me the way Estrella sees me.

"I'll always take care of you, my beautiful wife." My body is trembling as I drop my hand to her throat and apply the smallest amount of pressure. "Tell me about a kink you've always wanted to explore," I say.

Estrella's mouth curls at the corners when her eyes fall shut and she enjoys my touch.

"We've tried bondage, sensory deprivation, spanking, and overstimulation," I go on, and she gives me an eager nod. "Is that all you've ever wanted to try?" Almost immediately, Estrella shakes her head.

"There's more," she admits, her eyelids fluttering open again so she can look at me.

"Be my good girl and tell me, little star. I want to know," I say as I squat down in front of her, my grip on her throat tightening a bit, making her moan.

"Temperature play," she says after swallowing hard. "And roleplay," she adds, licking her lips. My gaze drops to her mouth, fixating on it as I restrain myself from kissing her.

"Which one would you like to do tonight?"

I don't want to overwhelm her by combining two new kinks she hasn't tried before. I've done both and love playing with temperature more.

"The first one. With ice cubes." I give her a soft kiss, showing her how proud I am of her for sharing this with me.

"Would you like to be tied up or blindfolded while we play with the ice?" I ask, watching her give me an eager nod. "Which one, Estrella?"

She shudders, biting her lip as I squeeze her throat again.

"Tied up, please."

I stroke her jaw with my thumb, taking another moment to merely study her face, the way she shakes like always when she's so turned on, and how carefree she looks.

She trusts me with her body, with her pleasure, and I will use any permission given to touch her, kiss her, take her mind off all the worries running around in her head.

"Take off your clothes for me, then get on the bed. I'll get the ice." I stand up, but she grabs my hand, remaining on the floor.

"James?" It's the first time she hesitates following instructions in the bedroom. I tilt my head down to look at her.

"Yes, darling?"

"Kiss me." Uncertainty fills her eyes when I hesitate. "Please," she adds, her voice breaking on the word.

My lips crash onto hers. There is nothing calm and calculated about the way I kiss Estrella. There is no rhyme or reason. There is only *need*. Pure, raging need to have her taste in my mouth, in my bloodstream, everywhere it can possibly go inside my body.

My tongue slips into her mouth to play with hers, but I pull it out to nibble on her bottom lip and make her moan. My hand moves back around her throat, squeezing gently. It's always gentle, never forceful. But I know she enjoys a little pain with her pleasure. So I reach up and tug on her hard nipple, making her cry out in pleasure.

"More," she begs, but I shake my head, breaking our kiss.

"Get on the bed. I'll give you more after," I promise, and she finally jumps up, reaching for her dress and slipping it off.

My cock is already so unbearably hard, looking at her undress has my self-control slipping through my fingers like sand. I barely manage to hang on to a few kernels and look away, stepping out of the room and toward the mini fridge/freezer thing they have at this hotel. I put some ice in there earlier because Estrella doesn't like to drink room-temperature water. She needs it cold, so I always make sure there is ice around or at least a fridge where I can stock water bottles.

I wonder if she's noticed.

But if she had, she'd know how in love I am with her. She'd know I'd give her my life, every portion of it, if it made her happy. She'd know my entire body revolts against the thought of getting a divorce from her.

Perhaps she has noticed. Maybe she even knows all of it. Maybe hearing the words out loud just scares her, but they don't scare me anymore. They used to. I fought against them with every fibre of my being, but not anymore. Instead of fighting myself, fighting the inevitable, I'll fight *for* her. For our future.

I take a deep breath outside of our room door, pushing all of those thoughts away. Tonight isn't about love and all of its complicated components. Estrella wants sex, to be distracted by pleasure, and as her husband and the man who worships the very ground she walks on, how could I possibly deny her a single thing?

Estrella is on the bed, completely naked and waiting for me. Her long brown hair frames her body in a way that makes me even weaker in the knees. There's a soft smile on her face, anticipation making her chest rise and fall abruptly.

"On your back, Estrella. Let me see how wet you are, how ready for me," I say, my own heart racing in anticipation.

My body is humming with need, my cock pressing against my boxers and jeans uncomfortably. It wants to be inside Estrella. Needs to be. But it's not time for that yet. We're playing, and I'm not going to slip inside my wife until I'm good and ready. Which will be after her first or third orgasm.

"Are you excited, darling?" I ask as I step toward my bag, pulling out the rope I always bring with me when Estrella joins me on trips. Just in case.

"Yes, sir. Very," she says as she leans back. "Let me show you," she adds before letting her legs fall apart, revealing her soaking wet pussy.

Her clit is swollen, and I lick my lips at the thought of pulling it into my mouth. Licking it. Playing with it until she comes all over my mouth. Flick my tongue over that piercing, too.

"Then let's get you tied up so I can put my mouth on you," I say, and she gives me another of those eager nods.

Whenever I tie Estrella up, I take my time. At home, it's easier because I have the loops on the corners of the bed to slip the rope through, but I have to be creative today. Meticulously, I wrap the rope around her wrists, careful not to make them too tight.

"Good?" I ask, and she grins up at me, flashing me that smile of hers.

Once Estrella's wrists are tied to the bed frame with the rope, I pull my shirt off and then my trousers. Her eyes focus on my chest and abs, tracing my body with her gaze. My cock somehow gets even harder, and I refrain from groaning because fuck, she doesn't even have to touch me for my body to react. A single gaze is all it takes.

"Tell me your safe word," I say to distract myself.

"Red flag," she replies. "Yellow flag if I want to slow down. Green flag to keep going. So very motorsport of us," she teases, and I smile back at her, my fingers itching to touch her.

"I'm going to use the ice now, okay? If you don't like it, we'll stop immediately," I assure her, reaching for the bag of ice.

"I know, husband. I know I hold all the power." Good. Because she does. "And I want this. Please touch me."

There is no wasting time, not when Estrella begs. I take an ice cube in my hand, the cold of it sending a thrill through me. I move onto the bed, straddling my wife's hips as I bring the ice cube to her lips.

"First, I'll give you the ice cube. Then, I'll replace it with my mouth," I inform her, pulling the cube off her mouth and putting mine on hers to make my point.

I feel her smile against me.

Then, I repeat the process with her neck and nipples. I circle her right one with the cube, watching it pebble from the cold. Estrella sucks in a sharp breath and presses her legs together, watching me as I remove the cube to suck her nipple into my mouth. As I play with it, I put the cube on her other one, then put my mouth on that one seconds later.

"Oh fuck!"

She's writhing beneath me, pushing her hips off the bed in search of friction. My cock is hovering perfectly over her clit, so she rubs against me, and I almost come in my boxers from the simple contact. I bite down on her nipple a little in warning, and Estrella cries softly, still rubbing against me.

"Estrella," I say, the cube now melted as I bring my hands to her hips to push them down.

"It feels so good. The coldness of the ice, the heat of your mouth. It feels amazing. Do it to my clit, please," she begs, but I shake my head.

"I'll do it to your clit once I'm done with the rest of your body."

"Will you at least let me grind against your magnificent thigh?" The naughty smirk on her face tells me everything I need to know.

"Compliments will not always get you what you want, little star," I say, but I'm moving around until my thigh moves between her legs so I'm straddling her thick thigh.

"But today they will?" I reach for another cube as she asks the question, leaning back again until my lips brush her ear.

"Today, yes. Rub your needy little pussy against my thigh, but don't come. I want you to come with my mouth on you and fingers buried deep inside of you."

She tugs on her restraints like she wants to reach out and touch me, and I smile as I nip at her neck, trailing kisses down her cleavage. Estrella grinds against my thigh as I run the cube over her chest, then lick the path of water left behind.

"Fuck. Yes. Oh fuck," she moans, her rubbing becoming more frantic as she rolls her hips faster and faster. "I don't think I can stop. I'm so close, James." I slide my leg out of her reach immediately, hearing a grunt of complaint from her.

"A little longer, darling," I mumble between licks and kisses.

I take my time. One, two, three more ice cubes melt as I make my way down her body, teasing her by putting the cube everywhere but on her clit. She trembles and whines, begging me to touch her clit, but I keep teasing her. I even remove my boxers to make her wait longer.

But eventually, I'm the one who can't deal with the ache in my cock anymore. I can't deal with my mouth watering at the sight of her swollen pussy, begging for my attention. So, I press the ice cube to it, hearing Estrella cry out before clamping her mouth shut to stay quiet. She's rolling her hips against the ice, and I add a bit more pressure before removing it and putting my mouth on her clit, sucking hard.

Estrella pants out several things in Spanish, rubbing against my face as her body keeps trembling.

There is something so very intimate about going down on someone. I've always enjoyed it, but I've never enjoyed it *this* much. I could spend hours buried in Estrella's pussy, making her come over and over. Study every inch of her. Play with her piercing.

I find myself grinding against the mattress to ease the tension in my cock as I lick and suck, slipping two fingers inside of her and curling them. She keeps tugging on the rope, pushing off the bed to get closer to my face and chase her orgasm. Her thighs bracket my head, but I love it. I love how she loses control when we're in this position.

"Come for me, darling. Let me feel it," I say right as I find her G-spot and stroke it. My mouth is still on her clit as she orgasms, and I keep licking, letting her ride out her pleasure.

And she does.

This might be the longest I've felt her orgasm yet, and I already want to make it happen again. I slip my fingers out of her and put my mouth on her inner thigh as she keeps trembling, still high from pleasure.

"James," she says a few minutes later, and I realise I was getting lost in tracing her pussy with my lips, kissing every centimetre of it and tasting her orgasm. She tastes so fucking good.

"Yes, my wife?"

"I want to touch you. Run my hands through your hair as you slip inside me," she explains, and my grip on her thighs tightens as I let her words roll through me. "Please untie me so I can," she begs, always such a fucking sweet sound.

"Okay," I manage to croak out, but it takes me a moment to turn my arms from putty back into muscles.

Then, I push off the bed and crawl up her body, still between her legs. My cock rubs over her clit as I undo the knots of the rope on her wrists, and I almost shake in response.

"That feels good," she says as she grinds against me, sighing at the contact. "You always feel so good. So hard and perfect." My hands fly to each side of her, gripping the pillows so hard, my knuckles turn white. But it's all I can do to keep from falling apart and spraying my cum all over her stomach instead of filling her up.

And I do like to fill her up.

"Estrella, stop playing. I'm trying to undo these bloody knots," I say firmly, cursing when she digs her heels into my ass to close the distance between us. The head of my cock presses to her entrance in response, and I shiver as a wave of pleasure rolls through me. "Keep it up and instead of fucking your pussy, I'll fuck my hand and make you watch," I say and she gasps dramatically, making me chuckle.

"You. Wouldn't. Dare."

There are no fucking words for how desperately in love I am with this woman.

"Test me, Estrella. See what happens."

She lies perfectly still after that. Once her hands are free, I guide them to my hair, and she doesn't waste a second to slide her fingers into it, tugging to get me closer.

"I need you," she says, pushing off the bed to kiss me. And I can feel she doesn't just mean right now. She doesn't just mean sex. She needs me the same way I need her.

"You have me," I promise her right as I press the head of my cock inside of her. "I'm not going anywhere." Another promise that falls from my lips with ease as I sink another centimetre inside of her. She clings to my cock, welcoming me and squeezing me at the same time. I'm breathless as I add, "For as long as you'll have me, I'll be right by your side. I'll be yours."

Estrella kisses me to shut me up, but it's just as well. I can't speak anymore. Pleasure is clouding my mind as I drive all the way inside of her, making us gasp at the same time.

My strokes are messy. They're fast, then slow. Hard, then soft. I spread her legs to go even deeper, and Estrella takes every centimetre of me with moans of pleasure and pure contentment. I'm so worked up from playing, I keep having to slow down to keep my orgasm at bay. But my perfect, naughty wife only uses that opportunity to squeeze my cock with her walls.

It's the sweetest torture.

Within minutes, she's clamping around me as her body shakes through yet another orgasm, but this time, she takes me right over the edge with her. My balls have drawn so tight that the release has me seeing stars. I keep fucking into her, keep going as I fill her with my cum.

Every time I'm inside Estrella without a condom, I lose myself to her even more. Because this is the only way I want to have sex anymore. With her, without a barrier.

We stay in bed for several minutes after I've cleaned my cum off her when it dripped out, right after pushing it back inside her with a smirk on my face. Estrella's moan was all the assurance I needed that she liked it as much as I did.

We're cuddling, our heartbeats perfectly uneven. I trail my fingers along the tattoos on her arm, and she runs hers over my abs, tracing them.

"Thank you for taking my mind off it," Estrella mumbles, and I press a soft kiss to the crown of her head, inhaling her floral scent in the process. "For taking care of me."

"I'm not done yet. We still have aftercare, and I plan on washing you and wrapping you in a blanket before cuddling again." She relaxes even further against me at my words, and I keep stroking her arm.

Then, I do everything I promised her, and I stay awake late into the night, watching my wife sleep and rubbing my thumb over her engagement ring and wedding band.

Chapter 48
Estrella

WE'RE MEETING BERT AND Jennifer for dinner tonight.

Our plan is officially in motion.

Nevaeh is at the hotel here in Miami, watching Leonora, Kieran, Daisy, and Damian. She insisted to stay with the kids instead of coming along today, and I couldn't be more grateful. Daisy is very comfortable around Nevaeh, so I know she'll be happy to spend some time with her... friend? *Tía*?

I don't know anything anymore.

I still haven't recovered from James admitting he loves her. From when he was about to admit he was in love with me. I'm not in denial. Even though I cut him off, I know what he was about to say, but my argument stands. Maybe having to be fake married is the reason he developed these feelings. And there is no way to know. Not while we *have to* be together.

"Take a deep breath, darling. For me," James says, lifting his finger to my neck to stroke his thumb along my nape in relaxing, circular motions. I inhale, my eyes fluttering shut. "That's it. Everything will be fine. I promise." I hate myself for believing him.

"They're late," I say through gritted teeth, my irritation settling everywhere. We have one shot at this because if Bert and Jennifer figure out what we're up to, we won't get what we need.

Proof.

"It's a power play," James says, still caressing my neck. "They think this intimidates us, but it does the opposite. It angers us, and the angrier we get, the more ruthless we will get." I let out a sigh when he rubs out a knot in my neck.

"I'm scared," I admit, and he gives me a few nods, acknowledging my words.

"I've got you. I'm not going anywhere. You're not alone."

I both hate and love it when he reminds me of that.

How could I feel alone with this beautiful man sitting beside me? The person who has never been loved the right way in his life. The husband I didn't need but want so much now, it makes my heart beat a little unevenly every time I think about not having a future with him.

"If I kiss you, will you slap me in the face for the bad timing or will it distract you like I hope it will?" he asks.

"Maybe slapping you will make me feel better," I say with a nervous laugh, and James bursts into laughter.

"Okay, but aim for the left side. The right side is my good side," he replies, but I close my eyes and lean forward to kiss him instead.

His hand lifts from my neck to my chin, cupping it as he deepens the kiss. My hands find his magnificent thighs, and I almost sigh when he nips my bottom lip and tightens his grip.

One kiss, and I'm somewhere else. I'm in the fantasy land James takes me to where worries don't exist and I can be happy.

But fantasies only exist for so long before reality comes crashing back in.

"Are we interrupting something?" I attempt to pull back, but James' grip on me tightens even more to keep me in place. Then, he kisses my lips one, two, three more times before leaning back and glaring at Bert.

"Do not interrupt me again while my wife is kissing me," he warns, his accent thick and his voice low. I almost shudder, but not in a bad way. Not at all. "You're late," he points out next, perfectly composed despite the angry expression consuming his features.

"Well, I was on the phone with my lawyer, telling him you wanted to meet us to discuss something. I told him I'm assuming it's about the money I was asking for," Bert replies.

"That's exactly what we're here for. So, why don't you sit down, shut your mouth for once, and let us give you the contract I had *our* lawyer draw up for this?"

Jennifer's eyes meet mine at that very moment. The eye contact is making me more uncomfortable than anything else. Especially because she gave those eyes to Helen. Daisy inherited them. Looking at hers for that long makes me feel things I'd much rather not address.

"Now that's good news! Finally, you've come to your senses. Let me see that contract," Bert says as he sits down, and Jennifer follows his lead and settles in the seat beside him.

"First, we need to discuss what this will mean," I say, feeling my heart race.

One shot.

We have one shot.

"You don't have to say it out loud, Estrella," Bert starts, butchering the pronunciation of my name again. "We're not stupid." I actually burst out laughing.

James snickers beside me.

"I beg to differ, so just to be safe, I'll dumb down the deal, and you'll let me know what you think of it. Okay?" The scowl he throws my way is downright dangerous, but I've never been intimidated by men like Bert.

The only thing I'm intimidated by is the judge I'm convinced he has in his pocket. Because no matter what I say, what evidence we bring, there is a chance they won't give a shit.

"We will give you ten million US dollars in exchange for you dropping this ridiculous child custody battle. Your revenge will be complete," I say, and James leans forward, staring at Bert with a scowl that has even me shifting in my seat.

"And we will get to keep our daughter where she rightfully belongs. In her home. With her brother and friends." My attention drifts to Jennifer, who looks at the table with a blank expression.

What is it with her?

Concentrating on her, on the pity I feel for her, is a whole lot easier than thinking about James calling Daisy *our* daughter. Calling Damian her brother.

"Yeah, fine. If we're ten million dollars richer, well, I don't have to tell you how it'll feel to be rich," Bert says with a laugh directed at James. "If you don't forget the feeling as soon as the money hits my bank account."

"And in a few months, I'll have made double as much. Let's just get this over with," my husband replies.

As much as I appreciate his nonchalance and confident, cocky demeanor right now, I know giving ten million dollars to Bert is a big deal. He has the money—of course he does, he's a fucking F1 driver, he makes more in a year—but no one would ever simply give it away.

"Sign the contract so we can be done with it," James adds, and I nod once, even if no one is paying me any attention.

Bert is busy reading through the contract, Jennifer is still staring at the table, and, even though his hand is on my thigh as he squeezes it reassuringly, James isn't looking at me either. But his comfort is enough. I place my hand on his, allowing myself to glance around the restaurant. Adrian, Valentina, and Gabriel are sitting at a table, all of them listening to this conversation. And so are Leonard, Chiara, Scarlette, Julián, and Cameron, who are at two other tables to make this place look like we didn't book it out fully to make sure it's just us here.

"I think I would like to up this number. Double it, since you're just going to make it in a few months." James leans back in his chair and snorts.

"Absolutely not. I know something's wrong with you, but this is too far. I can't give you twenty million. On what fucking grounds?" Bert slides the contract back toward James.

"Well, the mental health of a parent is very important in determining whether they are capable of raising their child. Estrella has a history of depression. We don't."

My heart sinks at the mention of my mental illness being used in such a way.

To take my daughter from me.

"It was only mild depression, and I didn't even get medication prescribed. You can't use that against me. I did everything right. I got help. I went to therapy. I have found ways to manage my symptoms so I can be the best parent for Daisy. All you've ever done is ignore her existence until you decided she was the best way to get revenge on your dead daughter and my dead brother," I rant, my heart racing as I stand up, too angry to keep sitting. "Going against their will isn't going to change the facts. Helen chose Pedro. She was happy with him. She chose him over you, something she wouldn't have even had to do if it weren't for your racist tendencies."

Bert is up and reaching for me as soon as the last word has left my lips. But he never makes contact. Someone has his arm behind his back and his face pressed into the table before he can do anything.

"Let me go!" he screams, and I almost smile when his face contorts in pain.

"No," Chiara says, shooting Jennifer a warning look. It tells her not to get involved, not that Daisy's "grandmother" made any attempt to protect her husband.

"I will sue you for everything you're worth," he barks, but Chiara merely cocks an unimpressed brow.

"You can try, but you won't get Daisy. Estrella and James now have eight witnesses that your reasoning for wanting to take their daughter away is revenge. Even a bribed judge won't be able to help you win that custody battle," she says and finally releases him, stepping back right as our friend group—our family—moves toward the table to glare at Bert.

"You set me up?" he asks after straightening out his back. I get a little satisfaction from the way he flinches when he rolls his shoulder and *a lot* of satisfaction from the panicked look on his face as he looks at my family. "It doesn't change a thing. I will—"

"Stop it! Just stop it, Bert. I can't do this anymore."

I almost fall backward onto the chair.

"Your plan isn't going to work. And it shouldn't. Daisy doesn't belong with us. She belongs with Estrella." Shock has my jaw glued shut, preventing it from letting me speak.

"How could you do this? How could you turn on me? Her family took Helen from us!"

"No, you did that. You pushed her away. You made her choose. And she died so far away from us. I didn't even get to say goodbye," Jennifer says before bursting into tears and throwing her napkin from her lap onto the empty plate. Val shoots me an unsure look, but all I manage to do is shrug. "We're not taking Daisy. I will call the judge to tell him we won't be fighting for custody."

This has Bert exploding into a rant about how horrible of a wife she is, but she's having none of it.

"I can't be a part of this anymore. I'm done. And I'm done with you, Bert. Goodbye," she says and stands up to storm out of the restaurant. He follows her, and I sink back into my chair.

My heart is racing. I'm nauseous. My head is spinning.

But…

"Is it over?" I ask James, and he drops back into his seat to take my hand in his.

"They have no case. They don't even have a functioning marriage, something we all just witnessed," he says, and I do my best to take deep breaths to hold back my tears.

"Okay," I say. "Okay."

I repeat the word several more times until I finally break down when James wraps his arms around me.

I sob even harder when more sets of arms follow, mumbling how grateful I am for them all. They probably can't hear me, but I need them to know anyway.

"I love you all. Thank you so much."

"We love you, Estrella, and we're always going to be there for you," Scarlette replies as I sob against James' chest again.

All of the worry I've been feeling for the past year finally lifts off my shoulders.

We're safe.

We're going to be okay.

No one's taking Daisy away from me.

Chapter 49
James

Estrella hasn't let Daisy out of her sight since the drama with Bert and Jennifer at the restaurant. Not that the little girl seems to mind. My wife has also been keeping my son extra close, and I can't help but stare at them instead of getting ready for the race.

"Let's go, Man-In-Love. You're starting from pole, and I'm going to need you to focus," Daiyu says, and I throw her a look over my shoulder, begging with my eyes to let me have another moment just staring at them, but she shakes her head.

"Fine. I'll focus."

I've got a family to make proud, after all.

Having Damian here, at his first race in years, has me giddy all over again. He's been talking non-stop about how cool it is that I'm number one. I tried to explain to him that I'm leading by twenty-four points—I had extended my lead, but we've had a race since summer break, and I only came in third while Cameron won. My son didn't care about the points.

But I care.

The points are important, especially with only seven races left. Over the years, F1 has tried to do more races a year, but all of us drivers were so burned out, they decided to go back to twenty. I know some fans were upset, but I actually think it's better this way.

We risk our lives every single time we get into the car. I'm glad we get to spend more time with our families now.

After kissing Damian and Daisy on top of their heads and placing my forehead against Estrella's as I mumble, "You mean everything to me," I get ready for the race. I don't give her time to respond because I know Estrella isn't ready to admit she loves me. She needs distance to see I would choose her every time.

Daiyu and I rush through my warm-up before I have to make my way to where we drivers have to line up to listen to the national anthem. Miami's heat is weighing heavily on all of us as we stand there in our racing suits, me with my sunglasses pushed up the bridge of my nose and everyone else with their team caps on.

"Cheer up, buttercup, you're starting from pole. Aren't you excited?" Adrian says as we line up on the grid to listen to the national anthem.

"Not particularly. Plus, I have a feeling that by the end of this race weekend, my wife is going to leave me," I blurt out, voicing my fear for the first time since Bert and Jennifer had their marital spat in front of us.

"Fake wife, you mean," Adrian corrects, but I shoot him a glare so foul, he takes a step back and raises his hands in mock surrender. "Okay, sorry, touchy subject. Anyway, I'm teasing, mate. Everyone can see this is as fake as my feelings for Nevaeh. Minus twenty percent," he says with a wink, his sunshine smile covering his face again.

"Is it obvious for everyone? Because I'm pretty sure Estrella would say the opposite, and I have no bloody idea how to make her believe none of what I feel is fake or the result of us being forced to be together," I explain, clearing my throat when Val and Gabriel appear.

I've apologised multiple times and bought her a new simulator setup, so she's no longer angry with me for pushing her off the track a few weeks ago. The tension between us isn't there anymore, but I do see the pity in her eyes that lets me know she heard what I said.

Her next words only confirm it.

"Sometimes, a bit of distance can put things into perspective. I know Gabriel thinks that when he left it was the worst thing he could have ever done, but it also showed us that we'd crack the Earth in half to be together," she says, and her husband's arms wrap around her.

"I knew Nevaeh was my future. I knew she was everything to me, but having that confirmation that the distance between us gave me didn't hurt. It only solidified my beliefs. So, Val is right. It isn't always a bad thing. Just make sure she knows it's not forever if you don't want it to be. Make sure she knows you love her," Adrian adds, and I shake my head.

"She won't let me tell her I love her. I tried to tell her and she slapped a hand over my mouth," I explain, and Gabriel raises both of his brows in surprise. "What?"

"Well, if I were you, I'd ask myself why she's so afraid of the words when we've all seen the way you show her how in love you are with her," he suggests, and it's my turn to pull my features into a surprised expression.

"What do you mean?" Gabriel takes Val's hand in his, lacing his fingers through hers just enough to stare at their rings side by side.

"I mean, everyone can see how in love you are with her. She knows. Your actions have spoken louder than any words, but it's the words that scare her, no? Why? If she already knows, why is that confirmation so terrifying?" This silences all of us, and when Cameron approaches, a skip in his step, he catches the serious vibe immediately.

"You all look like you're planning to kill someone. Who is it? I vote Adrian," my teammate says, making the blonde uncross his arms as his jaw drops.

"Me? Why not Mr. Pretty Boy over there?" Adrian asks and points at Gabriel.

"Well, he's been my best friend for over a decade. You've been a pain in the arse," Cameron teases, nudging Adrian, but Gabriel's the one to respond.

"And why the hell would it be me, Adrian?" Val is snickering to herself.

"Because I couldn't say my sister since I'd sooner die than let anything happen to her, and threatening James is like threatening a starving lion that already wants to rip your head off, which leaves you," Adrian explains, but we're all interrupted by someone telling us to line up for the anthem. "Thank God, I don't think the hole I was digging for myself could have gone any deeper," he whispers to me, and I burst into uncontrollable laughter.

The anthem is sung by a group of people, and as soon as it's over with, I make my way back to Daiyu. She's already waiting for me to finish our pre-race rituals. Since it's so hot, Daiyu tells me to lift my shirt to spray my chest with some cool water. The camera that records live footage for the television channels decides to point to me at the same moment Daiyu sprays me, and I can't help but chuckle.

Then, it's time to zip up my suit, put my balaclava on, and slip my helmet on my head. Once seated in the car, Daiyu hands me my gloves, and I let the whole word drift away to focus on this race. Cameron is starting second, which means he'll be fighting me from the first corner.

There aren't a lot of points between us, so today is important.

The formation lap passes by torturously slowly, but we're all lined up on the grid again long before I have the chance to calm my racing heart.

"Sky's clear. Plans are set. You got this," Ximena says, and I let out a shaky breath.

Light. Light. Light. Light. Light.

Then they all disappear.

My car shoots forward as I press the proper buttons on my steering wheel to shift into gear, pushing down on the gas pedal at the same time.

Everything is going well. I manage to keep Cameron behind me through the first lap, which allows me to create a gap between us to get my teammate out of my DRS zone.

Nothing spectacular happens, at least not that I notice.

But that's when I hear Ximena's voice.

"You've almost kissed the wall on your entry in the chicane twice. Be more careful," she says, and I grit my teeth as I make my way through three more corners.

"Don't call it that. I don't want my wife to think I kiss anyone but her." She doesn't let me hear it, but I know Ximena snorts at my response.

I do my best to avoid the wall by going more right in the chicane, but the second time I try to do so, my car doesn't react to me. My rear hits the barrier, and I spin until I hit the wall. The impact knocks the breath out of me, but there is nothing I can do except brace myself.

"James?" Ximena asks, tears stinging my eyes.

"No," I mumble, my breath coming out quickly. "No, no, no, NO!" I scream, hitting my steering wheel over and over. "Fuck!"

"James, are you okay?" Ximena asks, but I shake my head.

"I'm sorry. That's all on me. I'm so sorry."

It's my fault. I've just lost a race. My team is going to have to work and pay so much to fix my car. My championship lead could be completely eradicated if Cameron wins.

Tears stream down my face inside my helmet, and I let them.

This is all my fucking fault.

It's one thing to give interviews when you have a race result you're content with. It's another when you're angry at yourself for being the biggest fuck up the world has ever seen.

Add reporters who want to pour salt into my open wounds to the mix, and I am very quickly running out of patience, especially because I haven't been able to see Damian, Daisy, and Estrella once since my crash.

"James, it's nice to see you," Gillian from *Griffin Sports*, one of the worst reporters in F1, says as I approach him with my PR officer, Angie. "I'm very sorry about how your race ended. Can you walk us through exactly where you think you messed up today?" My eyebrows pull together on their own accord, so, truly, there is no stopping the unimpressed expression appearing on my face.

"Well, I knew I fucked up when I hit the bloody wall. How's that?" I ask, smiling at him despite wanting to punch him.

Gillian has the nerve to laugh.

"I would think so, yes. My next question is about the championship standings. Since Cameron won today and snatched the fastest lap point for himself, he is now leading by two points. How do you feel about that?"

"Not great. I had a lead, I started the season well, and now my teammate is first in the standings. Valentina has caught up as well. There are six races left, and I have to make sure I come out on top, so, honestly, how do you think I feel?" With all of this pressure, it's a wonder I'm still standing upright.

"What are your next steps?" Gillian asks instead of dignifying my response with one of his own.

"I'll have to watch the footage again and see what I did wrong. I also have to speak to my team to see what we can do next. Otherwise, there is nothing I can do. The race is over. The standings are what they are. All I can do is focus on Las Vegas."

Which is the next race. In two weeks.

Two weeks later, it's the Mexican Grand Prix.

One week after that is *Día de los Muertos*, and I wanted to surprise Estrella with plane tickets to her parents' house. She told me she hasn't been able to go back and celebrate this holiday with her family, but I was hoping she would like to with me by her side.

Now, I know nothing.

We haven't spoken, but I'm dreading our conversation because I have a feeling I know exactly what will happen. And I'm not ready to lose my daughter and the woman I've become very certain is the love of my life.

Because if she isn't, then that concept isn't real.

If she is, I don't think I could survive living a life without her as my wife.

Chapter 50
Estrella

Two weeks have passed since James' crash. We came back from Miami twelve days ago, and Damian and Daisy have gone back to preschool without a single complaint. I'm sure they were too excited to tell all of their friends about Disney World and the race weekend to mind going back. I've been working almost every single day, and James has been training even harder than ever before. He's in the simulator so much, he hasn't once slept in our—his—bed with me.

We haven't spoken much either. It's like we both know what will happen once we talk, so we simply don't. That doesn't mean he didn't join me in the shower before he left, bend me over at the waist, and fucked me until I came not once but twice on his magnificent cock. He gave me aftercare, too, but still, we didn't speak.

He left for Las Vegas a week ago, and all he said was, "Please take care of yourself and Daisy," like we were the ones racing dangerous cars around a Formula One circuit.

But he won. Daisy and I watched as he crossed the finish line in first place, five seconds ahead of Valentina. She was battling Cameron until the end and managed to snatch second place despite starting in fifth. Which means James, Val, and Cameron are all very close together in the standings now. Too close for my fake husband, I'm sure.

My fake husband, who is already on his way back to the house.

My fake husband, who I can no longer avoid.

My fake husband, who I've fallen in love with so deeply, there is no denying how I feel.

"Mamá, can I watch *Tangled* again?" Daisy says, pulling me out of my thoughts. I scratch Marbles' head where she's lying on my lap, hating that I'm going to miss her and Lollipop, too.

I hate it even more that I'm going to break Daisy's heart today.

I'll break mine and hers as soon as James comes home because things can't keep going on like this. I allowed it for two weeks, but it's time I face reality. I just hope my daughter will be able to forgive me eventually.

"Of course, *florecita*. I'll put it on for you," I say, smiling at the way she's holding onto Lollipop.

I turn on the television before going into the kitchen to get started on dinner. Daisy asked for *chilaquiles* and it's been a while since I've made them, so I've bought enough ingredients to try again in case I mess up the first time.

My phone rings right as I'm making the *salsa verde* from scratch, my mother's name flashing on the screen.

"*Hola, Mami,*" I greet her, not in the mood to talk. I love my mamá, but I'm trying to mentally prepare for breaking up with my fake husband, and I haven't built up the courage yet.

"*¿Qué pasa?*" she asks because sensing something is wrong with me is like her sixth sense. It's like she can sniff out my feelings even with an ocean keeping us apart.

"*Nada, Mamá, estoy cansada,*" I reply, lying through my teeth. I'm wide awake. I've never felt this awake in my life.

"*Mentirosa,*" she says, but it sounds more like a curse, which makes me smile.

"Did James upset you?" my father asks in our mother tongue, and I realize he's listening to our conversation.

"*Hola, Papá. ¿Cómo estás?*"

"Don't change the subject. Answer my question, my love. Was it James? If it was, put him on the phone. I'll give him a piece of my mind."

"*No te preocupes,*" I start, sucking in a silent but sharp breath. "He hasn't been home, so we've barely spoken," I go on in Spanish, but even I can hear how off I sound. "More importantly, I was wondering if Daisy and I can maybe come see you soon," I lie, wanting to change the subject.

Well, it's not exactly a lie. I've been thinking about going to them for months. Initially, before we all knew Jennifer would turn on Bert, I was thinking James, Daisy, and I could go to visit my parents after the Mexican Grand Prix. Now, I don't know anymore. I should bring Daisy back to celebrate with our *familia*, but I don't know where to find the courage to do so.

"Yes, you should come for *Día de los Muertos*, Estrella. Your Aunt Rosa and Uncle Julio are coming this year. And you know that your Mamá Elena and Papá Bruno would love to see you two as well," Mamá says, and I stop moving as a wave of emotion hits me straight in the chest.

I'm... homesick.

"I'll think about it," I promise them.

Our conversation ends ten minutes later, but I feel so uneasy because with every second that ticks by, James gets closer to coming home. After talking to my parents, my chest only feels heavier.

To distract myself, I put on Grupo Frontera and let their music attempt to cheer me up.

But that's when he steps into the kitchen.

I don't have to turn around to know he's there. I smell him immediately. His warm and intoxicating scent. I feel his presence like a gentle hug that holds me together. My back stiffens in response, but I manage to turn around and look at his beautiful face.

He wears the type of expression that says a million things without a single word having to be spoken.

He knows.

He knows what I'm about to say.

And he's fucking terrified.

"Hi," I say, grabbing the counter behind me and staring at the ground to avoid his gaze.

"I have a feeling that's the very opposite of what you truly want to say to me." My heart shrieks in fear, but I simply nod.

"Things can't go on like this, James. We can't keep dragging out the inevitable," I say, just like I practiced a million times in the mirror. It's his turn to nod. He walks around the kitchen island and leans against it right across from where I am.

"You love me," he states so dryly, I can't help but laugh.

"Do I now?" I ask even though he's absolutely right.

"Yes, you do. As a matter of fact, you don't just love me. You're *in love* with me. You feel everything I do, so I don't understand why you're running, darling." If only I had it in me to let anger take over, to start throwing lies at his head, but the truth is bad enough. There is no need to cover it with deceptions.

"I'm scared you're going to wake up one morning and realize the only reason you fell for me is because you had to. Because you had no other option," I explain, letting out an unamused laugh and covering my face with my hands.

He's in front of me with his fingers snaking around my wrists a heartbeat later.

"I know what I feel, little star. I know I'm in love with you because for the first time in my life, I understand what that means," he says as he pulls my hands off my face to make me look into his blue eyes. To make me look at him as he tells me he loves me for the first time.

"You didn't sign up to keep us forever, James. You didn't sign up to have another child. You signed up for a marriage with an end date. We weren't meant to last. Can you say for certain that you've thought about what your life will look like with Daisy and me constantly around you, no expiration date?" I ask, and he gives me a sad smile.

"My life would look exactly how I've always hoped it would, only with the right woman by my side and a daughter I could only wish for," he replies so quickly, my head spins a little.

"You need to be a free man in order to know if you want to be with me, James." He shakes his head like that's the most ridiculous statement in the world.

"No, Estrella. *You* need to choose *me* the same way I'm choosing you. Not because you have to. Not because of a marriage born out of convenience. You have to choose me because you want me, and if you need to take some time to figure out if that's the case, I'll give it to you. I love you and Daisy more than I'll ever be able to put into words. That won't change if you ask for a bit of distance. Nothing will ever change that."

He cups my cheeks and leans down to press his forehead to mine. I tilt my head up as tears run down my cheeks.

"I had a feeling this was happening today, so I already talked to Val and Gabriel. They offered me a room at their house. I'll stay with them until after I come back from Mexico. That's about three weeks from now." I lean away to show him my confused expression.

"This is your home, James," I say, but he shakes his head.

"No, little star, you're my home. This is merely a house. If you want it, it's yours."

His hand lifts to my chin as his eyebrows draw together. He looks like he's in pain, and that only makes more tears fall down my cheeks.

"But in three weeks, I'll be at that front porch with flowers and a pair of earrings. I'll still be in love with you, and I hope you won't be afraid anymore to tell me that you love me, too. In three weeks, I want you to choose me back," he says, his voice breaking on the word "choose."

Tears shoot into his eyes, but he doesn't blink them away. He lets them drop without hesitation.

"I need you to choose me back, Estrella," he whispers. "You are everything valuable in the world wrapped into one person. You are my shining bright light in a pitch-black galaxy."

"James," I start, my voice cutting off.

"I know," he says. "Three weeks. If you don't text me saying you realized your feelings were a result of the faking, then I'll be here. I'll be wherever you are." I place my hand on his stomach, craving to touch him for a little longer. "If you change your mind about us, I'll pick up Marbles and Lollipop and promise you'll never have to see me again."

He kisses my forehead as I cry, my heart shattering in two when his tears drip down my cheeks, mixing with my own. I hate myself for being so incapable of responding to every single sweet thing he's said in the last five minutes. I hate myself for making him have to be so understanding of my fears. I hate myself even more for wanting distance to assure myself he really wants me and Daisy.

He starts to walk out of the kitchen but stops in the doorway to look over his shoulder.

"You have me for life, Estrella Celeste Cortez-Landon. I hope I have you the same way."

With that, he steps into the living room to greet Daisy and let her know he will be gone for a little while. The front door shuts minutes later, and I sink to the ground to break down.

"Mamá?" My head snaps up at the sound of Daisy's voice. She's standing in the door frame with her stuffed kangaroo hugged to her chest, the ginormous one James bought her. "*¿Qué pasa*, Mami?" I attempt to stop crying to be strong for her, like I've done her whole life.

"*Nada, florecita, estoy bien*," I lie, but she walks to where I am on the floor and sinks to her knees to be at eye level with me. "*Lo siento, amor*," I say, wiping my tears, but she stops me and puts her tiny hands on my face.

"You always tell me crying is okay, Mamá," she says. "I can hug you until you feel better," my daughter adds before wrapping her arms around me, holding me.

I hug her back as fiercely.

"James will be back, Mamá. He promised me," she says, so I hug her tighter, hoping she's right.

Hoping I didn't just make the worst mistake of my life by sending him away.

Chapter 51
James

I FEEL LIKE A shell of myself. A hollowed-out version. I'm clinging to the tiniest sliver of hope that Estrella truly does love me and a bit of distance will prove to her that we can't live without each other. Fine, *I* can't live without *her*.

"You look like shit," Gabriel says as he opens the front door of his house, but I don't even have the energy to come up with a snarky comment.

"Okay. Can I look like shit inside the house or do I have to listen to you insult me on your doorstep?" I ask, making the amused smirk fall from his face.

"Fuck, how badly did it go?" he replies as he steps to the side to let me in. Chase, their very energetic rescue dog, runs toward me and immediately starts sniffing my trousers. He's done this every time since I got Marbles and Lollipop. I pet his head before leaving my suitcase at the staircase to bring up later.

"I need a drink," I say, walking toward the kitchen.

"James," Gabriel says right as I open the fridge door and pull out a beer. It's only after I close the fridge and pop the top off the beer bottle that I look at him. He looks concerned, like he actually cares about my feelings and hates to see me this way. "What happened?"

It's a simple question, and I miss the days when he irritated the living fuck out of me. I miss when anger used to take over when I was around Gabriel. It was so much better than the way tears jump into my eyes right now.

"I told her I loved her. I told her everything I've been feeling. And when I offered her space, she took it," I say, taking a sip of my beer in hopes it will hold back the tears. It doesn't. They fall down my face anyway.

That makes his features soften.

"Isn't that what you wanted? For her to realise she loves you on her own terms? That she wants to be with you even when she doesn't have to be anymore?" he asks, but I let out a dry laugh.

"No, Gabriel, I wanted her to choose me. I wanted the love of my life to think distance was as ridiculous a concept as I do. I wanted her to feel exactly how I feel, but it might just turn out that my wife truly doesn't desire to spend the rest of her life with me."

Silence fills the space between us as he considers me, but his gaze is so intense, I cower a little.

"James, you love your sister, right?" he asks, and I raise both brows in response.

"Yes, of course."

"And you love Adrian and Val, right? They're your best friends, as close as family."

"I don't understand where you're going with this," I reply, taking another sip of my beer. Gabriel's thoughtful expression stays on his face.

"Estrella is terrified of losing you. She's so terrified that she wants *you* to be sure of your feelings without a speck of doubt. She needs to know you've thought about this, about what it will mean to stay married to her. You'll have a daughter for life. A wife. She wants you to be a million percent sure so you don't wake up one morning and leave her." Gabriel walks up to me and places one hand on each of my shoulders. "Only a bit of distance will assure her that you have truly thought about all of this. Can't you understand that?"

"Probably not as well as you do," I mumble, my shoulders sagging in defeat.

"I've been known to run from my feelings, too, but look at me now. I have the smartest, most beautiful, and most badass wife in the world, and she's happy with me. It took us a while to get here, but I always knew we'd end up together. Don't you feel that way with Estrella?" he asks, and I let more tears drip down my cheeks.

He squeezes my shoulders before doing something... well, fucking strange.

He hugs me.

Gabriel Biancheri pulls me into a hug, and that's not even the strangest part. The strangest part is that I hug him back. I take the comfort he gives me.

That's how desperately I need it.

"I feel hollow without her, Gabriel. Like part of me is missing."

"I did warn you about losing your heart along the way," he replies, but all I can do is snort. "Come on, Landon, I know exactly what will cheer you up," he says when he pulls out of the hug, patting my right shoulder twice. He steps toward where his phone is in the dining room, dials a number, and then hangs up after speaking in French to the other person.

Twenty minutes later, as Gabriel and I settle down at the table on the veranda, my chaotic best friend appears behind the man I used to hate.

"Your savior is here!" Adrian announces, and the Loki reference has me bursting into laughter despite feeling like shit. "Aww, James, you don't have to look so sad anymore. I'm here now. You're not alone with this idiot anymore," he adds, using his thumb to point at Gabriel over his shoulder. He gives me a brief side hug before settling in the seat at the head of the table.

He takes in the deck of cards and mugs with hot chocolate Gabriel and I carried outside. His mouth forms a perfect O-shape before excitement covers his features.

"Oh my God, Gabriel. Are we introducing James to our special Adrian-Gabriel time?"

I've known about the way they meet up to play cards and drink hot chocolate whenever one of them feels down for years. I'm honoured they would even consider including me.

Gabriel scrunches his nose at his brother-in-law.

"Don't call it that. Makes it sound like we sword-fight with our dicks," he replies, and Adrian bursts into laughter.

"You fucking wish," he says, but Gabriel maintains the disgusted look on his face. "Well, perhaps not. You'd feel very self-conscious after seeing mine," he says with a grin, picking up his hot chocolate to take a sip.

"You're awfully quiet over there. Care to jump in?" Gabriel asks me, but I simply shrug.

"Can't jump in when he's making valid points. I've seen him naked. There is a reason he's so fucking cocky, you know?" I tell Gabriel, who rolls his eyes. Adrian's self-assured smirk only makes me chuckle.

"Well, poor Nevaeh." The mention of his wife's name has my best friend beaming.

"Speaking of Nevaeh. There's something I should tell you both," he starts, and Gabriel and I both turn to look at Adrian.

He smiles even more brightly.

"She's pregnant."

Chapter 52
Estrella

I've never been the kind of person who could hide under their covers when they were hurting. I wish I was. I wish I could allow myself to fall apart for a few days, weeks even.

But I can't. My little girl is counting on me to take her to preschool. She needs me to tuck her in every night. She counts on me to keep making money to put food on our table, buy her new clothes, and everything else that comes with being her mom.

And as long as Daisy keeps smiling, I know everything will be alright, and she does smile, quite a lot actually. Especially today.

In order to distract me, Valentina has helped me arrange an interview with the member of the Velocità Rossa team responsible for hiring the test drivers. I haven't heard anything from Hawke Racing, and, if I'm being honest, it would be a greater honor to test drive new cars from the same company that was involved in signing the first female Formula One driver.

"How are you feeling?" Val asks, and I appreciate the way she grins to let me know she's talking about the interview today.

"Nervous. I don't know why I'm nervous. Maybe I'm not nervous. Maybe this is excitement. No, excitement feels different. This must be nervousness," I ramble, making Nevaeh, Scarlette, Chiara, and Val give me concerned looks.

I hold onto Daisy's hand even tighter. She has headphones on her head as she watches her favorite show. She's been so patient all day. We had to drive five hours to Maranello and now we've been waiting for half an hour for the interview already. She hasn't complained once about how boring today must be for her.

"Here, smell Scar. It'll help," Nevaeh says, and Scarlette turns to her with a surprised look on her face. "What? You always smell like lavender. It'll calm her," the German explains.

"Alright, you can get a sniff, but don't tell my husband. He's told me he reserved the right to all sniffs a few years ago," she replies, and I actually snort in response.

"I'm good, but thank you for the offer. To be honest, I don't even know why I'm nervous. I have a job I love at the academy. This is just—" I cut off, searching for the right word when Val grabs my hand and squeezes it.

"A dream?" she asks, and I fight the lump that's forming in my throat.

"Yeah, I guess it would be a dream." I let my head fall backward, expelling an unamused laugh. "I'm not allowed those, am I? Shouldn't I be solely focusing on Daisy's dreams?"

I don't know why I voice the questions. I never have in the past. They were always thoughts gnawing at me when I was alone in bed at night, but these four women always make me feel so safe and loved. It's like they oiled my vocal cords, allowing words to slip from my lips.

"No. Your dreams are just as important," Chiara replies, and I don't know why, but hearing a mother say so means more to me than if the other three had responded. "Listen, *bella*, I have two children I love more than life itself. I would kill for them and I would die for them, but just because I'm their mamma doesn't mean I'm not also a business owner, an artist, a daughter, a wife, a friend, a sister, and more. You are allowed to be more than one thing. You are allowed to be whatever you want to be," she says, a reassuring smile slipping onto her face.

Chiara Tick is always an other-worldly kind of beautiful person, but she's even more so when she smiles because it's a rare gift she doesn't give many people.

"The question is, what do you want to be?" she asks next, and I fall silent as I let her question bounce around in my head.

"I want to be Velocità Rossa's test driver. I want to be a coach at the academy. I want to be Daisy's mom. I want to be a great friend, daughter, and sister, even with my brother no longer around. I want to be James' wi—" My voice breaks off before I can finish my last sentence.

No, no, no. I cannot go down this road right now. That man will not distract me and throw me off my game before this important interview. I will simply suppress any thoughts of him like I've done for the past week.

"Don't do that, Estrella. Don't shut off the part of yourself that wants to feel. Trust me, it'll only come out in different ways," Scarlette says, and it sends tears straight into my eyes.

"I can't think about him. If I think about him, I'll think about how deeply the pain of heartbreak has sunk its claws into me. If I think about him, I'll wonder if this past week has potentially changed his mind about his feelings for me, and I don't know how to handle that possibility when he's the person I love with my entire soul, heart, mind, and body. So, no, I won't allow myself to feel everything I need to because I don't have time to fall apart."

This is the first time I've admitted I love James out loud.

"Reya, you're running from a man who has shown how much he loves you and Daisy a hundred times over the course of your 'fake' marriage. He has not changed his mind because that's not how being in love works. You cannot simply make your mind up about how you feel. That's something your heart decides, and his heart chose you long ago. The question is, do you choose him?" Val asks. I run my hands over my face, doing my best not to burst into tears.

"You don't have to answer that, honey. We've all seen how you look at him. It's how we all look at our husbands. It's how a person looks at someone they never thought they'd find but would do everything to keep." Nevaeh's words have me staring at her with my heart screaming in fear.

"He hasn't told you he's realized his feelings were a result of our faking?" I ask Val, scared to hear the answer, but she merely gives me a compassionate smile.

"No. All he's told me is that he feels like he can't breathe without you. He told me he misses you and Daisy so much, he can't sleep at night. He told me he's never loved anyone the way he loves you," Valentina says, walking up to me to slide an arm around my shoulder.

"Then I fucked everything up, didn't I? I didn't fight for us. I just sent him away. I—" I cut off, covering my mouth with my hand. "I didn't even tell him I love him."

We all stay silent because there's nothing to say. They gave me a safe space to express my feelings, and now that I have, I've realized three very important things I can no longer deny.

1. My dreams are important, and I am allowed to fight for them.

2. I get to be whoever I want to be.

3. James Oliver Landon is the love of my life, and I don't want us to get a divorce.

It's been over a year since we met, and he helped me find ways to turn my life the right side around again. He's made me question everything while giving me clarity over so many things. He's even given me the space to grieve in a way I never had before. James has taken care of us from day one, even though I specifically asked him not to. Even though I kept pushing him away at first. Even though he told me he could never give his heart away.

He gave it to me.

"Estrella? Please, come on in," a woman says, and determination takes over every part of me. I give my daughter a kiss on the top of her head before heading toward the woman.

"Well, Estrella, after talking to you and reading everything on your resume, I can confidently say you're by far one of the most experienced and skilled drivers I've had the pleasure of interviewing," Joslyn says, and I smile from ear to ear.

"It's an honor to have been given the opportunity to speak to you. This would be a dream job for me, if I'm being honest," I reply. Joslyn tucks her dark curls behind her ears before standing up and holding out her hand for me. I rush to stand up, too.

"I hope to see you back here in a week for another interview and some on-track testing." Hope blooms in my chest like a flower that's been craving to see the sun all day.

"It would be a pleasure," I manage to croak out, trying not to get too excited.

We've just spent about forty-five minutes talking about my accomplishments in auto racing back in Mexico and my current job at Kids Like Us.

"The pleasure is all mine. My friend who works at Hawke Racing has been talking about setting up an interview with you for weeks, and when I told her you were coming in today, she was jealous. I have to make sure you get the best job offer at Velocità Rossa," Joslyn adds as we move toward her office door. *Hawke Racing is interested in setting up an interview?*

"Have a good day." I attempt to respond properly, but this new information has my head spiraling so much, all I manage is a mumbled "you, too."

There's no time to linger on my thoughts because every members of my family that came with me today runs toward me to bombard me with questions. I answer them all with the biggest smile on my face because I'm one step closer to getting a job where I'll sit in a car again.

I hug Daisy, and when she says, "I'm proud of you, Mamá," I finally let the tears fall.

Chapter 53
James

"You look absolutely miserable," Dominique says before she places a plate of food in front of me.

"Thanks," I reply with a snort, which makes Nicolette chuckle.

"Don't be that way. You know we worry about you," Dominique adds.

"You don't have to worry. I'm not a child," I assure them, but Nicolette takes my face in her hands to make me look directly into her eyes.

"You're family. That means we get to worry. Now eat your food and then you're sleeping in our guest room before you fly out to England, okay?" she says, and I deflate even more.

I've been an emotional wreck for the past week. Everywhere I turn, I see Estrella. It's why I decided to go to England before the race in Mexico. I need to get out of Monaco, away from all the places I went to with my wife. Away from the park we walked. Her favourite café. The Italian restaurant where I kissed her after a date.

Plus, Mum's been asking me to come and see her. I know Mia would also like to spend some time with me, so it's a win-win either way. Since I'm only going for a few days, Nicolette and Dominique told me they'd be more than happy for me to take Damian as well. We'll have a nice father-son getaway, exactly what I need right now.

This morning, Dominique, Nicolette, and I went to behaviour therapy with him. He's seemed much happier in the past few months as he's able to concentrate on finishing a task instead of getting distracted frequently. I think his medication is really helping him. All in all, my son is incredible and I'm so proud of him.

I will not repeat the cycle my father put me through. If he knew Damian had ADHD, he would make my son feel like there is something wrong with him. Just because he is neurodivergent doesn't mean he isn't still the smartest, most determined little boy I've ever met. He trains so hard at the academy because he has this dream of following in my footsteps.

"Eat," Nicolette says as she steps back into the kitchen, leaving Dominique and me by ourselves. She gives me a comforting smile that I don't quite manage to return.

"I miss them so much," I whisper, bringing my gaze to the steaming plate of pasta, which only reminds me of Daisy and Estrella too because they love pasta.

"I'm sure they miss you, too, James," she replies, reaching for my hand on the table.

"Estrella hasn't messaged me once. I doubt she misses me," I say, the weight on my chest multiplying as I say her name.

"From what you told me, her not messaging you is a good sign. You said she should reach out if she doesn't want to be with you anymore, and she hasn't. That's good," she reminds me. "You need to sleep more. You look like you haven't closed your eyes for longer than it takes you to blink," she says, then points to my plate. "Eat, then sleep."

I do as I'm told, no matter how ill I feel. Daiyu would be furious with me if she knew how little I've been eating, drinking, sleeping, and working out. Instead of preparing myself for the next race weekend, I've been lulling in my pain.

Estrella would be very disappointed in me. She'd tell me to get my act together. That I have a championship to win. And she'd be right. I'm barely ahead in the standings. I need to win in Mexico. With so few races left, there is no space for error.

"Daddy, can we play Mario Kart?" Damian says right as I finish my plate of food. Dominique takes it from me and nudges me in the direction of their living room.

I set everything up for us while he waits patiently on the sofa, his feet dangling from the ledge of it.

"Daddy, when are we going to see Daisy and Reya? I miss them." Tears shoot into my eyes at his question, but luckily, my back is turned to him. I don't want him to know I'm hurting for the sole reason that I want to protect my son from any pain.

"Soon, bud, very soon I hope. For now, we're going to go see your aunty Mia, okay? Your grandmother also wants to finally meet you," I say, turning around to see Damian tilting his head with a confused look on his face.

"I have a grandmother?" he asks, and I walk over to him with two remotes.

"Yes, and she is very excited to get to know you." This doesn't make him any less confused.

"She didn't want to see me before?" he asks, his voice taking on a sad edge.

"She did, bud, she really did, but your granddad, he isn't a good man. He was upset with me a few years ago and decided to stop speaking to me, so he kept your grandmother away from us, too." I never thought my mum would want to be a part of our lives again, so I hadn't planned on sharing any of this with Damian until he was much older, but he deserves to meet his grandmother. I love my mum. When she stopped speaking to me, my heart shattered.

Dad never liked me much to begin with, but Mum? She would have fought dragons for me.

That's why I'll do anything I can to help our relationship now.

"Why is Granddad like that?" Damian asks, not even caring about the game anymore.

"I don't know, little warrior. All I know is that no matter what happens, I'll always be there for you. You are never getting rid of me," I say and start tickling him as an evil villain laugh slips from my lips. Damian bursts into giggles, and I can't help the way a bit of warmth finally spreads through my frozen-over chest again.

We play for a little over an hour because Damian tells me he's nowhere near tired, but eventually, I can barely keep my eyes open and convince him to watch a movie with me instead. He nuzzles himself against my side as soon as it begins.

I think about when I was a child. I think about taking my father's hand and him telling me boys don't hold other boys' hands. I think about the toxic masculinity he harboured.

When I held my son for the first time, I vowed that he'd never have to feel as ashamed as I did for wanting affection from my father. I will never turn him away when he takes my hand or cuddles against me on the sofa. I will pull him closer instead, and I will tell him that when he's older, he can love whoever he wants.

I'm a bisexual man who didn't explore his sexuality until the toxic male figure in his life disappeared. My son will not experience anything like this. He will have acceptance and love and support.

"Love you, bud," I say before placing a kiss on his head.

"Love you too, Dad."

My heart might be aching, but as I hug Damian to my chest, it becomes a dull sort of ache, a more tolerable one.

And I finally manage to fall asleep.

Chapter 54
Estrella

It's been two weeks.

Two weeks out of three.

I went to Val's house yesterday, hoping to find James and talk to him, but she told me he took Damian to England to spend some time with his sister and mother. I booked Daisy's and my flight to Mexico an hour after hearing that.

I'm going to fight for the man I love no matter what.

Right after I get this job today.

"How's the helmet?" Joslyn asks, and I give her a bright smile.

"Amazing. The suit, too. I'm so excited to drive this car," I say, stepping toward the new Velocità Rossa 579S.

It's bright red with a glossy finish, and I can't help the way my mouth waters at the sight of it every time I look at it. Much like the Hawke I drove, this one is all sleek with smooth edges. Unlike the Hawke, this one looks like the kind of beast that you'd find in the wild and run from.

"I'm happy to hear it." Joslyn gives me one more smile before walking away.

Nevaeh and Daisy wave at me from where they're standing in the garage, the other three women giving me a single nod of encouragement. I wave back at them, trying to fight the wave of pure relief when I see my daughter's bright smile. Daisy knows how much this means to me, and I'm starting to understand that she wants me to be happy as much as I want her to be happy.

"Ready?" a mechanic asks, handing me a pair of gloves.

"Absolutely," I reply. I slip them onto my hands and take several deep breaths as I settle down in the car.

It feels like this seat was molded to fit my body perfectly. There's a wave of nostalgia ebbing and flowing inside of me, but I embrace it instead of trying to push it down.

I was born to race. I was made for it.

"You're good to go, Estrella. Show us what you've got," Joslyn says through the earpiece I put in my ear earlier, and I smile as I shift into gear and push down on the gas.

The car drives like a fucking dream. All these new upgrades made to the cars in the last half-decade since I raced already astonished me when I drove the Hawke. But Velocità Rossa is lightyears ahead with their sports cars. I practically fly down the track. Every corner is a smooth glide compared to what I was used to back then.

It took me a long, long time to get into motorsport. As a woman, being a racecar driver is a dream you have to fight for harder than any man. It is a dream that even when you live it, you constantly have to prove yourself. You have to be and do twice as much as men. You have to fight for respect every second, and you have to make sure you don't do anything to turn people against you, which happens quickly since they're always looking for a reason to undermine you. It was always different for my male peers. I knew a driver who harassed women, groping them without consent, and he kept his seat for years. Me, on the other hand, I almost lost mine for crashing out in my second race.

These double standards aren't news to any woman. They weren't to me, but I have to admit, becoming friends with Valentina Romana has taught me many things. Most importantly, she has shown me that it is possible to bring about change if only you continue to fight without holding back. You fight for your place in this male-dominated world. You fight against the men who undermine you. You fight for the respect they try to deny you until there is nothing they can do anymore to take your dream away.

Val's living her dream.

And I'm driving this beautiful car straight into mine.

By the time I bring it back to the pits, I feel like I'm glowing. My lap times must have been quite fast because Nevaeh, Valentina, Chiara, and Scar all have proud looks on their faces. Somehow, I manage to peel myself off the seat and get out of the car, my legs pure jello. It's a wonder I don't fall face-first onto the track. I love the adrenaline rush when it hits my bloodstream, but when it wears off? Sometimes it feels like a truck has hit you several times.

"*Eso fue glorioso*," Valentina says as she approaches me to take my helmet. She also very subtly places a hand on my arm to steady me, and I love her a little more for it.

"Thank you," I reply, my cheeks burning from the permanent smile on my lips.

"Estrella, I have to say, well done!" Joslyn compliments as she walks up to us. "The control you had in the car, the lap times you set, and the focus I saw in your eyes…" She trails off to shake her head and smile proudly. "It would be Velocità Rossa's honor to hire an amazing driver like you to test our cars. I'll have the official offer to you on Monday," she adds as she holds her hand out, making a wave of unfiltered joy hit me straight in the chest.

"The honor is mine," I manage to reply, but luckily, Joslyn leaves before she can see the way my legs wobble again. "I got the job," I whisper to Val as she grabs my arm once more. Tears flood her eyes as she grins brightly.

"You did, Reya. You got it." Her tears drop and then her arms are around me. I find myself clinging to her.

"I did it," I repeat right before another four voices fill my ears.

"We're so proud of you, Reya," Nevaeh says.

"Never doubted you for a moment, *bella*," Chiara adds.

"Daisy is so lucky to have a role model like you," Scar says, and I feel my little girl hugging my leg tighter. I put a hand on the crown of her head and take several deep breaths.

I got the job.

I got the best daughter in the world.

STRAIGHT TO THE CHAPEL

I got a beautiful family made up of strong women and their partners who would destroy this world to protect every single one of us.

Now, I just have to get my husband back.

CHAPTER 55
James

My trip to visit Mia and Mum went well. We had a great time, despite me walking around like I've got a permanent thundercloud above my head. My chest still feels unbearably hollow, and being in Mexico without Estrella and Daisy only hurts more. I keep hearing Grupo Frontera songs that Estrella used to sing along every time she was cooking in the kitchen. I was offered *horchata* yesterday and almost bawled my eyes out because it didn't taste as good as my wife's.

I've always loved Mexico. The culture here is so beautiful, and the people are wonderful, but my body hurts from how desperately I wish Estrella was here.

I miss everything about my wife, and these bloody reminders aren't helping.

"Hey, Landon," Javier Morales says as he approaches me on our way to stand on the track to listen to the national anthem of Mexico.

"Hi, Javier," I reply, doing my best to fake a smile, but I don't succeed. My face stays as serious as it's been since Estrella asked for some distance.

"Where's your wife? I haven't seen her or heard about her from you in a hot minute," he says, his accent thick. I glance at him for a moment, not sure what he's trying to achieve.

"It's none of your business," I say as I continue walking, but he runs to catch up with me.

"Uh oh, trouble in paradise already? I thought the first year of marriage was supposed to be the best." I stop dead in my tracks, placing a hand on his shoulder.

"Listen, kid, I know you're a rookie and you have a lot to learn, so I'm going to let this interaction slide. Now, don't ever mention Estrella again." I'm about to walk away when he says something that makes my stomach turn upside down in anger.

"Can't blame me for being curious about a beautiful woman like her." A smile I don't mean curls the left side of my mouth, but I know it's more dangerous than friendly. His grin falls as he takes it in.

Good.

"Yeah, my wife is very beautiful. She's also very intelligent, kind, funny, strong, compassionate, and one hell of a racecar driver." I take a step toward him, towering over him. "You know what else Estrella is?" He swallows hard, and I keep my threatening smile in place as I add, "She's very mine and very off-limits." His eyes widen visibly in fear. "I suggest you remember that, or next time I'll show you why the world has painted me as the bad guy of Formula One." I leave him standing where he is, irritation gnawing at me.

This fucking rookie is really testing my self-control today.

"Good God, I think he just wet himself, mate," Adrian says as he approaches me, walking beside me with that little skip in his step that he's had since he married Nevaeh.

"He deserved it," I reply, grinding my molars together.

"He really did," Gabriel chimes in, squeezing my shoulder once as he joins us, too. Cameron rolls his eyes.

"I don't get Javier. One moment, he's flirting with me until my cheeks turn the shade of Adrian and Val's car, the next, he's asking you about your wife," Cameron says.

"What do you care? I thought you didn't want another relationship," Gabriel says, challenging his best friend.

"Who said I want a relationship with him?" Cameron's eyebrows shoot up his face to mock Gabriel's challenging look.

"Your face did," Gabriel replies, making Cameron's cheeks turn pink.

"Well, I don't. He's just—He's—" The Australian cuts off, but I nod understandingly.

"Pretty. He's very pretty," I finish for him, making his shoulders sag in defeat.

"Yeah, and infuriating. Considering he was with his last boyfriend for three years, he's certainly acting a lot like Adrian did before he met Nevaeh. Flirting with everything with a pulse." Cameron smiles a little at Adrian's shocked expression.

"Hey, I was practicing for the day I met Nevaeh. How else do you think I swept her off her feet?" Adrian scoffs, and Gabriel grins right before he answers.

"Your millions? Your good looks? Anything other than your personality?" Adrian should be offended, but instead, he smirks at his brother-in-law in that confident way he always does.

"I've always known you find me attractive, but it sure is nice whenever you remind me." Gabriel rolls his eyes and shakes his head before turning to face the person who is about to sing the Mexican anthem. Adrian does the same, keeping his smirk in place. Cameron is looking at the ground, a thoughtful expression lingering on his face.

"Estrella and I were sending each other mixed signals for a long time. Hate and attraction. Irritation and intrigue. Mixed signals are caused by a lack of communication. Because as soon as you realise what *you* want, you can tell the other person. But be careful, because if you're like me, your feelings may never be reciprocated," I say, hating myself a little for dragging the mood down so much.

"You are one bloody fool if you can even think Estrella isn't madly in love with you, James. Have you not been paying any attention to the way she looks at you? To the way she takes care of you? To how she searches for you in every single room she enters and when she finds you, her shoulders go from tense to dropping in relief? To the way she fucking shines as bright as a star right after you kiss her?" My throat has closed up entirely. "She may not have said it, but she has shown it. You're just so convinced no one could ever fall in love with you that you refuse to see it."

The national anthem starts before I can reply, not that I have anything to say.

STRAIGHT TO THE CHAPEL

I took pole yesterday with Cameron in second, Val in third, Gabriel in fourth, Javier in fifth—even though I don't like the rookie, I'm happy for him for being so high up on the grid at his home race—and Adrian in sixth. I'm ahead of Cameron by eight points, which isn't a lot with five races left.

"How are you feeling?" Ximena asks as we wait for the light to tell us to take the formation lap.

"Nervous yet strangely confident."

The car has been feeling great all weekend. We were fast yesterday, and the free practice sessions showed us that we have a lot of potential to have great race pace.

"Don't get cocky. You know what happened last time," she says, and I almost snort.

"Thank you, Ximena. That helps." Silence is all I receive in return, but it's most likely because the lights flash on, signaling for us to take our formation lap.

I suppose if Estrella hadn't kept it, my heart would be racing right now. Instead, all I feel is my stomach doing several somersaults. I've never been so nervous before a race. It feels like today means more than all of my other races combined, and it isn't because of the championship standings, not entirely. It's because I want to make my wife proud and win her home Grand Prix. I want to take home the trophy for us. I want to hold up the Mexican flag for her and make her smile in the way that has my soul sighing in relief.

Then again, all I truly want is her.

Fuck the championship.

Fuck finally holding the trophy.

Fuck winning.

If I've lost Estrella forever, then what's the point of it all? Who am I winning for? Myself? No, this has never been about me. This dream was always my father's, but he manipulated me until I believed it was mine, too. It wasn't until I met Estrella that I realised what my dream truly was.

I want to be happy. I want a family. I want a spouse and kids and all of the things that come with it. I want to be loved, and I want to give all the love I have in return.

Yes, I still want to win, but that's a goal.

That will be an accomplishment, not a dream come true.

Estrella, Daisy, and Damian are a dream come true.

My dream come true.

I take a deep breath, going into tunnel vision. This is what I've been trained to do. Forget about everyone and everything else and focus solely on racing. On *winning*. My father's voice usually bounces around in my head, screaming at me to get my act together and stop being a little shit. I've always tried to ignore it, but it's been there, in my subconscious, warning me of the consequences should I lose again. But not today.

Today, all I hear is Estrella.

You got this. I believe in you. I'm proud of you.

As I line back up on the grid, in first place where I qualified, her words are all that matter. As I take another deep breath, I let her soothe me.

The first light turns on as soon as the person waving the flag in the back walks past, and I hold my breath, waiting for the rest to turn on.

When all the lights vanish again, I feel how quickly I react. I anticipated it better than ever before, and I hit the throttle as I shift into gear, pressing all the corresponding buttons on my steering wheel. I shoot forward without a threat from Cameron while he fights off Valentina. She slips ahead of him. I have no time to watch them battle as we head into *Moisés Solana*.

As I take a deep breath, I hear Ximena's voice, knocking it straight back out of me.

"Cameron, Adrian, and Gabriel crashed."

"Are they okay?" I ask, feeling fear and panic course through me in equal measures. Yellow lights flash at the sides of the track where the fences are, letting us know to slow down and stop overtaking.

"Checking," she says, which is not an answer that satisfies me. "Safety car is being deployed."

"Ximena," I say, my voice cracking.

"I can't tell you things I do not know, James. Give me a moment." I check my mirrors to see Val swerving behind me, trying to keep her tyres warm. "Adrian and Cameron got out of their cars, but Gabriel hasn't. Apparently, he's on the radio, groaning in pain," she says and I swear several times.

"Please keep me updated."

We drive past the crash site, and I notice the front of Gabriel's car is wrecked. He is getting out of his car, though, which I take as a good sign, even if he's holding onto the marshals a little more than I'd like.

I look into my mirrors again, Val's Velocità Rossa a dangerous sight. Maybe it's because I've known her for so long, maybe it's because we're family, but I can feel the way her panic and frustration slowly turn into ice-cold determination.

"Ximena, shouldn't this be a red flag? Three cars in a dangerous spot? What are the stewards waiting for?" I ask, still following behind the safety car.

"They're discussing it," she replies, and I furrow my brows.

"This should be a red flag."

"I don't disagree," she says, but it's in a way that lets me know not to discuss this over the radio. We wouldn't want to get in trouble with them for speaking our minds and undermining their ability to make these decisions themselves.

We drive another lap before Ximena says, "Red flag," and I notice all the lights that were previously yellow turning red.

Then, all of us make our way back to the pits.

Chapter 56
James

Gabriel is okay. They're taking him to the hospital to make sure there is no internal bleeding and that he doesn't have a concussion, but, according to his team, he was already making jokes and is doing alright. Adrian and Cameron are fine, too.

But Val is pissed.

I saw her standing at the pit wall with Lorenzo Mattia, her team principal, and she looked ready to tear someone's head off. From what I've seen, the crash was all three drivers' combined fault, so I have no idea who she's mad at. I won't ask. I'm doing my best to stay in my zone while we wait for the hardworking marshals to clear the track of any debris and the cars.

"This is going to be a very long race if there's already a red flag within the first couple of laps," I tell Ximena, my body feeling heavy and sweaty. Now that the usual adrenaline rush has subsided, I feel like lying down and taking a quick nap. Adrian's done it once during a red flag, and I'm seriously considering doing it as well.

I might only be twenty-eight, but this sport makes me feel like an old man.

"That was an unfortunate crash between three *idiots*. Now that they're out of the race, it should be smooth sailing," Ximena says with a small smile, trying to cheer me up, but I feel as irritated as Val.

"It shouldn't have happened." She nods in agreement, then nudges my shoulder.

"Hey, everything is going to be okay. You're going to win today. Plus, a little birdie told me they arranged for a local racing legend to do the post-race interview. Isn't that exciting?" Again, I know she's trying to cheer me up, but I couldn't care less.

My unimpressed look must tell her exactly that.

"Ah, we've got an official restart time," she says, her attention drifting to the screens in front of her. "You've got ten minutes, then it's time to go racing again."

I nod several times before walking over to Daiyu.

We spend the next ten minutes getting me ready to get back in the car. I get another glance at Valentina, who looks at me with a stern look and curt nod.

Fuck.

She's going to throw everything she has at me.

We're in our cars, ready to do another standing start. The crowd cheers and screams for us, and I let their energy spur me on, reigniting my adrenaline rush. All of us line back up on the grid, ready to start this race again. I feel calmer yet more on edge at the same time with Val being the one to chase me down.

It's an eerie feeling, and I don't know what to do with it.

The restart goes well for me, and I manage to gain a second on Val before they enable DRS. My tyres feel great and so does my car, but Val doesn't give me a second to breathe. Seven laps after the restart, she's less than a second behind me again. She's fighting me and dancing on the lines of the rules, her car almost touching mine as we head through every corner.

By the time our first pitstop comes around, I'm drenched in sweat. I managed to gain two seconds on Val, but she follows me into the pits, her team ready for the stop, too.

My crew can't get one of my tyres off. I'm standing and standing and standing, my rival already done changing her tyres. A frustrated groan escapes me right as I get the green light. I move away from my crew, cursing over and over as I drive to rejoin the track.

Val is in first.

I'm in second.

"FUCK!"

I'm three seconds behind her, according to Ximena, so for the next twenty laps, I go from charging my battery to attacking Val and back to charging my battery. Eventually, I'm close enough to smell the victory.

"You took point three seconds out of the distance between the two of you in the last lap. Keep it up. There are four laps left." Ximena says.

"Leave me to it," I reply breathlessly.

Val's car is so close to mine now, I have to be careful not to drive into the back of it. I also have to be careful not to pull the same shit as last time. It's one thing for the world to hate me for the way I drive. It's another for my family to think I'm unnecessarily risking their lives.

"Three laps, James," Ximena warns, and I grit my teeth.

"Not helping."

Val and I are side by side a lap later. My car is faster. I have been proving it the whole season, but she's been managing her tyres better than I have. She's the better driver.

She—

Val goes wide. She brakes too late and goes wide, allowing me to slip ahead of her. By the time she rejoins the track, I'm long gone.

I make it all the way to the end of the race without a single threat from her.

A rush of endorphins releases as Ximena screams that I have won, and tears sting my eyes. I did it. I won the Mexico Grand Prix.

I have extended my lead.

And if I'm lucky enough, no matter where Estrella is, she is fucking proud of me.

I see a fan holding a Mexican flag through the fence for me, so I stop right next to them. With the help of a marshal, I'm able to get the flag, and, once secured in my hand, I keep driving. It flies in the wind, making the crowd roar. This win is for all the fans here who are wearing my colours, and for Estrella, her parents, Daisy, and Pedro.

Once I've parked my car in front of the first place sign, I take a moment to scan my team for the one person I need most, but she's nowhere to be seen. It's a habit I've developed since marrying Estrella, and I doubt I'll ever shake it. But I let the victory send more happiness and pride through my veins. I wrap the flag around my shoulders and raise my arms to my side, earning another roar from the crowd.

I hug every single member of my team before getting weighed and taking off my helmet. I hand Javier, who came in third, the Mexican flag, and he shakes his head as tears collect in his eyes. I wipe my face with a towel and take a sip of my water, smiling at the way the fans are shouting my name.

There is nothing like winning an F1 race.

Except for...

"Estrella."

Her name leaves my lips in a plea, a sigh of relief, and a vocal embodiment of all my pain. Her brown eyes meet mine from where she's standing holding a microphone, clad in a dark green pantsuit. My gaze immediately drifts to her left ring finger, another wave of relief shooting through my system when I see she's wearing her rings.

Plus, a little birdie told me they arranged for a local racing legend to do the post-race interview. Isn't that exciting?

Ximena knew the person interviewing us would be my wife. My wife, who is a racing legend here. My wife, who I love so much and am so frustrated with, I don't know what to focus on. My wife, who came to me.

I can't help myself. I take quick strides toward her and wrap her in my arms, desperation leaking off me in uncontrollable waves. I cling to her, swallowing back more tears when she hugs me back as fiercely.

"I'm so sorry, James." I lean back to press my forehead to hers.

"Can I kiss you? Please, Estrella. I've been dying to put my mouth on yours for the last two weeks." Her response is lifting her hands to cup my cheeks and pressing her lips to mine.

Everything seems to fall right back into its proper place as soon as she kisses me. As soon as I know she didn't come here to tell me we're over. As soon as I know this is it. This is where she chooses me. And I don't care if the whole world is watching. I love my wife. I'm not afraid to show every single living creature that I'd rather die than live in a world without her in it.

"I love you in every galaxy, James Oliver Landon. I choose you. I will always choose you. I'm sorry I didn't tell you that before. I'm sorry it's taken so long, but I'm hoping you'll still have me," she says, doing a much better job at keeping her tears at bay. Mine have started rolling down from the second she told me she loves me.

"You're my shooting star, Estrella, and I wish for you and Daisy to stay in my life permanently. Not because of a marriage of convenience. Not because we're faking. I don't want this to have an end date. I want this to last forever."

"I want this forever, too, *bebé*. I want you."

I kiss her several more times before hugging her to my chest, unable to let her go. She chose me. The love of my life chose me. She's going to keep choosing me, not because she has to, but because she wants to.

"I think I should interview you now," she says after a while with a little laugh, but I don't manage to peel myself off her.

"I think you'll have to step away, little star. I won't manage to," I admit, so she does, leaving my hands twitching to reach out to touch her again.

Somehow, I restrain myself, instead watching her walk over to where the interviewers usually stand. She waits for Javier, who has the flag wrapped around himself now. He's grinning, and I don't blame him. He's a rookie who earned a podium in his first season driving in F1 in his home country.

I watch Estrella with tears lingering in my eyes, barely even registering Val's appearance beside me until she speaks.

"I knew she was coming today, but she made me promise not to say anything."

"Of course she did." I wipe away a rogue tear as it runs down my cheek.

"What a glorious feeling, isn't it?" Val asks, and I look at her to see she's staring at Estrella, too. "Finally coming home after weeks of being the kind of homesick only people in love will ever understand."

"Yeah," I reply, bringing my attention back to Estrella. Javier speaks in Spanish to the crowd, and they cheer his name.

Val is up next, and I go back to studying my wife. She looks so heartachingly beautiful. Her long, dark hair is in a messy, yet perfectly styled updo. Her smile is bright and contagious. Her brown eyes are filled with the kind of joy I hope she'll always feel with me from this day on.

"Daddy!" Another piece inside of me stitches itself back together at the sound of my little girl's voice. I spin around to see her sitting on Nevaeh's hip, grinning.

"*Felicidades!*" I take her in my arms without hesitation. She throws hers around me, and I kiss her temple.

"*Muchísimas gracias, princesa,*" I reply, which makes her giggle.

"*Muy bien, Papá.*"

At this point, I wish someone would hand me some fucking tissues because I'm sure if I keep this up, my racing suit will be a soaking-wet combination of sweat and tears in two minutes.

"I've missed you so much," I say and hug her a little tighter.

"You're squishing me," she complains at the same time I hear Estrella announcing my name.

"I'll be right back," I say as I lift Daisy back over the barrier to Nevaeh.

Sprinting over to Estrella, I make sure to wipe my face very quickly. I take the microphone Val hands me, a smile finding its way onto my face as I turn to face my wife. This setting, being here as a national pride in racing, has her glowing in the most wonderful way, and I'm so mesmerised by it, my mouth falls open a little.

"What a sensational drive, James." She smiles, so I return it, looking directly into those shining eyes of hers. "How does it feel to have won today despite having a much slower pitstop and struggling with tyre degradation toward the end?" God, she's so gorgeous when she talks about racing like the pro she is.

"It feels incredible. Winning in Mexico has always felt special to me, but having family here that I can make proud with this win only adds to the magic."

Her gaze softens visibly at my words, but she stays professional the whole time, asking me more and more questions about the race.

Eventually, she comes to an end and says, "Anything else you'd like to add?" I look at the crowd as they cheer for me, feeling nerves creep in before I manage to speak again.

"*Gracias a todos por su apoyo. Es un honor el haber ganado esta carrera rodeado por algunos de los fans más asombrosos en el mundo. Significan mucho para mi,*" I say in Spanish, internally thanking Scarlette, Val, and Julián for teaching me every chance they get. Then, I turn to Estrella and add, "*Gracias por ser mi esposa.*" Shock has covered every centimetre of her face.

I want to stay with Estrella, but I'm ushered away and into the cool-down room. Minutes later, we're making our way onto the podium where they play the English national anthem and then the Austrian one for my team. They hand me the trophy for first place, but all I can look at is Estrella and Daisy.

My girls.

I may just be the happiest man in the world right now.

Chapter 57

Estrella

I OFFERED FOR ALL of us to go out for dinner to celebrate his win, but James insisted we go back to his hotel and spend the night with just the five of us—I brought Marbles and Lollipop because I can't leave my babies at home.

Gabriel has been discharged from the hospital with minor injuries, and Adrian and Cameron were cleared, too. As soon as James found out, he put his phone away. All he can focus on is Daisy and me. He's been hugging our daughter since he came out of his room freshly showered. James also constantly finds a way to take my hand and either hold it or place it on his cheek or kiss it.

He tucks Daisy in when she falls asleep before he struts back out of her room in the suite. I stand up to walk to him. As soon as I'm in front of him, he leans down to press his shoulder against my stomach, and then I'm draped over it as he carries me to the other room.

"James!" I squeal, giggling the entire time. He smacks my ass playfully once before gently placing me on the edge of the bed. Then, he kneels in front of me, looking up at me like I'm his goddess and he's getting ready to worship me.

"I'd like to talk," he says, making my heart palpitate.

"Uh oh," I reply, trying to sound like I'm not scared of what he will say. He senses it immediately and shakes his head.

"It's nothing bad, I promise," he says. "Darling, I would like to talk about us and our future together." I cup his cheeks, tracing his high cheekbones.

"Okay," I whisper, still a little nervous. His blue eyes trace my features for a moment as his hands caress my thighs.

"No more rules. I'm all in."

"So am I," I reply, my thumb rubbing along his jawline.

"I want to stay married. I want you to keep coming to races when you have time. I want everything we had, but I don't ever want you to wonder if it's real or not. It's always been real to me." He swallows hard, and so do I. "I don't want to be apart from you unless it's necessary. I want to entangle our lives further, in every way. I want us to allow ourselves to feel whatever it is we need to feel. I want all your happiness and sadness. I want your pain and pleasure. Give me everything, Estrella."

"You can have everything, James." A tear drops down my cheek. "Every piece of me. Every part of my soul. You can know every bit of me. Because I want everything you're saying, too," I say, and he lifts his hands to snake his fingers around my wrists. "I need you to know that being apart from you was excruciating for me, too. I wanted to be with you every second, *bebé*. I love you. I have loved you for so long. Please don't ever doubt that."

He sits up and kisses me before wrapping his arms around me, hugging me to his chest. We stay like this for a while, simply holding each other as our heartbeats find a perfectly even rhythm, but there is more I'd like to say, more he has to get off his chest.

"Are you angry with me for needing the space?" James places a kiss on my neck, working his way toward my mouth.

"I was, but when I saw you today, all of it faded. There's no need for misplaced anger, darling, because I was never upset with you in the first place. I was terrified you didn't love me. There's a difference."

His lips brush mine, a soft touch. A hint of what he hungers for. Intimacy. More of me. To catch up on the time we've lost.

"What have you been up to for the last two weeks?" I ask, running a hand down his torso. He grabs it before it reaches his lower abdomen, lifting it to his mouth to kiss my pulse point.

"Mostly lie in bed and cry," he replies, but because he smiles, I give him a semi-amused snort. "What about you?" James asks, rubbing his thumb over my wrist before placing my hand on his left pec.

"Well, actually, I got a new job," I say, turning my head to meet his gaze.

"You got the job at Velocità Rossa?" A wave of pride ripples through his eyes.

"You knew about it?" He tucks a curl behind my ear as he gives me another one of his devastating smiles.

"Do you even have to ask that?" My eyes flutter shut at the way he traces my jawline, then my lips. "I soaked up any little update anyone was willing to give me." I melt a little.

"Will you come with me to my parents' house for *Día de los Muertos*?" I ask, and he kisses me again, this time deeper, longer.

"Yes. I'll go anywhere with you, Estrella."

It's my turn to kiss him then. I tilt my head up to deepen the kiss, desperate to have his taste rush through my bloodstream, but he leans away again before I've had my fill.

"James," I whimper. He places his hand on my throat, squeezing only a little to keep me from kissing him again. "Please, more."

"There's something I need from you," he says, but his other hand is already guiding my body further against his, pressing me fully against him.

"Anything," I reply, my breathing hitching as heat settles between my legs. His hardening cock is pushing into my stomach, and I'm dying to take it out and guide it inside of me.

"There are four races left. If your work schedule permits, I want you to come to every single one of them. Please." He says the last word right as he repositions to rub his bulge against my aching clit.

"Try to stop me," I reply breathlessly, partially from excitement and partially because he's increasing the pressure on my neck.

"Good, because those will be the four most important races of my career, and I need you there," he says, still rubbing against me. It's been so long, my body starts trembling seconds later. "Are you close already, darling?"

"Yes, sir." The response falls from my lips with so much ease, he groans loudly.

"Have you missed my body, darling?" He rolls my hips forward until I cry out softly.

"Of course I have." I shudder from pleasure as he nips at the sensitive skin on my jaw.

"Don't come yet. I want you to come with my mouth on you," he says, releasing my throat. He crawls down my body, saying, "Take off your shirt," as he goes to slide down my shorts. He undoes the string of them with his teeth before removing them and my underwear.

Every inch of my skin is on fire, need coiling deep inside of me and tightening all my muscles. I've always craved James more than words can describe, but all those times don't compare to right now. I would do almost anything to have his mouth on me, which is probably why I moan when he places my legs on each of his shoulders, kissing the inside of my thigh.

"Look at you, little star, already soaking the sheets from how desperately you need me." I rip my shirt off, palming my breasts right as he places his mouth on my pussy, rubbing his tongue over my clit and playing with my piercing.

"Yes! Fuck!" I slam a hand over my mouth, screaming against it. James flicks his tongue again and again, pushing two fingers into me. I'm so wet, they slip in with ease, and he curls them at the perfect angle to play with my G-spot. "Oh fuck, oh fuck, oh fuck, oh fuck," I moan over and over, my legs shaking on his shoulders.

James eats me out as if he's been starving. I fall apart moments later, but he doesn't stop. He licks the length of my pussy, tasting my orgasm like he's never had anything so sweet in his life. All I can do is place my hand back over my mouth to let out more screams. I have a love-hate relationship with being overstimulated. On one hand, I can't get enough and want him to keep going forever. On the other,

I can barely handle it. But I've got my safeword, and I don't want to use it. James knows my limits. He won't push me too far.

After my second orgasm, he pulls back to kiss up my body, pulling my right nipple into his mouth.

"James, please, I need you inside me. I need you to come, too," I say, practically clawing at his back to get his mouth to mine and his cock closer to my pussy.

"I won't last long. I need to make sure you're satisfied first," he replies, moving to suck my other nipple into his mouth, but I grab his face to make him look at me.

"I'll be satisfied when your cum is dripping out of me."

"Fucking hell, Estrella," he mumbles, dropping his head on my chest and groaning. "You unravel me and put me back together in the same breath. How is that possible?" He nips at my nipple, but I feel his hand slipping down, reaching for his pants. Meanwhile, I drag his shirt over his head, needing his skin pressed against mine.

As soon as we're both naked, he repositions himself so he's hovering over me, my thighs bracketing his hips. His forearms and knees hold him up as I lift my head to claim his mouth. I dig my heels into his ass, pushing him further against me until the head of his cock rubs over my clit. Pleasure clouds my mind almost instantly.

"More, please," I say when he does nothing other than kiss me for a moment.

"What do you need, wife? Hard and fast, or slow and soft?" he asks, one of his hands cupping my breast as he sinks another two centimeters inside of me.

"I'll take whatever you give me."

"I know you're my good girl, Estrella, but I want what you want."

"I want both," I manage to admit, breathless all over again as he sinks fully inside of me.

I don't know how much time passes; I lose all sense of it. The first time, it's hard and fast and even sloppy. His strokes are messy and somehow still hit the perfect spot inside of me. I come so hard, he slips a hand over my mouth to silence my scream. Right before he comes, he slows down, slipping out of me.

He kisses me for a long time before thrusting back inside of me.

The second time is slow and sensual, and I come just as hard, pulling him over the edge with me. Feeling him fill me with his cum drags out my orgasm until we're both shaking and moaning. I dig my heels back into his ass to keep him in place, but James doesn't move to pull out either. He nuzzles his face into my neck, trailing kisses along my sensitive skin there.

James traces my tattoos, as if he wants to make sure he memorizes all of them. He's done this almost a dozen times since we got married, but I'll never get sick of it. Just like I'll never get sick of the way he traces the rings on my finger.

The ones he put there.

"Where did you learn how to speak Spanish?" I ask him after a while of silence, and he chuckles.

"How horrible was my accent?"

"Not as bad as you may think, but it could use some work," I reply with a laugh, which makes James hide his face in my neck again.

"You can blame Julián, Scarlette, and Val. They didn't tell me it was so noticeable."

"It's okay. I'll teach you from now on."

"I'd love nothing more," he says, pushing off the bed enough to place his mouth on mine.

"I love you," I whisper once he leans back. He presses his forehead to mine, and I can practically feel him smiling.

"I love you so much, and I'm never letting you go again."

"I'm never going anywhere again."

Chapter 58
James

IF I HAD TO describe Estrella's parents in one word, it would be "wonderful." Her whole family is. Ever since we arrived yesterday, they have been doting on us. I met her mamá and papá, who welcomed me with open arms and warm smiles. Afterward, they introduced me to Mamá Elena and Papá Julio, Estrella's grandparents. Tía Rosa and Tío Julio showed up an hour later with their children, and they were ecstatic to see Daisy and Estrella.

More family members came to welcome my girls back home and to meet me. Estrella's cousin greeted me with a, "*¿Qué onda, wey?*" which made me furrow my brows and my wife giggle. She told me it's a way of greeting in Mexico.

As someone with a small family that always has some sort of problem, this big, beautiful family's endless stream of love made me a little choked up last night. Especially when Mamá Elena took my hand and led me to their *ofrenda* to show me all the people they've lost and are honouring on *Día de los Muertos*. She explained to me that along with photographs of them, they put their favourites there on the altar like Papá Emiliano's favourite cigars or Tía Alejandra's favourite sweets.

I also can't help studying Pedro and Helen's pictures for a little longer than the rest, for the first time seeing what they looked like. Pedro and Estrella are identical, and Helen has the same blue eyes my little girl inherited from her.

There were also some sodas, alcohol, and more. Estrella's mum and her sister were also preparing lots of *tamales* and other foods to put on the altar and for the family to eat.

Mamá Elena explained that there are very important components for the *ofrenda*. There is the *flor de cempasúchil*, which she also called *flor de color naranja*, the *pan de muerto*, and there are *velas* and a *copal*. She said that the smoke from the *copal* helps the souls find their way to the house where the *ofrendas* are.

After she finished explaining it, she gave me a few petals so Daisy and I could help her with the *camino de pétalos de flor de cempasúchil* that leads from the entrance of the house to the altar. This is also for the souls to find their way.

Daisy and I also helped Papá Bruno and Tío Julio hang the *papel picado*, but my beautiful wife pulled me away to show me *calaveras de azúcar* and more sweets that are very common on this holiday. She gave me some *pan de muerto* and I found myself constantly asking for more because it was delicious, especially paired with Estrella's *horchata*. Usually, the pan is served with hot chocolate, but I'm addicted to Estrella's *horchata*, something my wife keeps smirking at.

Today, we're all going to the cemetery. It's a very important tradition, too. For Estrella's family, they spend some time at the graves to spend time with the people they lost. Some of her family members make music because Pedro and her other grandparents used to love music.

I notice Estrella's hands shaking as she zips up her dress, something I offered to do for her but since it's on the side of her body, she didn't want help.

"Are you okay, darling?" I ask, rubbing my hands over her bare arms. The embroidered dress she's wearing is a mixture of a lot of vibrant colours, and she's wrapped a scarf around herself, too.

I already loved Mexico before I started being taught about this holiday, but now? It's just so lovely. They celebrate death while I was taught to fear it. They mourn, yes, but they also spread joy on this day.

Estrella told me there is a saying they use here. "*En México, nadie muere realmente,*" and I think it has become my new favourite saying.

"This is the first time I'm going to visit Pedro and Helen's grave in years. I don't know if I'm ready," she admits, taking my arms and placing them around her.

"I'm here with you, my love. Whatever you need, I will give it to you. If you need a moment of privacy today, I will take Daisy and we can go to that little *plaza* you were telling me about where the *mariachi* are performing tonight. I'll do whatever I can to support you," I promise, watching her eyes flutter shut in the mirror in front of us.

"Thank you."

"There is nothing you need to thank me for. I'd give you every single piece of my strength if I could, little star. Without hesitation."

She reopens her eyes to look at me, a small smile slipping onto her face.

"I know you would. It's why I'm so glad you're here," she says and spins around in my arms, lifting her hands to my neck.

"Nowhere I'd rather be." I kiss her lips, lingering until we hear Daisy's voice.

"Mamá, Papá, *estamos esperando,*" she says, and I love the way I can understand her nowadays. Daisy takes our hands to lead us out of Estrella's childhood bedroom and down the stairs to where the whole *familia* is waiting for us, just like Daisy said.

Then, we all make our way through the small town and toward the cemetery.

Chapter 59
Estrella

There's a weight on my chest. It was slowly lifting with every second I spent with my family, but it's getting heavier again with every step toward the cemetery. Everything I see reminds me of Pedro. When I put his favorite soda on the *ofrenda* yesterday, I started crying. When I gave James a piece of the *pan* Pedro used to love, I felt my heart drop into my stomach. When Mamá and I made his favorite food, I spent several minutes hugging her.

My parents have found a way to live with their grief in a much better way than I have. My way was mostly suppressing it because I had no reminders of my brother around me except for my tattoos and my little girl. Yes, I went to therapy, but it didn't prepare me for this gut-wrenching pain when I arrive at his and Helen's grave. I barely manage to breathe past it as I watch my family starting to decorate the grave similarly to how we decorated the *ofrenda* and our house.

"Estrella," my mother says, her fingers lacing through mine. "Take a deep breath, *mi amor*. It'll be okay." She wraps an arm around me, pulling me against her side as we wait for our family to finish setting up everything.

My Tío Matías starts playing his guitar, and I get this weird nostalgia feeling combined with immense sadness because Pedro used to ask him to play all the time. I force my gaze to shift to Daisy and James where they're standing with Papá Bruno. Daisy is giggling and James has his hands on her shoulders as he listens to my grandfather tell them a story.

"*¡No inventes!*" my little girl squeals in response to whatever Papá Bruno said, giggling to herself.

"It's okay to feel hurt but remember that Pedro would want you to enjoy life for as long as you are given it. That you'll get to see him after." My brother would say that. He would tell me not to linger on pain. He would tell me to choose happiness because it is a choice sometimes. Not always, but sometimes. For me, this is sometimes.

"I love you, Mamá," I say, feeling her kiss my temple a moment later.

"I love you, Estrella."

"I love you both the most," Papá chimes in, hugging us from behind. He places a big kiss on my cheek before doing the same to Mamá's, making me chuckle.

My family and I spend hours at the grave, sharing stories, listening to music, and so much more. James keeps his arm around me at all times, and Daisy keeps switching from sitting on my lap to going to look at the other graves with her cousins. She looks happy to be here for the first time since she was a baby. She doesn't remember anything about our town that I didn't share with her. Most of our family didn't get to meet her until yesterday, but she's quickly becoming some members' favorite. Not that I'm surprised. She's the cutest little girl in the whole world.

My husband listens to every single story—some shared in English so he can understand, some in Spanish because a few of my family members don't speak English.

It's during a rather long story from my Tía Rosa that I turn to him.

"Do you understand it all?" I whisper because she's speaking rather fast in Spanish, and I doubt his months of lessons are enough.

"Not all of it," he admits, and I give him a reassuring smile. "But I enjoy listening to her. She has a very soothing voice."

"That she does," I reply, leaning my head against his shoulder.

My family and I tell the stories of the family we've lost to remember them. We remember them so they can cross the bridge between the land of the living and the land of the dead on this sacred day. So that when we put up their pictures on the altar, their souls can find their way back to us.

It's late into the night when some of my aunts and uncles start leaving to put their young kids to bed. Daisy is sleeping in James' arms, and even his eyes keep fluttering shut with exhaustion more frequently than a few hours ago.

"Why don't you take Daisy home? I'll be right there," I assure him, and he gives me several nods before kissing me and standing up to take our daughter home. Mamá and Papá each give me a kiss on the cheek, too, following James out of the cemetery.

I wait until I'm the only one left at Pedro and Helen's graves. Closing my eyes, I place a hand on the gravestone with their names, letting the tears I've kept in all night finally drip down.

"*Los extraño tanto,*" I say in Spanish. "*Espero que estén orgullosos de la madre en que me he convertido,*" I add, my hands shaking from pain. "*Espero ser todo lo que siempre desearon para Daisy en una madre.*"

Silence fills the area around me as I sink to my knees, still crying because I have to let it out once and for all.

And maybe it's that pain.

Maybe it's the story Pedro shared with me of hearing voices when he walked past the cemetery on *Día de los Muertos* all those years ago, but I could swear I hear his voice say, "*Eres todo eso y más.*"

My head shoots up, tears still trailing down my cheek.

"Pedro?" I ask, sobbing uncontrollably.

"*Mamá tiene razón. Nos veremos de nuevo un día. Por ahora, ve a vivir tu vida. Estaremos aquí cuando estés lista.*"

Goosebumps appear all over my body, and I wrap the scarf I wore tighter around myself. This can't be real and yet, because my brother believed things like this were possible, I don't question it. It could very well be my brain making this up, but it feels too real. It feels like he's right here, and when all of a sudden I sense something pressing down on my shoulder, I know it's his hand.

I look over my shoulder and, though I can't see him, I know it's him.

STRAIGHT TO THE CHAPEL

"I love you both so much. I promise I'll come back more. I promise to show Daisy more of her home. I promise to live my life." Suddenly, as soon as the words have left my mouth, the weight I was feeling since coming here lifts off my chest so abruptly, it knocks the air out of me. I keel forward, my hands barely catching me.

"We're so proud of you, Estrella."

The feel of his hand disappears, and I think his soul does, too, but a part of it will forever live on in me. In Daisy.

And one day, I will see him again when I cross the bridge I never believed existed more than I do right now.

Chapter 60
James

WE'RE ON THE SECOND to last race of the season, and I've gained such a lead that if I win today and Cameron comes in second, I can win the title before the last race.

In the past, Leonard petitioned for them to change the Qatar Grand Prix schedule so instead of having it during the hottest time of the year, it would be when the temperature was a bit more bearable. But since everything has been thrown around this season, it's back at the end of the season, right before Abu Dhabi.

I'm already sweating.

During Quali yesterday, I almost got a heatstroke, so today will be a lot of fun.

Estrella, Damian, and Daisy are here, which is like a constant flow of determination and strength hitting my system. I'm sitting in my car, letting their presence fuel me. I qualified second. That means the start will be crucial. I have to overtake Cameron. I have to create a gap.

Because of the point buffer I've managed to gain by winning the other races, I'm less nervous than last year when I was this close to victory. Even if I don't win today, the championship won't be lost.

I'll have another chance in Abu Dhabi.

"Ximena, I'm boiling in the car," I say, more sweat dripping down my temple.

"They're aware of it, but there's nothing we can do if they don't decide to call it off," she replies, making me grind my molars in frustration.

"Yeah, copy."

This is going to be a tough race.

STRAIGHT TO THE CHAPEL

Once our teams clear off the track, we wait for the lights to flash on so we can take our formation lap.

There's something very liberating and sad every time I realise this is the second to last race of the season. On one hand, the winter break will make me miss racing. It's what I've been breathing for my entire life. On the other, I breathe for my family now. I can't wait to spend as much time with Daisy and Estrella as possible. Watching my wife teach at the academy or test drive new cars. Picking Daisy and Damian up from preschool. Hopefully marrying Estrella again because, this time, I want there to be no ruse, no pretense.

I want her to know it'll be forever when I say "I do."

Not to mention, I'm very excited to see what the off-season brings. Adrian and Nevaeh's baby shower—still can't believe that wanker is going to be a father. Chiara's new art gallery opening. Potentially Leonard's announcement to get back into F1 as a team principal—which is not confirmed but wishful thinking on my part. Scarlette and Julián moving to a new house. Val and Gabriel taking Chase on a trip around the world. And who knows what Cameron will come up with, too.

The lights finally appear above us, and Cameron drives ahead, leading the rest of us around the track. It's Cameron, me, Adrian, Val, Gabriel, and Javier before the rest of the grid follows. The five of us top drivers have not been this close together since the race where Adrian, Gabriel, and Cameron crashed in Mexico.

It makes me a little nervous.

They say I'm the driver who pushes boundaries, the one who knows the rules so well, I know exactly how to bend them to my will, but the fact is this: the man ahead of me and the three drivers behind are just as much of a lion hunting down their prey as I am.

This sport is about winning no matter the cost. It comes first, before safety, before reputation. But I want to win the right way.

The Formula One fandom is split between those who hate everything about me and those who love me. It's time I prove the ones who defend and support me right.

I am a driver worthy of the victory.

I am a driver who is fair and wins because I earn it.

I am a driver they can be proud to wear the Hawke colours for.

I take several deep breaths, waiting, waiting, and waiting for the lights. Fear and determination wrap their hands around my heart, squeezing until I wheeze for a single breath. It's painful, but it's a reminder of what I could achieve here today.

The first light appears, and everything vanishes. It's a different mindset drivers go in when we race. It's almost like a superpower, and it's one I desperately need at this very second.

The start is a mess. Cameron manages to stay ahead of me while I chase after him with the front wing of Val's car almost touching the rear of mine. I grit my teeth, adrenaline coursing through me. Val has to back off a lap later when Gabriel overtakes Adrian and hunts her down. It gives me the room to go after Cameron.

Since we're fighting for the championship, our team has given us the green light to battle. Hawke has basically won the Constructors' Championship already, so this is all about our individual standings now.

"Cameron keeps swerving on the straights," I say to Ximena through the radio.

"I'll deal with it," she replies.

Cameron and I head into the sixth lap of the race side by side. DRS has been enabled, so I have the extra speed advantage to help me push ahead. I overtake him, but he fights me in turn one, pushing me off the track in order to take back first place. Shock consumes me as I watch all four of his tyres slide off the track, too.

My heart drops as I hit the gravel, but there is no time to waste when my car is not stuck. I'm losing time, but I'm still in the race.

Except, now I'm fifth.

Fucking Cameron.

"What the hell is that wanker doing? He has to get a penalty for that," I tell Ximena, outraged by how he shoved me out of the way in order to get back in first place. He even went off himself, the dickhead.

"On it."

"Check if there's any damage on the car, too. It felt like something came loose," I say, breathless and irritated.

Rage has consumed me, but, again, I can't linger on it. I've got a job to do.

"No damage, James," comes through the radio a minute later.

Laps over laps follow. I overtake Adrian and am now chasing down Gabriel. Cameron is under investigation, but I need him to get a penalty so I can figure out where the hell I have to finish in order to win this championship. It shouldn't be what I'm focusing on because I'm supposed to only be concentrating on closing the distance between Gabriel and me, but I can't help it.

I want the win, and I want it today.

My body is exhausted. This is a two-stop race. We haven't even made it to the first stop.

"Cameron has received a ten-second penalty for the move he pulled. He will serve it during his first pitstop," Ximena informs me, which is already a relief.

"I want to go with Strategy D," I say because that strategy involves us undercutting the rest of the grid, which may be my only hope to overtake Val and Cameron if they keep up their pace and I stay stuck behind Gabriel.

"Understood. I'll get back to you."

While I wait, my tyres slowly degrading, I chase down Gabriel. It takes me several laps once I'm behind him to finally overtake him because, well, Gabriel is a two-time world champion for a reason. I'd probably have no chance if his car was as fast as mine.

"Box, box," Ximena says right as I approach the pitlane entry, not giving the other teams a moment's time to react.

I practically smile.

My pitstop goes flawlessly, and, even though I end up in seventh, by the time the rest of the grid ahead of me pits, I'm in second place, Val leading. Cameron's stop made him come out in tenth place, and a bit of *Schadenfreude* has settled in my chest. I don't need to win anymore if Cameron ends up sixth or lower, but I want to win.

It's a brutal battle between the heat and me for the next ten laps. Val keeps a steady lead of more than a second ahead of me, but I'm not trying to overtake her yet. I'm saving my battery and tyres.

The only problem is, Val pits before me, which means that instead of being on the offence, Ximena and I go on the defence, reacting to Velocità Rossa instead.

"How many more laps do you think you can do on these tyres at this pace?" Ximena asks while I'm cursing at Val's early pitstop.

"A few, not many."

"Use your warm tyres to create a gap, more than a second." More than a second because that's how much Val was leading so if I make up that time, I will come out ahead of her in the second pitstop, even while she's trying to undercut me.

Three laps pass before I hear my race engineer's voice again. "Box, box."

I must have gained enough time, but now everything is on the pitstop. My heart is racing as I stop in the spot surrounded by my pit crew. The front and rear jacks lift the car so the other members can take off the old tyres and screw on the new ones. The light turns green about two seconds later, and I let out a sigh of relief as I make my way back onto the track.

"You'll come out ahead of Valentina," Ximena says right as I rejoin the track, and I look in my mirror to confirm her words. Val is behind me. "Let's hope there is no safety car."

A snort I don't mean leaves me. A safety car would be the worst thing for our strategy right now because there are four cars ahead of us that have yet to pit, and if a safety car is called for and we're all told to slow down, they'll stay ahead.

It feels like I'm simultaneously holding my breath and breathing too heavily. My car is a sauna, causing more and more sweat to roll down my back.

No safety car comes.

Once all four cars ahead have stopped, I take first place. At this point, the only thing I'm battling against is myself and the heat. Black spots appear in my vision from sheer exhaustion and overheating, but I push past it.

I push and push and push and—

"James, you can slow down now," Ximena says softly, her voice full of emotion, and I feel my heart sink all the way into my stomach when I see fireworks going off in front of me. "You've done it. You are Champion of the World."

It takes every last piece of energy I have left not to break down in my car and stop driving at the same time. I'm so tired, all I manage to do is wave at my fans as tears fall down my cheeks. I bring my car to the finish line for the first time as World Champion, stopping it and climbing out very slowly. I step toward the nose of my car, sinking to my knees and bowing to it because, fuck, I wouldn't be here without this rocketship.

I don't manage to get back on my feet for several minutes. Disbelief, shock, happiness, utter exhaustion, all of it has its claws in me. So, I kneel there, my helmeted forehead pressed against the front wing of the car.

Arms wrap around me from behind, and I turn my head just enough to see Adrian hugging me. Then follows Val and Gabriel and, even though I know it pains him because he's lost the title to me, Cameron hugs me, too.

"Congratulations, mate. It's so deserved," I hear Adrian say, his voice muffled.

"You did it, James," Val chimes in, making more tears stream down my face.

"Well done," Gabriel says, squeezing my shoulder.

They hug me for a moment longer before a burst of energy goes through my body and my wife's name escapes my lips.

"Go get her," Adrian says, smacking me on the arse when we stand up.

I sprint toward where I think Estrella is with our children, ripping my helmet off at the same time. They're standing with my team, headphones on Daisy's and Damian's ears to protect them from the loud noise around us. My eyes find Estrella's, who is crying as visibly as I am.

Once I'm finally in front of my family, I hug all of them, needing to be as close as possible. Estrella kisses my lips, cupping my face in the way that makes my knees weak.

"You did it, *bebé*. You won. You're the champion," she says, tracing what us racers call helmet lines that stay on our faces for a while after our races. It's that simple, gentle motion that centres me even as my heart and soul are overcome with pride and joy.

"I did it," I whisper, pressing my forehead against hers while still hugging Damian and Daisy. With my wife's hands on my face, and my children's arms wrapped around my legs as the world celebrates my accomplishment, I truly have everything I could ever wish for.

Months ago, Adrian told me I'd find my happy ending. He said everything would one day make sense, and this very moment, this is what he meant.

"Go. We'll be here to celebrate with you after," Estrella promises, so I kiss her lips and our children's heads one more time.

"You're my happy ending, Estrella." I kiss her again, lingering with our noses still touching.

"And you're mine," she replies.

Our story may have been far from a fairytale, but we did save each other. We fell in love, and we gave our hearts to the right person for the first and last time in our lives.

Epilogue
James

Estrella proposed to me the first time we got married.

It's only right that I propose to her, too.

Chiara and Leonard helped me arrange the whole thing. They're two of the kindest people, and letting me use Chiara's art gallery because of the immersive star exhibition she has in one of her rooms here in Monaco only proves that. They also prove it by letting Daisy have a sleepover with Leonora so Estrella and I could have the night for ourselves to… celebrate.

"Promise me, James, if you're going to fuck, do it on the blanket you've brought," Chiara says, and I almost choke on my own saliva.

"Oh, um, I wasn't planning on—"

"Trust me, sometimes it just happens. Chiara and I were celebrating in her gallery in England for hours the day she got it, and—" The Italian woman slaps a hand over her husband's mouth.

"Point is, not on my floor, Landon. I'll turn the security cameras off, but stay away from the art, okay?" Chiara says, her usual scowl in place.

"Why would you let us do that?" A laugh slips free because I'm genuinely so surprised.

"Well, there's nothing quite like making love under the stars, is there?" Leonard chimes in, wrapping his arm around his wife and guiding her out of the room where I've put a picnic blanket on the ground with a champagne bottle and two glasses as well as a little basket.

This room truly is perfect for proposing to my little star. Chiara has placed hundreds of star-shaped stickers that glow in the dark on her walls and ceiling. On top of that, she has cut even more stars out of a sturdy material—perhaps cardboard or something like it—and hung them at different heights throughout the room.

It's wonderful.

Once I've set up everything, I text Nevaeh, Val, and Scarlette, asking them to bring Estrella to the gallery. They were keeping her occupied all day so she didn't realise I was running around to do this. Estrella doesn't suspect a thing, which makes this ten times more exciting.

I have had my championship title for a little over two months now, but it would be meaningless without the woman I call mine.

"Why are we here without Chiara?" I hear Estrella say from the main entrance.

"Um, well, she's meeting us here. Come on," Scarlette lies, and I listen to the sound of their footsteps as all four women step toward the room I'm in.

Fireworks go off inside my chest when I see her. Estrella is wearing a dark green coat and the beanie I've given her, a perfectly content smile on her face. It's only when she spots me that it falls, giving way to the shock turning her lips into an O-shape. My hands are shaking as she covers her mouth, nerves running through me.

We're already married. I don't know why the bloody hell I'm nervous. She's not going to say "no."

"James," she says, taking a step toward me. Nevaeh, who's holding her little baby bump, gives me one wink before leading the other two women out of the room. "What are you doing?"

"What I should have done the very first time, darling." I get on one knee when she's in front of me, taking her hand as I sink to the ground. "Estrella Celeste Cortez-Landon, you are the very definition of a soulmate for me. You are the reason I breathe like I've never been more at peace in my life. You hold my heart in your perfect hands, and I don't ever want you to place it back inside my chest."

She sinks to her knees in front of me, tears filling her eyes, which makes my breathing shudder.

"I belong to you in a way I never thought I'd belong to a person. You belong to me in a way I never thought anyone would give themselves to me. You're the love of my life, little star, and every single day you choose me is a day I'll spend consumed by the type of love I've always wanted. You and Daisy are everything to me. Everything and so much more."

I hold both of her hands as I say my next words.

"My sweetest Estrella, would you do me the honour of marrying me again? This time, without a prenup and rules we came up with? Without anything that says I don't want to be with you for the rest of my life?"

She nods before I've even finished talking, but she waits patiently until I've finished before she says, "Yes, James. I do." She flings her arms around me and kisses me like I'm the best thing in the world, and I drink in her feelings as our tongues tangle. "You're the love of my life, too. I love you in every galaxy in our universe. I love you like the stars love to illuminate the night sky. I love you, plain and simple."

I take out the ring I bought, the box heavy in my hand. Estrella's brown eyes drop to it, but she immediately lifts her gaze again to show me the sadness in them.

"Are you going to make me give you back my other rings?"

"What? No, darling. Never. This is for your right hand," I say and lift the lid of the velvet box—shaped into a star, naturally—to reveal the ring. The sight of it makes Estrella chuckle.

"Am I not supposed to wear your initial around my neck?" she asks as I lift the ring with the letter J placed on the top of it out of the box.

"Perhaps, but rings are more our thing, don't you think?" I ask, reaching for the other velvet box I brought. "Well, rings and earrings," I add, lifting that lid to reveal earrings shaped into the letters J and L. "A matching set." Estrella giggles the entire time she places them on before waiting impatiently for me to slide the new ring onto the ring finger of her right hand.

"So, this is like the promise ring step that we skipped. Very thoughtful," she says, still grinning. The lighting of the room is dim, but I swear, Estrella shines so much, she brightens it up effortlessly.

"We skipped a lot of steps that I'd very much like to catch up on, Estrella. I hope the rest of our lives will be enough time," I say as both of us stare at her new ring.

"The rest of our lives sounds good to me," she replies, leaning forward to bring her lips to mine. She stops right before she kisses me, her eyes meeting mine. "Should we start with our first time having sex in an art gallery?"

"It's like you read my mind," I reply, flipping us around so she's on her back with me between her legs on the blanket.

Spending the rest of my life losing myself in Estrella might just be the best thing I'll ever do.

The End

Translations

florecita - little flower

Espérame aquí, florecita. - Wait for me here, little flower.

No puedo dormir, Mamá. - I can't sleep.

Eres un chico malo. - You're a bad boy.

No siento las manos. - I can't feel my hands.

¿Puedo? - May I?

¿Quieres decirme qué pasa? - Do you want to tell me what happened?

Hola, mi amor. - Hello, my love.

¿Cómo estás? ¿Y cómo está Papá? - How are you? How's Dad?

Vete al carajo. - Go fuck yourself.

Estrangularé a mi marido. - I'm going to kill my husband.

Pinche idiota. - Fucking idiot.

¿Qué pasó, florecita? - What happened, little flower?

¿Quieres manejar los karts? - Do you want to drive the karts?

Sí, por favor. - Yes, please.

¡Ya voy, Simón! Cállate la boca, idiota. - I'm coming, Simón! Shut up, idiot.

¿Qué quieres? - What do you want?

No te atrevas a reír. - Don't you dare laugh.

Page one

Translations

¿Para qué? Son igual de inútiles que una bolsa de arena en el desierto.
For what? They are as useless as a bag of sand in the desert.

Ahorita vuelvo. ¿Está bien? Quédate con Daiyu.
I'll be right back. Okay? Stay with Daiyu.

Es algo bueno. - This is something good.

Sí, florecita, es algo bueno. - Yes, little flower, this is something good.

¿Por qué? Porque eres un hombre muy difícil y no quiero pelear.
Why? Because you are a difficult man and I don't want to fight.

¿Mamá, puedes repetir los nombres de todos los equipos?
Mamá, can you repeat the names of the teams?

En Fórmula Uno hay Velocità Rossa...
In Formula One there are Velocità Rossa....

¿Y el Qualifying? Cómo funciona? - And how does Qualifying work?

Tomen, estos son para ustedes. - Take these, these are for you.

¿Qué están haciendo ahora?- What are they doing now?

Mamá, mira. - Mamá, look.

¿Estás bien? - Are you well?

¿Te lastimaron? - Did they hurt you?

Está bien. Vamos. Las llevaremos de vuelta a su hotel.
It's okay. Let's go. Let's get you back to your hotel.

Page two

Translations

Estamos contigo, corazón, en las buenas y en las malas.
Siempre nos tendrás a tu lado, siempre.
-
We are with you, heart, through thick and thin.
You will always have us by your side, always.

figlio di puttana - son of a bitch

Te ves feliz. - You look happy.

Odio estas pinches cosas de turistas. - I hate these fucking touristy things.

Bueno, no es lo único que haríamos. - Well, that's not the only thing we'd do.

¿Qué pasa? - What's wrong?

Nada, Mamá, estoy cansada. - Nothing, Mamá, I'm tired.

mentirosa- liar

Hola, Papá. ¿Cómo estás? - Hi, Papá. How are you?

No te preocupes. - Don't worry.

Nada, florecita, estoy bien. - Nothing, little flower, I'm fine.

Lo siento, amor. - I'm sorry, love.

Eso fue glorioso. - That was glorious.

Felicidades! - Congratulations!

Muchísimas gracias, princesa. - Thank you so much, princess.

Muy bien, Papá. - Very good, Papá.

Translations

Gracias a todos por su apoyo. Es un honor el haber ganado esta carrera rodeado por algunos de los fans más asombrosos en el mundo. Significan mucho para mi.
-
Thank you all so much for your support. It's an honor to have won this race surrounded by some of the most amazing fans in the world. It means a lot to me.

Gracias por ser mi esposa. - Thank you for being my wife.

¿Qué onda, wey? - a Mexican way of greeting a friend

En México, nadie muere realmente. - In Mexico, no one really dies.

Mamá Papá, estamos esperando. - Mamá, Papá, we're waiting.

calaveras de azúcar - sugar skulls (a Mexican tradition on Dia de los Muertos)

¡No inventes! - Stop joking.

Los extraño tanto. - I miss you a lot.

Espero que estén orgullosos de la madre en que me he convertido.
-
I hope you are proud of the mother I have become.

Espero ser todo lo que siempre desearon para Daisy en una madre.
-
I hope to be everything you always wanted for Daisy in a mother.

Eres todo eso y más. - You are all that and more.

Mamá tiene razón. Nos veremos de nuevo un día. Por ahora, ve a vivir tu vida. Estaremos aquí cuando estés lista.
-
Mamá is right. We will meet again one day. For now, go live your life. We will be here when you are ready.

Acknowledgements

First and foremost, I would like to thank the person that spent a lot of time on this book with me, teaching me about their culture, and being so patient with all of the questions I asked. Leo, thank you so much for all of your help. I know I was probably super annoying, but I am so thankful for every bit of your culture that you shared with me so I could represent Estrella respectfully and accurately. I also want to thank someone who introduced me to the Mexican culture when I was still very young. Gera, thank you so much for everything you taught me all those years ago. I've always held such a deep appreciation for Mexico and the Mexican culture because of everything you taught me, and I want you to know how grateful I am for you. I also want to thank all my sensitivity readers, especially Clyo, for taking the time to read, comment, and share more about their culture to make this the best version of Straight to the Chapel with the best representation that it could be.

I also want to thank every single one of my beta readers who spent hours and hours reading and commenting in order to give me the feedback that made me fall in love with the story all over again and perfect it at the same time.

A so very special thank you goes to Sunel, Halie, Sami, Gemma, Jess, Kayla, Solène, Makayla, Melanie, Emma, and Tanisha. Thank you for everything, and for beta reading STTC and giggling with me over how cute they are (and crying with me at the tough scenes).

I'm also so incredibly grateful for Vicky, Sophie, Martina, Alyssa, Apoorva, Beth, Hali, Renee, Mais, Hannah, Brittani, Julia & Mareike, Victoria, Aroosa, Nesi, Jane, Ruth, Salma, Javi, Eliza, Mariah, Katherine, Isabella, Briana, and more amazing people who have supported me for so long and are always there for me when I need a confidence boost. You all are so amazing, and I don't ever want you to think I take you for granted. I am so lucky to have all of you in my corner.

Ams, as always, you get a very special thank you because you make me a better writer, person, and friend all in the same breath. I'd be lost without you. Teigan, you are a shining bright light in a pitch-black galaxy, and I am eternally grateful for your friendship. Esha, thank you for always teaching me and inspiring me. I'm so lucky to call you a friend, too. Natalia, this is like the hundredth book of mine you've read (kidding, of course, but it feels like that) and I'm so glad you haven't gotten sick of my writing yet.

As always, the biggest thank you goes to my favorite person in the entire world. My sister. Without you, I'd be a girl with a dream that would never go anywhere. With you, I've published more books than I could have ever dreamt possible, and I know we're going to make it big very soon (as we all know, as soon as I write it, it becomes true). And again, I need to highlight that she is the one who edits, formats, makes the covers, takes photos and everything basically that gets my books out of my drafts and into your hands.

Lastly, I always want to thank my grandparents, mom, and Robyn and Miriam for being there every step of the way and being the kind of emotional support system everyone should have because it is the best thing in the world. I love you all, and I'm so very grateful you continue to read my books.

All my love,

Bridget

About the Author

BRIDGET L. ROSE IS a half-German, half-Italian author, who was born and raised in Germany until the age of thirteen. She fell in love with books from a young age, and soon discovered her passion for writing as well. She likes to spend her free time with her family, reading a book, or writing one herself. She also adores the sport Formula One, which led her to write her Pitstop Series.

Books by Bridget L. Rose

The Pitstop Series

Jump-Start

The Inside of a Rainbow

Rush: Part One & Two

Chase: Part One & Two

Reserved

Diffuse

The Last Championship (Novella)

From Angels to Devils Series

From Devils to Angels